Sunrise Descending

SUNRISE DESCENDING
Copyright © 2011 by Kevin Shoemaker

This book is printed on acid free paper

A Shoemaker Labs Book
Lafayette, Colorado

e-mail: Shoemakerlabs@gmail.com

ISBN 978-0-9815092-4-2
ISBN 0-9815092-4-X

Registered with the Library of Congress

Grateful acknowledgement is made to those who have given permission for the use of previously copyrighted material in this book. Every reasonable care has been taken to correctly acknowledge copyright ownership. The author and publisher would welcome information that will enable them to rectify any errors or omissions in succeeding printings.

Cover Art courtesy of Auzigog
Chapter Artwork courtesy of NASA, the Shoemaker family and Wikipedia

First edition December, 2011
Printed in the United States of America

To Judi, Leah and Stephen
for their inspiration and support

Acknowledgment

I would like to sincerely like to thank Mary Landahl for her editing and comments. Also, I would like to thank my friends Grant, Jason, and Eliot for their editing and comments. Finally, I would like to thank my lovely wife Judi, daughter Leah and son Stephen, for their encouragement and patience.

Author's note

Only certain types of music sound right in space, ask any astronaut. Vivaldi is one, Enya of course and probably Johnny Cash should be added (this came from the older astronauts). Although hundreds of songs and symphonies have been heard while floating in orbit, only a few have had that three dimensional quality that belongs floating among the stars.

But why is this true?

It's true because humans belong in space, and many artists inherently know this. Look at Kandinski's work, listen to 'Echos from Space' the NPR program. Humans not only dream of our inevitable place in the realm of the nebulas but they are physically and emotionally prepared for it and I can prove it to you....

What happens when a person is given the chance to fly into space? A hundred years ago we flew for the first time, a hundred years from now there will be many safe, inexpensive ways to venture into space. Let's pretend its a hundred years from now. There will be hotels in space and shuttles between these hotels and Earth. As the reader of these words, would you go? Would you go if you knew other people who went? Would you want to get married in space? Do you see my point? It will be just another interesting place to go and see, space travel marketed by large companies and raffled by organizations trying to raise money for various causes. It will be part of the natural course of events.

~ Sunrise Descending ~

Table of Contents

Introduction

This world has turned billions of turns, every day for 365 days a year, for approximately 4.3 Billion years. From the sun's perspective, the Earth's leading edge or terminator rotates towards the sun and appears different every day. The sun peers over this line as it creeps away from the remaining darkness. The Sun observes the remains of the previous day and the efforts of those who live on the planet. The cycle of daily life begins at this line as most of the creatures of Earth start their day, see the sun rise, have their morning meal and begin a new rotation.

This is the story of some of the lives lived during a particular period of Earth's rotations. One special life became significant as is continuing through many many generations. It was whimsically called a "happenstance," where the confluence of several lives in space and time caused a major change in one particular person. He is still out there in the Universe and it appears he will be out there forever. Whether or not this is good or bad is up to the reader. The purpose here is only to report what has happened.

~ Sunrise Descending ~

There are others like him, as it turns out, but their lives are too complex to provide a continuity of events that would be relevant. His life is enough.

Think of this from the perspective of the sun, looking out upon the brightened faces of its students, who watch intently. They rotate slowly revealing new details of themselves in the early morning, excited by the day, calmed by the night.

At the Boat, Call From Houston

Searching my heart for its true sorrow; this is the thing I find to be;

That I am weary of words and people; sick of the city, wanting the sea

- Edna St. Vincent Millay

~ *Sunrise Descending* ~

It was a little after dusk. A flock of birds flew left to right in the evening twilight like a collection of dark stars forming ever evolving constellations, much like those in space but at a quicker pace. The temperature was a non factor, neither hot nor cold but periodically punctuated by a cool breeze sent from a descending bubble of clean high altitude air. Stephen Daedalus lounged on the bow of his boat, watching the remnants of a bait ball. A thousand small fish formed into a sphere with only the very highest portion at or above the surface. The fish swam frantically in circles eating, mating or both, the effect of which was a slight boiling motion sprinkled periodically along the creek and waterways near the marina.

Stephen sipped his drink, found it low in the glass, then put it down on the deck box cushion and started observing the newly forming stars. Faintly, in the distance, the bait balls gurgled, wings of birds coerced the air, a dog barked. Otherwise silence, the boat perfectly balanced between the pilings, lines arced. In this condition, the slightest push if patiently applied could move this 66,000 pound boat as if on ice within its caternary cradle.

The balance of the boat was symbolic of the balance needed in life. The six inch step from dock to deck allowed Stephen to release his connection to the stress and concerns of daily existence, to find peace and healing time from the bruises and lacerations of the week's activities. Not that the wounds were unwanted or un-needed.

A tinge of salt was in the air, life's chemical, conveyer of nerve activity. Salt allowing the senses to function, allowing the moods to change, allowing the heroes to play. Stephen flared his nostrils for more then examining his cup tasted the last remnants of his drink and stood up.

Satellites appeared in the sky showing off their supreme flying skills compared to the occasional airliner negotiating the air waves. Straight and true were their course, such is the reality of flying in space. Stretching, Stephen walked aft to the door leading the salon attached to the helm. Darkness had really set in, that and the quiet had really given the boat a sense of being suspended in space. Through the door to the right, pausing for a moment to view the world from the helm, he quietly stood, relaxed, at peace.

Then the flashes came, as they had before, in this same area of the boat. Fine, periodic flashes of light, colored like the star Sirius, sometimes blue, sometimes red, continuing throughout the spectrum. Typically observed when looking to port, these lights gave Stephen yet another reason to day dream. What were they really? Maybe they were the portals of vision from the future, used by time travelers to replay the past. He wondered why, if time travel was possible, even tens of thousands of years in the future...why had we not experienced our curious future onlookers? He assumed that they would only venture to the most interesting places and events. Smiling, he thought, maybe they were here to view him before he made an important discovery or caused a catastrophe. "Well okay, whatever," he spoke for the first time in an hour. Going below to the forward salon Stephen paused to look at a computerized picture frame showing one of 256 pictures every 3 seconds. Images of family, everyday life, trips, water and space. This was yet another opportunity for daydreaming, but Stephen was thirsty and continued into the galley to refresh his drink. Walking back on the occasionally squeaking floor he ascended to the helm and then around the corner back to the deck outside. The stars were brighter now, planets were ablaze and satellites obvious in the clear sky. He sat down, adjusted his weight for comfort and looked up. As he did, he heard a sound much like that of a glider on final approach. There was a slight hissing sound changing aspect as the shape moved in the air. Thirty feet away, a large heron reached its legs out, flared for a landing and touched down on a finger dock. Folding its wings, it looked at Stephen, conveying the idea that it wanted to be left alone to go to sleep. Stephen decided to obey the sentiment and quietly resumed musing about the stars.

Mars was in Sagittarius, it had been over a year since he had landed on the red planet. Landed, explored, worked and left without a full crew. The experience of leaving Benjamin and Judy, running into the Spheront probe on the return voyage, landing back on earth full of distracted people, left him numb. No hero worship, only questions followed his return.

Nancy had wandered off to hopeful obscurity in the space agency reviewing proposals writing specifications for future missions. Stephen on the other hand, was a commander and was expected to justify his commands; this was part of the job description. The experience had rid the room of joy, as it were, with countless meetings, debriefings and questions. It wasn't until a few months ago that he was able to get to a beach, or better yet, to the boat, for badly needed de-compression time. Being officially exonerated for his actions during the inaugural flight, he always felt a slight pall over his meeting and dealings with the managers after the mission. Flight Control looks down on independent thinking and autocratic decision making. In the end everyone understood but there was the possibility that everyone was not in full agreement.

Quiet descended on the marina, the water was like glass and the animals were asleep. Stephen took in a deep breath, enjoying the clean air and oxygen. Sleep was stalking him as well and he made plans to get up from the settee and move inside. During his initial movements to retire the phone went off. The light from the display shocked him and the world around him. Grabbing the phone and squinting his eyes from the bright back lit display, he noticed the area code of the the originating call: 281....Houston.

"Rats," Stephen spoke aloud, the first vocalization in many hours. "Now what?"

The Previous Week

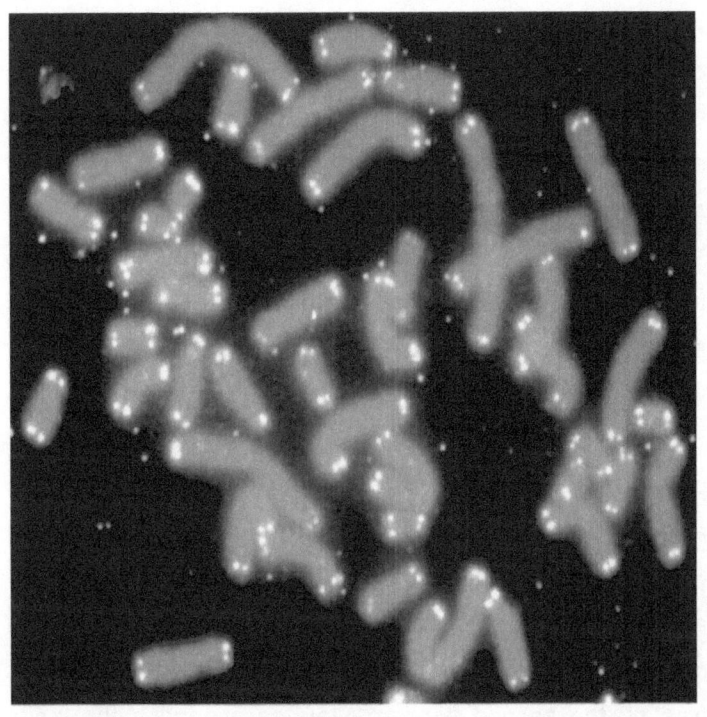

As we grow older, we become ourselves, only more so – J. Morosohk

Before his period of reflection on the boat, a simple but life changing event occurred. Stephen had no idea at that time of the long term implications of the experience. He was back in Colorado, visiting friends when he received a call from a flight physician he once had and with whom he become friends. The physician asked for a meeting at his office, Stephen responded enthusiastically, as he had not seen his friend for several years.

On the appointed day Stephen drove for several miles to a recently built medical facility. His friend retired so it seemed interesting that either he was back in practice or was borrowing someone else's office. He pulled up into a parking space, put down his coffee and opened the car door. The walk to the main entrance was about 30 meters away. It was cold and crisp outside in mid September. Stepping up to the sidewalk, he entered the building, automatic doors sliding apart revealing an open area with a coffee vendor to the right and stairs to the left. The office was on the second floor so Stephen ascended the stairs and looked for the proper entrance. As he went in he found that there was no receptionist or nurse. He was not sure if he should sit or stand or even if he was in the right office. That question did not linger long as his friend soon appeared from the door to the laboratory.

~ Sunrise Descending ~

"Stephen, how great to see you," the doctor opened with.

"Roger, great to see you too, its been way too long, I have lots to tell you."

"Of course you do, I have been following your adventures for the last several years, what an amazing experience, including the unexpected ending."

"Surprised me as well, although in retrospect, being slightly anonymous has its perks."

"Yes, exactly, and in fact, that is why I contacted you."

"Oh?"

"In fact, why don't you sit down? We have some things to talk over," said the doctor as he moved over to a desk and chairs near a window overlooking the Rocky Mountains.

Stephen did as asked, moving to a chair facing the desk. The desk and office belonged to another physician. This was interesting if for no other reason than it was mid day, middle of the week and in he was in a fully functional abandoned doctor's office.

The doctor continued as he looked for a fresh piece of paper and a pen on someone else's desk. Sitting down, the doctor started to draw the double DNA helix complete

13

with the enzyme rungs. At the ends of the DNA strand he emboldened the drawing, looked up at Stephen and started.

"Are you familiar with this part of the DNA strand, Stephen?"

"Are those the Telomeres?"

"In fact they are; these particular strands as you know, coordinate the replication of the cells within our body. As we grow older these strands begin to loose their ability to replicate perfectly and thus our bodies start to degrade. The reason we are meeting today is to talk about these telomeres."

Stephen looked up from the crude drawing and was wondering what would follow. He knew the doctor to be dedicated to the medical profession, had worked a long career as a general practitioner, flight physician and surgeon. He had also obtained a PhD in medical research and as a result had an amazing ability to track down obscure diagnoses with patients who had seen many other physicians but without relief from their maladies.

The doctor began, "First I need to establish a confidentiality barrier." He looked at Stephen and continued, "what I am about to the tell you will be the most important words you will ever hear. You need to understand this clearly as this will effect your life forever. Okay?"

14

"Okay, keep going."

"For many years now research has been conducted on the ability of the the cells to replicate perfectly, as you know, we concentrated on the actions of the telomeres and in fact now understand how they work. As you can imagine after we understood the basic principals we started to experiment with lab animals. This was done after we had made some gene sequencing adjustments and performed what we call sub-micro surgery. This is a combination of chemistry and micro biology, the research took place in a remote area of Utah. I can't go into many details yet, as you can imagine, this is a very closely guarded secret. The important thing for you to realize is why you are here. I am part of a plenary group that has recommended that we take the next step in the science. The mice we tried the gene manipulation on have been successfully changed and are healthy."

"Healthy but what," interrupted Stephen.

"Healthy but immortal," answered the doctor.

"And so...."

"Please let me continue, this is very important Stephen. The results of the experiments were successful. We now need to take the next steps with human tests. All of us on the board were allowed to make suggestions as to

15

who would be best suited to live for a long time. This was no easy decision as you can imagine. Who can tell if the chosen person will go insane or become a despot? It took significant reflection to decide who was most stable, who would be able to adjust to very new experiences and most importantly, who would we like to represent us in the future. My choice was you; (for all of these reasons) you fit all our requirements because of your experience on your trip to Mars a few years ago. The board agrees with my decision and they want to know if you are willing to work with us?"

"Um, in what way?"

"By helping us take the next step. By starting treatments that will extend your life."

"Sounds interesting, I have always felt our existence on this Earth was too short. There is so much more I could do. Tell me, what will happen? What will I feel? Will I become frozen at this age or will my body start to feel the ravages of time?"

"This is something to consider in a very serious way. We are not sure what will happen as far as your final age or even if you will change over time. The subjects of our last tests, the mice and monkeys, appear to have been frozen at their present age. Micro cellular analysis shows that their cells are replicating perfectly, but we cannot say what has happened to them mentally, in other words how they feel about themselves and others, or if they can even tell the difference. Your responsibility will be to work with us while we can....and chronicle your life thereafter for researchers in this field. Are you willing to do this? And before you answer, are you fully aware of the implications of this decision?"

"I have a good feeling that this is the right thing for me to do. My life has been a little strange after the Mars voyage. Its going to take some time for me to get back to being productive."

"Yes, we know; this is an opportunity for all of us. Actually, I am not the only one to think that it was a good idea to get you involved. Several of us are in agreement that you are the best subject to complete this work. There are several layers of reason for this decision......"

"I am not surprised, lets get started."

"Okay, you're sure about this?" The doctor knew the answer to this question before he asked it and while asking started to prepare the medicine. He walked over to a stainless steel cart with a syringe and a rubber stopped vial containing a multi million dollar concoction of life changing fluid.

Placing the syringe in the rubber stopper, he drew fluid into the chamber and turning towards Stephen, prepared to inject.

"Looks like sea water," commented Stephen.

"Funny you should say that," returned the doctor as he swabbed Stephen's shoulder and painlessly injected the serum.

"Roger," started Stephen, "I've known you for over 20 years, you saved me from a very rare disease, which no other physician could understand. All of your advice on health care for me and health care for my parents was perfectly correct. We were saddened by your early retirement. I should have known you didn't go home and start watching TV."

"Oh, of course not. Although I have to say that Oprah was sometimes interesting. Some of the subjects she covered were timeless. However, you are right and to be honest, I immediately went into research, made a lot more money, had a lot less headaches and soon found myself in the company of several very forward thinking researchers. Two of them are Nobel prize winners."

"Were you smarter than they were?"

"Only every once in a while would I show I might be smarter. Genius at that level is hard to comprehend even for the highly educated."

"Granted, but it must have been thrilling in a way to work with them."

"It was, in fact it ultimately taught me a very important lesson."

"Oh, yeah, what was that?"

"Humans are capable of anything. You know, most people just follow the life cycle of being born, reared by their parents, getting a job, retiring and dying. But there are a very few who make huge impacts on civilization, all based on their intellect and drive. Its amazing actually that there are those who are very capable but have little or no drive, they don't amount to much. Then there are those who are very capable and have drive, they go far in this world, but then there are those few who are incredibly capable and have extreme drive, they are those change the course of civilization."

"How do you interact with them?"

"Actually its very simple....simple from a human perspective. Just accept them and what they do, that's it."

"Well, that makes sense, but in a way you have to qualify to interact with them on their level or else they get bored."

"True. But they are human beings as well and in fact usually seek acceptance in the same way as you and I."

"Well, that is logical, although life in their company is probably at a higher pace."

"It is, and you need to be assured that all of us considered many things before we decided to offer you this opportunity."

"Oh, I am okay with this, believe me...and by the way, what is going to happen next?"

"Not much actually, you probably won't notice anything for months. But what you will notice is that your physical and mental state will not coincide with those of your age. You will get the sense that they are growing older, remembering less, not as physically active as you are and there will be other things."

"Other things?"

"Yes Stephen, you are married, what you find normal in your relationship with your wife will not change, but what she feels as normal will change, so be prepared."

"I can imagine. She might not be very happy with this decision of mine. But in her case she will be understanding. I won't violate my oath and take care of her until the end."

"Yes, we know."

"How much of my life did you predict?"

"Only enough to realize that it was a good gamble to give you the serum. We ask only that you remember us and chronicle your life for others, especially others like us, who will see you in our last moments as you are today."

"Okay then, I guess the die is cast; actually I am kind of looking forward to this, thank you for the opportunity."

"You are moving into uncharted territory, Stephen. We all hope you fare well."

With that, the doctor rose from his chair, gathered his syringe and vial, carefully cleaned up the area and adjusted the room to appear that nothing had happened. The doctor looked at Stephen when he was finished and expressed his feeling that it was time to go.

Stephen rose, put on his coat, felt his arm where the injection was made and moved towards the door. He wondered still about the lack of people in the office during a work week. The doctor led him outside the office, pulled the door behind him, not locking it. They walked down the hall where at a descending staircase the doctor stopped,

21

motioned Stephen to take the elevator and said: "I will contact you in a few years for a checkup, enjoy."

Stephen did not know exactly what to say, as the impact of what was going to happen started to sink in he thought about what his next century would be like. "Thank you Doc, I look forward to seeing you later."

The doctor disappeared, Stephen made it outside and as he walked to the car he tried to sense if anything was different. He felt nothing, rubbed his arm again and remembering the words of the doctor about the subtlety of the upcoming changes decided to get back to his life. First and foremost was to get back to the boat for some needed R and R. The previous months had been harrowing and he needed to relax and decompress.

On Mars, Cold, Isolated, Stressed, Fantastic

This earth of majesty, this seat of Mars,
This other Eden, demi-paradise,
This fortress built by Nature for herself
Against infection and the hand of war,
This happy breed of men, this little world,

~ Sunrise Descending ~

On Mars, it was still cold. Pockets of 30 to 50 degree temperatures had been found but in general it was just cold, in the negative numbers, challenging equipment and inhabitants alike. Benjamin and Judy spent a good amount of their time concerning themselves with insulation, heat production and maintenance.

The robotic spacecraft brought a significant amount of equipment, living supplies and even objects of comfort. The factories and engineers on Earth did a very good job of creating deployable structures, heat engines, oxygen generators, water pumps and other necessities for life on Mars. Along with each load there was always a special "gift." One which motivated Benjamin to quickly find the spacecraft after it landed, bring the cargo modules to the base camp and start work on extricating the contents. The gift was always packed first and therefore was the last to be found.

As a consequence of the the frequent supply flights, 32 buildings had been erected, 20 generators of various kinds were installed, some generating oxygen, heat and electricity for the camp. As the camp grew, the interconnected modules became warm and noisy, giving the flavor of an Arctic outpost on Earth, habitable but predicated on the proper functioning of the integrated equipment.

The gifts were anything from a common table lamp to special food to holiday decorations. It was amazing how such gifts made the pioneer inhabitants feel comforted. It reminded them of the wagon train pioneers of the western migration in the United States. Most of their possessions were practical, but some, a very few were meant only to remind them of the positive aspects of their old homes.

"We have a little city now, Judy," Benjamin reflected. He did this as he looked out of one of their many portholes. The shanty town looking high tech area appeared at first random but all of the buildings' layouts were purposeful.

"Do you think its time for more people, Ben?" asked Judy.

"Definitely, you and I were in some ways lucky to have made it this far, it has not been easy. This town needs more life, so we can relax a bit. NASA is considering this idea now. The problem of course is how to move the bureaucracy into action, especially with the design of new spacecraft for the 'immigrants.' I wonder what they are going to do, especially now that they have competition from to many commercial entities."

"Good question, hope this happens soon, maybe they should dust off Thales."

"Nah, never happen. In a sense that was like flying a biplane across the
Atlantic, it could be done but there are so many better ways of getting here. Most of the robotic craft made it."

"Yeah and two of them are out there, stuck in the dirt, with my ice cream aboard."

"Someday, we or someone we know will find them and get the ice cream."

"Yeah, but...."

Her reflections were interrupted by the radio with the voice of mission control.

"Mars one, this is mission control. We have a text message for you inbound on channel 9. Please advise after your review. Mission control out."

~ Sunrise Descending ~

Judy and Benjamin looked at the radio, then observed a small light on the panel indicating a text message was being downloaded to one of their computers.

Problems in Houston, Problems with Equipment

Courage is the price that Life exacts for granting peace. -
Amelia Earhart

~ Sunrise Descending ~

On the boat his phone was vibrating, making a disturbance in the once delicately quiet night. Hesitating from fear of the unknown, Stephen moved slowly to answer the call.

"Hello, this is Stephen"

"Stephen Daedelus?" asked the caller.

"Yes."

"Stephen, this is Norm Belke, associate administrator of the NASA Mars Mission Directorate, Houston, I apologize for the late call...but we have a problem."

"Sure, I remember you, it must be a challenging problem for you guys to be up at....2 a.m. Your time."

"It is in fact a significant problem and the consensus here is that you would be the best person to help us."

"Okay, what's the deal?"

"Well as you know, people here in Houston were somewhat, lets say, taken aback when you returned from Mars empty. We all know and acknowledge that it was your prerogative, its just that it was not according to the expected flight plan, and that makes the controllers nervous. And of course they had absolutely no intention of letting you fly for us again because of that unpredictability."

"Yeah, I know; it was a tough decision but I really felt it was the proper one, Norm."

"Well, Stephen, that is all water under the bridge now....somethings come up."

"Oh? Have all the people who do not trust me retired?"

"Not exactly."

"What then?"

"It's best if you come in for a meeting, none of this needs to go over the air waves."

"When?"

"Tomorrow."

"Wow, must be important, do you want me in Houston?"

"That would be best, Stephen. A private jet will meet you in Richmond, next to the flight museum tomorrow morning at 0700."

"Well, okay. How long will I be needed?"

"You're right about that, see you tomorrow."

The phone went dead, with Stephen trying to understand what had just happened and why he did not answer his question. He sat on the bow of the boat for a bit, considered another beverage but realizing the lack of sleep he was about to experience he thought better of it. He gathered his things, rose, looked around to make sure all of the lines were secure and the covers on the settee were properly placed. He walked down the starboard side towards the entrance to the rear salon of the Chris Craft Constellation. Turning right he walked down the steps towards the forward salon and paused briefly looking at the book shelf on the port side of the boat. The moon was full and filling the cabin with that slightly blue light and making the air smell a bit differently, as the presence of the moon typically does.

The books were illuminated by the blue, late night light and Stephen thought about the authors, both living and dead; in fact, mostly dead; casting their impression and snippets of life from earlier times. The historical snapshots from these books formed the lattice like bridge to the past, for the most part, these books were the only commentaries of the various ages long gone. Not just history, in fact, in the case of the books on the shelves, mostly social, philosophical, personal, political and scientific observations. All state of the art during their particular time periods. What was so fascinating about these books was that these were the chronicles of the authors past, allowing the succeeding authors a shoulder to stand on for their new views of the world.

Stephen continued to walk to the forward area of the boat, down another flight of stairs to the kitchen or galley. He cleaned his glass and looking up from the sink thought about the old boat, some 40 years old now, and how still in good shape. The wood mellowed the bumps during the multitude of voyages the boat had experienced. The wood absorbed the atoms of all of the people who had owned it and spent time on the boat. The wood as a result looked good from the experience. The electronics were old, but the engines and systems all worked and had been kept in good shape. A few previous owners had in fact lived on it and called it home. One of the owners was a Tuskegee Airman, hero of the second world war. The wood had absorbed the traces of many parties, musical events, sleep overs and other rhapsodies.

He loved this thing, not just for its history and beauty but also for its spirits. Those voices and murmurs from passing salt water and laughing people. He never wanted to leave it, but now he had to prepare to do so yet again. This meant securing the hatches, sea cocks, electrical systems, water systems, heads, plus a general clean up. He worked for the next hour doing this, in silence.

What was it about old boats and old airplanes? Kept in good shape they last forever. Can this be said of more modern things? Only time will tell, but aircraft from the 1920s can still be flown and there are many boats on the water that are hundreds of years old.

Stephen's last act before retiring was to go out on the bow one more time and look at the stars. As he did so, peering upwards, he remembered that the universe above was gushing discoveries. Hopefully his trip in the morning would allow him to help the process of discovering.

He would not be disappointed.

Mars Life

We are all...children of this universe. Not just Earth, or Mars, or this System, but the whole grand fireworks. And if we are interested in Mars at all, it is only because we wonder over our past and worry terribly about our possible future. - Ray Bradbury

~ Sunrise Descending ~

Judy and Benjamin watched the download activity with marginal interest. This activity happened at least once a day. The support excitement for the pioneers on the red planet had been reduced due to budget problems. The general public was on to other concerns back on Earth. So what was left was the two people on Mars, fending for themselves with low level support from "home."

"Wonder what's up?" Mused Benjamin.

"Its a little early for a message today, I'll get it while I get some tea." Judy said while getting up and gliding over to the communication rack.

Although they had been doing their prescribed exercises, Judi and Benjamin had slowly adapted to the Martian gravity, which was 38% of Earth's, and as a result, had muscular changes to compensate. They were thinner, their hearts pumped slower, their food intake was much less. These were the consequences of living on another world; one adapts and in this case the adaptation would not allow them to ever leave their new home. Few people had thought about this when the exploration fury was in full swing. The new Martians were forever Martians; their children, of which they had two, were diminutive by Earth standards and would be in physical distress if they ever visited Earth. They however and their parents had some distinct advantages that few had predicted. Although their bodies were a bit smaller from the experience, their cranial cavities had grown, especially the children. Also, the oxygen rich atmosphere from the multiple greenhouse air processing network, aided in their mental capabilities. In addition to the changes probably the biggest difference was that they discovered that they were aging at a much slower rate.

They both liked to run through the evergreen forests in the greenhouses. They could leap 10 feet at a time and run for an hour through the interconnected buildings they had built.

Robot ships had provided a constant stream of building materials, which kept them very busy. At the end of the day however they would look out of their windows over the village and wonder when the others would arrive. Slowly over the months the idea that more pioneers would arrive to do the science and continue the infrastructure began to morph from a solid schedule to a hopeful banter.

On Earth the causes were complicated. There were thousands of space industry workers that planned, built, tested and launched the robotic ships that made their way to Judy and Benjamin, but it was getting more expensive to continue these flights. World economies were having problems adjusting to a strictly capitalist philosophy as the drive for lower personal wages coupled with greed caused a significant division between owners and workers. As a result, the economies of many countries were unable or unwilling to support an expensive space program, replete of profitability and supporting only two people. The robot visits became less frequent and the quality of the cargo was lower. The whole program was headed for a major funding cut unless one of two things happened:

The Mars colony became completely autonomous

or

There was a financial incentive to continue the robotic trips.

The tide was changing and Benjamin and Judy knew it. It became obvious that they needed to talk privately with someone at NASA they could trust. This is why they took notice when the red message light was illuminated. It was a message from a friend.

Judy walked over the machine and reading the text, spoke aloud.

"This is from Jack, he says that things are getting worse at the Space Agency....'much has happened even in

37

the last few weeks and I am concerned. Money is drying up and the administrators are working hard to provide the support you need to continue. They have identified two possible scenarios that you need to think about. Namely, live in a more isolated way or come home. All of us would prefer you stay, as the science you have provided has been invaluable, more importantly, having life on another planet is a huge psychological benefit. While you live on Mars, there is hope that there is a better life elsewhere. I say this in light of the fact that in some ways we here on Earth are returning to the Dark Ages, as only a handful of people own most of the wealth and wield most of the power. Money is the real focus on any decision that is made and because the powers that be don't understand the greater benefit of having you on Mars, they are cutting back on the support. What has really happened here is that the powerful corporations and vested interests have enough influence on our national governments that all activities are viewed in a cost/benefit way. Your mission is costly, the benefits are not so obvious to the capitalists, unless of course you find gold. I want you to know this so you will be prepared for an important conference call you will be getting next week. The questions are can you manage by yourselves or do you want to come home to Earth. I am guessing that those will be the only choices for you. ' Regards, Jack."

Judy looked away from the monitor to see Benjamin's reaction and observed a blank face, unemotional.

"What do you think?" she asked.

"Not sure just yet. But I know that we need to talk about this. I was hopping that we would have more people here to join us. I am not sure if we can or should stay here alone."

"The problem dear is that we are acclimated to the Martian gravity and climate, such as it is. To go back could be problematic, even dangerous. We are thinner, our hearts work slower and the kids were born here and might not fare well on Earth."

"True. I am worried about this myself. You know Judy, we thought about this years ago before we decided to stay here and realized then the scope of our decision. It was not easy, but we felt compelled to try. I know that we could make it here by ourselves but it would be a struggle. What will happened to our children? Would they be the last Martians?

"Well for now lets think about the options, the powers that be won't discuss this until next week and then we might have a different view. I will call Jack and tell him to stand by for our decision."

"Okay."

Judy sat down at the communications terminal and started typing a note to Jack. After a few moments she rose to join Benjamin at the dinner table to think about the future. Life on Mars had not been that bad actually, just different; it was like living in Northern Canada without the snow. The oxygen had been generated by thousands of plants and trees.   The excess was vented   off to the Martian atmosphere. Years ago scientists had calculated that this process would eventually lead to an atmosphere with clouds, warmer temperatures and the ability to go outside with an oxygen mask only, not a full spacesuit. But these days were getting farther away as the effort to colonize Mars was slowing down.

If they left, the automatic watering systems and venting systems would eventually fail and their work would be in ruins.

If they stayed, they could become fully isolated and life would be very problematic. Especially with two siblings procreation would not be an option.

Could there be another solution?

~ Sunrise Descending ~

A significant amount of people on Earth were thinking about this too. It was a heated topic amongst the space industry workers as well as the general public. The only people not thinking about this were the industrialists who had made their minds up long ago...no profit, no reason to pursue.

The conversation would effect Stephen Daedalus's life.

Back to the Boat, then Destination Houston

There is a tide in the affairs of men, Which taken at the flood, leads on to fortune. Omitted, all the voyage of their life is bound in shallows and in miseries. On such a full

sea are we now afloat. And we must take the current when it serves, or lose our ventures. - William Shakespeare

Stephen slept well on the gently rocking boat. In the morning, he rose, had his tea, ate breakfast and secured the systems on the boat. This entailed closing the sea cocks below in the engine room, shutting off the unnecessary electronics and doing an inspection of the outside of the boat to make sure the lines were set. Gathering his bag and backpack, Stephen left the boat and walked down to the dock; this always began the worst part of being on the boat: leaving.

He rubbed his arm where the doctor had given him his injection, wondering if anything was happening to him. He certainly did not sense anything although it had not been a long time since the visit to the office. The experience still haunted him to a degree, with the empty office and the strange promising story about freezing his life at his present age.

Reaching the end of the dock which started where the boat was moored outside on the open water and wound its way through a long covered portion to the marina office and the parking lot, he turned right to find his rental car, parked a few hundred feet away and continued until he came to the left side of the car. Pushing the unlock button on the key fob, the car beeped and he opened the rear passenger door to throw his bags in the back seat. Closing it he then opened the driver's door, sat down, paused to look at the bobbing boats nestled in their slips looking like horses ready to leap to the race. He really did not like this view as it meant he was really leaving for a while, maybe a long while. Stephen drank it in for a few long moments, then looking down, started the car. Driving the circuitous route back to the airport, Stephen could faintly hear and smell the boat, which was starting the long wait for human occupation.

The airport was small but busy, but he did not have to spend any time in the main concourse, but find his way to the General Aviation (GA) terminal where a sleek white Citation X jet was waiting for him. He dropped off the rental car and made his way to the GA terminal, located the jet which was sitting there whining with the auxiliary power unit on. There was a flight attendant at the door in a suit. Stephen walked up the air stairs and inside to an empty plane. He took his place in one of the plush seats and buckled his seat belt. The flight attendant pushed a button to retract the stairs and close the door; this happened at the same time the starboard engine started to wind up. The door shut and as the attendant took seat next to Stephen, the aircraft started to taxi.

"Want something to drink before we take off, Mr. Daedelus?"

"Sure, how about some coffee?"

"Coming right up, sir."

"The attendant rose and moved towards the galley on the right side, disappeared for a moment and returned with a porcelain cup and saucer."

"Cream? Sugar?"

"Cream please."

10 seconds later, Stephen was leaning back in his seat, the flight attendant was strapping in to her seat and both engines were lit. The aircraft taxied quickly and was number one for departure. The jet lined up on the North/South runway and straightened up on the centerline. The engines spooled up and the acceleration was brisk pushing the occupants of the jet down in their seats. Within a few seconds the nose rose to a high attitude and the jet was off into the wild blue. At one hundred feet above the ground, the jet rolled to the left to a westerly heading and with the gear coming up, accelerated to 350 knots. Even

though it was below 10,000 feet, where the speed limitation on aircraft is 250 knots, this particular flight was given no speed restrictions. The engines seemed to be at takeoff thrust levels for several minutes as the clouds whizzed by and a few light bumps gave way to smooth high speed flight. The climb was direct to 50,000 feet, where the nose arced over to a cruise angle of about 10 degrees and finally the thrust of the engines diminished a bit to keep the jet from going supersonic. This particular aircraft was capable of .92 Mach or 640 knots true air speed. It appeared from the cabin that it was flying to its potential. The sky outside appeared very deep blue if not black at this lofty height.

The attendant rose again and offered lunch and another drink. Stephen took advantage of the offer and selected Filet Mignon as his main course followed by crème brulee desert. Too early for alcohol, Stephen selected ice tea. The meal was perfect and by the time the formalities of serving the meal was over it seemed that the jet was starting its descent. Relaxed, Stephen waited for the long descending flight path to culminate in a landing in Houston. The flight took a total of one hour and fifteen minutes as the jet was given priority routing and no speed restrictions in any phase of the flight.

~ Sunrise Descending ~

The NASA airfield was ready when they arrived and after a smooth touchdown the jet quickly taxied to a hangar where one engine was shut down on the way and after it entered the cavernous building the other was shut down. By the time the aircraft came to a stop, the only sounds left to hear were from the door opening and the air-handling fans slowing to a stop. Once the cabin door was fully open and the air stairs deployed, Stephen stepped out to a waiting group of people eager to take him to the main office complex where the future would start to unfold.

A waiting car took the group to the main NASA headquarters and they entered a side door and moved directly to check in at the security office. A badge was issued along with a compensatory FBI background check. All was in order and Stephen was issued the standard instruction regarding movement inside the facilities and the required escorts in certain areas.

"You are not authorized to go to floors 5 and 6 without escort." directed the head guard.

"Understood." replied Stephen. In some ways, being in a secured facility like this was a privilege and in other ways a restriction of freedom. Today Stephen simply wanted to get this over and find out what all of the ceremony was about. He did not mind the constant companions and the parting of the groups of people as they walked to a conference room. As they walked down the hall towards the conference room he heard the familiar techno speak of so many aerospace facilities.....

"We are PDR minus 30 as of today; we have to finish the peer reviews and mod the CDR for compliance."

"We are out of limits on the simulated bell temps, we need a hired gun to come in and help us."

"The FAA hacks are on us like a cheap suit, I don't care if they are right, we need to relax the specs to move on."

Stephen smirked at this talk, as he had been a part of the culture for so many years. Things got so complicated in this line of business that cost overruns and sliding delivery dates were the norm. The general idea of aerospace engineering was to have every detail scrutinized (which makes sense) by several engineers and ultimately one engineer would be the guru of one finite detail and represent his specification in hundreds of meeting before any metal was cut. Although on the surface this was safe, the philosophy of not leaving any details to chance crippled the progress of designing and testing spacecraft. Everyone worked very hard but having 45 engineers design a small radio was too costly in terms of time and money. The outgrowth of too many failed or slowed space projects gave way to the lean and mean approaches of the smaller more nimble companies that could move quickly and keep the risks to themselves.   In part that is why Stephen was walking down this hall today, although for what exact reason he did not know.

Turning the corner to the right and aiming for the conference room a hundred feet away, Stephen saw a women thirty feet ahead going in the same direction. He noticed her fluid stride and how she moved outside as well as inside her clothes. It had been a while for him, and this mesmerization although a bit Neanderthal was taking over his more reasonable senses. It felt natural in to almost stare, it may have been crude, but he was having a hard time noticing anything else. She had an aura of confidence punctuated with obvious women hood. He started to wonder.....

"I see you have found the director." said another women who was standing closer to Stephen having watched the display of behavior unbecoming of an officer.

Stephen snapped back into reality.

She continued. "She is too far up on the food chain to be interested in you pal. Especially when your drooling." The women turned to go into another office with a bit of a sneer on her face. Had it been that obvious? Especially for a total of 12 seconds of staring. How could anyone else notice, but then again women, Stephen found out, are observant. He sobered up and walked to the large conference room and looked for a chair.

"Please, over there." said the women Stephen had been staring at as she pointed to an end chair, opposite her's.

"Okay, thanks," stuttered Stephen. He moved towards the assigned seat after looking for ten milliseconds at her face. She was actually quite attractive except for a very serious look of purpose, which raised Stephen's eyebrows and reset his brain for serious work.

She continued as the attendants were sitting down and starting their laptop computers. "Lets get settled everyone. Please close the door and lock it. Okay everyone, we have Stephen Daedalus here with us today, we need to get right down to business and tell him why we are here and how he can help us." The room quieted a bit with the exception of the low level tapping of the keyboards. To the right of the director a man focussed on Stephen and began to speak.

"Stephen, I am Dr. Hyatt, deputy director for space missions to Mars. In this room are the director and managers of all of the divisions responsible for flying missions to Mars. They support the activities of the people that live there. By that I mean Benjamin, Judy, and their two children who chose to stay on your mission several years ago in Thales. We are all in agreement that to move forward on this mission, and we need your help." Dr. Hyatt paused for a moment, allowing Stephen to view the others in the room, several whom were looking at him. Stephen could sneak another glimpse of the director who has studying him. Thales was the name of the 747-400 that was modified with a rocket engine that flew to Mars, landed and flew back.

Dr. Hyatt was referring to a mission Stephen had commanded years ago which culminated in leaving two people on the red planet. Upon Stephen's return from Mars he intercepted an alien probe. The results of these two events changed everything, especially how Stephen was treated upon his return. The space probe became top priority as it contained messages for the inhabitants of Earth as it's planet of origin had detected life here. Stephen was just another pilot when he landed the 747 at Cape Canaveral and walked out to a meager group of technicians assigned to "safe" the aircraft and moth ball it in a lone hangar at the Cape. After that it was a combination of small contracts and life on a wooden boat. It really wasn't too bad, just lonely at times.

The deputy director continued, "We in the room are the decision makers. Dr. Captiva, to my right, is the director and principal scientist in this mission, her decisions are final. The other people in this room specialize in logistics, propulsion, robotics, communications and public relations." Stephen, while listening, decided that the object of his affections, Dr. Captiva was probably just a drone. She was acting like a company drone and examining him with anything but curiosity. Probably no fun at all. He shifted in his seat to start the long process of getting the rundown of why he was brought here and what they wanted. At this point it looked like work to him.

"Okay here are the details", Dr. Hyatt started while the other directed their attention to Stephen. "We have been working a mission for the last several years that in essence you started. As you know it was not planned and NASA had to scramble to address the problem as well as support the two people left on Mars. It was not easy and continues to be a significant financial drain for the agency. Because of some serious pressure from Washington to cut the budget and move on to more science oriented missions, we need to resolve some major questions relative to our activities. We have a mandate to roll back the mission activities by 90% in the next year which gives us but few options. In fact two options, make the inhabitants on Mars autonomous or bring them back. After due consideration, bringing them back is problematic, they have adjusted to the gravity on Mars and the medical staff believes that it would be extremely risky to have them try to live on Earth. So our recommendation is to fly more people there, willing to live without support from us unless there is an emergency. We intend to have a rocket available on standby for such contingencies. The regular missions however, will stop. NASA will cut back all but the most essential communications and move on to other priorities. You're here to help us with our decision to go back to Mars, bring more people and hopefully jump start a colony."

The voice echoed in the room a bit while Stephen drank in the words and considered his place in the universe. Unconsciously he rubbed his arm were the good doctor had injected him weeks ago. There was no sensation, just some remote psychological reason, probably wondering what if anything would happen. He forgot about is quickly as the idea of flying back to Mars started to seep in.

"Fly back in what?" Stephen asked.

"Thales, we want to refurbish the spacecraft and fly it back, all of our other plans are seriously delayed and over budget. We had to make a decision based on economics and timing. We think this is our best bet." explained Dr. Hyatt.

"Well, you know what I am going to ask, what have you done with Thales? What are you going to do with Thales? That spacecraft will require some major refit to get it ready for the mission. And of course, we have to fly it beforehand to make sure it is capable of making the journey......and let me get this straight, you spent billions on failed rocket designs and have decided to resurrect a 30 year old airliner/spacecraft hybrid that was designed for a single mission? What am I missing here? Asked Stephen incredulously.

The participants in the room stopped typing and either looked at Stephen or Dr. Captiva. Dr. Captiva started, "Its like this Stephen, its the decision we had to make and now is the time we have to make it, as we have mentioned before, there are pressures from Washington and pressures from within the agency. We do not have time to go over all of the details, suffice it to say that this mission has full NASA and White House support. We are going to execute this mission with or without you. We would prefer to do it with you as you have all of the necessary experience to make this mission a success. Now, do you want to think this over for a bit before giving us an answer?"

"No, I can give you answer now, but first, what would be my role?"

"Commander of the mission, you would be in charge of flying to Mars and returning the spacecraft safely back to Earth."

"Would I have authority, responsibility or both."

"Both, but you have to work within the confines and structure of NASA, just as you have before. And I need to warn you, no more cowboy management will be tolerated."

"Lady, do you know what the first rule of flying an aircraft in the rule book states?" "No, enlighten me," said the director with a slight scowl. "Rule 91.1 of the Federal Aviation Regulations states that the pilot in command is the final authority as to the safe operation of the aircraft, in this case a spacecraft. I don't mind working with you, but I will do what's necessary to be safe."

"Understood, as long as you work with us. No surprises this time."

As she said this, she actually looked human for a second. She waited a few moments for this to sink and then said:

"And I am coming with you."

Stephen was not exactly happy to hear this. "Listen, I don't care if you don't trust me, its more important that I have someone who knows what they are doing in a sophisticated aircraft. This thing cannot be handled by a single pilot."

"Its not about trust," was her reply, "its about the fact that this mission cannot fail, and we do not have the time to get you up to speed, more details will be given to you while we are on our way. Also, I have over a hundred hours in sim on your aircraft."

"Thats not enough for this bird, honey. She flies like like an ocean liner in the air and like a Porsche in space. We will be doing 40,000 mph two hours after we leave orbit, one slight miscalculation and we go to Jupiter instead."

"Correction," she looked directly at Stephen, "55,000 miles and hour, we have made some modifications. I know about them because I directed the re-work as well as 35 other upgrades. You are the one that might need more sim time."

Stephen thought for a few moments. It was a strange combination of wanting to do this mission and not wanting to do it. Fundamentally though, he realized that he would certainly would regret it if he did not try. Sitting on the bow of the boat, although very relaxing would not hold the same value as going back to Mars, even with a overly serious director looking over his shoulder at all times. Also, he was interested in what modifications had been done to the ship. It was time for the big decision but it seemed obvious which way he was going to go.

"Okay, lets do it, when do we leave?"

"Tomorrow morning, first light, we have a lot to do....think you can still fly a T38?"

"Of course, stick or automatic?"

His joke did not go far.

"Cute, but we have serious things to attend to, Stephen, think you can keep up?"

"I am not worried about that, Dr. Captiva. Lets just get the job done and try to have a civil time doing it."

"Agreed, see you tomorrow at Hangar 4, 0600."

With that the meeting came to a close, all participants rose, gathered their things and moved towards the now open door. The director waited, as did Stephen. Some people moving past Stephen said "good luck," but Stephen did not know exactly what to think. Was the challenge going to be in the execution of the mission or living in close quarters with someone who appeared to be extremely serious and probably no fun. He had decided to get in a few words with the director in an effort to be open minded and get to know her better.

She was picking up her notebook and looking at Stephen when she said, "don't mess with me."

Hearing this warm comment encouraged Stephen to reply, "As you wish, doctor."

Now he was worried, although she was still cute, she was obviously very concerned about something and she was overflowing with important confidential information. Stephen was the last to leave the room and while waiting he decided that this was business and the chances of knowing her personally was nil.

Off to the Cape

Men acquire a particular quality by constantly acting a particular way... you become just by performing just actions, temperate by performing temperate actions, brave by performing brave actions. - Aristotle

The next morning came quickly, Stephen rose at 4:00, showered, ate and by 5:00 was at the airfield getting on his flight suit and selecting a helmet for the flight to the cape. He looked around for Dr. Captiva, who he assumed would be flying the T-38 Talon as well to the Cape. This old fighter trainer jet had been around for a long time; it was used to give the commander and pilot of a mission recent high performance experience before a space flight. The jet was actually basic in nature, with steam gauges instead of a glass cockpit, like most modern fighters. It looked fast even on the ground Stephen thought as he walked to the waiting jets on the tarmac. The ground crew was moving around two of the them with ground carts attached and various personnel performing a walk around to insure they were ready. As he got closer, Stephen located the crew chief and walked over to talk to him.

"Good morning, Chief."

"Good morning, Commander, nice day for a flight. Your partner is waiting in her aircraft, she's waiting for you to take off. We have done an inspection of the jet and its ready to go."

"Thanks, I appreciated it chief, however, I always do my own walk around, a habit I learned as a flight instructor."

"As you wish, the Doctor is anxious I might add."

"Don't worry I will keep the inspection to less than an hour."

The crew chief smiled at this and acknowledging that Stephen had the reputation of being a good stick and rudder pilot moved aside to allow him his walk around."

Stephen walked methodically around the craft and looked over the wings, engines and fuselage for any problems.   He found none but felt better about having performed the function himself. At one point he looked over at his "partner" and saw that she was looking at him behind the darkened visor of her helmet. He could only guess at her mood but assumed it was as dark as her visor.

He stepped into the cockpit and adjusted himself to be comfortable, strapped himself in and attached the various hoses and cables to allow for breathing and communication.   He looked up at the crew chief for a second and asked,

"What is the inter-plane frequency?"

"Channel D on your communications panel." The crew chief pointed while saying this and smirked at what Stephen might be thinking of doing. To the crew chief, Stephen was just another hot shot jet pilot, full of himself and cocky. Stephen reached down and placed the switch in the proper position, then verified that the avionics was functional.

"Good morning, sweetheart, been waiting long?"

"An hour or more now, are you satisfied that your Cessna is not going to fall out of the sky?"

"Looks okay to me honey, but I can see from here you left the covering of your pitot tube on, and thats gonna make your flight kinda interesting don't you think?" Stephen smiled inside his visor at this. The channel went dead as she switched over to another frequency to get the ground crew to remove the covering.

"Just wanted to see if you were awake." she said.

"Oh, yeah, ready to hit the wild blue. Wanna lead or follow?"

"Your the commander, if you can get that thing started I will let you go first."

Stephen smiled, and with that initiated the start sequence for the jet's two after-burning engines. The check list was followed exactly and when complete , the commander called ground control.

"Ground, this is Nasa 64, flight of two, at hangar four ready to taxi with information Hotel."

"Nasa 64, flight of two, taxi to runway 35 left, monitor tower."

~ *Sunrise Descending* ~

"Monitor tower, Nasa 64 on the move."

Stephen advanced the throttles to the start the jet rolling, he pressed right rudder to turn it and passing the other jet, noticed it had started moving as well. They taxied to the appointed runway and halfway there....

"Nasa 64, flight of two, cleared for takeoff, climb to seven thousand, heading one two zero degrees, squawk 4323, departure frequency will be 128.15"

Stephen repeated the instructions back to the controller and when he was finished configuring his cockpit for flight, rounded the corner from the taxi way to the runway. He advanced the throttles to max without afterburners and accelerated briskly down the left side of the runway. Behind him and to his right was the accelerating second jet, with his partner; she held a tight formation from the point of advancing the throttles to breaking ground to climbing and turning to the assigned heading. The landing gear on both aircraft snapped up at the same time. As Stephen would eventually find out, she was a master pilot and comfortable in any flying machine.

The pair of jets climbed quickly to their assigned altitude and made their way down the Gulf Coast towards Florida. The conversations were minimal and within a few minutes they were getting priority vectoring to the large North/South Cape Canaveral Shuttle Runway.

Touchdown was smooth and they taxied in unison to the ramp and the the awaiting flight personnel. Exited, Stephen walked over to the second jet and as the canopy was lifting, Dr. Captiva pulled off her helmet and motioned Stephen over.

"Nice flight, you held your altitude pretty well, by they way, you and I are very good friends as far as these people as concerned, lets not make them change their minds."

"Okay," Stephen said reluctantly, "I will do my best."

With this, and the approaching line personnel, Dr. Captiva alighted from her jet and smiling gave everyone present the sense that all was well, and the new mission, the most exciting one as far as she was concerned, was just beginning. Smiles everywhere, even on Stephen, who thought it best to keep up the charade until he understood what was really going on.

They moved inside to shed their flight suits and put on the official NASA astronaut clothes, a blue jumpsuit with patches and zippered pockets. They walked confidently amongst the NASA personnel and waved to those who waved from afar. This was the astronauts' way of doing things. They had all walked down these paths and through these buildings in the past, all made history as well. They ended up walking to a waiting van and drove to the Vehicle Assembly Building (VAB for short) for their first pre-flight meeting.

The trip did not take long, and even when they started the enormous building was in clear view. Built on eight acres of land, standing 526 feet tall with it own internal weather system, one cannot be but awed at looking at it or being in it. Built in the 1960s for the Saturn Rocket which took astronauts to the moon, it had been converted and re-used for many other missions including the Space Shuttle.

Their van stopped in front of one of the giant 456 foot doors to the building, Stephen and Dr. Captiva got out and stopped to look at the enormous structure. Stephen mused that it looked like two enormous hands with a thousand steel fingers wrapping around an interior.

"Its interesting that the steel that was used to make this came from ships, automobiles and other structures that were used in the second world war and after a long and interesting history were melted and reformed into this building," Stephen said to his mildly interested partner.

"Its an amazing structure with a thousand stories in it," she returned.

65

"Yep."

They needed to return to work and promptly walked into a conference room inside the enormous building that was reserved for the Thales II mission. It was away from the mainstream NASA activity in the other on site buildings so there would be few distractions. They sat down together and looked at a group of space workers, some with hard hats on, that would be the ground crew for the new mission.

"Well the crew is here, what the hell is going on?" Asked a rather acerbic ground operations manager.

Dr. Captiva began, "ladies and gentlemen, this is a new NASA mission that was conceived of very quickly and has the full support of the NASA directorate and the White House. All of you have been selected to work with us based on your experience here and more importantly the high level of security clearance you all possess. It is imperative that this mission be executed smoothly and quickly. You will be given all the resources you need be they material or human. Get only the best most trusted people and the best equipment. If you need something that is in (for instance) Antarctica right now, it will be sent on its way to you this afternoon. This mission has the highest priority of any mission NASA is working on currently. Put everything else aside, make your plans and get moving. All of you in this room have had a separate briefing of what is expected of you. Some of you have already started your tasks. The Thales spaceship will be brought out of mothballs immediately and refurbished for a new mission. This means new engines, avionics, cabin and scientific instruments. All of these components will be here in the next week. We have to integrate and test them and start test flights in less than three weeks from now. Everyone has been cleared for extensive overtime pay as we need to launch in two months. Cancel your barbecues, we need to get started. Any questions?"

Several hands went up.

"We are going to need a bunch of people just to change out the engines."

"Then call Boeing now, they are on board with this mission and will send you all of the personnel you need. The engines will be here very soon and if it takes ten people to change one out then get forty people here immediately."

"Where are the mission headquarters if we need to coordinate our efforts?"

"Right here in this room, Stephen and I will be living in this building and can be reached twenty four seven. Your information packets have our cell numbers. Any other questions?"

67

She received no replies, just bewildered looks reacting to the immediacy and intensity of this new mission.

"Alright then, lets get to work."

All of the workers rose and headed for their assignments. Dr. Captiva opened her laptop and connected to the local internet, started the process of following progress on the individual tasks. Stephen, watching her, decided to do the same. The room quickly emptied and the two partners became engrossed in the details of the mission. Stephen reviewed the personal and cargo manifest and the general flight plan.

"Who are these ten people we are taking to Mars?" was one of his first questions."

"A carefully selected crew, willing to stay and try to exist on the planet without assistance from us. They are all skilled infrastructure people. Engineers and technicians mostly with a few medical personnel and an astronomer."

"An astronomer?"

"Yes, for the most part the Martian atmosphere is pristine and the transmissivity is excellent, much better than Earth's. Observations there will all reach the diffraction limit or ultimate resolving power of their telescopes. NASA will send robotic spacecraft to the planet with mirror sections that will be assembled into a large segmented offset reflector. This way there will be no aperture blockage and the images will be pure. As you know, many other planets have been discovered but our earthly instruments cannot resolve features or determine in detail the gases prevalent in their respective atmospheres. A large Martian telescope will be able to do so."

"And discover life on another planet?"

"Exactly."

"How much support are we going to give them after we leave them there?"

"Not much, emergencies of course and periodic science missions, but nothing like we have been giving them. Its time they tried to make it on their own. Do you know how much they have accomplished since they have been there?"

"Well, I have followed some of the details but in general, no."

"They have built a self sustaining village also they have completely acclimated to the Martian gravity and cold. They have more water and food there than they can use and have really done an amazing job in colonizing that planet."

"Good for them."

"Using their building techniques, we think we can triple the size of the village to accommodate more people in the future. NASA however cannot support them anymore due to budget cuts and political pressures."

"They don't make any money for anyone here on Earth, huh?"

"Not my place to say, not yours either."

"Okay, I understand we just have an assignment to follow."

"Exactly."

With that, Stephen realized that there were probably more stories to tell, but this was not the venue. He spent another hour on the flight plans. He noticed the effects of increased performance from the upgrades. At some point he realized that he was getting tired and it was close to dinner time.

"Dinner tonight?" He asked, guard down.

"I told you not to mess with me, Stephen, we have no time for socializing especially when we are making every one else work their tails off and by the way, I have little interest in fly boys with Neanderthal attitudes and sexist opinions."

"So...I guess that means no."

"Your catching up."

~ Sunrise Descending ~

"How do you know I am sexist?"

"Its in your eyes and your mannerisms. Look, I don't have time to peer into your soul and tell you what went wrong in your mis-spent youth. Suffice it to say we have a mission to accomplish and I am not going to let your drooling interfere with the proper execution of our tasks.

"Okay, okay, I hear you. Hands to myself.....so now I am confused, you knew my history I'm sure. What made you choose this mission, especially with a handsome Neanderthal like myself?"

"Just lucky I guess."

Stephen thought he was getting mixed messages from Dr. Captiva, but at this point in the conversation was very clear about her non interest.

"Okay, its too cold in here for me, I am going for a walk, maybe I'll find some humans."

"Make it quick, we have a lot of work to do."

"Aye, aye."

Stephen walked off, wondering what had just happened. It would not worry him to much except for the fact that he was attracted to this women who seemed like she was mad most of the time. He would have to be in close quarters with her for the flight there, four months and the flight back, four months. He wondered for the first time,

71

was this was really a good idea. It became apparent to him that he needed to resolve this issue before they launched and that he might have to make a very hard decision quickly.

For now he walked to the hangar that housed his old plane, which had worked so well a few years ago, getting him and others to Mars and safely home again. It really was a remarkable spacecraft in that it was designed for Earth bound work but was easily adaptable to space. They had attached skids on the underside of the craft for a high speed landing on one of the deserts of Mars, this had worked very well, so well that the takeoff was uneventful. The rocket engine from Boeing had about 100,000 pounds of thrust and easily got them out of Earth's orbit as well as successfully off the Martian surface. It was throttle-able and had a smooth response.

Stephen walked towards the main hangar and thought about all of the history at the Cape, from the 1950s on, heros were made here, not just pilots but engineers and flight controllers as well. He smiled at this thought as he walked in the warm Florida sunshine. Nearing the building he slowed to soak up more sun and rounding the corner found the entrance door to the hangar and ultimately to an aircraft he had not seen in years.

~ Sunrise Descending ~

The door was on one of the sliding sections of the hangar door and when opened, revealed darkness inside. Stephen moved in following the main hangar door to a supporting wall. There he looked for the light switches. After a few moments he found them, turned them all on and heard their ballasts start to begin the slow process to full brightness. In the dim light he could see the tall tail of Thales in the far corner, behind several other jets and test equipment. He walked over to get a closer look. The lights continued to increase in brightness and by the time he got to the aircraft details were easily seen.

The aircraft was filthy, covered in dust and probably had birds living in it. The scorch marks of the underside of the aircraft from re-entry were still there. As he walked around looking at the bottom side of the craft he heard footsteps near the hangar door. They were getting closer and constituted at least three people. As they neared the aircraft they found Stephen and addressed him.

"She's dirty isn't she?"

"Filthy, when is last time she saw the outside?"

"Years ago, its time to change that. By the way, my name is Brian, chief mechanic for this hangar, these are my technicians, Phil and Bob, they are here to bring her out and clean her up. Later today, we will have about a hundred people in and on her, tearing out systems and putting in new ones. It will be a twenty four seven operation and I can assure you when we get done she will look real pretty."

"Thanks, I look forward to that," said Stephen

The large hangar doors started to open, revealing several more people in tugs or holding tow bars all ready to start the extraction process. There were about five jets and two helicopters that needed to be removed before Thales could be moved. Birds fluttered about as Stephen reached up and touched Thales for the first time in many years. His fingers revealed a lot of dust and grime. Looking out to the sun outside he noticed that there were ladder trucks waiting as well to wash the years of accumulated dust and dirt onto the tarmac below. Stephen expected to see an inch of dirt on the ground when it was over and his quess was actually pretty close.

Slowly the other planes came out and it seemed that the process was bringing fresher and fresher air to the deep insides of the hangar where Stephen was waiting. Finally a technician approached with a tow bar and connected it to the 747. Pockets of dust fell to the floor as he did this. The tug approached slowly, lining up with the long axis of the plane and moved towards the steel ring at the end of the tow bar. The connection was made and when the other techs cleared the wing tips and tail the tug started to slowly pull the great bird out to the sunshine. The tug labored as this was by far the largest aircraft in the hangar. They (Stephen, the tug and the technicians) moved at a slow pace towards the open hangar doors. The wheels of the plane rumbled over the steel tracks of the hangar door and finally they moved out to a central position on the tarmac. Looking at the aircraft in the full sunlight a light brown coating was revealed. Stephen was motioned away from the plane as the cleaning trucks moved in to start the process of washing it down. This would take close to an hour with several cycles of cleaning and rinsing which needed to take place. During this time Stephen spoke with the technicians and engineers who had gathered a few hundred feet away. There was a plan to clean, position air stairs at the forward entrance door and eventually open every door and hatch to air the thing out. The aircraft would be placed back in the hangar at sunset and the work would continue on the retrofit. The other planes and helicopters would be taken to other hangars, leaving Thales alone for the first time in years. Alone in the cavernous space but covered in NASA "ants" for the next several weeks.

The air smelled dirty while the trucks drove around the airplane and applied industrial strength detergent followed by clean water rinses. By the second round, the air started to smell cleaner and the plane started to shine a bit, revealing its true self. Finally, the trucks completed their duties and drove back to a staging area, the airplane was dripping thousands of droplets of clean water. The noise of the drips waned over a period of about 10 minutes. The quiet was followed by the starting of an air stair truck which drove slowly into place at the forward passenger boarding door. A lineman motioned the truck into place and stopped it when the rubber tube at the end of the upper walkway touched the clean fuselage of the plane. Hydraulic feet extended to stabilize the stairs. Then someone came over to Stephen and motioned him to join the technicians that were going to open the craft for the first time in years. No one knew what to expect but Stephen was the most experienced person on the tarmac. He knew what to expect because he with what was the last to leave the ship. Due to the frantic activity surrounding the discovery of the Spheront probe on the maiden voyage of Thales so many years ago, Stephen stepped off of the aircraft and it was immediately sealed until there was time to go over the interior and record the aircraft's condition; that time never came, until now.

Stephen was apprehensive but curious at the same time and alighted the stairs with the techs. The leader of the group made his way to the hatch and grasped the handle turning it counter clockwise, pulled hard, and yanked it open. He moved the door to the forward outside position and peered in.

"It smells pretty rough in there," the technician said as he looked at Stephen.

"I understand it was never cleaned out, there should be a lot of old food and garbage in there."

"How about putting an air evacuation hose in there and running it a bit before entering?"

"Good idea."

Another technician put a breathing mask on and reaching down to an awaiting air-conditioner trailer, pulled a hose into the interior of the plane about 150 feet, near the center. He returned in a few moments.

Removing his mask he addressed Stephen, "Looks like some of the aircraft I have seen in the Arizona Boneyard for aircraft. Not too bad, its just obvious that no one has been in there for years."

After a few minutes Stephen entered tentatively, followed by several other NASA workers. They fanned out to address the situation in their respective areas. Some coughed as the air was slowly filtering out. During this process, other technicians had attached a standard air

77

handling hose to the air conditioning pack access area on the belly of the aircraft. Within a few minutes, fresh air started flowing out of the many vents inside the aircraft. At the same time, electrical power had been connected, energizing relays and allowing power to be applied to the lighting systems. Stephen made his way to the cockpit and hesitating, switched on the overhead lights circuit breaker. The plane started to come to life as air was circulating and lights started coming on. A few were not operational but for the most part the plane was now alive with air, lights and people.

"Looks good," commented Stephen to himself.

For the first time in the last few days, Stephen felt happy. He was now doing something, self actualizing and getting caught up in the new mission. Life blood now coursing through his veins. He smiled and had a wave of confidence regarding his position in life. He took in a deep breath of semi stale air and started checking out the various systems on the ship.

Hours later the internal air was clean and fresh and several systems were up and running. This included the navigation and communication systems.

"These people make good equipment," Stephen mused, thinking about the aerospace engineers who had provided him and the rest of the Thales I crew with excellent systems.

By this time over one hundred personnel were working on the craft, inside and out. They were removing the rocket engine mounted on the lower aft fuselage of the aircraft and pulling avionics boxes out of the electronics bays. Every activity appeared orchestrated and efficient. All moving surfaces of the wings and empenage (tail) were removed for overhaul. Several machining areas had been set up in the hangar for this purpose. At some point observing this beehive like activity Stephen stepped out of the aircraft to take a break and view the action from afar. As he move outside to the top of the air stair platform he saw Dr. Captiva on the tarmac looking up at him. The night was crisp, the moon was full, and Stephen, even with all of the previous uncomfortable conversations was still taken by her, standing on the tarmac which was wet and shiny from a short rain shower minutes before.

"Ship doesn't look too bad," Stephen said hesitatingly, although he was really thinking she did not look so bad herself.

"Was it a mess before?"

"A bit, but hard work and patience always wins in the end"

79

"Hmmm."

"Would you like to visit your new home?"

"In a bit....first I would like to talk to you....privately."

"Okay, I'll be right down."

Stephen started walking down the stairs hopeful that this next conversation would not blow up like the last. He made it to the tarmac and with the Moon casting blue and gray shadows on the surroundings and Dr. Captiva illuminated softly by the same lunar glow, waited patiently for his arrival.

"Its nice out tonight," he started

"Beautiful," was her reply.

"Look," he continued, "I really don't want us to be at odds with each other, its really important for the mission but more importantly, I just feel like I would like to get to know you for who you are, not just the scientist director who is responsible for this gigantic undertaking.

"I have a lot of things on my mind and I am not sure I have time to get personal."

"No problem, one step at a time. I just think that if we both lowered our weapons for a moment the mission would have a better chance of success."

She thought for a second, and it seemed like a layer of ice might have melted off.

"Okay, but not too fast. I agree that we need to get along to allow the efficient execution of this mission, its just that I am not in a place for anything too personal."

"Fair enough. Like I said, one step at a time; no pressure."

They turned away from the now illuminated aircraft which seemed covered with people pulling parts off its exterior. They walked down a path made of crushed seashells, like so many other Florida paths, and walked slowly towards the ocean. Stephen thought is would be wise to be quiet and drink in the beautiful evening and look forward to seeing the shimmering sea. The temperature was perfect. They walked further down the path and eventually came to the Atlantic Ocean, whose expanses here had witnessed many rocket launches, some explosions and a few tragedies.

"Stephen, I have to tell you something," she began after many minutes.

"Go ahead," he replied.

"This mission has many layers to it and you will find the details out soon enough but suffice it to say that it has to work...it has to work because there will be no others."

"I'm not sure what you mean."

"The powers that be do not like scientists who do basic research, unless of course it produces profit in the end. So it has been decided that we have to finish the Mars colony support....now. If our mission fails, there isn't a viable back up plan. The colonists will be cut loose from all but emergency support and that will always be months away. Many of us at NASA wanted continuous support, especially since the colonists had been doing a wonderful job of building the infrastructure necessary for further human habitation. But now that is done; we can deliver a few more people to Mars and then thats it. The people who have signed up are under no illusions about this mission; they know that it could lead to their demise if they are not successful in creating a self sustaining city on Mars. We did not have as many volunteers as we have had in the past for this mission. Everyone knows its one way."

"Okay, fair enough. I appreciate you being honest with me."

"Well, you would have figured it out soon enough."

"Then, if I may ask, why are you going on this mission.....do you intend on staying?"

"Interesting question, Stephen. Between you and me, and this really has to stay confidential, I am not sure exactly what I am going to do. Officially to complete this

82

mission I need to return. I am concerned however as to what I am going to return *to*."

"Hmmmm, okay, I promise to keep this conversation to myself. To be completely candid with you, I am only interested in completing a safe mission. You can make any personal decision you want as long as it does not compromise that aspect of this mission."

Dr. Captiva nodded in agreement and turning her gaze out to the moonlit sea becoming deep in thought about her future.

Stephen, unable to ignore her beauty, watched the gentle warm breeze move her long hair to expose and sometimes cover up parts of her perfect face. He was overwhelmed by the moment.

"What's your first name?"

"Zsa. Please only call me that in private, I have an image to protect."

"Okay, that works for me. And now that we are being honest with one another, I would like to move away from our initial brash conversations and begin new ones based on mutual respect."

She looked at him directly. "Sure you can handle that cowboy?"

"I promise to do my best."

"Okay, but in public it has to be nothing but professional, and I really mean that. A thousand eyes are on us now. Ones that you know about and ones that you don't. We have to work perfectly together and strictly by the book. If anyone senses a friendship between us we will take a lot of heat for it."

"Okay I can handle that, in fact its better for me to do my best when I don't have to wonder if you are going to stab me in the back."

"Well the night is young."

Stephen and Zsa fell silent again for a few moments. Stephen had the urge to step toward her but knew this was not the time for her or the mission."

"We need to get back."

"You're right, lets go."

~ Sunrise Descending ~

The Beast Awakens

Engineering is not merely knowing and being knowledgeable, like a walking encyclopedia; engineering is not merely analysis; engineering is not merely the possession of the capacity to get elegant solutions to non-existent engineering problems; engineering is practicing the art of the organized forcing of technological change... Engineers operate at the interface between science and society. - Dean Gordon Brown

They walked back in the moonlight to the hangar which was buzzing with activity. It was a perfect Florida evening. They separated several hundred feet from the hangar; Zsa, or Dr. Captiva now, walked back to the conference room which was now mission control and Stephen went back to the hangar to observe and coordinate activities. They both felt better and more at peace than they had an hour ago.

Dr. Captiva entered the Vertical Assembly Building or VAB, found the conference room, sat down at her computer and started updating the schedules. She started to coordinate the activities of at least thirty groups of people, setting up teleconferences and coordinating the logistics of the retrofit.

Stephen entered the high bay hangar and started what would be his typical "rounds," where he would visit each group working on a different aspect of the cleaning or retrofitting of the aircraft. Once clean it actually looked pretty good, but now access plates were all open, flight control surfaces were missing, flaps were completely deployed and she looked a mess. His face contorted to show his discomfort at the sight. He realized however that this was just a machine, although any good pilot will tell you that when they really get to know their aircraft it will reveal a

86

unique personality. A good pilot will know how the machine needs to be treated to exact the best performance. So in a way the aircraft takes on a life of its own.

The nose radome was off and a new radar was being attached. New infrared, millimeter and optical sensors were being attached to the upper and lower fuselage. The old rocket engine was being replaced with a newer more powerful version. New antennas were being added and most interestingly, the wing to fuselage attachment point was being covered with a new larger skin, to allow flight much closer to the speed of sound. A multitude of "speed mods" were being added. Over even the few years that the ship was not flying, new more efficient designs from the computer simulation software packages were being added to the old airframe. This would increase speed, lower fuel consumption and increase the absolute altitude the aircraft could fly. Some of the modifications looked too strange to be of any help, but fluid dynamics is a funny field, the unexpected happens often. Stephen walked up to a technician.

"What does this module do?"

"This is a passive radar array, it takes the signals emitted by other transmitters like TV and FM radio stations and examines the multipath between the transmission tower and the reflected signals from say, other planes, and calculates their position, course and velocity. You get a three dimensional picture of the airspace."

"This won't work very well on Mars, though."

"Not true, sir, the colonists have a beacon on the surface, with it and this antenna you will see the moons, Phobos and Deimos, as well as mountains and hills. You will also be able to see gradient changes in the atmosphere revealing gust fronts and wind movement."

"I knew that...well, make sure it's in correctly." Stephen walked off a little embarrassed and wondered what other fantastic equipment was being installed.

He decided to go up the air stairs and examine the activities inside the aircraft. Everything in the main cabin was being removed, which he expected, but as he walked upstairs to the cockpit he was dismayed to find that the whole area was now gutted, no chair, no instruments, no wires. It was almost down the metal. He found a technician who might know what was going on.

"Where do I sit?" Stephen said, pointing to the empty room up front.

"Oh, a lot has changed since you flew this plane last, sir. We realized to upgrade the cockpit, it would be

88

easier to gut it first then put in the new avionics and flight control systems."

"What about my chair?"

"We are going to replace it with a better chair."

"I spent twelve months in that chair, it knows me and I know it, I don't want another chair."

The technician looked at Stephen in a way that projected "you don't get it," but finally realized he was talking to someone whose experience spoke volumes.

"You'll get your old chair sir, I will make sure it happens."

"Thank you. Its nice to know that one thing won't change. This aircraft flew perfectly last time. You must understand why I am nervous about changing everything; it means we need to start from scratch, no legacy, and thats very risky. You know we made it to Earth's Moon many times with one rocket, the Saturn, and it never failed We then went to a much more complex booster system, the Shuttle, that failed several times. Guess what I think about that."

"Sorry sir, you're right."

"Damn right. Do me a favor and pass that little pearl of wisdom on to your buddies, and while your at it, tell them this old clunker could have made it back to Mars without any changes."

"Yes, sir."

"Who was it that said 'the more they improve the plumbing the easier it is to stop up the drain'?"

"Don't know, sir."

"Scotty."

"I don't know who Scotty is, sir."

"Scotty, the engineer from the Enterprise, of course."

"What Enterprise?"

"From Star Trek of course....oh never mind, get back to work."

The technician backed away, confused. Stephen left the cockpit to examine the rest of the mods. He had a few other entertaining opinions about the work that was being done. He felt like an old man, even though many of the technicians were older than he, but Stephen had much more experience with flying machines and was concerned about making so many changes at one time. There is a rule in engineering that goes "change only one thing at a time, then test until satisfied with the mod." Its the safest way.

Stephen decided it was time to find the crew chief, that person who was responsible for coordinating all of the changes to the aircraft. Stephen left the plane and looked for someone everybody was going to for answers. He located a person at a bench with a variety of laptops in front of him and talking to several people at once. Stephen walked over and waited for a break in the action he asked:

"You in charge?"

"Yep, whatcha need, pal?"

"Some sanity, what is going on here?"

"And, who are you?"

"Stephen Daedelus, I am going to fly this machine, or whatever it has become."

"Oh, sorry I did not recognize you, Stephen; I know you're a good pilot and I promise you we are not going to change any of the primary systems. The aircraft will have the same feel as before. What we are changing is just about everything else. There are new communications requirements, navigation requirements and power plant requirements. This old aircraft will have significantly better performance. I can assure you that all of the new systems have been throughly tested. There is nothing theoretical on this aircraft; each part has legacy."

"Okay, we'll see. What's your name?"

"Jack Fox, but you can call me Enzo."

"Enzo? Like the car?"

"Exactly, I am going to get one of those when I grow up......so you want to know what we are doing to your baby?"

"I'm not sure, it looks like your gutting the poor girl and putting new fancy electronics in her, are you confident that all the new stuff is going to work? It seems to me that all of these changes will require a lot of test flights. I don't know if we have a lot of time here."

"You have enough time; we have scheduled four test flights a day starting early next week. Test technicians will be on board to take all of the new equipment through the paces. You and the flight crew will be given test cards, which you will have to perform precisely. The flights will be two hours long followed by an hour on the ground."

"That's a lot of flying for one day, Jack."

"We need to do it to make schedule. You don't have to fly every test flight, we will rotate in fresh crews every four hours."

"Okay, but I need to be kept up with the progress on each change."

"We assumed that, so we have set up an office for you to observe and coordinate the flights you do not personally fly."

"I can live with that."

"So, lets get started, over here we have all of the details of each upgrade. You can start with those manuals." Jack said, pointing at a shelf of four inch wide binders near a wall in the hangar.

Stephen walked over to the book shelves and started with the navigation upgrades. Sitting down, he started the long process of catching up to the leading edge of aerospace engineering.

Meanwhile, Zsa or Dr. Captiva was busy coordinating all of the details of a major interplanetary mission. She soon had a staff of very busy people running around keeping up to her demands. The process, although rigorous, was time tested; it minimized the number of people involved and maximized well proven techniques and procedures.

At some point that evening both Stephen and Zsa independently looked out towards the moonlit ocean and smiled.

****

Over the next several days, the aircraft was transformed into a highly sophisticated spacecraft. Plans were made for the maiden flight; Stephen would be the first test pilot. Instead of custom flight suits with mission patches and insignias he was handed a standard flight suit off the shelf. He approved of the suit saying:

"Good choice, now lets get to work."

Then, one fine morning, the aircraft was fully ready for its first flight. A tug pulled the plane out of the hangar and into the sunlight. The air was clear and still. The weather was forecast to be mild. Stephen, the flight crew and fifteen engineers and technicians, climbed up the air stairs and into the plane. The stairs were pulled away and the door shut for the first time in two weeks.

The crew took their positions and over the next forty five minutes, powered up their equipment and checked and re-checked all systems. Stephen made his way to the cockpit and smiling at the sight of his old chair, sat down in the left seat and strapped himself in. In the cockpit was the standard captain and first officer positions with the addition of two more seats that included the flight engineer and communications officers. This ironically was a through-back to early years when all major intercontinental aircraft had these positions. There was always a sense of greater safety with more flight crew. The positions had been eliminated over the years due to advancing technology and especially the airlines' needs to cut costs. Stephen felt a lot more comfortable with this arrangement.

"Pre-start checklist."

"Switches set, starting number one."

With that, the first improved turbo jet engine starting turning, bringing new life to the beast that had millions of miles on the odometer. The whistling turned to singing then to roaring as the fuel was introduced to the turbine section of the large engine. After it stabilized, the second engine was lit followed by the third and forth. To the ground crew on the tarmac with the ground felt like it was vibrating. Vibrating with new life from the old beast as well as new life in this ambitious mission.

Dr. Captiva came out to see the plane start up and take off. She was content that the first step of two hundred had been successful. Its possible that Stephen looked up from the gauges and screens to see if she was there, but no one now remembers. Within a few minutes, the beast's engines increased in thrust, following the commands of the throttles with Stephen's hands on them. The aircraft with basically new everything started to move slowly down the taxiway and towards the runway. The throttles were retarded a bit to keep the extra thrust from moving the plane too quickly.

"Thales two, cleared to taxi to runway three three, monitor tower, squawk 5412, departure frequency 132.45, on departure fly heading zero niner zero, climb and maintain flight level five zero zero."

The first officer repeated the departure instructions and advised the Captain that all pre-flight check lists were complete.

"Thales two, wind three five zero at five, cleared for takeoff."

"Cleared for takeoff, Thales two."

Stephen lined up the now 800,000 pound ex-airliner on the center line of the runway and slowly advanced the throttles to the max takeoff position. The thrust from the new engines pushed the crew members back in their seats at least an inch as the acceleration increased due to the ram air into the four turbo fan engines. As the aircraft accelerated a phenomenon known as ram air recovery increased the thrust of the engines as more and more air fed the compressors in the intakes. Unlike piston engines, jet engines increase in power as they go faster, especially in the initial phases of flight.

Within what seems like a few seconds, the first officer announced:

"V one, Rotate, V two." in rapid succession.

~ Sunrise Descending ~

Stephen pulled the control yoke back several inches until the nose wheels left the ground to aim the aircraft skyward. As the plane gathered more speed, the main gear left the ground.

"Gear up."

"Gear coming up."

He set the climb angle to fifteen degrees and looking at his air speed indicator, realized that the beast was accelerating much faster than Thales one had. He pulled the throttles back to the max climb power setting. Even with a healthy climb angle, the aircraft was still accelerating rapidly.

"Thales, two, tower, no speed restrictions during climb."

"Thales two, roger, no speed restrictions."

The plane blew through 250 knots well before reaching 10,000 feet which was the normal "do not exceed" airspeed. After that point the cockpit did not have to be "sterile" allowing the flight crew to talk a bit more freely.

"These new engines are something, the sim did not give me an accurate feeling of the g forces I was to expect. I'm at 44% N1 and still accelerating."

"New engines, new wings, new fuselage contours makes for a fast slippery plane, captain."

They climbed directly to 50,000 feet, leveled off and started a series of detailed performance tests designed to verify the operational expectations from the new modifications. The flight crew and especially Stephen were very impressed and found themselves not wanting to return for a landing.

Test after test was performed, most were completed successfully. The remaining issues were logged and would be addressed after landing. After two hours on station it was time to come back to base, the aircraft banked toward Cape Canaveral and approach control was contacted.

"Canaveral approach, this is Thales two, flight level five zero zero, inbound for landing with information alpha."

"Thales two, Canaveral approach, descend and maintain one eight thousand, heading two five zero."

"Out of five zero zero to one eight thousand, heading two five zero."

Stephen pulled the throttle almost back to idle and started the descent. He noticed instantly that the aircraft did not want to stop flying and was forced to deploy the speed brakes to allow a normal descent.

"She's happy up here, huh?"

"Yep, your probably going to have to use the speed brakes all the way down, certainly at this distance. The simulation software warned us about this as he wings are so much more efficient after the mods."

They finally made it back to 18,000 feet. The first officer got back on the radio.

"Canaveral approach, Thales two level at one eight thousand."

"Thales two, approach, turn left to one eight zero, descend to ten thousand."

"Ten thousand for Thales two."

They turned towards Miami and could see the light blue Caribbean Ocean in the distance. After a few minutes....

"Thales two, approach, turn right to three zero zero, descend to three thousand, intercept the glide slope for runway three three, cleared for the ILS approach."

"Right to three zero zero, down to three thousand, intercept the glide slope and cleared for the approach, Thales two."

They did as they were asked and soon had the approach flaps out and the gear down, everything was working perfectly. The virtual navigation systems showed many details down to the buildings and towers on the final phase of fight. Then about ten miles out.....

"Thales two, approach change to tower frequency approved. See ya."

"Have a good one....Thales two"

"Cape Canaveral tower, this is Thales two, outer marker inbound for runway three three."

"Thales two, Canaveral tower wind zero three zero at six, cleared to land."

With that, the final landing checklist was completed, Stephen took the aircraft off of autopilot and hand flew the beast to a smooth landing with the mains touching down at the thousand foot marker.

"Grease."

"Thank you, that was a good flight."

They turned off the runway near the end and taxied down the taxiway back to the hangar. At least thirty technicians and engineers were waiting to down load data and make any necessary adjustments.

The beast was officially alive.

The air-stairs appeared and were placed on the left side passenger entrance as the engines were shut down and the aircraft systems put to rest.

It had been a long but successful wait for rebirth.

Departure

Strong Reasons make Strong Actions – William
Shakespeare

Two weeks went by, nearly one hundred hours of
flight time was accomplished during this time and the new
rocket engine was fired several times.

Things seemed to be going well as the bugs were being rung out of the complex flying system. The captain's seat still felt good to Stephen and his concerns about making so many changes were starting to be allayed. Meanwhile, Dr. Captiva was working furiously on the flight plan and logistics, no easy chore. She and Stephen saw one another rarely as each was fully concentrating on their work. Both seemed to work from 7 am to 10 pm every day. It was a major grind but it had to be done, just as so many other major projects have required.

The final flight crew was chosen, Stephen would be the commander and three other competent pilot/astronauts were added to share the workload. Dr. Captiva would head up the science section and manage the day to day operations of the ship during their forecasted four month journey. Twelve total crew-members would make the voyage. They were carefully chosen based on skills, stable psychological attributes and the clear understandings of the risks of this mission. Most of the crew had scientific background ranging from medicine to astronomy. Many had authored books and papers, which gave them an edge during the selection process as the people of Earth wanted a chronicle of human life on Mars. The final crew joined the preparation activities and their ability to work together under stress was observed. Due to the careful screening process, everyone worked together well and it was noted that they all appeared anxious to be pioneers on another world. People who do these types of things and have a special personality which does not allow them to acknowledge defeat. They always look for alternative courses of action during trying times. This crew would be the optimum group to fly with on this mission. There was an inherent trust among these crew-members.

The twelve were divided evenly between male and female and all between the ages of 25 and 35. The exceptions were Stephen and Dr. Captiva, who were older, more experienced and as a result the natural leaders for the mission.

The start of the third week of tests found the crew close to exhaustion so Dr. Captiva mandated days off for each member, staggered of course to minimize any interruptions. This included both herself and Stephen, the process of selecting who would have time off and when was done by a random number generator in her laptop. As fortune would have it, both Stephen and Dr. Captiva had the same day off. The rest of the crew and NASA technicians knew nothing of their possible friendship so when the "days off" register was published no one had any suspicions. But

Stephen noticed the fortuitous event. When he had a chance to go to the VAB for real business, he found a private moment to ask Dr. Captiva (Zsa) about plans for that day, he said:

"Let's go somewhere together."

"Oh, I don't think that is appropriate, it would be fun but too risky now."

"Well before you reject the idea completely, think about this.....I can meet you at a small airport with a small plane and we can get to someplace in Florida that will be close enough if we have to return quickly and far enough away to allow us to relax. What I am thinking about is flying for no more than an hour from here. Some of the options are Key West, Sarasota, Clearwater and St. Augustine."

"I will think about that, but I am still not sure I like you."

"It would not be exactly a date, you know; separate rooms, time to yourself, no pressure."

"Hmmmm, maybe, we'll see."

"Okay, I have the plane reserved for next Wednesday at a local sleepy airport. I will have the plane ready to take off at 7 am. It will be fun, I promise."

That was all the time they had together in a private moment before someone found them with a question. They quickly went into professional mode and continued with their normal activities.

The appointed day came quickly, Stephen was not sure if she would show up but hoped she would. He woke early, went to the airport and pulled out a TBM 850 single engine turbo prop from a large clean hangar. The air was crisp and clear as he performed the walk around, looking at all of the flight surfaces and inspecting the fuselage. He did this slowly and methodically, for two reasons, the first to be a safety conscious pilot and the second to give as much time as possible for Zsa to show up. About half way through his inspection he bent down to examine the underside of the aircraft and refocused on a pair of legs on the other side of the aircraft. He rose and looking over the top of plane saw the face of Zsa.

"I'm glad you made it, its a beautiful day to go flying."

"I decided to take my chances, just don't assume anything, and remember, I have a pilot's license as well, so don't try anything cute."

"I wouldn't dare, I can't afford to upset my boss, especially when we are going to spend months together in a small tin can in outer space."

She smiled a rare smile, which looked good, "Keep that in mind, cowboy, now lets get out of here before anyone sees us and gets curious."

"Hop in, I am almost finished here and will join you in a second, hide under any seat."

"Very funny," with that Zsa entered the cabin, stowed her overnight bag and moved into the cockpit to settle into the co-pilot's seat. Stephen smiled to himself and looked forward to spending time with his possibly, new girlfriend.

When the walk around was complete, he looked at the plane one last time, walked in the aircraft, turned completely around, pulled the stairs up and by pulled down the upper hatch. He locked it in place, turned right and moved forward to the cockpit. Zsa had already pulled out a headset and placed it on her head. She then started to look for the phone jacks on the instrument panel. Stephen joined her and pointed to the lower right so she could plug in and talk to him during the flight.

Stephen settled into the left seat and finding the check list proceeded to get the aircraft started and avionics initialized.

"I appreciate you being meticulous when you fly, its the sign of a good pilot."

"Thank you, I have always been careful; you would be surprised how many things I have caught."

"How long is the flight, oh and where are we going?"

"I filed for an airport near Sanibel Island, thought you would like the beach, its very quiet and peaceful. The flight will take about 30 minutes in this plane"

"Sound perfect, lets go."

"You got, it," Stephen said as he had gotten to the point in the checklist where he could start the engine. The props started to turn more and more rapidly and at about 20% of engine speed, he introduced the jet fuel to get the engine running and stabilized. This particular plane had a 900 shaft horsepower engine that could propel it over 350 miles per hour to their destination. At that speed, it would be a very quick flight, basically up and down.

He started to taxi, and as he finished the before takeoff checklist and moved closer to the active runway he pushed the talk button on the radio.

"Cocoa Beach traffic Tocata November 5423 Alpha taking runway 34 for departure to the West."

Hearing no reply, he scanned the skies for any traffic in the pattern and seeing none moved the plane to the numbers and lined up on the center line of the runway.

He advanced the throttles to the takeoff position detent and felt the g forces increase quickly to the takeoff speed of 75 knots. He pulled back on the control column and broke ground. The speed increased rapidly as the turbo prop increased in output power due to the ram air recovery. Maintaining 170 knots indicated, he called Center."

"Good morning Jacksonville Center, Tocata 5423 Alpha out of Cocoa Beach climbing to 5000 heading 270."

"Tocata 5423 Alpha, Jacksonville Center, radar contact, fly heading 260 for traffic, climb and maintain flight level 210."

"Up to 210, Tocata 5423 Alpha."

The aircraft was streaking through the air at over 200 knots with a vertical speed of 2,500 feet per minute. Soon he closed into his assigned altitude and leveling off, he trimmed the aircraft and engaged the autopilot.

"Jacksonville Center, Tocata 5423 Alpha level 210."

"Tocata 5423 Alpha, thank you, cleared direct to Ft. Myers VOR."

"Direct Ft. Myers, Tocata 5423 Alpha."

Their true airspeed increased to well over 300 knots and then within what seemed like a few minutes, it was time to descend. Stephen pulled the thrust lever back about half way and followed air traffic control's instructions for a descent and a handoff to the local tower. The landing gear came down and full flaps extended in anticipation of a smooth landing, which Stephen performed nicely. Due to all the activity the flight actually felt like a quick drive to the local store. They tied the aircraft down in the transient parking area and made their way to the rental car agency on the field. They chose a nondescript Ford and found the road to Sanibel Island. The temperature was perfect and rolling down the windows they inhaled the good fresh air of the ocean.

Within 20 minutes they were pulling up to a beach cottage resort. They stopped, got out and made their way to the office. Stephen paid for both rooms, and interestingly, Zsa did not object. After receiving the keys, they walked outside into the Florida sunshine and towards their rooms.

"This is perfect."

"Absolutely."

Zsa asked, "where do we meet for dinner?"

Stephen was taken aback for a second, not sure how warm she would be on this trip. He intended to be completely neutral (if that was possible with such an attractive companion) and give her all the space she wanted.   It seems that sometimes being cool can be attractive.

"How about the restaurant near the clubhouse?" he answered pointing to a building about 50 meters away.

"Okay," she said smiling, "how about six?"

"Perfect, see you then."

Now Stephen was getting light in the heels, he had been concerned that she would be all business and that any personal feelings might not evolve for many months.   He had decided that the wait would be worth it, but this response was more that he had anticipated and it made him smile, both inside and outside.   He almost danced to his room, which was in a different building than hers.   He entered his room, hung up what clothes he brought with him and tried to relax for the next few hours.   It would not be easy and after about 15 minutes of pacing, Stephen decided to go for a walk on the Beach to try and calm down. Changing to more appropriate beach attire he left the room and walked out the side door of the building towards the beach.   It was about 80 degrees, warm when away from the beach, but as he got closer to the water the sea breeze made the temperature perfect.   Looking at his watch, he decided to walk in one direction for half an hour then return to his room for a shower and nicer clothes.   While walking, he found himself thinking about her, the mission and his life in general. Unconsciously, he reached up and rubbed his arm again, caught himself in the act and wondered if the doctor had been right, if his life was frozen at this age and what that might mean for a long term relationship. At this point it did not matter, as he felt too excited about the prospects of getting know Zsa. That was the focus now, the mission would go smoother in his mind if they got along well. If not, it could be a mental drain that would have deleterious effects over the long flight phase of the mission. Was it worth a try for this reason or should he be totally professional and not try? Fundamentally, his spirit and soul needed something like this, it had been too long and he wanted someone to talk to and be with, at least a soul mate.

His walk continued while he thought about the details of the mission and his decision to open the door for Zsa. Hopefully she would reciprocate, life might be good if she did.

All too soon, he found himself coming out of a thought daze and realizing that he had gone in one direction for almost an hour. He might be late for dinner and this could not happen. He turned back and started jogging back to the resort. The sand that had just been wetted by the lapping sea felt the best to his feet. Every once in a while he stepped on the receding water and made a nice splash as he did, the water did not make it to his body on its way up as he was moving too quickly to get wet. He found himself in more than a jog, almost bounding. He had the energy and felt no pain. Every once in a while he increased his speed to something just below a sprint and got his breathing rhythm to coincide with every other step he took. He felt like he was flying down the beach.

At some point during his race to happiness, he realized he had made it all the way back to the resort and needed to slow down and warm down before he stopped completely and had a shower. He took his last quick steps on his way inland from the beach towards his room. Walking the last 50 meters he breathed heavily but with a significant sense of satisfaction. There is nothing like the feeling after you have exercised beyond what you thought you were capable of doing. Nothing like it in the world. He was smiling on his way into the building, smiling and sweating profusely. He found his room, entered, removed his shoes and socks, and still full of energy had to walk around for a while before he could sit down. Because of his run, he now had several more minutes to get ready for dinner. At some point while relaxing he knew he could take a shower without sweating any further. The shower felt perfect and after drying he found his best clothes for dinner, He paced himself to be ready at exactly the right time.

Zsa had found her room and during the time Stephen was walking and running. She made herself a cup of tea, sat on the balcony soaking in the sun and let her mind slowly wind down to a murmur of activity. So many things had layered themselves up in her thoughts. She wanted to make sure she made room for the possibility of finding someone she really liked and wanted to be with. To her, Stephen had initially been brash and a bit chauvinistic. She hoped it was just a defense mechanism and not a true reflection of how he really was. She sensed his attraction while he settled into a more reasonable person. Sometimes working very hard like they were doing can expose one's true personality. You see them react to other people during times of stress and you see them make decisions. A selfish person and a selfless person are easily distinguished. She knew that Stephen took this mission very seriously, he was not working on his resume and he was not trying to impress anyone; he genuinely wanted the mission to be a success. That was important to her which made him important to her as well.

At some point on the balcony she looked up from the book she was reading and saw someone running down

113

the beach. He was quite a distance away but she could not see who it was. She watched this person stretch out his legs and it seemed that every step was five meters long. He looked comfortable and graceful, the sight made her smile.

"Nice form," she thought.

Back to her book and then a glance at her watch, she realized it was time to get ready for dinner. She rose, put the book face down on the bed and went to her closet to select something to wear. Classy or sexy? Hard choice to make, but this was just the first date, she did not want to show her cards too early and certainly did not want to give the wrong impression.....

She chose sexy.

Why not? He seemed reasonable enough to accept her ultimate decision.

She put on a dress and some shiny red high heeled shoes. Looking in the mirror she decided she looked and felt better than she had in months. She grabbed a shawl for the final touch and checked her makeup for perfection. Grabbing a small purse, she left her room and walked down the hall towards the lobby. She got her first evaluation when she passed two, 30 something, men in the hallway, they just looked at her without a word, then she could hear their necks turning when she passed them. She had made knockout status, which made her smile. Now it was time to blow someone's doors off.

She walked through the lobby and outside to a path that led to the restaurant. As she got closer, she saw the Tiki lamps lit and the palm frond roof covering a very nice wooden building. It was perfect. Up the stairs and into the waiting room she went. As she neared the Host, whose blood pressure had obviously risen in her presence, she was happy to find Stephen there waiting for her.

"Wow, you look beautiful."

"Thank you, and you clean up nicely yourself."

He smiled and looking at the Host, indicated that they were ready to sit down and have a wonderful evening.

The host led them to a corner table, which was round and had a flickering scented candle on it. The silverware glinted in the candlelight and the linen was spotless. The host helped Zsa to her seat and Stephen sat down to face a women whose beauty transcended all others. He had to take a deep breath to keep from staring, she liked what she saw as well and relaxed in anticipation of good food, drink and conversation.

A waiter appeared with a wine menu and asked the standard question.

Stephen looked up at Zsa.

"Red Bordeaux?"

"Perfect."

"Chateau Laffite 59 please."

"An awesome selection sir," the young waiter said.

After the bottle was fetched and the first drinks poured, Stephen offered a toast.

"May you live as long as you like and have all you like as long as you live."

She smiled, they touched glasses and both carefully tasted of wine. Realizing that the wine was smooth and perfect, they both smiled again.

"Nice," she said.

"Nice indeed."

They then started some small talk which morphed into a bit of business talk and eventually they, while periodically looking into each other's eyes, remembered some lighter moments in an otherwise hectic schedule.

"Remember when Jack dropped that field generator on his foot? He didn't know whether to be horrified or in pain."

"Yeah, I remember, his mouth just opened, nothing came out."

They both began to laugh.

~ Sunrise Descending ~

Other anecdotal stories were remembered and the conflict of so many very serious people with the humor of silly mistakes made them laugh further. They finished the bottle of wine together and shared a perfect meal. Time was dilated when what was really hours felt like minutes. Stephen took a deep breath and looking at her in the candlelight said:

"You really do look wonderful tonight, I hope we can share more moments like this."

"I feel the same way, Stephen, this has been a perfect evening. I am not very tired, would you like to walk on the beach?"

"Absolutely."

They finished up, paid and walked out the door towards the beach, which by now was lit up in that blue glow only the full moon can project. The phosphorus in the water made the foam and breaking waves visible. The sea birds either clustered in groups sitting on one leg or moved up and down the shallow water looking for fish. The birds for the most part ignored the couple walking now down the beach. She held her shoes in her left hand, he walked to her right holding his. The beach was theirs tonight and maybe the whole universe. They walked slowly for perhaps a mile in one direction, sometimes letting the surf touch their feet and observing the seagulls watching the two in semi interest. At one point they saw a sea turtle coming out of the water. They stopped as it made its way inland and began to dig a hole to lay a clutch of eggs. When the turtle was finished, she covered the eggs with sand and slowly made her way back to the sea. It was an astounding sight.

"If we come back in a few weeks, we can see the hatchlings make their way to the water; its quite a sight. The sea is their safety but the birds and other natural predators get a lot of them before they make it."

"Wow, I want to come back and see that."

"Okay, consider it done."

At some point, they realized it was getting very late, as the moon had made its way over quite a bit of the sky.

"We should get back, unfortunately we need to get back tomorrow night."

"Tomorrow night?"

"Yeah, its the weekend and we both have two full days."

"Wow, thats great, how did you swing that?"

"Manager's prerogative. Everyone knows you and I are working our tails off, actually they all think *we* need a break but in reality it will give them a break, if you know what I mean."

"Yeah, I know what you mean, we ride them pretty hard. Okay we can go back tomorrow evening, flying over Florida during a full moon is very nice."

"I look forward to it."

"Its getting late, maybe we should retire."

"Oh, yes....we should."

Then came that pregnant silence where the next move could not be predicted. After a while...

"Its been a perfect evening, want to meet for breakfast tomorrow morning."

She responded with, "sort of."

A New Dawn

The meeting of two personalities is like the contact of two chemical substances: if there is any reaction, both are transformed. - Carl Jung

The next day they awakened into a new world; one of promise and hope.   She rolled over to face him and closed her eyes to continue basking in the afterglow. He was as calm as calm gets and wanted to stay there forever.

Eventually, they decided to have some coffee or tea to greet the new day. The ocean breeze was wafting into the room, the curtains swayed in the breeze melodically and the birds sang a new tune.

"Good morning."

"Good morning to you."

"Sleep well?"

"Perfectly."

"Breakfast?"

"In a bit, coffee first."

He rose and brought her a cup, sat down near her and watched her sip. The dawn gave her a angelic glow.

Eventually, he rose again to get a cup of tea, she remained in bed and closed her eyes once more. Getting his cup ready and not wanting to disturb her peace, he walked over to the balcony and looked out at the ocean lapping up on the beach. The birds had been awake for some time now and were busy trying to find something to eat. A lone Heron, with long legs and neck, walked purposefully in the shallow water looking for an unsuspecting minnow or small fish to dine on. It did not have to wait long as the water was teaming with life.

Stephen decided to walk down to the beach, he put his cloths on and kissing Zsa on the cheek, told her he was going down to the water. She nodded in understanding.

Once at the water's edge Stephen reflected on the evening and on the future; all things were different now. He smiled at the change while looking at the water changing every moment. As he stood there breathing the new day's good air Zsa came up behind him wrapped in a bath robe, she put her arms around him. No words needed to be said.

At some point they turned and walked back to the room to dress and go to breakfast.

The rest of the morning was filled with packing and checking out. They found their car and decided to drive down the beach roads back to the airport. They ate lunch in Venice and stopped afterwords for an hour or so to view the beach and talk further.

"The last few days have been wonderful Stephen, but before we go any further I need to tell you something."

"Go ahead."

"I am religious."

"Thats okay, I can accept that, however I am not. Is that going to cause you concern?"

"Probably not, are you fiercely anti-religious?"

"Oh no, I have my own understanding about it, I think I understand why others have religious feelings, it doesn't bother me that they do so unless they try to pressure me to adapt to their beliefs."

"Fair enough, I won't do that but I would like to feel comfortable in my ways of respecting my religion and those who practice it. It keeps me at peace. What do you believe?"

"Well, I believe in history, geology, astronomy, archaeology, anthropology and human psychology. And all of these studies give me concern about the myths and legends of major religious figures. First there is the historical view; for instance, none of the people who wrote the bible knew Jesus personally, the old testament came before and the new testament came after his life. I agree that he existed and of course is legendary but stories like the parting of the seas and talking bushes and the barbarity of many stories in the old testament make me believe that the writings are more myth than reality. There is a disconnect between what archaeologists have found and what is written in the Bible. Also, there were many more "chapters" of the bible than what has been published. From the standpoint of anthropology, starting at least 100,000 years ago, we were animists and believed in spirits that were responsible for the things we did not understand like lightening, rain and earthquakes. There were objects that these people made that represented such things as fertility (the Venus of Willendorf, 22,000 years ago), or of hunting spirits, of forest spirits or ocean spirits. This gave way to the polytheists like the Egyptians and the Greeks, who had many gods that represented more sophisticated concepts, like love, war and the seasons. One of these Gods, Zeus, rose to the top as someone who had many human qualities but was omniscient and omnipotent. The Greek Gods evolved into a single God, Zeus and this single God became a standard for many many succeeding religions. This is historical truth. Why we have need for an omniscient being is still a subject of debate. Some say we all feel better if we know someone else is in charge, others say that God is a projection of ourselves and depicts the perfection we all crave. The whole story is interesting and important but hardly over. My problem is that some people take their religions very seriously and as a result look down on others. This ethnocentrism causes problems, deaths and wars. History proves this point without a doubt. Now I will say this, I have met people who are at peace because of their religious beliefs. I certainly can't fault them for that, but I have to admit that some religious practices make me uneasy, like playing with snakes, gesticulations, repetitive body movements, uniques diets and the like. I think in a way this feeds the ethnocentrism, makes them part of an exclusive club and leaves others out. The horrible truth is that human beings are more alike than different and throughout history, when differences are amplified, bad things tend to happen. I am Christian and you are not, I am Suni and you are not, I am Serbian and you are not.....I am Nazi and you are not. Finally the line between oral tradition and historical truth is always blurred. The same goes for allegory and truth. For instance Plato's allegory of the cave serves to tell us about the difference between truth and perception. Does the biblical story about the burning bush do the same? Did either event really happen?"

Stephen paused to catch his breath and hoped his view point did not turn off Zsa, who patiently listened. She did however have a response.

"That is certainly a rational way of thinking and even I will admit that there are a lot of irrational practices in religion, but several very good byproducts of religion are missed. I agree that there are a lot of religious people who are at peace with themselves and this of course is good. I don't think they care about any academic reason for this they just appreciate being in this state. I will remind you

125

that many charitable agencies and charitable people have religious roots. St. Francis of Assisi is a good example as is Mother Teresa. They both came from a religion that produced the Inquisition, but you wouldn't say *their* religion was a bad thing. Many people look at our world in wonderment when they see the beauty of nature and sometimes they witness coincidental events that they attribute to a higher power. I would advise you not to take the actions and words of extremists in any religion as a comment on the rest of the believers. Most Israelis and Palestinians just want peace, but there are people of the Jewish and Muslim faith that act out of the boundaries of acceptable behavior and cause lots of problems. Many, if not most people in this world believe in a supreme being of some sort, maybe it is psychological or sociological, I don't think they particularly care. Its natural for people of similar beliefs to gather together, it's a confirmation to them. So most people believe and maybe there is something to it. I am guessing (or maybe hoping) that in the future there will be harmony between all beliefs and harmony with all people in general."

"I guess we'll see," he replied.

"Well I don't think you'll be around then, dear."

He looked at her with a will to tell her more about the doctor and his potion, but felt it was not the time.

"Its just that I want to be frozen and awaken in the distant future."

"And who is irrational?" she said smiling.

Smiling back he said, "okay, maybe that is a little out there, and by the way I think you are right about extremists. We seem to hear about them all of the time. Didn't someone say once that, "when we amplify all of the extreme views that we end up not hearing anything?"

"Yeah, I've heard that."

The drive and the conversation went on until they made it back to the airport after dinner. They both felt that they had so much more to learn about each other and were willing to put in the time to do so.

At dusk, they were loading their bags onto the plane and Stephen was doing a thorough walk around. The blue taxi lights illuminated as did the white runway lights as it got even darker. Finally they were ready to depart, Zsa climbed aboard followed by Stephen. They settled into their seats and while Stephen was finding the check list Zsa leaned over and gave him a kiss. He smiled at this and continued to prepare the cockpit for flight.

Within a few minutes the engine was started and they were taxiing to the active runway. Permission was given for takeoff and they rolled down the runway to an unpredictable future, although they both were looking forward to it their new adventures together.

Banking left they saw the Moon just coming out of the Atlantic Ocean and illuminating the water and earth below. It was an awe inspiring sight.

"Maybe you're right," he commented.

"About what," she queried.

"About a lot of things."

"Who knows...maybe."

Their ride was glass smooth while the Moon rose up the right side of the flightpath. All too soon they were vectored to the sleepy little airport near the Cape. She thought about the work that would commence in the morning and felt that it might be just a bit easier to handle.

Stephen made the final turns to line up with the runway, lowered the gear and made another smooth touchdown. The airplane was put away in its hangar to wait for another flight. Stephen and Zsa went to their respective cars to drive home; each a bit changed from the whole experience.

Looking Down the Runway

Friendship makes prosperity more shining and lessens adversity by dividing and sharing it. - Cicero

The next morning they were back at work and both were impressed by how much had been accomplished during their absence. It is harder to see progress when immersed in daily tasks.

The end was in sight with regards to the retrofits and upgrades. A furious amount of work had been accomplished and the tests were proving that the new aircraft would indeed be better and safer. The insides had been modified for more people, for instance, the food bays were increased in size. One major change was a larger "g" section, which incorporated an internal ring that rotated fast enough to create the sense of gravity; it could be adjusted for Earth or Mars by changing the speed. All in all, it was more comfortable as well, with several much larger windows installed and more private areas. The crew quarters were designed for single people as well as couples.

Test flights proceeded and sorted out problems, one by one the ship became ready for a serious mission.

Near the end of the effort it came time for the commander and crew chief to have the 'conversation.' They would sit down together, away from the others, to get the most honest appraisal about the readiness of the plane.

Jack 'Enzo' Fox was approached by Stephen.

"Lets talk a bit, when you get a chance."

"Sure, how about after lunch?"

"Meet you in the cockpit."

"Okay."

~ Sunrise Descending ~

A few hours later Stephen made his way to the cockpit and found Jack waiting for him.

"Well, what do you think?"

"She's in good shape, most of the test expectations were exceeded. The only concern I have is that the center of gravity is a little bit aft when you're fully fueled. This will improve when you get to the flight levels. After the inflight fueling it will be about perfect for orbital insertion. The computers will be busy shifting fuel loads around for a few minutes then you'll get the green light. So all I am asking you to do is be patient."

"No problem, I tend to check and re-check at times like that, there should be plenty of time for things to settle down. By the way, thanks for your diligence and dedication on this project. You should sign your name somewhere in this bird."

"Already have, when are you planning to make final preparations?"

"One week, the mission specialists are due to arrive in two days. Final electrical tests will be done and the final navigation downloads will occur as well. Everybody is ready to go and anxious to start the mission. I like the fact that we are not tied to a rigid schedule and can launch exactly when we are ready."

"Know what you mean, its help us a lot as well, we have the time to go over details several times. Can I come with you?"

"Sure, you can sit jump seat, you gonna tell your wife before or after we break ground?"

"Before, I'm sure she will let me go for a few days, then I have to come back and take care of the dog."

"That will work, I'll feed it into the flight management system."

Jack smiled and started to get up to go aft and check a few last details.

"Before you go, I have one more question for you."

Jack paused and settled back down in the first officer's chair.

"Go ahead."

"Rumor has it that you are in periodic contact with Benjamin and Judy. I just wanted to know how they are holding up."

"Well, its not been easy for them. Its been a long wait and they are concerned about the changing status of the program. They would like more emphasis on the science and of course a lot more people would be nice to really get Mars colonized properly. I talked to them recently about our progress and the fact that you would be on your way very soon. They are definitely looking forward to your arrival. And by the way, I have left a special present for them in the aft cargo bay; it has my name on it so please make sure it is delivered properly."

"Oh, I will, I promise."

Stephen smiled at Jack, whose expertise, experience and good nature made this ambitious project a success.

"Okay, I am out of here," Jack said as he left.

"Later."

Stephen paused in the empty cockpit for a few minutes to look at the new layout and think about the advances that had taken place in the last few years. The aircraft looked and smelled new. I seemed to stand a bit taller, almost as if it was proud.

"I think she is alive and smiling," thought Stephen.

After a few more minutes he felt like it was time to leave; the ship murmured with life as pumps and fans made their quiet noises and gave the sense that the aircraft was ready to go.

****

~ Sunrise Descending ~

Days of tests passed without any major problems, then the full crew showed up, both the flight crew and the mission specialists. Stephen was finalizing some navigation downloads in the cockpit when the co-pilot came in with his flight bags and placed them behind the right seat. Looking up he addressed Stephen.

"Eric McIntyre reporting for duty, sir."

"Welcome to the front office, have a seat."

Eric sat down and viewed the control panel and displays.

"This layout is a bit different than the sim I have been living in."

"Yep, it is...complements of Jack the Crew Chief. He is a bit of a pragmatist and has given us some extra controls in the cockpit for redundancy. I think its a good idea and I will take you through the procedures while we do our final shake out flights. Your resume looks impressive. You moved right through school like it was a minor bump in the road. Although I know that you have a brain the size of a planet, I gotta tell you that I want you to fly this machine like its part of your soul. It will take us to the flight levels like a graceful swan then it will take us into space like a bucking bronco. You have to be comfortable with both types of flying."

"No problem, I have aerobatics, glider and tilt rotor experience. Put wings on a washing machine and I'll land her smoothly."

"Every fly a Cessna 172?"

"Soloed in one, couldn't wait for my instructor to get out the plane."

"Oh yeah, how come?"

"He went on and on about how he was trained by someone who earned the distinguished flying cross in the Army and was also trained by a member of the 99s, a group of women who were taught by or flew with Amelia Earhart. I hear all these stories about Rickenbacker and Bob Hoover. He was a good instructor but some of that other stuff bored me. However, I will have to tell you that he was the one who suggested I consider becoming an astronaut."

"Hmmm, his name wasn't Kevin was it?"

"Yeah it was, you know him?"

"He taught me how to fly as well. Those stories started to make sense about 20 years after I got some advanced flying certificates. Did he ever take you through the 'bad' night?"

"Yeah, we were flying instruments at night over Colorado and he was pretending to be air traffic control, then all of sudden things started to fail. The radios went out, instruments were failing, fuel was low, I thought I was lost; but then he taught me to always have a plan 'B'. I will always appreciate that."

"Helped me as well. I had some serious emergencies flying commercially a long time ago and although he wasn't there, he kept me focussed."

"Guess in a way he is going with us on this trip."

"Yeah."

"I looked at the flight plan for tomorrow, it looks pretty extensive....inflight refueling, emergency ops, engine out landings...sounds like fun," Eric said smiling.

"It will be a blast. It will be our version of the 'bad' night," replied Stephen.

Eric settled in and started to assist Stephen in programming the flight management computers and setting up the navigation waypoint. They worked in silence for about 30 minutes until Zsa walked into the cockpit. She and Stephen made eye contact. Zsa asked, "Stephen may I speak to you in private?" Stephen rose and the two of them moved to an unoccupied cabin just aft of the cockpit.

Stephen asked, "Hey, how you doin?"

"Fine, I see the pilot is on board; we have all of the mission specialists on board as well, they are settling into their posts and setting up their systems. I understand we are going to have a fun flight tomorrow. Want to give me any hints as to what to expect?"

"I wish I could but the boffins on the ground are looking forward to causing mayhem for us. Advise everyone to be cool and take care of their areas of responsibility. In a way, this will be a human test flight, where you and I evaluate these people under stress. It will be a harbinger of how they will real act up in space when things go wrong."

"Okay, sounds like fun, I hope."

"What do you think of them so far?"

"I think they are a great bunch of people, well educated, professional, good temperaments. I look forward to flying with them."

"Do you think they will follow orders, even if they disagree?"

"Yes, I do, but tomorrow will be a good test," she said smiling a wry smile that spoke volumes to Stephen."

He smiled back, "see you later?"

"Sure."

Stephen walked back into the cockpit. Eric, having witnessed this conversation and observing their body language, was confused.

"Um, who was that?"

"Oh, I don't really know, maybe a technician or something."

Eric looked right at Stephen, who was smiling.

"Yeah right, but that's okay, just keep your pilot in the dark."

"Remember what your instructor used to say about girls?"

"He would say that pilots talk about girls when they are flying and talk about flying when they are on the ground with the girls."

"Well that's it, maybe I will tell you about her on our way to Mars."

"Looks like it will be a story and a half."

With that they completed their tasks and rose to exit the cockpit and do a preliminary walk around. They walked down the air stairs and over to the main landing gear.

Outside, they viewed the activity, which included loading of pallets in the belly of the plane.

"What's in those containers?"

"Food, equipment for the people who stay on Mars and the skis."

"I understand we perform an EVA to attach the skis."

~ Sunrise Descending ~

"Yes, about half way to Mars three of the mission specialists will don spacesuits, go outside and attach these skis, which by the way, worked really well last time. We will land in the same area as before, then 'roll' out over several miles. The skis cushion the landing and distribute the weight nicely which as you know will be about 39% of what we would experience on Earth. The landing will be critical; the sims you have been training in give the look but not the feel of flying on Mars. It will be strange to see the ground rushing by at 250 knots and the airspeed indicator showing 140, just above stall. These skis will ablate a bit during the landing so we can't do 'touch and goes,'" Stephen advised with a smile.

"For tomorrow's flight how close will we be to gross take off weight?"

"Very close, so the procedures in the cockpit have to be crisp. Think you are ready?"

"Absolutely, I have been through so many emergency procedures in the sims I can handle them in my sleep. It's not going to feel right if everything goes as planned."

"Well then, lets hope you feel horrible when we land."

They continued walking around the aircraft, examining the new attachments and making sure the access covers were secured properly. Half way through their journey they found Jack who was busy instructing several mechanics on how to properly pre-flight the plane. When he was finished he turned to and addressed them.

"Top of the morning to you."

"Good morning, how's the plane?"

"Most of it works," was the response.

"Nice, gonna tell what doesn't?"

"Na, it won't matter anyway, everything will be perfect tomorrow morning."

Stephen smiled at this and knew, unlike Eric, that all would be well when Jack signed off the aircraft.

He looked at Eric, "Don't worry, he knows what he is doing."

"Yeah, I've heard."

They continued to walk along the plane, taking note of the changes and quality of the technicians' work. Everything looked perfect, especially the attachment points for the skids. Eric imagined how the mission specialists would have to exit the cargo hold with a lot of equipment and coordinate the assembly of a complicated structure while in space. He looked forward to the details. The specialists would rehearse a bit before and have a detailed list of steps to perform once outside.

Some technicians were polishing the aircraft and making sure it looked its best; its a well know fact that if an aircraft looks good it will fly faster. Thales was no exception to this rule. The metamorphosis from hangar queen, dirty and dusty as it had been several weeks ago, to the polished state of the art example is what now made the pilots smile.

Soon enough, it was time to go home and relax, possibly to review the flight plan for tomorrow's flight but mostly to savor the last few days on Earth. The next many months would be fascinating as well as perilous. Every member of the crew took time to look at the sunsets, the plants, the animals and other typically ignored details of life on this planet as they all knew full well that they would not experience these treats for a long time, in some cases never.

The next morning was pristine and clear, as so many Florida mornings can be. The crew members assembled and listened to Zsa describe the mission for the day which comprised of a multitude of tests including inflight refueling and operations near the absolute ceiling of the aircraft. As Jack had predicted the plane checked out perfectly and was properly fueled when Stephen and the other flight crew showed up. It had been pulled out and looked ready to work in the clear morning air. The tug operator was taking off the tow bar as the full Thales crew entered the aircraft; this was actually the first time the whole crew had actually been together in the ship. Most of them sensed the uniqueness of the moment.

Stephen and Zsa entered, took their places, started their equipment and waited for the announcements from the flight crew about the progress of the flight plan.

"So far, so good," Stephen said to Eric as they were finishing the pre-start check lists. "Everyone is in their place, Zsa is on board, this is an important moment." He said this as he reached up and pulled out the Engine Number One starter enable switch. The aircraft began to have a life of its own now and would soon be disconnected from its umbilicals in order to be ready for flight. Quickly the other engines were started and settled into a comfortable idle.   The flight crew set the rest of the switches, programmed the flight management system, checked and re-checked the environmental controls and made ready for flight to 50,000 feet.

"This is your captain; we are ready in the cockpit and checking the status board from your stations it appears you are all ready as well. I want to welcome you to our first of several shake out flights, we all have a lot of work to perform and I look forward to professional execution of each of your duties. Any 'safety of flight' issues are to be reported to the Captain, any mission relevant issues are to be reported to the mission commander. You will all be able to follow our progress on the mission pages. Good luck to us all."

As he clicked off the PA switch Stephen reached to his right and advanced the throttles about an inch to initiate movement of the spaceplane. Within seconds the four 55,000 pound advanced high bypass ratio turbines had the 800,000 pound behemoth moving. This required the Captain to retard the throttles a bit to keep from going too fast. Many of the crew members at their stations looked out their windows to see a small crowd of technicians, engineers and mechanics waving. The aircraft had flown many times within the last several weeks but now it was getting serious. In a few days they would be given permission to fly to Mars. The new spaceplane was ready; hopefully the crew would be in as good a shape as the plane.

As they taxied to the runway, the flight crew getting their final flight instructions from the air traffic controllers. Pre-take off check lists were stowed, the pilots settled into their seats and the 747 was taken to the center of the runway stripe. 15,000 feet of runway lay before them. Stephen took a breath and slowly advanced the throttles to the take off setting. The gauges had the proper readings as the spaceplane started to accelerate. Within seconds the engines were starting to increase in power due to the ram air recovery. This added yet more thrust as more compressed air was becoming available every moment. At 200,000 pounds of total thrust the aircraft quickly found the rotation speed.

"V R"

Back pressure was being applied to the control column.

"V 2"

The nose gear was rising to a preset angle of 15 degrees; the main gear quickly followed. A distant thump was heard in the cockpit as the landing gear found their full extension stops.

"Positive rate, gear up."

"Gear coming up."

Another thump was heard as the gear found their stowing positions and locked in place. The landing gear doors closed perfectly.

"Flaps 1."

"Flaps to position 1."

"Thales 2 this is Cape tower, no speed restrictions on your climb out, contact departure, have a good flight."

"Cape Tower, no speed restrictions, changing to departure, good day."

Two mike clicks were heard as the First Officer changed the radio over to the departure control frequency.

"Cape Departure, Thales 2 out of 2 thousand for flight level five zero zero."

"Thales 2 Departure, good morning, turn right heading one four zero, maintain best climb rate, no speed restrictions to altitude."

"Thales 2, roger."

With that they switched over the autopilot and flight director to fly the ascent profile perfectly. The aircraft was cleaned up (flaps retracted fully) and was maintaining a steep climb angle to keep a speed of 350 knots. In a lot of ways, compared to other commercial aircraft, this one felt like a rocket ship. It had better engines and the modifications on the wings and fuselage allowed it to slice through the air effortlessly.

After the plane passed 10 thousand feet, Stephen turned to Eric, "this thing is really moving, even at these high outside temperatures. What a piece of machinery!"

Eric responded, "I am amazed; this is performing better than the sim led me to believe."

"No kidding, our last several flights were pretty good but they performed some major tune ups recently. I can really tell the improved handling and power."

On the ground Jack and the rest of the small crowd watched the plane take off and climb right up into the sky.

"Boy that sounds good," Jack remarked as the aircraft was climbing away. The sound of the 4 engines at take off thrust reverberated in the cloudless sky for at least a full minute. About 30 seconds after take off, the plane banked nicely to the right to continue its climb to the southeast. Most of the ground crew stayed outside until the spaceplane was long gone. They had a lot invested in this mission and more importantly, they had built a machine capable of flight in space. They all felt proud, especially since the management of the project was handled correctly and there were no surprises. The work was hard but work into the very late hours was never needed; the pace was just right.

A contrail of the climb-out remained several minutes after the sound had dissipated. The ground crew slowly disbanded and moved back into the hangar to follow the progress of the flight on their monitors.

~ *Sunrise Descending* ~

Images on the flat screens inside the hangar showed the mission specialists concentrating on their tasks. The flight crew was busy at work coordinating the flight test card with the map of the flight over the Atlantic Ocean. The flight would last a little less than three hours with about twenty flight profile tests that needed to be performed. Due to the pace of activity, the whole flight felt like 20 minutes and all too soon the plane and it's occupants were headed back for a landing. Knowing this the ground crew came out at the appointed time and watched the spaceplane descend into the traffic pattern and turn to final approach. They watched the aircraft lower its landing gear at the outer marker, flare for a landing a the end of the runway and touch down gently at the 1,000 foot marker. A few claps could be heard from the ground crew. They moved to their assigned places and waited for the large plane to taxi in and come to a stop. The wheels were chocked and the plane shut down. The engines were still winding down when the air stairs was brought into position and the mission specialists started to emerge from the forward passenger door. As they descended the stairs they were smiling and looked satisfied as to the performance of the Boeing. The flight crew and Zsa were the last to emerge from the plane and as they did they found Jack waiting at the base of the stairs.

"How was the flight," asked Jack.

"Perfect," answered Stephen

"Perfect," answered Zsa, at the same time.

"Well, okay.....are you sure you didn't run over any curbs or anything?"

"Not this time, last week maybe, but now we are swinging wide at the turns," quipped Eric.

The aircraft was secured, a power plug was attached and after about an hour of securing the internal electronics the aircraft was pulled into the hangar. A debriefing of the flight was still taking place when this happened as the numerous details of the flight were being discussed. In general it was declared a success and many felt that after another flight or two it would be time to launch into space.

Breaking the Surly Bonds of Earth

In space one has the inescapable impression that here is a virgin area of the universe in which civilized man, for the first time, has the opportunity to learn and grow without the influence of the ancient pressures. Like the mind of a child, it is yet untainted with acquired fears, hate, greed, or prejudice. - John Glenn

~ *Sunrise Descending* ~

The day finally arrived, one especially crisp and quiet. The ground crew was a bit sullen, the flight crew more focused, the mission specialists separate and in their own worlds. All things alive seemed to be watching the astronauts as they milled around and made themselves busy. Many of the mission specialists would not return as they would settle on the Red Planet.

The spaceplane was more ready than the crew but that would change in an hour or so; humans need to mentally prepare for bold efforts. They wandered around a bit, smelled the air, looked at the grass and ocean. At some point though, it was time. Intuitively they moved towards the shiny plane and congregated towards the bottom of the air stairs. Without any fanfare or obvious communication they started up the stairs.

Stephen looked at the stream of people going into the plane, then he looked at Jack.

"Looks like they're ready."

"Yep, it looks like its time to say goodbye. The ship is ready, fully fueled and completely signed off. The mission control people are ready as well."

"No time like the present?"

"No time like the present."

~ Sunrise Descending ~

With that they shook hands, Stephen took in a deep breath, smiled inwardly at the notion that Zsa would be close to him for the next several months, and walked toward the aircraft. He ceremoniously would be the last to board. Pictures were taken as he turned at the top of the stairs before he entered the craft and waved goodbye. Within a minute after he entered the door was shut and secured, the air-stairs were pulled back and the ground crew began the start up process.

Stephen entered, turned right and made his way to the back of the aircraft to see how everybody was doing and if indeed they were completely prepared for the long mission ahead. After making eye contact with all of the crew, and speaking to most, he was satisfied as he made his way forward that they were ready and anxious to start the journey.

The last place he stopped was where Zsa was sitting, she looked radiant as she looked up at him and smiled. Stephen felt himself getting flushed and for a moment, could not speak. However he overcame his momentary euphoria and commented:

"I am looking forward to this trip, Zsa."

"So am I, Stephen. Lets light this candle."

Smiling, he said, "You got it babe."

Some of the specialists heard the comment and many more saw the body language between the two. Anybody who had any aspirations for either one of them dismissed their thoughts immediately.

After another moment of silent communication Stephen turned and went forward.

He entered the cockpit, brushed off his seat, looked over at Eric and smiled.

"Ready for this?"

"Been waiting years for this moment, Captain. How about you?"

"I can hardly wait."

With that the professional side of flight took over as Stephen sat down and buckled in. Eric pulled out the pre-start check list and the process was started to take them to Mars.

The engines were started, voltages checked, pressures confirmed and a smooth, complete check out of the aircraft systems was completed. The cockpit crew performed as if they had flown together for 20 years. All procedures were executed flawlessly and soon the aircraft (or really spaceplane) started to roll towards the takeoff. This was the last time the landing gear would feel full gravity for a year. Communications were established with mission control, final weather checks were performed and the plane made its way to the runway for the takeoff. Permission was given, the tower wished the mission good luck, brakes were released and the aircraft accelerated down the runway to a smooth take off and climb. The ground crew listened until all sound was gone and they could no longer see the aircraft climbing away to the Southeast. Mission control took over, vectored the plane to a inflight refueling of liquid oxygen for the hybrid rocket engine attached to the underbelly of the 747 and vectored them to the orbital insertion spot near the equator.

On a geosynchronous stationed satellite, the high resolution cameras slewed over to the spot where Thales lit the rocket engine and smoothly entered orbit. The trajectory was perfect as the satellite relayed the view to the mission control engineers on the ground. A white line over a normally blue sea showed the transition

This had been the most successful, lowest cost entry into space for decades.

Meanwhile on the Thales, the g forces had pushed the whole crew inches into their seats, for some reason most of the people in that craft were smiling. They reached orbit, shut down the rocket engine and started the ion / Biefiel-Brown thrusters that would take them out of parking orbit in a few days and then accelerate them to the Red Planet.

By this time Jack had made it to his desk, opened his laptop computer and e-mailed his friends on Mars.

"They're are on their way, sent a present."

This message was more important to the two people on the Red Planet than the official channels relaying the mission status. They knew that once the spaceplane broke orbit it would establish contact with them and keep full time communications. They kept a full time watch on the progress and performed their daily chores keeping the little city ready for more people. Now however, they were finally assured of having some company.

"They're on their way, sweetie."

"I know, I am really excited, it's going to be a long six months though."

"Plenty of time to get the party ready."

The Mars colonists 'puttered' about, doing their duties but subtly made sure things were getting cleaned up. There was a lot of dust on Mars and it gets everywhere, but no matter, robotic vacuum cleaners worked most of the time picking it up and taking it back outside. Interestingly they had made a small hill from their efforts over the last year or so. The rest of the facility hummed along, alive, empty, lonely with a rare visit from the two inhabitants. Every once in a while, Nancy would look out into the greenhouses or other open spaces and imagine people walking about, talking, dropping things on the floor, just generally living. She thought about how long they had lived there alone, how long it took the space agency on Earth to make up their minds and execute a plan. Now she had hope.

On Thales, the whole crew was busy, which was amazing; amazing because they would have to keep themselves occupied for 6 months. There were all kinds of experiments going on, daily meetings, inventories, scheduled exercise sessions, dinners, all types of disciplined life. Stephen wondered how long it would last, especially since his last voyage to the Red Planet, with much fewer people, broke down in the end and bordered on anarchy. He hoped this would be different but was concerned about so many different personalities. It wouldn't surprise him if the second half of the trip was significantly different than the first half.

But as he watched over the next few months things seemed to work out, a testament to the power of society.

Days turned into weeks, weeks into months. The routine continued which brought some unexpected discoveries from the science teams. As a consequence of not be distracted the researchers were able to work on their projects as long as they wanted. Weeks into the voyage the astronomical imaging team claimed the discovery of a multitude of new planets, some with tell tale signs of life. The first "marker" was that of methane, which could be detected in extra solar planets using a large telescope and a sensitive spectrometer. Weeks of imaging and measuring allowed the astronomers to detect this methane on their instruments in enough quantities to qualify for the possibility of life. The other way methane is emitted is from the cores or mantles of new worlds. Methane has biological origins as well and as a consequence was one of several ways the astronomers could use to confirm the presence of life. The other markers include Carbon Dioxide in small quantities and several other gases that indicated the presence of a life cycle, either animal or plant. After many images were taken of a particular candidate, the scientists would sit down and debate the probability of organic activity. They would take two sides of the debate and argue both sides strongly. The person who made the initial discovery would be on the pro side along with a group of believers and the other side would be made up of qualified scientist who could bring up all of the potential objections to the idea. There were strong personalities in both groups. Each had to stop "hissing" at each other long enough to give a percentage grade to the candidate planet and move on. Of the (ultimately) dozens of potential life harboring planets only a handful that had the highest potential were given names. Names like Aphrodite 4, CoRot 7b, L'quacious 5, Benthic 2 and Hebe 6. These names were constructed from the star system and the orbital position of the planets. The 5 named planets above had significant chances of having life as they gave off a multitude of greenhouse gases, had evidence of night time activity in the form of lights and had radio emissions. Scheduled observations of these planets were performed during the voyage to gather as much data as possible about these planets; as history would record, these planets would all be visited and extraordinary details of the indigenous life would be discovered. The excitement of this and other discoveries about Thales kept the crew active and engaged.

Another thing that would keep Stephen and Zsa engaged was their new love for each other, which did not go un-noticed by the rest of the crew. There was no doubt in several people's minds that these two belonged together. They handled stress, conflict and daily routines well. They represented the senior management of all activities on board the spacecraft. Their word was respected and final. In most cases they made decisions together and always listened to one another's point of view. In cases of safety of flight issues, whomever was the most conservative won the argument. The comfort and style that the two emoted while running the ship's affairs gave a sort of calm to life on board. This fact was extremely important as no one could leave or get another job. "Water seeks it own level" someone said long ago. In this case it meant a natural harmony was created onboard the ship allowing everyone on board to look forward to the next day, week and month.

Over half way to the Red Planet the crew isolated themselves from Stephen and Zsa one day and discussed an important subject amongst themselves. Stephen and Zsa were asked to stay in the cockpit with the door closed for almost an hour while the crew gathered in the commons area. After this long period a member of the science staff came to the cockpit and asked Stephen and Zsa to join the rest of the crew. It felt strange to them as they made their way to the open area where the crew had gathered and as they entered all eyes were upon them. They were asked to "sit" on one end of the large room as a representative of the crew addressed them.

"Stephen and Zsa, we have asked you to come here to discuss an important issue for us. We have decided after due consideration, that you two should get married.

Normally it would be up to the two people in the relationship but in this case we as a crew are too close to each other to not feel the sense or aura of your love for each other. If you are willing to follow through on this request we will designate Eric temporary Captain of this vessel which will give him the right to perform the ceremony. If you are not willing to follow through on our request we will understand but will note our objections."

Stephen and Zsa were a bit shocked to hear this declaration from the crew and were silent for a bit in the corner of the room.

Zsa spoke first, "We did not know that our affection for each other was so obvious."

The spokesperson replied, "it is more obvious to us than the fact that we are in an aluminum spaceplane on its way to Mars."

Stephen continued the conversation, "Can Zsa and I talk about this alone?"

"If you must." This last comment was followed by several smiles.

The crew broke up and everyone went back to their stations, each would watch the intranet to blog about the decision or any other actions of the Mission Commanders.

Normally a couple makes this decision themselves without the aid of others. Considering who they were as a pair would allow them to deal with the world. In this case things were reversed. The crew, or in this case, their little world thought Stephen and Zsa would be better together than apart.

"Shall we go back to the cockpit to discuss our options?" Stephen asked a bit facetiously.

"It doesn't look like we have any choice."

"Oh, we have a choice, we could live a lie."

"Well, I don't want to live a lie, I want to live with you."

"I want to live with you as well. I can think of nothing I would rather do."

"Then its settled. Let print some invitations."

Zsa had not thought about details like this and stopped to consider the decision she and Stephen were making. In some ways simple, in other ways complex.

"Are you sure about this?"

"Very."

"It seems impetuous."

"It seems right. And if it doesn't work out they will call another meeting to dissolve the marriage."

Zsa smiled at this, but in her heart knew that this was the right thing to do. She felt too comfortable, too content and too happy to think of anything else.

"Okay, I'm game."

Stephen assembled the others, stood in the middle of the group, "Okay, we concur, you may proceed."

The spokesperson replied smiling, "Excellent, we are all very happy for you. Sorry about the formal nature of this; we all felt you two belonged together, for your happiness as well as ours. When would you like to have the ceremony?"

"On the Vernal Equinox."

"That will be two weeks from now and it should be enough time to order flowers and a caterer."

The crew again broke up and returned to their work. Stephen and Zsa watched them disperse and then looked at each other.

"I have no doubts about this."

"Neither do I. I love you."

"Love you too."

They embraced and walked together back to their work area to bask in the thought of life together, its unique beginning and the confirmation of the people around them.

Stellar Bound

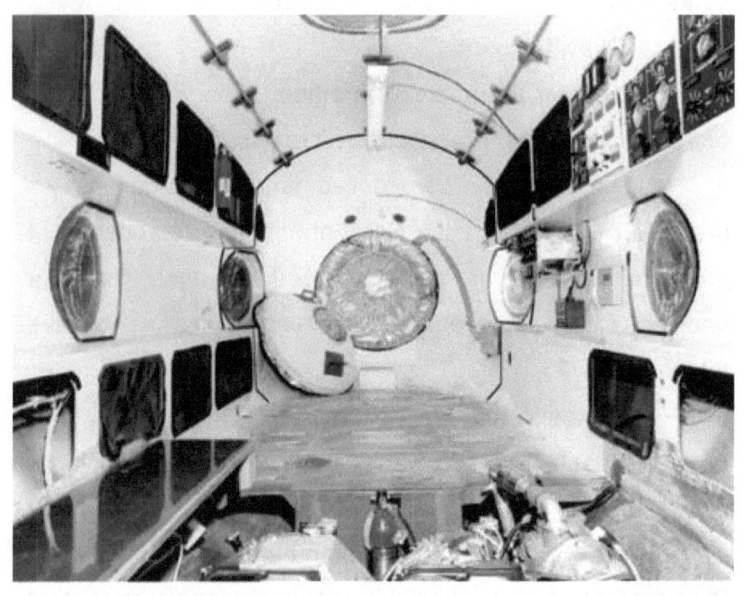

I used to believe that marriage would diminish me, reduce my options. That you had to be someone less to live with someone else when, of course, you have to be someone more. - Candice Bergen

Within two weeks preparations were complete. Thales was completely cleaned and made ready for a party.

~ *Sunrise Descending* ~

To the degree they could, the crew dressed up and manufactured a bridal suite, which was nothing more than two adjoining rooms opened up into a single room.

Eric was promoted for 24 hours to the rank of Captain, as Stephen and Zsa were given a day off for the honeymoon. The ship was oriented so that the sunlight projected into the left side of the ship and filled the cabin with light.

In the hours leading up to the ceremony there seemed to be a settling in the universe as every component of the spacecraft was working perfectly. They were precisely on trajectory and a little ahead of schedule, a full day in fact. As a result the crew felt a day off was completely justified. They were up early cleaning, cooking and creating a bit of illegal alcohol by finding clandestine bottles and allowing the technicians with some chemical background to ferment certain food stuffs. It was a day off everyone needed.

Stephen and Zsa prepared by getting their best uniforms and embellishing them with ribbons and patches. It was a bit light hearted as dresses and tuxedos were not available.

The wedding incorporated as much ritual as possible from all of the crew members, especially the

163

international ones, who had interesting twists on the bonding ceremony. Their customs were woven into the proceedings in an artful way; everyone as a result, felt included.

At the appointed hour everyone gathered in their finery into the largest commons area. Eric was in his temporary Captains's suit, slightly elevated above the rest. This of course was relative as everyone was weightless; they chose a "floor" and tried to make sense of who was above and who was below. When everybody settled in Stephen and Zsa appeared and floated down the aisle between the two groups of people, his "family" and her "family." The image was angelic as they were moving at about one foot per second. At the end, they grasped railings to slow down and positioned themselves facing Eric, who after everyone was settled down, began to speak.

"We are gathered here in front of all things in this Universe to witness the bonding of these two people. Never before in human history has this been accomplished in the presence of such an important group of people, on their way to settle a planet and start a new civilization. This bonding is symbolic in many ways of who we are as a species and who we will become. This is an historic wedding because of these facts. More importantly, Eric smiled at this point, we are here to bond these two souls who belong together and not apart. This is as natural a phenomenon as the planets orbiting their suns and should be appreciated for what it really is....love's gravity, with that and the complete concurrence of the crew of Thales I ask you to affirm your love for each other until death do you part."

"I do."

"I do."

They were looking at each other and completely in their own new world. Kissing, they sealed the bond. In their eyes the Universe was now a better place.

Cheers went up in the crowd and from somewhere deep in the congratulating group, came a bottle of champagne. As if on cue, packets were produced to sample the drink in zero gravity.

The newly married couple made their way around to all of the well wishers until the Master Alarm system went off and brought the festivities to a screeching halt. Everyone sprinted for their stations. Eric was the first to discover the problem by deftly navigating the computer system.

"We've been hit!"

"Hit by what?"

"We are loosing pressure in the forward science section. We are also loosing water in tank number four. Looks like a meteorite went through us."

The flight crew and several engineers made their way forward and quickly found a one centimeter hole in the fuselage, hissing air. One of the engineers placed a patch over the hole and sealed it.

The others were looking at the water tank to find the leak, within a minute they found one hole but not another, or exit hole.

"Found it, but only one. Someone get me an insta-patch."

"The device was produced quickly and applied to stop the water leak."

"That was close. What happened to the projectile?"

"I don't know, it could be in the tank. Lets get a fiber optic and search for it."

The alarms were silenced and all other systems checked out. The holes were sealed and a small robot was dispatched to make a permanent patch on the outside of the fuselage. Within fifteen minutes the fiber optic found the meteorite. It was a small chrondrite, pretty rare, and certainly unexpected in this part of space. They fished it out with a grasping tool. After drying it off and examining it under the microscope, they paused and decided that the timing was perfect for a stellar wedding present. The engineers and scientists found a way to mount it in an aluminum vise like device. It had two pincers that were tapered and shaped like question marks. The points were set against the rock and the bottom portions of the question marks were attached to a block of material. It looked a bit like the devices that were used to hold lunar rocks from the original Apollo space flights.

After the present was finished they all got up, found Zsa and Stephen and with the other members, presented the cosmic present to the newly married couple. What was once dangerous was now fortuitous. The couple accepted the present from crew and from whomever sent it. They placed it in their new room in a prominent place. A memory of the amazing day with their friends and family (in essence) with an unexpected cosmic visitor. A day no one would soon forget.

Eventually, as they still had a portion of the free day left the party continued and a good time was had by all. That evening as the lights were dimmed and the orientation of the craft was brought back to normal the crew relaxed and looked forward to the following work day. Stephen and

Zsa retired to their honeymoon suite. The rest of the daytime crew retired as well, happy and comfortable.

Over the next few days all was well, no new cosmic visitors. At this point in the voyage attention was given to the preparations for landing. They were over half way and there was a faint sense of urgency as they had to attach the skids during an EVA, finish up their experiments and individually consider their futures. It was at this moment that the communications with the people on Mars was much more frequent. Preparations on the surface were getting taken care of and the tenor of the work was just a bit different.

Stephen was on one of these days, working in the cockpit getting the ship prepared for an extensive EVA when Zsa came in and sat down beside him.

"Feels like we are on the down hill side of this ride."

"Yep, definitely feels like somethings changed."

"How is everybody's mood?"

"Good, anxious, excited, even though we are still a month or so away. I wonder how many are going to stay there?"

"Not sure, they are all invited to make their homes there, certainly enough room for them all. They did give them an out if they wanted to come back... no problem."

~ Sunrise Descending ~

"They are all good people; the ones that stay will make a great little city."

"Thats for sure."

They worked in the cockpit for another half and hour, at one point in time they each individually thought about their future together, wondering if they would come home in an empty plane.

The next few weeks went by even quicker, the EVA was performed flawlessly, several long term experiments were concluded and secured. Thanksgiving was shared on one evening; the crew melded together and had warm feelings for each other as well as families and friends back home. Several screens in the common area showed families in their homes eating traditional meals.

Soon meetings were held to discuss the landing preparations and the landing itself. After that, all activity was focused on communicating with the people on Mars and securing the loose items in the cabin. The cargo holds were also secured at this time.

A few final trajectory burns were performed to line the spacecraft perfectly into an orbit that would be decayed into a approach path. As some point during these preparations the crew members one by one finished their tasks and could relax until the final burn for orbital insertion.

Both Stephen and Zsa relaxed as well and now had time to reflect on their upcoming lives. Most of the specialists had decided to stay; some of them had decided to make a decision after they experienced the place. Crewmembers were experiencing very similar thoughts that went through the pioneers of the 1800s that crossed the Mississippi Westward in search of new lives. The same type of thoughts as the people who crossed the oceans in the 16 and 1700s in search of new worlds. It was a combination of excitement and anxiety. They looked out of the windows on the spacecraft at the ever enlarging image of Mars and appreciated its beauty and its starkness. Now every revolution of the planet allowed the settlement to be viewed on the powerful telescopes onboard the Thales. The crew had adapted to the Martian day, 24 hours 39 minutes in length. An interesting question amongst them was whether or not they would live longer because of the slight stretching of the circadian rhythm. The lower gravity would also contribute as there would be less physical stress on the body. Blood would flow easier, muscles would be stronger and the skeletal frame would be under much less load. A grave consequence of the adaptation to Mars would be the inability to return to Earth. This was a major commitment for these people, but they were strong in disposition as well as focus; these were the right people for this mission. They looked out the window and felt nothing but sincere joy.

Landing

For every takeoff there must be a landing –
Common Flight Instruction Lore

The day arrived with a combination of "too soon" and "its been a long wait" which is always a strange combination. The flight crew had been very busy and unavailable to communicate. Mission control on Earth was now far away in terms of communications range which by this time was over ten minutes away. This meant the communications delay was long in terms of a coordinated interaction. They could only monitor and answer long term questions due to the fact that the round trip for communications was over twenty minutes. That meant that the complete final phase of the flight was controlled by the flight crew in the spacecraft.

An orbit was achieved on schedule, above the orbits of Phobos and Deimos the two Martian moons. Slowly the spacecraft descending towards the surface. The computers predicted exactly which orbit would experience the atmospheric interface. This is where the surface of the spaceplane would start to heat up and speed would start to bleed off. As calculated, the spaceplane made its many revolutions and along with heating up started a very subtle buffeting. Although much less than light turbulence, it felt uncomfortable initially considering the crew members had experienced many months of glass smooth flight. They soon got used to it as the sensations really meant they were getting close to landing.

The plan was to take five days to continuously dip into the Martian atmosphere until the speed was slow enough to point the nose down and set up for a landing. The flight path would be identical to the last flight of Thales when the aircraft would be flown over the North Pole towards Olympus Mons (the largest extinct volcano in the solar system). After flying over the southern point of the mountain; the aim would be to turn towards a series of smaller (relatively speaking) mountains that would mark the final descent point to a long smooth stretch of land conducive to landing with the skids. The amazing part of the landing would be the very high ground speeds that would be necessary to support the wings of the aircraft due to the thin atmosphere. Another interesting fact was that the aircraft would only be able to make small attitude adjustments based on the atmosphere; the control surfaces of the plane would deflect significantly and in some cases thrusters would be used. The flight path would be very straight at the final phases of the approach.

In the cabin all loose things were stowed; the crew "flew" around inside sometimes bumping each other and sometime feeling the airframe buffet and lurch in the tenuous atmosphere. All experiments were now concluded and secured. The equipment was stowed for transfer in aluminum containers. Anything that could be left on the surface was also stowed. The plane cleaned up nicely and actually looked a bit empty as they started to pick up some consistent light turbulence. For the most part, over the next 18 hours before landing the crew kept seated with their safety harnesses on. Periodically the plane would take a good moderate bump and lift them off their seats. Stephen elected to put on the "fasten seat belt" sign, a holdover from the plane's previous life, to make sure everyone stayed safe.

The bumps continued at the six hours to landing point, now few of the crew members left their seats. Stephen alerted everyone that within an hour the ship would start the final descent. The bumps would continue to grow until the ship started to slow down; an hour before landing the ride would be relatively smooth.

As planned, the ship's nose and tail thrusters went off, the nose of the plane dipped, and the fun began. Outside the crew watched as ionized gases and electrical discharges ran up and down the wings. The display was awesome, beautiful and strange at the same time. As they were on the night side of Mars when they started their descent the light show was even more brilliant. Pretty soon the lights diminished along with the bumps and now all that could be heard were the fans and other equipment in the plane. Outside the landscape of Mars moved by at a tremendous rate as their true airspeed, that was based on altitude and outside temperature, was well over the speed of sound on Earth. The turns were gentle and Olympus Mons, the largest volcanic formation in the solar system, moved briskly by the port windows as they lined up for touchdown. An announcement was made on the PA system to get everyone prepared and braced. Within a few minutes, continuous announcements were made regarding distance to touchdown, altitude and speed. These were made by Eric, the first officer. During the last minute of flight, a computerized voice took over as Eric got busy with the final checklist.

The computer voice:

"On glide path, three miles to touchdown, 1000 feet."

"On glide path, two miles to touchdown, 500 feet." The nose of the plane rose a bit.

"On glide path, one mile to touchdown, 200 feet." The nose rose a bit more.

"On glide path, 50 feet.

"20 feet."

10 feet."

"five, three, one"

~ *Sunrise Descending* ~

The touchdown was so smooth that the crew felt no bump. All they experienced was a hissing sound as the sand was rushing under the skids at 200 miles per hour. The forward velocity started to slow, gently pulling the crew member away from their seats when three large parachutes were deployed. This effect lasted for less than a minute before everyone on board realized that the landing roll out was almost over. The ship finally slid to a smooth stop. The dust kicked up by the landing event was catching up to the ship and overtaking it with slowly moving wisps of red dust. It laid a film over the wings and powdered the windows as the crew started to unbuckle and feel the gravity of the Red Planet. Stephen and Eric were still very busy up front securing the systems and shutting down all non-essential components of the spacecraft. Solar cells that had been attached to most of the upper fuselage before launch started to provide enough energy to run heaters to combat the extreme cold that would be experienced on Thales while it was on the surface. Temperatures of -80 Fahrenheit were possible at this spot. Aircraft of this type can easily handle outside temperatures of -60, temperatures lower than that could cause problems. The heaters would take care of any issues and keep the electronics in good working order.

~ Sunrise Descending ~

The first band of mission specialists started to suit up for the walk to the settlement. There weren't enough suits for everyone so the plan was for ten crew members to make the trek, then one would return in a Mars rover to transfer the suits to the next group. The disembarking process would take several hours. The flight crew and mission commander would be last once they were convinced that the ship was safe to leave. On board telemetry had already been established between the ship and the settlement command center. Voice communications had also been established; the voices on the other end sounded very excited and talked of awaiting food and drink. Words about a party were offered to smiling, tired crew members. Some of them actually felt like they were home.

Ten people were now suited up and checked out for an EVA or walk to the facilities. They could see several structures about a mile away, many with lights, one with a beacon inviting them in. They looked through their visors out of the port holes of the cargo deck at the distant empty village and were anxious to visit and explore.

At the appropriate point the air was evacuated from the forward cargo hold where the group was standing, A red light turned to green announcing that the pressurization between inside and outside was equalized. The group leader reached to her right and pushed a button to open the cargo door. It smoothly and silently moved up to reveal red dirt and rocks twenty feet below them. Two other specialists pushed out a landing stairway and let the end float to the surface. The slow motion impact sent up two small dust clouds. The upper end of the stairway was secured and the railing that was attached was brought up to the vertical position. With but a few seconds hesitation, the leader started down the stairs, noting any flexure or bending. It turned out to be secure enough for more specialists to follow the leader down. Within a few minutes all ten were outside, some looking at the ship with a sense of thankfulness, some looking at the village anxious to get going. Once the members were ready they set off for the mile walk. In 39% of Earth's gravity the walk was effortless. Some skipped, some jumped but most tried to walk in a coordinated manner which was not easy after so many months of weightlessness. The mile was covered quickly, mostly due to the fact that the crew was anxious to see their new living area. Rooms and common areas would feel as large as football stadiums after the confinement of Thales over the last many months. The crew walked loosely in formation with their new freedom. Every once in a while

179

one of the members would walk off in a separate direction to explore something or get a bit of space.

Eventually they found themselves at the air lock. They filed in and discovered two faces looking through portholes at the end of the chamber. Both of them were smiling and the Thales crew, in a way felt that they had just come home after a long journey. The outside door closed, the pressurization cycle started and within several minutes the inner doors opened to reveal two very excited adults and one child.

"Welcome to Mars."

"Thanks you, it feels like it has been a long time coming."

"Good, please follow us; we will take you to the living areas and command center. The next crew will arrive in about fifteen minutes."

They walked down a wide corridor with a roof of plastic sheeting and a floor of hard red sand. At the end was what appeared to be a concrete wall with an aluminum door built into it. The door was opened and they all filed through. Behind them the door was closed and sealed and the new crew hesitated a bit to take in the view. It was a large room; the largest they had seen in months. There were tables, couches, monitors, food, chairs and children's toys.

"Sorry about the mess, we had everything in order until our child got excited and pulled out all his toys."

"No problem, its good to see children again, reminds me of...."

"Of home?

"Yeah, just like it, kinda funny in a way."

"Well, welcome to our home, now your home; please note the laptops sprinkled around the facility. We have over one and a half million feet of floor space. The laptops are in every major area and connect to the intranet incase you need to contact us or find your way around. Each of you has your own room, which you can find by typing in your name into the search engine."

With that Benjamin and his family started back to get the next crew. The first group looked around in wonderment. It was a comfortable area just like a nice lobby in an hotel found on Earth. Some of the people moved to the laptops to see the facility layout and locate their rooms.

"Cool, I have a window. My room is near the kitchen area as well, perfect. I am going to go over there and drop off my stuff."

181

"Okay, see you at dinner."

With that and other conversations the crew broke up and started to explore their new world. They fanned out in many directions, some to find the greenhouses, some to find something to eat, some to their quarters. It was a relief to many to be alone for a few moments after too many months in close proximity.

Power was plentiful, there seemed to be at least 50 rooms and at least 10 greenhouses. Light was everywhere, although not as bright as that on Earth, it was close due to the tenuous atmosphere. Benjamin had paid particular attention to bringing in solar light using fiber optics connected to a small telescope; he was able to port the light into most rooms. The light had a very slight red tinge but was bright enough to feel warm if you put your hand on the output aperture of the fiber optic.

The rooms were warm as well, a consequence of good thermal management by using the water they found in abundant quantities just under the surface. Once warmed into liquid form, they used electrolysis to separate the oxygen from the hydrogen, then they recombined the gases and ignited the mixture to provide significant heat that powered their electric plant. The by-product of this combustion was steam, which of course was condensed to

182

provide water for the plants and people. It was as simple as the use of steam for locomotives in the 1800s and 1900s. In fact the whole facility was a study in simplicity. Initially, when Benjamin and Judy first came, they built a home in the available caves. The entrance was in the lower portion, which allowed the upper portion to hold breathable air and keep the temperature comfortable. They started building greenhouses to capture more heat and make food. They learned to make bricks and mortar by using the indigenous soil and water. All of the outside surfaces of their buildings were made this way and were extremely strong. The water in the bricks also was a natural barrier for the solar radiation that rained down on them due to the lack of atmosphere and magnetosphere.

Water provided the heat, life and protection for the new village.

The second group arrived as happy as the first. The third and finally the flight crew came after securing the aircraft and establishing a radio link to monitor the status of the plane. Stephen and Eric both wore monitoring devices to keep close track of conditions on the craft. Once they arrived they found most of the mission specialists completely at home and taking over specific areas both to start their work and to start their new lives. It was actually amazing how easy it was for these people to go to a new world and so quickly own it.

Stephen found Zsa while Eric looked for his room and some dinner. Zsa had the same impressions as Stephen. They both were amazed at how easy it was for the new people to call this place home.

Benjamin and Judy and their son were ecstatic about the new visitors, correction, neighbors, and felt for the first time that their mission and efforts were worth it. It had been a long lonely road for them. There had been a lot of ambivalence about whether or not they had done the right thing and whether or not NASA would continue to take care of them. With the advent of the the new people it seemed that all would be well.

Eventually the dog Astro, who had been delivered on a previous freight flight, came out and greeted everyone. It had been a pretty quiet place for him over the last many months but now he seemed comfortable with the new sounds, smells and people. He walked around to every person, smelled their hands and allowed several to pet him.

The place seemed a bit warmer, now with all of the humans generating heat. Benjamin went over to the environmental monitors and confirmed that it was true. This lowered the power requirements for the facility however more people increased the food needs. Benjamin and Judy had grown food over the past 16 months and had stored over 90% of it; they had significant amounts of wheat, corn, vegetables of all sorts and fruit. The past several freight runs contained dried dairy and meat products. A significant amount of freeze dried foods were sent as well. For the most part, the pioneers would be eating a vegetarian diet, with a small amount of dairy and meat every once in a while. The freight flights from Earth would continue for a while but it was incumbent on the pioneers to become completely independent. With Benjamin and Judy leading the way this could easily be done.

Village life started in earnest, water sought its own level as everyone found their space, assumed their responsibilities and just lived. Couples formed, marriages ensued, kids were not far behind. All of this happened reasonably quickly over the next several months. The reduced gravity had its effects on everyone, Stephen and Zsa worked out hard every day to mitigate as much muscle degradation as possible. To them, there was no question about returning to Earth, for all the others, including Eric, they were happy to stay. Eric found his way into the astronomy group and applied his formidable skills in data acquisition and electrical engineering to help design and make an amazing telescope. Due to the rarified atmosphere they were able to use this instrument to probe the skies in a way no Earth bound telescope could. The people who without a doubt, would stay minimized their exercise time and maximized their work time. They fully intended to create a safe, comfortable village. They prepared to grow and spawn other villages on the Red Planet. Those who might be ambivalent about staying exercised a bit more, but eventually succumbed to the fact that they (for now) had more than ample strength to get around. Benjamin and Judy had made their commitment and as a consequence were a bit thinner and a bit taller than the rest. Their kid also was taller and thinner than kids his age on Earth.

The window for departure would come in a few months for Stephen and Zsa. They worked hard in anticipation of that day and wondered how many people if any would come back with them.

The days rolled by and life on Mars was as normal as normal gets. It became apparent to most of the people now that this was just as viable as anywhere else to live.

The daily activities included meetings during breakfast, assignments of tasks, discussions of any hazards or safety issues and upon finishing their meals the new Martians attended to their assignments. Soon the inevitable sociological issues rose and more meetings revealed the need to move people to other quarters and/or reassign some of the tasks. Cliques were formed of course and during meals and meetings certain groups of people stayed together. It was a microcosm of the cultural backgrounds left on Earth; most people retained some level of ritual in their lives, some practiced their religious beliefs as well. Areas were eventually set up for contemplative thought and prayer. Zsa spent some time here thinking about home and family as well as the cosmic significance of her journey.

Again the days rolled by and the mini society shifted about for its own comfort. In a way the new villagers seemed to look at Stephen and Zsa as visitors. They knew the couple would leave someday and now someday soon.

The Return Voyage

The fatal metaphor of progress, which means leaving things behind us, has utterly obscured the real idea of growth, which means leaving things inside us. - G. K. Chesterson

That day did arrive, the day in which everyone felt strangely ambivalent. Those who would stay sealed their fate. Those who thought of going back to Earth were in flux. Stephen and Zsa of course were committed and went about their duties as if there was no looking back. Eric had decided to stay and become a permanent member of the astronomical division. Their new telescope had already made many discoveries and the excitement from such work was overwhelming to him. He called it a "discovery machine," as if when it was used properly it would yield much new information about our universe. The thin atmosphere of Mars virtually eliminated the twinkling of the stars and allowed the telescope to often perform at its diffraction limit. This is the best any telescope can do and is achievable only in space or on planets with very thin atmospheres. There were dust storms on Mars however, which limited observation time; but for the most part it was clear. Eric also designed a radio telescope, One that had very wide bandwidth and a very high frequency of operation. The plentitude of craters on the surface allowed for catenary reflectors to be made like the telescope in Arecibo, Puerto Rico. The low gravity was conducive to minimal structures and minimal deflection from wind. Some of the craters Eric considered were miles in diameter and would become the largest single radio telescopes ever made by humans. Other crater antennas could be added in the future to combine, in what is known as an interferometer, which is capable of resolving radio features in the Universe in very minute detail. The absence of radio interference like that on Earth helps as well.

Stephen and Zsa had the ship unpacked completely and then repacked with enough food for 4 people during a return flight. All of the fuel levels were checked and augmented as necessary. The chemists amongst the mission specialists had separated the Hydrogen and Oxygen from the water found on Mars to produce a significant amount of rocket fuel as well as fuel for the furnaces for the living areas. Although difficult to separate, the Oxygen in Carbon Dioxide is plentiful and this is what makes up the Martian atmosphere. Plants of course thrive on this and the key to long term survival on Mars is to plant as much as possible. The greenhouses had manufactured enough Oxygen from the plants to allow spillage to the outside. At some point in the distant future Mars would have another atmosphere capable of allowing plants to grow outside, probably lichen and other similar hardy varieties. Mars could and would be tamed.

A day was selected for takeoff back to Earth. The day had many meanings to the crew. As it approached the final decisions were made and final commitments were acknowledged.   On that day Stephen and Zsa stood amongst the others and wondered if anyone was going to join them.   It turned out that no one did,   which was somewhat expected.

"Well, thats it then, all of you are going to make a new world." said Stephen. "This has meaning to the entire history of Earth, it has been in the minds of science fiction writers for centuries and in the eyes of the astronomers who mapped this world and now in the souls of its people."

Zsa continued, "all of us at home pledge our support and wish you the best of luck.   With the new arrangements in NASA I believe that there will be periodic shuttle flights between the planets and, of course, the freight flights will continue."

"Have a safe flight," was the response from the newly appointed Mayor of Lowell, Benjamin.   Percival Lowell had been chosen to be the name of the first Martian city, after the 19th Century astronomer who spent a significance amount of his life trying to map and understand Mars.   He thought that there were canals on Mars. He formed the beginning of the effort that led to the discovery of Pluto 14 years after his death. The choice of the name Pluto and its symbol were partly influenced by his initials PL.

Stephen and Zsa shook hands with everyone, looked around one last time and headed for the air lock that led to Thales.

"I wonder what this place will be like in twenty years?" mused Zsa.

"Successful, I am sure." answered Stephen.

They got into their flight suits, placed their helmets on and entered the air lock. Within a few minutes the pressures had equalized and they started the mile long walk to the plane. They looked back every once in a while to view the peoples faces in the portholes as well as the new living city. They smiled upon doing this.

Once at the plane they climbed the air stairs, pulled them inside the cargo hold and closed the cargo door. After the door was secured the lower fuselage of the plane was pressured allowing Stephen and Zsa to remove their helmets and move upstairs to the cockpit. On their way they examined the inside of the main cabin and made sure that everything was secure and ready for takeoff. Although they had done this many times before in preparation for the flight, one last walk through was always prudent. This was especially true as Zsa was now the co-pilot and could not attend to the main cabin.

~ *Sunrise Descending* ~

They checked all systems and all back up systems. The fuel was checked visually and a pre flight inspection was done on the rocket motor that would send them back to Earth.

After everything seemed flight worthy, Zsa and Stephen made their way to the cockpit and strapped in to their seats. The auxiliary power units were started and the fuel cells were engaged. They worked down the pre-flight check list which consisted of at least one hundred steps. Once finished, they sat back, looked at each other and then Stephen reached over to a switch on the center panel, flipped it, which ignited the rocket engine. Once ignited it was at a very low thrust level and only showed its return to life with its subtle rumbling and slight vibration felt in the floor plates. Stephen looked up from the displays and advanced the throttle a bit to get the big bird moving. Slowly it started to slide forward. Stephen engaged the smaller thrusters on the wings, tail and nose to coax the plane around in a circle back towards the indents of the skis left in the red dirt from the landing. Once in the the groove, Zsa made a radio announcement.

"Thales is on the takeoff run."

"Roger Thales, good flight," was the response.

Now that the plane was stabilized in the grooves, Stephen advanced the throttle to maximum, the thrust was much more impressive than the last takeoff he performed so many years ago.

"Airspeed is alive."

"Eighty knots."

"One twenty."

"One fifty."

At this point Stephen pulled back on the control yoke and the nose of the plane began to rise. He stabilized the pitch at about three degrees and waited for the wings to start working. Their forward speed was well over two hundred knots when the ground started to fall away. At this point the nose was pitched up a bit more, the airspeed hit three hundred and the acceleration was now past one g. Soon after that the airspeed dropped to zero as they reached the edge of space. The acceleration maintained however for a few more minutes until they reached a safe orbit. At this point the rocket engine throttled down.

"Okay, now a few orbits and we will start the rocket again and go home."

Stephen engaged the flight director, autopilot and flight management system which took over the flight from this point until they were on the final flight path for a landing at Cape Canaveral.   The g forces decreased to zero and they became weightless.

Stephen felt a slight discomfort in his arm and rubbed it a bit; he noticed over the past few months that this slight discomfort had slowly permeated over his entire body. He actually felt like something was going on in his brain as well. He had not told Zsa about his shot a year or so ago.

"Okay?" she asked.

"Yeah, fine, no problem."

"How long will we be in orbit?"

Stephen looked at the flight management system display.

"Oh, a little over an hour, then the autopilot will light the rocket engine again, we will feel the g forces build, then the maneuvering thrusters will point us home.   In this configuration, about twenty minutes after the burn, the Earth will slowly move from underneath us to be centered in the windshield.   After that, a few months of boredom followed by few minutes of terror." Stephen smiled after his attempt at a joke.

"Very funny, Stephen. I can hardly wait."

"Well, we will have to keep ourselves occupied somehow," said Stephen with a wry smile.

"Oh, you're right about that, there is a lot to clean, we have to do an inventory, check out all of the systems every day, just soooo much to do."

"Well actually I was thinking about something else, sort of, kind of."

"Don't worry we will have plenty of time for that when we get back to Earth."

"What?"

"Just kidding, monitor your gauges."

With that suggestive interchange, Zsa unbuckled and floated back to the main cabin to check things out. Stephen was left alone in the cockpit to go through the checklists for changing to en-route status. He became very busy and lost track of time. When the rocket burn was five minutes away an alarm and announcement was heard. Stephen looked over to the co-pilot's seat and became a bit nervous.

"Zsa? Zsa, you need to come up here quickly and strap in!"

He turned a bit more to look down the corridor to the main cabin and saw Zsa, suspended in air, floating towards him.

"Be right there, I don't want to go so fast that I go through the windshield."

~ Sunrise Descending ~

"Okay, be careful, but we don't have much time."

She floated into the cockpit area, where Stephen caught her in his arms and maneuvered her into the seat next to him. It took a while for her to get her legs on the floor and find the straps as they had floated in all directions since she left. Soon, she was about done when..

"Thruster engaged, 100% power," came a computerized announcement.

They were pushed back in their seats, then the smaller maneuvering thrusters came alive and started moving the nose to an attitude that would take them out of orbit. Zsa had a much harder time finding the last straps to put on as the artificial gravity was getting intense. Finally, she was buckled in and sighed a relief.

"That was close."

"Yeah, I was worried. You okay?"

"Yep, no problem, next time I'll come early."

"I hope so. Now the engine is going to be a full thrust for another forty five seconds then we will be back to weightlessness. So far its a perfect burn. Can you contact the people on Lowell after the burn and give them an update?"

"Sure."

For the next forty seconds the rumble and g forces continued. Stephen and Zsa surveyed the displays and followed the progress of the burn. At the appointed time the rocket was shut down, g forces diminished to zero and silence surrounded them.

"That was a perfect burn, we are right on track and have plenty of fuel left."

"Good, I will contact the others now.

"Lowell Base, this is Thales, how do you copy?"

"We have you loud and clear. What is your status?"

"We had a successful burn to leave orbit and are on track for Earth. All systems nominal."

"Excellent, we watched your progress here on the telescopes and telemetry, everything looks great."

"Its a bit lonely up here, just the two of us."

"Thats the way it was meant to be, remember this moment for the rest of your lives as others will a thousand years from now."

"Roger that, Lowell Base, we will. Best of luck and we will contact you tomorrow at the same time."

"Thank you and good flight. Lowell Base out."

With that and the surrounding silence sans the air distribution system and a few cooling fans Thales sped towards Earth and an eventual landing months from now.

198

~ Sunrise Descending ~

Stephen and Zsa started up several experiments and began to re-acquaint themselves with Earth life from a remote connection to the Internet. They could see already the divergence in cultures between the two worlds; one seriously trying to succeed and the other bathed in history and complexity.

Over the next many weeks they found themselves in a daily routine of exercise, research and starting up the communication channels to those back home. Days seemed to filled with activities. Work progressed into the evening many time a week. They did pause for meals and some entertainment, especially new movies and news in the evening.

Because it was important to have full time coverage of Thales operations, Stephen and Zsa had separate sleeping schedules; their lives overlapped for eighteen hours every day. Stephen was awake from 7 A.M. To 11 P.M., Zsa from 3 P.M. To 7 A.M. Sometimes their schedules slipped but under no circumstances were both of them asleep at the same time. The ship's safety systems were reliable enough and on many previous missions, including the Shuttles, all astronauts would sleep at the same time; the difference of course was the real time monitoring of all systems by full time mission control operations. If anything went wrong the astronauts could be awakened immediately. In the case of any Mars mission the communications time could reach up to 20 minutes. This was long for taking care of an emergency quickly.

The days and weeks rolled by, the routines became routine. However about three months into the voyage there was an incident.

"Zsa, have you been monitoring the solar telescope displays?"

"I check them out daily, have you seen something?"

"Well, I am looking at the Hydrogen Alpha display and there is a very large prominence on the leading edge of the sun. This thing looks massive. Are we close enough to monitor the solar satellites in Earth orbit?"

"No, not yet, but I have pulled up the sensors on the ship and they are just starting to move up. This could be a major storm."

"Yeah, your right, could be huge. I haven't seen a prominence that large in decades."

"We should set the instruments to monitor this in real time and set the alarms for rate of change as well as high values."

"I agree, Zsa. Also, I think we should prepare to move into the shelter. I just brought up some Interned solar monitoring sites and the chatter from the scientists is starting to get intense. They are comparing it to solar storms from April to June of 2010. These were CMEs or Coronal Mass Ejections, which caused havoc with satellites and power grids. Some are saying that this one is much larger. We need to prepare."

"Okay, Stephen, I'll get the check lists out and move us into the shelter quickly."

As they started to recognize the gravity of the situation the particle and radiation monitors started to record increase activity at an ever increasing rate. Stephen and Zsa saw this and started moving very quickly to secure the ship's systems and move into the aft area of Thales, near the tail, where most of the water was stored. The water tank was actually built into the walls in the form of a very thick walled tube, with cylindrical water tanks on the ends with spaces between them and the tube to allow access. While inside, there was no direct line to the outside without "looking" through water. Many thousands of gallons of water were stored here. It turns out that water is a very effective insulator against intense radiation; this was one of the reasons so many nuclear reactors were placed in large water tanks. Inside the tube there was a working and living area which had basic connectivity to the ships intranet and communications systems. They could control most of the ships functions from a pair of laptop computers inside this safe area. In addition there was enough food for weeks.

Stephen and Zsa worked quickly inside Thales, while radiation monitors started to go off. Soon, even the Earth bound mission control engineers were trying to warn the crew. Within thirty minutes they had all of the systems secured and had moved to the safe area. They brought in three laptops, two for real time operations and one spare. They hooked everything in and started to monitor the solar displays while the outside monitors continued sounding off.

Within a few days of sequestration the radiation levels outside of the safe zone were so dangerous that to go out for even a few minutes could prove fatal. They hunkered down and obeyed the sensors, which was not easy. After a week or so, the flare had subsided and the dangerous levels started to subside. It had been a very long camping trip but as soon as the monitors started to get quiet, Stephen and Zsa emerged for brief periods to check everything within the spacecraft. No major problems were found during these excursions but just to be safe they spent extra time in the safe area until there was not any residual radiation detected. The whole episode took seventeen days. For the most part, Stephen and Zsa were bored as they waited; every once in a while they had to get inventive.

Three weeks after the radiation storm, Zsa found Stephen and sat down near him with a pensive look on her face. After a moment, he noticed her and her unusual look.

"Hey, Zsa, is anything the matter?"

"No, nothings the matter," was her short reply as she remained quietly looking at Stephen.

A few moments passed, then Stephen knew something was up. He stopped his work and moved towards Zsa, taking her hand he asked:

"I can tell something is going on, are you okay?"

"Oh, yes, wonderful in fact."

"Alright," he said slowly, "I can play this game. Are you felling wonderful because we are going home?"

"Sort of."

"Are you feeling wonderful because your experiment with the fungus is going well?"

"Nope. Not even close on that one."

"What then?"

"We are going to have a baby!"

Stephen's face lit up. "Wow, a baby, our baby?"

"No one else was with us in the safe area several weeks ago, so yes it is ours."

"Wow, I am so happy. What are we going to call him....Stormy?"

"No, we will call her 'Star' as she is truly a star baby."

"Hmmm, okay, I can live with that. This is really wonderful Zsa. How did you find out?"

"Well, its hard to explain, lets just say that I had a feeling. A feeling of change in my body. It was very subtle but I had a feeling that we were not alone."

"Well thats a bit cosmic. Maybe it was just the fact that your internal chemistry was changing."

"Well, I am sure it is but this was actually something else. Like I said, it is hard to explain." She looked at Stephen now aware that he thought this might be a bit irrational but also aware that he would accept the explanation.

He looked at her with undying love and considered whether or not she had an extra sense of perception.

"Well we need to take care of you. I don't know if there has every been anyone pregnant in space. Considering that we still have a few months to go we should be monitoring you carefully."

"Well, I don't think that we should worry about it so much; this has been going on for billions of years. I am sure I will be okay."

"Well, alright, but let me know how you are feeling."

"Of course I will."

"I love you, Zsa."

"I love you too, Stephen."

With that they both seemed to recline and contemplate their new future.

Coming Home

Life is a voyage that is homeward bound – Herman Melville

Stephen and Zsa made their way back to Earth in cruise ship like fashion, in other words, relaxed. There was something soothing about having a child that set the tone for their last month in space.

The routine continued of course, but there was something different in the air. Zsa felt fine but Stephen was more attentive. In a strange way both Zsa and Stephen wanted to clean up an area of the ship and make it ready just in case. This nesting behavior of course was completely irrational but they felt more comfortable doing it, most likely to show their commitment to each other and their new family. The baby would be born months after they landed but just in case there was an emergency they both were prepared.

One evening, when they were both awake, they were sitting in the cockpit looking at the image of Earth in the windshield.

"Its getting closer."

"Definitely, the blue is getting intense. I am really looking forward to getting back."

"Yeah, its been a long trip, I'm looking forward to getting back as well."

"You know, a lot of changes are going to occur once we land, get de-briefed and go back to our jobs."

He looked into her eyes for a moment.

"Your right, lots of changes."

207

~ *Sunrise Descending* ~

By this time Stephen had really started to feel a change in his body. The decay of life has ceased, although subtle, it was measurable in the fact that nothing was changing, he always felt fine. He discovered that everyone else finds the slow degradation part of life and normal, once this is not a normal expected experience, it is noticeable.

Now, he considered the consequences of his actions. He for once considered what would happen if in fact the treatments he took so long ago would freeze him at this age and what would his life be like if his wife and child aged and he did not. There was a strange dichotomy in his thoughts as he stared out the forward windshield, with Zsa at his side. On the one hand to see the future would be amazing, on the other, to see friends and family age into oblivion would be close to a slow living nightmare. Was this a selfish act or one of courage? Now that the die was cast and assuming that the doctor was correct in his science, there was only one path towards the future. He looked over at Zsa and thought about whether or not to talk to her about the treatments; after a while he reconsidered as he wanted to make sure about the biological changes before he worried Zsa. She looked beautiful in the moonlight streaming through the cabin windows; an almost iridescent glow encompassed her face as he looked at her. He realized he would miss her terribly if he lived forever, her memory after a hundred years would be one of adoration, aging and loss.

Sitting back in his chair now, he saw that in fact the Earth was getting closer still and with in a few weeks the formal preparations for landing would start.

"Tomorrow we should start cleaning up."

"Little early, don't you think?"

"Yeah, maybe I'm just getting anxious, lots to do before landing and lots to think about after we land."

"Well, thats true darling, we can get started tomorrow; just getting the food in proper order will take a lot of time."

He smiled, "I'll put out the garbage tomorrow."

"For now, I have to go to sleep," she said this while getting up from her seat and starting her way back to the sleep area near the water tanks.

"Good night love."

"Good night."

Stephen was left with his thoughts which at this point were too complex for complete understanding. He checked the vital gauges, looked up at the Earth blue and white, looking like a marble suspended in space, and took in a breath.

"I wonder what's going to happen?"

From fifty feet behind him came the faint reply, "Good things."

Turning to look behind him, he saw her preparing for sleep, suspended in the middle of the common area, smiling at him.

For the rest of the "evening" Stephen ran through his routine, checking systems, quantities and voltages. He spent eight hours in silence going through his checklist, periodically daydreaming about the landing, life afterwords and life afterwords.

~~~~~~~~~~~~`

Within the next few days the spacecraft was getting cleaned up and loose items were being secured; it was a bit early but they were anxious about getting home. News from Mars was good, everyone was happy and working hard towards establishing a new world. News from home was good as well, with the usual political issues, skirmishes and wars. Stephen quietly looked forward to the day that these actions were seen for what they were, non sense. Zsa continued her seemingly incessant work, mostly due to her new found energy from being pregnant. Stephen watched for the most part and participated periodically. His body was not changing as much as hers. The doctors back home felt as though everything would be okay due to the early stages of the pregnancy. Stephen and Zsa were of course a bit more reserved as the child had been conceived and experienced its first trimester without any influence of gravity. Ultrasound equipment on board Thales was modified to be able to verify the health of the baby. These images were sent down to the doctors for examination. No concerns. Zsa continued to nest but added baby health literature to her reading lists. Stephen was encouraged to do the same but ended up scanning a few articles and feigned a massive workload in preparation for landing.

Another two weeks passed and most preparations were complete. They spent a lot of time sitting in the cockpit watching the Earth's disk get larger. Soon enough though they were passing the Moon's orbit. They had but several days to go and it was time to start slowing down. They rotated the ship 180 degrees around to engage the main rocket engine to start the deceleration. The body of the spacecraft rumbled for several minutes as the ship slowed to enable it to start grazing the atmosphere which would slow it down even further. This technique had been used before, first ironically on Mars, then again on Earth.

211

The spacecraft could be slowed enough to allow the thrusters to slowly enter the atmosphere. Temperature sensors in the nose and leading edges of the wings controlled the descent angle, managing the temperatures on the fuselage. It took patience however as the skipping part of the maneuver could take many hours and several orbits around the planet.

"We are thirty minutes from interface."

"Confirmed, all systems nominal."

"Good, there will be some buffeting, which will last a while, maybe a few hours, then it will smooth out at about 70,000 feet. The air will be thick enough for flight at 50,000 feet and the engines will be started. At some point we will feel gravity, especially when we pitch up to allow the wings to generate lift. After that it will be a thirty minute descent to landing, where we will smell the fresh Florida air. Are you ready?"

"Oh, yes."

"Okay, here we go."

A few minutes later a slight buffeting could be felt, just as predicted. They contacted mission control and confirmed that they were being tracked by radar. The transponder in the cockpit started blinking for the first time in over a year. The buffeting was now combined with the operation of the reaction control jets, which went off seemingly randomly to keep the spacecraft (soon to be aircraft) at the proper attitude and speed. The buffeting and firings continued for almost an hour, whereupon the magnitude of the buffeting increased and the rocket firings almost became continuous. Gravity was definitely being felt by the flight crew at this point, they could see and felt themselves sinking into the seats quite a bit now. The altimeter came alive and started to unwind from the 99,000 mark it had settled at so long ago. At 70,000 feet the nose rose a bit and they could just sense the wings attempting to use the now thicker air for lift. At 50,000 feet the nose rose at least ten more degrees and the sound of air rushing over the skin of the airplane was noticeable. It was at this point that the autopilot had the aircraft stabilized and the flight management system started engine number one. After a successful start the other engines were started in sequence, stabilized, then after a brief warm up, brought up to power necessary to sustain flight without the help of any rocket power.

"We're stabilized, temperatures normal and under autopilot control," Stephen said into the microphone to mission control.

"Roger that Thales, we have you on track to start your profile descent. Telemetry is nominal, we see that you have plenty of fuel for the approach and a missed if necessary."

"Mission Control, we concur, nice to smell air again."

"Roger that."

All of the air gauges were now active; a welcome sight after months of dormancy. Stephen changed the heading command control twenty degrees right to fly to their first descent checkpoint.

"Thales, cross Grissom at flight level two four zero. Slow to three hundred knots"

"Cross Grissom at two four zero, slow to three hundred, Thales one."

Stephen pulled the throttles back to fifty percent. He then set the altitude command control to 24,000 feet. The nose of the aircraft dipped and the sound of the engine tones diminished a few notes.

After several more minutes, they had passed a three dimensional point in the sky at the right speed and heading. They followed a predetermined path to the next waypoint, named "Glen" and to their final point, named "Lovell."

214

"Thales one, turn right, heading two seven zero, reduce speed to two fifty."

"Two seventy on the heading, two fifty on the speed, Thales one."

"And Thales one, be advised, two F22s will join up with you for escort."

"Roger that, control."

"Thales one, turn right, heading three one zero, intercept the localizer for runway three three zero."

"Right to three one zero, intercept the localizer, Thales one."

They banked over to intercept the radio beam aligned with the Shuttle Landing Runway which was now in sight. The sky was clear and blue, with hints of real air coming into the cabin, both Stephen and Zsa smiled at the sight and smells. The landing flaps came out in sequence and at the outer marker of runway three three zero, the landing gear came out for the first time in many thousands of flight hours.

"Landing gear down and locked, flaps five."

Stephen brought the aircraft speed down to one hundred and forty knots, which would be their landing speed at their present weight. Contrails started to curl out from the wing tips and flap tracks as the moist Florida air was condensing at the places near the wing where the air pressure was lowest. Soon they were over the threshold of the runway and the final flair was initiated to place the main gear on the thousand foot markers. The aircraft experienced a slight thump as the mains touched down; the nose gear soon followed about the same time as Stephen pulled the throttles fully aft and reached up to engage the thrust reversers. The auto-brakes engaged and Stephen and Zsa felt like they were being pulled away from their seats as the deceleration was brisk.

Within a few moments, it was all over. The aircraft was at taxi speed. The air in the cabin was now purely Floridian and the after landing checklists were being performed.

"We made it," Stephen said as he took a brief look at Zsa.

She reached over and touched his hand still on the throttles.

"Yes, we did, what a journey."

They taxied the aircraft over to the hangar they had departed from so many months ago. There were a throng of people waiting, most of whom they knew. The aircraft came to a stop and the wheels were promptly chocked, umbilical attached and an air stair pushed into position on the left

216

side. Stephen and Zsa finished their checklists, observed that external power was now attached and unbuckled themselves to exit. The gravity was almost annoying as it took real effort to move around. They held on to the walls and any rails present to steady themselves as they made their way to the opening cabin door. Once there, they found a group of smiling faces waiting for them.

"Welcome home, you guys are heros."

"Thank you, its great to be back. Thank all of you for your support and amazing work on this aircraft."

They carefully walked down the air stair to an awaiting van, which would allow them a much needed rest as well as some cooler air. The van drove about a quarter of a mile to another building where they would be debriefed. On the way over Stephen and Zsa realized they were famished and exhausted. The driver and front passenger periodically looked back at their now famous passengers to make sure they were okay. The van rolled up to the new building, the front van occupants quickly got out and came over to the side doors to help Stephen and Zsa out of the van and into the building. They walked slowly and called ahead on their radios to have doors opened and (after prompting from Stephen) some food ready.

Once inside more people were waiting and beaming at them. This was a bit different from Stephen's last mission where he was greeted by a much more serious and somber crowd. Stephen smiled at the change.

"Welcome home, please come in, food is on the way and drinks are waiting for you," said the mission director.

"Thanks, its good to be home, but I think its going to take a while to get used to the gravity."

"About two weeks," replied a nearby flight physician.

They sat down in comfortable chairs where the medical team came over and did their preliminary examinations. Blood pressure, blood samples, temperature....and about thirty other tests. While this was going on the flight team sat down near them and started the de-briefing.

"You had an excellent mission, the Mars colony is doing well and the the aircraft is in good shape. Over the next week or so we will go over the mission in greater detail; for now and the next few days the medical team will make sure you are acclimating properly."

"Thanks, its good to be back. Its amazing how tired we are after all of that. I assume that the gravity has had a huge effect."

"It has, more on Zsa than you, based on our initial blood tests. You seem completely unaffected from the trip, aside from the gravity issue. Zsa is having a more normal reaction. You will start feeling better soon, though."

"Good."

For the next several hours they answered questions about the mission. The flight logs were simultaneously being downloaded from Thales, which had been towed into the hangar. The medical crews hovered over them, X-rays and CAT scans were taken. After the major tests, fewer people surrounded them and by early evening Stephen and Zsa were allowed to walk around if they felt good enough. By nightfall they had been left alone for several moments.

"Wow, that was a day."

Zsa looked over from her arm chair. "Yes, it was. I am exhausted."

She stood up gingerly and walked over to Stephen. Putting her arm around him she said:

"Welcome home, I think they will let us go back to our house tonight."

"Good, I haven't heard any dire predictions; I think we are just tired from the trip and our new weight."

Stephen then got the energy to stand up and together they moved toward a window and looking out they viewed the blue skies, clouds and vegetation they realized they missed for so long.

"Lets go outside."

"Okay."

They found a door and relishing their brief anonymity walked outside and viewed the surroundings.

"Remember when we walked over near the dunes that one evening?"

"Yes, I do. It was a beautiful night and I thought you were rude and obnoxious."

"Yeah, I was sure I didn't like you either."

"Things have changed a bit."

"Yeah, a bit, you have come around to see it my way." She smiled at this comment. He winced a bit.

"Do you think our car is still in the parking lot?"

"I dunno, lets go look."

They walked a bit carefully towards the parking lot, passing a few people who looked slightly surprised at the the returning astronauts just walking towards a car lot like they were at Walmart. They knew the medical staff was looking for them by now but the excitement of escaping overwhelmed them. They walked as fast as they could, which was really not that fast. It seemed that they walked a little bit like they had too much to drink, pausing every few cars to lean on them and steady themselves.

Finally, they made it to her car, which was dirty and looked dusty inside. It was at this point that they realized that they had left the keys in a locker in the vehicle assembly building. Smiling at their loss of memory, Stephen walked over to another person getting out of his car to start his shift at the Cape.

"Say, could you help us? We are a bit sore from the walk, could you do us a favor and get our keys from the VAB locker room?"

"Sure, aren't you Stephen and Zsa from the Mars mission? I heard you just got back, congratulations on a successful mission. What an adventure."

"It was quite a trip," he said smiling.

"Okay, stay right here, I will be back in a few moments."

Stephen and Zsa tried to look nonchalant leaning up against her car in the sun. A few people detoured to say hello, chatted for a while. In a few moments the person with the keys returned.

"Thanks you so much," Zsa said smiling. "Hope it starts."

"Don't worry, I will stick around to make sure."

They got the doors opened and made their way inside. Zsa inserted the keys and seeing a moderate glow in the status lights, engaged the starter. The motor turned over slowly but finally caught. They both sat back a bit and smiled. A bit of smoke came out of the tailpipe, after a minute or two it subsided. The engine ran smoothly after a few minutes as well. Looking up at the person who helped them, Stephen said:

"Thanks, we appreciate the help."

"No problem, don't tell them I helped you guys escape."

"Deal. Are you coming back tomorrow?"

"Yeah, for a while. You know...sign a few papers, go on vacation."

The Cape worker smiled and waved goodbye. He also looked around a bit to see if anyone observed him assisting the get away.

Stephen and Zsa managed to make their way to the exit of the parking lot and past the guard station. They managed to get to the main road and off towards her apartment. Driving was an experience after a multi-month space voyage, but they managed. At times it took both of them to do a decent job. After about twenty minutes they found her place and drove into the parking lot. They managed to get out the car and to the elevator to the second floor. The idea of walking up a flight of stairs scared them. Once at her floor they made their way to her apartment, then realized they had no key to enter.

"Crap."

Back downstairs they went to the manager's office, who was happy to see her and wondered why she unexpectedly showed up, without fanfare, and without a key. They gave a few excuses and once the manager was convinced she gave them a spare set to get in. They left thanking her and again made it to the elevator and upstairs. Attempt two was more successful and they made it into the apartment, which of course was in the exact condition it was left in.

"A bit musty, do you have a beer in the fridge?"

"Used to, go ahead and check, bring me some water please."

"Got it."

He found a beer, hopping it wasn't too old, he opened it and sat down in front of the TV. Some things never change.   She opened the curtains and viewed the world from a completely different perspective.

"It looks so nice out there, I am happy to be home again."

"Me too.   Hey, we have some decisions to make, Mrs. Daedalus."

"Yeah, I guess you're right.   Well first off, no football."

"What? Thats criminal."

"Just kidding....I guess we need to decide about our living...."

Just then the phone rang and they both knew who it was.

"Hello?" Yes, we did. We just needed some space (no pun intended) and had to leave.   We will be back tomorrow morning. We feel fine, don't worry."

She hung up the phone with a flair.

"I don't think they ever had two astronauts escape before; they seemed a bit....concerned."

They both smiled, Stephen got the remote to work and started to look for a football game. They ordered pizza and Chinese as they now realized the day had taken its toll and they were starving. All the types of food they had not had in a long while was exactly what they wanted so they ordered too much. The food came in about forty five minutes, by then they had cleaned and prepared the table for dinner. They ate, cleaned up again and within minutes needed to retire. Sleep came quickly, the next day came quicker still.

Back to Life

When your work speaks for itself, don't interrupt. - Henry J. Kaiser

As it turns out the next day was Monday. Compete with that slight dread of a full week ahead. They would be very busy as well as in a recuperative state, but they made it to work, past the curious guards and into the area where their offices once were. Everyone gave them double takes as they made their way down the hallways and into their former work areas. It was a bit strange in the sense that they felt like it was a normal day, but people kept their eyes on them as they walked the halls and got comfortable.

"I feel better today, less effort."

"Same."

"Well, what shall we do? Answer e-mails today?"

"I think that once they discover that we are back, there will be plenty to do."

In fact she was correct. Once they got near their old offices, more people seemed to be present. The medical staff was waiting as well as their supervisors from way up in the food chain. As they rounded the last corner...

"Well, your back. Nice of you to return. May we continue to check you out and debrief or do we need to restrain you?" This from the Director of Cape operations.

"No need, we will be here all day and for that matter, all week."

"Why, yes you will. Please sit down, both of you."

The doctors and nurses took over again, this time while a member of upper management was present. This would continue through the day as more tests were performed and the long process of discussing the mission details ensued. At several points during the day Stephen and Zsa were separated; usually for the purpose of getting

227

objective observations about the details of some facet of the mission. They were however, treated well. Lunch was sent to them in the closest conference room. A stream of friends and family came through during this day and the following days. Life slowly returned to normal. The inter-planetary wedding was approved and the proper paper work executed. Stories about the wedding and other events on the voyage became legend as Stephen and Zsa walked the hallways within their own auras.

The doctors however whispered amongst themselves as they found Zsa's medical condition to be as expected after such a long voyage. Stephen's however was remarkably better. In fact, specialists who had worked with Stephen during the initial astronaut training period looked through their old notes and records and found a few interesting developments. For instance, pockets of calcium normally found in his heart had dissipated. Cholesterol levels were at a minimum. Mental activity was exceptional. Although confused, the doctors interviewed Stephen several times about any unusual occurrences during the voyage in an attempt to rationalize their findings. Stephen was not able to help them, or more accurately, not willing. These conversations went on for several weeks and the doctors had to at some point stop chasing the mystery and get back to their normal jobs. The notes and records were put away for later follow up, if necessary. Meanwhile Stephen and Zsa continued their everyday lives with, if nothing else, a sense of pride regarding the mission.

Zsa continued the cycle of pregnancy having frequent examinations confirming the health of the baby. Stephen found a nicer home and they both moved out of their apartments and became more suburban.

The baby was born several months later. All previous life experiences were relegated to history as the new family dealt with new family issues. New life has a habit of taking on a new life. With that tautology, they lived on, going to work, eventually school and eventually retirement.

Retirement became a real problem as a result of Stephen's medical changes. It was obvious that he was not aging at the same rate as everyone else. Five years after their return Zsa really noticed the difference and became concerned about her husband. Stephen had not told her details of the medical procedure for two reasons. First, he was never sure that the changes were real, at least until several years past with no discernible aging. Second, he feared losing Zsa as they grew apart in age. It would be alright for a while but certainly ten years after their marriage the differences would be too obvious to ignore. Friends and family took notice as well and they too had not been informed. Stephen was left with a very difficult choice. Tell everyone and be the object of criticism and curiosity or tell no-one and set the stage to disappear. Neither option was attractive but something had to be done.

At about the seventh anniversary of their return Stephen took Zsa out to dinner and started the process of letting her know what happened. They had received their drinks and just ordered their meals when Stephen started:

"Zsa, darling, I have to tell you something."

"Oh, oh, this does not sound good. If its about your new cute secretary, let her know that I will be over someday to 'talk' to her."

"Oh, no, nothing like that Zsa, this is actually more important."

"Okay, what is it?"

"Well, years ago, before I met you and well before our last mission to Mars, I had some treatments that potentially could keep me from aging."

"Really? What kind of treatments?"

"The treatments modified my cells to enable them to replicate perfectly. It was in the very early stages of trial when I obtained the test serums from my doctor."

"Hmm, so that explains a lot. My friends and family were impressed and tease me about marrying someone much younger than myself. I told them that I was younger than you, but they don't believe me. I am not sure what to think about this; of course it impacts our whole family. Why did you do it?"

"Well, some people want to live forever. In my case that idea was only part of the decision. The other parts included curiosity and the need to learn as much as possible. If this is really working, I will have a very unique perspective on humanity in say fifty years."

"Well, yes unique. And I hope relevant. This is a huge move on your part, especially if the treatments really work, we will not have a marriage or for that matter a family for much longer. You and I will grow apart. I will have no partner."

"Well, we can continue to live together for a while but in many ways I wish I had not had the treatment. I didn't think I would meet someone like you."

"Hmm, doesn't help. I have to think about this for awhile."

With that came silence and an issue that might not be resolved anytime soon. Their relationship now had a kink in it. To themselves, they both thought about their child and the impact. Stephen thought about being available for his son for a long period of time. Zsa thought about leaving her son behind.

This experience highlighted the issues related to being immortal. For the hydra, lobster and jellyfish, being immortal is not a huge issue, but a society expecting a life cycle versus a human witnessing a thousand generations creates some problems. What of the mind's capability to take in a thousand years of knowledge? What would an immortal think of a seemingly struggling nascent society of people destined to have but a few decades of productivity. The constant cycle of education, occupation and retirement could drive this person to bitterness. One would guess that they would seek out the brightest people alive at any one period to both seek relief as well as offer productive advice, much like a mentor. Stephen was headed for this unknown period of discovery. Zsa was headed for a strange trip with a younger and younger husband knowing that at some point the father would be younger than the son. This disturbed her quite a bit and it would take some time for her to rationalize their future life together. She loved him however and would instinctively try to work things out. He was attentive and supportive and certainly did not have eyes for any other women. She hoped this would last and if it did she could make due.

After a few days of contemplation Zsa found Stephen out in the garden deep in thought while turning some sandy dirt over for the next generation of annuals.

"We are going to have to move every few years."

Stephen looked up for a long moment, not directly at her but straight ahead and replied.

"Yes, you're right, thats the best solution."

"I think that what you did is in some ways noble but in other ways selfish. Considering you did this before we got together and life was different then; I can see the attraction. I only ask you for one thing."

"Anything, Zsa." He was now looking directly at her.

"Never forget us."

He paused before he said the obvious. He regretted the hollowness that he would experience in the far future.

"Never, Zsa."

She stood up and went back to their house to prepare a meal for their son. Stephen was in a reflective mood and felt one of the drawbacks of immortality. It was not part of the human condition; not part of the resonance that influences our lives.

Beginning the Journey

Its not true that life is one damn thing after another; its really one damn thing over and over. - Edna St. Vincent Milay

~ Sunrise Descending ~

They moved several times over the next several decades. She retired from NASA. He trimmed his resume and worked his way up to management positions but wisely decided to move up no further as he needed to remain an obscure member of a large group of professionals. Becoming director of NASA would be too public even though he was capable. In addition he changed his name around a few times and was able to adjust his medical records as needed. As long as his long line of physicians did not talk to each other his secret would be safe.

As far as Zsa was concerned he remained in love with her but she of course was a slowly changing person. Outside they were at first an oddly matched couple, she being much older than he, then after another move, he was portrayed as her son. Their real offspring dealt with the issue as well during the ensuing years. The strange part of course came when Stephen became younger than his son. They had a private birthday party on that day. The son for some reason thought it was cool to know someone close to him would see the Universe unfold.

Another few decades and several more moves later Zsa was at the end of her life. She slept for most of the time. Stephen continued to work and take care of the house; known to the outside world as a stay at home bachelor. He did on several occasions have the opportunity to rectify the situation with another women but always refused. His love ran deep.

At some point the inevitable happened and Zsa passed away leaving Stephen in a quite house as their son and his family flew in for a funeral. Stephen walked around the home having mental images of Zsa doing something here in the kitchen or there in the living room. The home was filled with sound and smells from the past. For some strange reason Stephen did not feel too lonely and at one point walked over to the window that viewed the street in front of their home. He observed people and especially children whose lives could be almost predictable. He looked at a particular kid riding a bike and imagined him growing up, having a family and career, getting old, all of this while Stephen observed from a distance. Another life, another life to be followed by another life, ad nauseum. Backing up from the window he considered his next move. As far as work was concerned he was completely bored with directing peoples' activities and dealing with short sighted decisions. Their bank accounts were doing very well from his constant promotions and careful investments. With prudence he could sell everything and travel for several years, staying inconspicuous and exploring the world. A few temporary relationships could be experienced as well. He would of course keep up with his now older son and his children, who then would someday be older than he. The strange part would come as the families genes grew and spread about. How would they feel hundreds of years from now with someone showing up from the blue and announcing that he was their great, great, great, great grandfather and appeared younger? Oh, and then prove it with a genetic screening. He decided to make that decision later as he knew that science would make incredible strides by that time and could alter his decision to become public.

His family did arrive eventually and a funeral was performed for his wife. It had to be a small funeral. His son was conciliatory and understanding. Afterwords, Stephen told him of his plans, which made complete sense to his son. They parted after the ceremony with the promise of frequent visits.

Stephen followed through on the house details and after making a bucket list of destinations, packed his luggage and left for his first port of call, Patagonia.

Over the next many months Stephen flew around the world and saw as many wonders of the world as possible. Then he purchased a sail boat and sailed around the Mediterranean,   then to Iceland, Greenland, Nova

Scotia, Maine, New York, Baltimore, Norfolk, Charleston, St. Augustine, Miami, Key West, Clearwater, Panama City and New Orleans, where he stayed for two months. Then, after the sea beckoned again, back to the Caribbean, South America, Africa, up to the Suez, Abu Dhabi, India, Darwin, New Guinea, Cannes, Sydney, New Zealand, Fiji, Tahiti and Hawaii, where he again stayed for several months. By this time he had met several other sailors willing to help him with the sailing and happy to have a free ride on a nice sailboat. The ephemeral relationships worked best. This vagabond existence worked for many years as it kept his secret protected. He kept in touch with his son, who now was older than he. Amazingly, the family secret would be kept until the son's death. After that no one would know. Stephen continued to live on investments and retirement (at least for awhile). The investments would blossom into major sources of money in several years and keep him from having to get a long term job. He did in fact have grandchildren, who at this time did not understand who he really was; he would follow their lives as well as their offsprings' and their offsprings' at least for several generations.

The years and the decades mounted, at his first hundred year birthday, he celebrated with a member of the doctor's family who he had befriended. She did not know who he was but they did have a chance to talk about the doctor's legacy and his interest in extending life spans. There were no records of his work, just rumors. She was convinced that the work had been more theoretical and no real experiments had been performed. Stephen had to contain himself as he wanted to let her know that her great great grandfather had been successful. The problem of course was that the secret would be exposed and that could have dire consequences. After dinner, Stephen left with a somewhat hollow feeling in his heart; these were the beginnings of isolation from humanity in general.

The real challenge was in keeping himself occupied, at some point, he had actually visited every country on Earth and lived for long periods in many of them. He had also sampled hundreds of occupations and because of his unique experiences in having lived through recent history he became a professor of history and taught at several universities. His courses became legendary as the students fell under his spell and had the sense that he had really lived through the events and times in which he spoke. Little did they know that in many cases he had. He took advantage of his experiences by also writing about them as a historian would, except for the fact that the papers and books were first hand knowledge, not interpreted or a result of research. The interesting part came when other historians disputed facts that Stephen knew first hand to be true. He had to interact with their objections carefully and needed backup documentation to prove himself correct in these matters. Academic egos can be formidable sometimes and on more than one occasion he had to let the accusers feel like they had won the battles. This was more important than proving his immortality.

After several multi-year stints as a professor his colleagues started to comment on his constant youthful appearance as they aged. At this point he had to leave the profession and do something completely different.

He did however observe a few constants of human behavior after his many many years on Earth. Humanity moved forward in a generally optimistic manner with the appreciation of good food, music and art. There was always creativity, always a leaning towards the future and the taking care of new generations. This was a gratifying discovery for Stephen who had witnessed a significant amount of wars, poverty and hate.

On yet another sojourn to another country he worried about what he could do next. The answer came in the announcement of the *Gaea* project, which was a multi national attempt to build an interstellar spaceship. The project would take decades to complete and would transport a select group of individuals to several candidate star systems to explore any life there. The ship would be built mostly by robots and would be assembled in Earth's orbit. The idea was to take about a thousand people on a voyage that would last about a generation long. In this way the younger people who started the trip would be able to return to Earth. Many people would be born during this time and many people would die. The science behind this project was simple. Einstein and Newton had been right; you cannot exceed the speed of light and you cannot get more reaction out of action. Once these precepts were accepted the *Gaea* project was started. The ship would in fact achieve a good fraction of the speed of light but would have to slow down significantly to explore other worlds.

With all of this in mind Stephen made a major life decision.

Voyage to the Stars

Though my soul may set in darkness, it will rise in perfect light, I have loved the stars too fondly to be fearful of the night. - Sarah Williams

~ *Sunrise Descending* ~

The object was simple, find a way to get on board the ship when they launched, keep the secret contained for thirty plus years and find a way to move on, hopefully to another world.

Stephen had realized that the only true path for him now was to explore the heavens. He had nothing but time on his hands. To that end he moved back to Cape Canaveral where *Gaea* mission control would be. He took a job in an ancillary support company that would allow him to keep track of the progress. *Gaea* would be a huge endeavor, a ship miles long, containing at least a thousand people. He carefully plotted how to become one of them. This might in fact be the easy part as once he was on board his secret would be more noticeable. A thousand people sounds like a lot until you spend thirty years with them. By then most everyone will know most everyone else. Inevitably Stephen's lack of aging would be obvious to someone.

For now the emphasis would be on grooming himself to be selected for the voyage, either this or he would have to become a stow away. Stephen chose to prepare for both contingencies. First he found work in the medical records section of a small company tasked with developing the software that would keep the medical records of all on board. Stephen was able to become one of the software developers and as such able to devise software subroutines that would be obscure enough to remain hidden for decades. They were designed to allow his age to be updated every few years while he was on *Gaea*. After he achieved this he got himself promoted to be a software installation technician responsible for installing and updating the routines inside the ship. This would require that he transport up and spend a significant amount of time in space. With his impressive amount of tribal knowledge regarding this software and his good health, preparations were made to have him shuttled up to the spacecraft.

After some training and preparations for space travel Stephen was ushered into a commercial shuttle for launch into space. This was the first time that he had been in space since his flight to Mars in Thales, which of course was not on his resume. He was however a very good student, to others it seemed as if he had done it before. The day came for the launch Stephen had all of the software he needed for a several week stay on the unfinished spaceship. He donned his spacesuit, was ushered aboard the shuttle and within thirty minutes was on his way back to space. He smiled at the thought and smiled at the thought that this was his first step to the exploration of the galaxy. Being an immortal had its drawbacks but he resigned himself to make the best of it with this new mission. What would one do with this "gift?" Given the great expanse of time to do things, what would any of us do? Stephen made a choice that many humans far in the future will do, explore the bounties of the Milky Way. It takes thousands of years to do this kind of thing, but if you have thousands of years to do it, well....

The shuttle rumbled skyward, arcing and accelerating. Within eight minutes the sky was black and the shuttle passengers and crew were experiencing weightlessness. Within several hours, and after a nice lunch, the great spaceship came into view. The dimensions were awe inspiring. The robotic assemblers looked like ants moving all about the frame and substructures of the ship. One side of the craft was lit by Earthshine and the other by a combination of Moonshine and Sunshine. The colors glinting off of the beast were impressive. Stephen was certainly impressed as even the large size of Thales paled in comparison to Gaea. It looked like a world unto itself.

"I could get lost in there," he thought correctly.

Within another hour the shuttle was lining up to a docking port. Enough of the great ship was complete to allow up to a hundred workers and technicians to live on board and build the infrastructure. Once the docking was complete the cabin door was opened and the cavernous insides were revealed. Some of the passengers had already visited the ship before and showed little emotion upon landing. The others, who were visiting for the first time, were wide eyed and excited at the experience.

They filed out weightlessly and started to find their individual working areas. After settling in they reconvened to have a safety briefing and get acquainted with the crew members of *Gaea*.   After the meetings they fanned out again to start their work routines. Stephen found his way to the medical wing of the ship, introduced himself to the people present and after locating a work station, started uploading software.   This   software   included   his inconspicuous subroutines. Within a few hours the main components of his upload were complete. The next several working days would be consumed with working out bugs and making sure the different types of computers could use the software correctly. As he finished his initial upload he knew that stage one was complete. He rose from his workstation and being completely independent and un-supervised he decided to explore the ship and find his quarters. Portions of the ship had been set in motion to create an artificial gravity. Getting to one of these areas was a relief to Stephen. Once there he walked around and slowly made his way to his room. Then he checked in with his co-workers on the surface and let them know the initial systems were on line. After that he found the cafeteria and got a snack. Sitting in the dining room he imagined living in this ship for a few decades as he explored the cosmos and made his way through time.

The large extent of the ship would lend itself nicely to a covert existence. If his subroutine worked out he could change jobs and find obscure un-public places to work. The layout of the ship included many different "neighborhoods" and living areas separated by great distances. If worse came to worse he would have several opportunities to stay on a newly explored planet. Stephen knew the plan could work it just depended on getting an invitation to be a crew member. He now had enough time to formulate a strategy to make sure it happened.

The first task was to make sure he had access to the computers, both in the ship and upon his return. This he did by making a special login and password, one that would have administrative control but not so obvious to the real administrators who ultimately would be working with the computers. The solution was to have a log in name work with two different passwords. Once the code was in place and compiled it would be near impossible to detect. As the computers were in a highly protected environment isolated from the Earth's internet by firewalls and sophisticated servers. To those on the inside of the system fewer precautions were taken as they assumed there would not be any substantial problems. This fact was taken advantage of by Stephen and his secret subroutines.

The internal designs of the ship where also available and Stephen studied them in detail just in case he had to stow away. This would only be a last resort as eventually someone would find out and their would be consequences to pay.

He spent the next few weeks finishing his work, testing out the software loads and making sure the ground engineers had easy access to his work. At the appointed time he packed his things and made his way down to the space dock to take a shuttle back to Earth. The seed had been planted.

The shuttle departed and within several hours was on final approach to the Cape. Flying to and from space was a lot easier these days, almost like common airline flights. He looked out the windows to see that familiar high descent angle of shuttles see on the landing approach. He looked forward towards the cockpit door just in time to let his peripheral vision see the flare to landing transition. Moments later the main wheels touched down. He knew the pilots were probably smirking at their good work. The shuttle slowed as brakes were applied. They turned to the right to leave the runway environment and taxied to the hangar. It all looked so new and modern compared to so many years ago when NASA was in trouble. It was really good to know they were doing much better now. They now passed the hangar where he and Zsa first met and ultimately took their trip to Mars. This was so long ago now but the images, smells and sounds were the same. He welled up a bit at the thoughts and these intense feelings of loneliness after her passing. At these times he felt sure he had made a mistake in becoming immortal. Now he had to avert his eyes to stop the flood of memories and try to think about something else. In the background, the intercom of the shuttles monotonically described the departure procedure and where to find one's luggage. Stephen came back into focus, unbuckled and got in line to depart the spacecraft. He wiped a tear from his left eye, grabbed his jacket and started walking; smiling, he remembered how different gravity felt when Zsa and he landed Thales so many years ago, unbuckled and departed to a waiting throng of Cape personnel. There were so many good memories of the past, although he had made a million more, none were so vivid as those with Zsa.

The door to the shuttle was now right in front of him; he lowered his eyes to begin the descent down the air stairs. No throng this time just a walk to the parking lot where he left his car. The emotional wave that had overtaken him was past now but left a residue he would have to deal with over the next several weeks. Ultimately it strengthened his resolve to get on *Gaea* as he rationalized that Zsa would have wanted him to move on with his life and do what made him happy. Now happiness was defined as getting away from Earth and its memories for a good long while, maybe forever.

He found his car, a bit dusty from some recent dirty rains. The engine started and as he settled in, it became smoother as mechanical things do not like to be left idle for long. A few moments later he looked up and placed the transmission lever into drive. The gravity just sitting down was still a bit strange and as the car moved the lateral g forces felt a bit different as well. Minutes later, he found himself driving down the highway towards his apartment complex. Once there, and a bit relieved, he made his way into his apartment, went in, shut the door and quickly found a beer to relax. It was now time to plot his permanent return to the "Mother" ship. The path was reasonably clear as he was the expert in the medical software he installed. They would need someone to maintain it and he had the credentials (whether known or not) to become an astronaut (again).

The next day Stephen went to work, settled in, had a good de-briefing and looking at his boss, decided to work extra hard to seal his place on the flight roster. This meant weekends and long hours during regular week days.

In time he was recommended again for a shuttle flight to install more software, this time for a longer stint.

Soon that day came, Stephen was ready, took the flight and spent a month on the near complete *Gaea*. This time he met and befriended many of the flight crew who were spending months at a time on the great ship. They learned of his unusual intelligence, experience and hard work ethic, which of course created a recipe for getting named to the permanent flight crew, a process which was just beginning. He was offered an interview with the senior flight staff and it was at this point he answered their many questions like a veteran. Everyone was impressed and Stephen was inducted to the first round flight crew.

251

Relieved, Stephen informed his boss, who was thrilled as their software would now be a permanent fixture on the ship as well as their worker being one of the crew. This made the stock holders happy too.

At the first opportunity, Stephen cleared up his personal affairs, including saying goodbye to some now distant relatives, sold his possessions and became (again) a NASA employee. He drove to the Cape parking lot, parked, located a young, just out of college worker, handed her the key and title to his car.

"What is this for?" she asked, wide eyed.

"I am going into space for a few decades and you look like you would appreciate a fine old car."

"Why, thank you so much. Your'e on the flight crew of *Gaea?*"

"I am in fact, leaving in six hours. The car is that black one over there."

He pointed, she squinted her eyes.

"What? What kind of a car is that?"

"A 1990 Bentley Turbo R. Low mileage in a sense. Very fun to drive, great for going to parties or out to dinner."

"Isn't that like a hundred years old? I have never seen anything like that except in books. Its probably worth a lot of money."

~ Sunrise Descending ~

"Oh yeah, its worth a lot, take good care of it. I drove it for over eighty years and its been very reliable."

"Eighty years, that can't be true, your in your thirties."

Stephen smiled, did not answer and left a confused new antique car owner standing in the parking lot staring at him as he walked into the staging area for the initial flight crew.

"Crew orientation is in the main hangar," said a voice over the intercom.

Stephen and his one bag walked over to the appointed area, found a seat and dropped his bags.

The orientation speech was like many others, do this, don't do that. It was over in thirty minutes. Stephen and the rest of the crew rose and started to drift towards the dressing areas where they would don their suits and test their safety gear. In about an hour the crew was ready. Some talked on their cell phones to a loved one or friend. Some looked a bit sad, some defiant. Stephen was just happy at taking the next step in his very long journey, one to the stars.

The crew finished all preparations and were led in their flight suits, to the shuttle. Their belongings were be sent to a cargo hold and given to them later.

~ Sunrise Descending ~

They strapped in and looked out the windows for one more glimpse of Earth. Stephen did not as he was a lot more interested in his new life in space. After a few checklists were gone through, the shuttle's engines started and a few seconds later they were accelerating briskly to the required seventeen thousand miles per hour. It was always a thrill to break the surely bonds of Earth. Always a thrill to reach out and touch the face of God.

Their journey took them into space, around for several orbits, and eventually right to the giant spacecraft hovering in the heavens.

The shuttle lined up as it had before and slowly closed the distance to the docking ring. A slight thump announced their arrival both to the passengers in the shuttle as well as the inhabitants of the great ship. Pressure was equalized, the door opened and again for Stephen the filing out process began. He had been here twice before and knew his way around well. He helped a few newcomers and eventually found his way to his new permanent cabin. Due to his low ranking it was small and without a window, that was okay though as he wanted not to stand out in any way. He arranged his things, sat down to a small desk and logged into the computer system. With a few unique key strokes he verified that his clandestine subroutines were still active. Then he shut down the computer and made his way to the dining area which at this time was just completed and had a huge series of windows that looked down on the Earth. As he walked in the light level was quite high, several people inside and most of the workers had sun glasses on. The Earth was huge from two hundred and fifty miles above the surface.

Stephen sat down and ordered lunch. Once relaxed he viewed his former home from a distance, thought about his life there, Zsa and when or if he would ever see it again.

Once done with lunch he rose and made his way to his new workstation, which was in the records section of the medical wing. Again it was a nondescript room, no windows and the vast majority of the organizational chart above him. He settled in, typed the password into the computer and started his routine of software maintenance. Every day for the next many years would be the same: sign in, run reports, answer problem calls, fix software. The trick would be how not to stand out and then, if a suitable world was found, how to get to the surface. These were problems to be worked out, not solved at this time. For now, he just felt successful.

Cruising

For my part I know nothing with any certainty, but the sight of the stars makes me dream. - Vincent van Gogh

After a few weeks on *Gaea* the final checklists and preparations started to be performed. Flight crews ran around securing and verifying every system on board the ship. It was now fully loaded and fundamentally ready for flight. Each of the engines had been started individually, but now it was time to light them all at once. In this case they were low thrust ion engines that could propel the ship to very high velocities, but at a slow rate. Once they were all running it would still take several days to get the ship out of orbit. After that they would slowly accelerate for the next year or so to get up to full speed. Slowing down would take an equally long time. There were however a sprinkling of vectored thrusters that worked on more standard chemical propellants but these were to be used in emergencies only.

On liftoff day an announcement was made on the intercom. A very slight humming was detected by those crew members who were in the aft part of the ship, otherwise it was just another day. Within about eight hours the people in the areas with large windows did notice a difference in the size of the Earth. The blue planet was definitely receding. After several more days the much smaller Earth started to move aft and became visible only on the camera monitors. The humming continued and would for a year. The flight to the moon took over a week, to Mars three Months and to Jupiter a year.

During this time Stephen kept to himself and was known as a bit shy. He did have acquaintances but had to remove himself from any serious friendships. He knew that after five to ten years he would have to move to a completely separate part of the ship or make a decision about living on a planet. He usually ate by himself and avoided all parties and get togethers.

Work was still mundane but he kept his sanity by being very detailed about his tasks. He documented everything and wrote programs to organized his work and optimize the software for which he was responsible. For that he was respected. He did however not seek any promotions and would come in late or make small mistakes to keep this from happening. It was a tough disciplined life. On several occasions during the years of travel Stephen felt like he should reveal his secret. He thought:

"Who would care....what could they do?"

But after every bout of introspection he would weigh being a object of interest and living a quiet life away from the spotlights. The quiet life was ultimately more appealing.

After a few more years loneliness started to take its toll and he decided to make friends with someone from the lowest echelons of society on the ship. He spent months making a decision on where to go and possibly find a friend. What would be especially appealing would be someone from a completely different culture. One that might have a completely different view on life than the standard crew compliment. After a long period of research he decided to try out a few places. What would be best would be areas that were rarely occupied during the second or third period of work. The first thing he did was ask his boss to allow him to change to the graveyard shift when most people were asleep. After he became acclimated to this time he started to explore the ship's least accessible areas. As the ship did in fact have a top and bottom this meant the bottom holds where cargo was held as well as most of the infrastructure equipment. The air and water purification plants were here and many individual power plants as well. The personnel in these areas tended to be mechanics and technicians.

As he explored these areas, which were vast, he learned to feel comfortable in the less public areas of the ship. The denizens of these areas had the same borderline anti-social way of life that Stephen liked. They actually formed a sub-culture that the "upstairs people" only told rumors about.

He started to visit these areas on a regular basis and at one point found his way to the front of the ship, albeit under the floor, and found someone with a very special talent. This person was also "under the radar," and worked in a mundane job maintaining air handling equipment. He was a supremely talented musician named Koichiro Takamizawa. Somehow he was appointed to be on the ship, carry out menial tasks and then perform periodically. Koichiro had not yet performed after several years in space, which was curious, but he did not seem to mind. In fact, he did not seem to mind about anything. He was completely at peace with himself, settled, happy. Stephen found him to be an oasis of calm and started to visit periodically. Koichiro was from Kamome, an island off of Hokkaido. In 1615, a group of merchants raised a shrine on the island to honor the god of the Sea of Japan, and in 1868 it was renamed into Itsukushima Shrine. In 1814, a monument to Matsuo Basho the most famous poet of the Edo Period in Japan was installed near the shrine. It had also been a gathering place for Buddhist monks for thousands of years. The island had beautiful beaches and eventually became a tourist resort. When Koichiro was born there had been a solar eclipse during a very sacred Buddhist ceremony. The alignment of moon and star was the harbinger of something very special.

Koichiro grew up in a good family that nurtured his musical talents. He was, at great expense, sent to the best teachers. He settled on the Koto as his instrument, a thirteen stringed instrument made of wood and having moveable bridges to affect different tunings. The instrument was very hard to play, but Koichiro's persistence and focus brought wonderful music to many people. He studied music until he was asked to come aboard Gaea; unlike the others he did not apply. The reason he was asked was to be able to remind the crew members about their home on Earth. Koichiro had a wonderful ability to paint scenes in music to remind people of waterfalls, birds, the ocean, and many other Earthly features. A very high ranking NASA director was astute enough to sprinkle the ship with objects from Earth as well as add art and a particular musician. Special compensation had been paid to Koichiro as his quarters had the only forward facing window on the lower decks.

Stephen and Koichiro got along very well as Stephen's deep level of wisdom, based on his real age, and Koichiro's natural comfort with everything, melded well. They both talked in a language few others understood. Deep reflections on existence and essence. Observations of life on Earth and other star systems. In a way, their philosophic credentials defined the roots of the tree of understanding with regards to the cosmos. These many moments of inspiration they shared was beyond science and emotion. They decided their knowledge was important enough to be recorded and formed what became known as the Space Testaments. These writings discussed the human interpretation of life outside of Earth as well as the non-human; together they formed a clearer picture of cosmic consciousness.

Stephen knew that Koichiro would not care about his immortality and more than any other would appreciate it. In fact, Koichiro believed in Rebirth. Rebirth refers to a process whereby beings go through a succession of lifetimes as one of many possible forms of sentient life, each running from conception to death. Koichiro was a Buddhist. Buddhism rejects the concepts of a permanent self or an unchanging, eternal soul, as it is called in Hinduism and Christianity. According to Buddhism there ultimately is no such thing as a self independent from the rest of the universe (the doctrine of anatta). Rebirth in subsequent existences must be understood as the continuation of a dynamic, ever-changing process of "dependent arising" determined by the laws of cause and effect (karma) rather than that of one being transmigrating or incarnating from one existence to the next. To Koichiro, Stephen's view of life was consistent with the teachings of the Buddha Siddhartha. He detected that Stephen had a very seasoned view of the present and the past. This was a wisdom that appeared only possible from someone who had actually lived many lives. Stephen never elaborated on how he came to have this wisdom it just seemed like a natural way to be.

They discussed many subjects over the ensuing years. Subjects like life in the past, life now and life in the future. There was, in both their minds, a continuity based on the past that would direct them towards the future. Koichiro had no illusions about dying. Stephen had no illusions about living. Interestingly they had very similar observations about the present as a result.

Even after many years Korichiro never made a comment about how young Stephen appeared even though Koichiro was visibly aging. It was almost as if he knew the truth but in no way did he care.

The voyage went many years before the first advanced life civilizations were found. For each inhabited planet they found chronicles were written, which Stephen read in detail. Stephen was not sure what he was going to do with the exception of getting off the ship at some time.

Meanwhile they visited Aphrodite 4 where the inhabitants, much like very intelligent reptiles, were at a stage of development many years behind Earth. This did not feel like the right place to live another lifetime.

~ Sunrise Descending ~

Next they stopped at a planet called CoRot 7b whose orbital inclination made for a constantly light side and a constantly dark side. The people on the light side never slept and did not know about the stars, the people on the dark side led reclusive lives, but understood time. This too did not feel like the right place.

Then they went to the next inhabited planet named L'quacious 5 where the people had merged with computer technology to such an extent that they were constantly on line, as they had electronics medically inserted into their bodies. Their logic and mathematical organization left creativity and art in the long distant past. They hungered for these things and with the advent of a visit from *Gaea*, they told the crew members of their needs. The crew members responded with gifts from many eras of Earth's history; they left art, music and literature for the L'quacions. These things were left without interpretation in an attempt to foster creative thought. Stephen found their needs too intense for him to live comfortably.

Benthic 2 followed, which had a rich advanced culture of empaths. They rarely spoke as verbal communications were inefficient. The reports on these people intrigued Stephen, however the idea of having many people reading his mind was a little uncomfortable. In addition, the sole pilot who visited this world brought back a companion, one who may or may not have been real. There were a lot of unknowns with this planet and more study was needed.

Last on the major list of inhabitants was Hebe 6, a most appropriate place for Stephen.

The Story of Hebe 6

That which does not twinkle is near – we must take this truth as having been reached by induction or sense-perception. - Aristotle

~ Sunrise Descending ~

Gaea had 'turned the corner' in her explorations, which gave the crew a sense of going down hill. Many of them looked forward to their return. One of the worlds they passed on the way back was worthy of a closer look. This world was the 6th planet in a sun like solar system, which the astronomers called Hebe. Named after the Goddess of youth, dispenser of ambrosia to the Gods, particularly Aphrodite. The astronomers thought this world looked young and fresh. After due consideration the management staff decided to change course to Hebe 6, go into orbit and possibly send an away team to land on the surface if the environment was conducive.

Once in orbit the imaging team found land masses, oceans, vegetation and evidence of cities or at least villages. They flew down for a closer look. Once there they found some curious details about the inhabitants who lived in villages.

There seemed to be an absence of elderly versions of the villagers. In fact the vast majority of the people here looked about the same age around their mid 30s. On the surface a language expert named Angela learned to converse with the people in the villages. One evening she was talking to one of the leaders and during the conversation she had to make sure she understood something very important that she had just learned.

The mission leader found her after the event and asked her what had just transpired.

"Well, I asked the leader of these people several times about their lifespan. He replied in no uncertain terms that this particular group does not have a lifespan. In fact they have no idea how old they really are. They remember hundreds or maybe thousands of annual cycles, which I think is close to our definition of a year. They remember geological events and the evolution of their flora and fauna."

"What about the younger ones?"

"Well, this particular group has had thousands of children. They grow like we do and age as we do, until they die. There are many villages around here that have normal life cycles, this one does not."

"Wow, do they attribute their long lives to anything particular?"

"They're not sure. The technology is not advanced enough for them to understand genetics or advanced medicine. From what I understand they have common colds like we do, break bones and sustain other injuries, but their bodies, unless the injuries are very serious, just heal.

This group was much larger in the past but natural disasters and accidents have claimed many of their people."

After a few mores days of conversation Angela had more to say.

"I believe that they feel that in some ways the long lives that they have experienced has been a curse. They have outlived so many loved ones that they are in a way lonely. None of them are married. They tell me that the lack of change in their lives is stressful. They have no life changing experiences to share with a mate. They stay together because of their common attributes. Many have tried over the years to live in other villages, but end up feeling very uncomfortable as they outlive everyone and cannot establish meaningful relationships. I don't think they want to die particularly, just move on. So yes they are very interested in what we can discover about them."

"That's amazing, you would think that immortality would be the key to discovering the universe."

"They lack the motivation to do so and are very comfortable here. In a way, their minds are full. They have experienced millions of events and because of that new things become ephemeral."

The villagers were probably thinking that the new knowledge of their "affliction" would allow them to

269

experience the final chapters of their lives. They looked forward to grow old like their ancestors with grace and dignity, slowly giving their mental faculties to the specters of illusion and repetition, to become themselves, only more so.

Strange, it seems that as humans the crew members, who had not experienced such long lives or known anyone who had, would see life as unfortunately short. There is a point in time for all humans when immortality seems like a very attractive option. Later, of course, the chemicals in our bodies conspire to convince us of our Autumn and to move us aside to allow the young ones to do the hard work. The "ancient ones" here in the village had been stuck in the working age and had not had the option of being the old masters directing the younger members in the arts of life and creation.

"Its rather amazing," a medical technician reported after several tests, "our preliminary results show they have the ability to correct abnormalities in their genetic code. As our cells reproduce minor mistakes occur during the copy phase, after many generations, obvious changes take place, which result in aging. In our case the telomeres, which are the end components of our chromosomes, help to replicate our cells, but sometimes not perfectly. In their case, each time their cells go through the copy phase the results are perfect. So, as a consequence, they do not age and all injuries are healed. In fact it might be possible for them to grow back an organ or a limb if it is injured or removed. Quite remarkable. In fact....."

Their leader had walked up to the crew members discussing their findings.

"We're the Nereids."

"I'm sorry," said the expedition leader, we are not familiar with that term."

"We are the offspring of the fifty original Nerieds, the daughters of Nerius and Doris the Oceanid, in the history of the Earth's Greek culture. The daughters married the young men of the indigenous inhabitants of this world. We are the offspring and share their traits. Some of us did not live as long because of the sharing of genes. But we, the ones in this village, carry the original gifts of the ancient gods of Greece."

The team leader asked, "But the time of the Greek Gods was so long ago, how did your parents find their way to this planet? We thought the Greeks were not capable of traveling through space."

"An advanced culture from a distant solar system set about to discover the inhabitants of worlds near their own. They built a large ship and spent several generations exploring space. During the voyage scientists onboard their ship discovered how to control the reproduction of the cellular structure and as a result the original members of that ship became what you would call immortal. Really nothing more than the progress of science. Compared to many cultures they met during their journey this was magic. Upon discovering Earth they decided to introduce themselves to the inhabitants of Greece, as they were the most advanced at that time. The fact that they did not age caused the Greeks to believe they were Gods. They stayed for a few hundred years and as the political climate changed and the impact of their presence became a problem they left and came to this world."

"An interesting parallel to our journey," observed the team leader, "several cultures we met probably thought *we* were gods."

"Of course. Its common across the cosmos. Cultures are all at different levels. It is the nature of living things to be in awe of life at a higher level."

"What will you do here? Here in paradise?"

"Continue to live simply and improve ourselves. We believe that it is written in the starlight and in the lines of our palms that we should live in deeds not years, thoughts not breaths, feelings not measurements from a scientific instrument. We count our time in heart throbs and believe that he who lives the most the one who thinks the most, feels the noblest and acts the best."

After the revelation about the villagers the personnel from *Gaea* gathered, made copious notes and recordings about their experiences on this planet, got in their shuttle and departed for the Mother Ship.

Debriefings were made after their return and as the crew members of *Gaea* were anxious to return to Earth only one more quick trip to the surface was performed. This was only to sample some of the vegetation and geology as the first group did not have time to do so.

Stephen, after reading all of the reports about the Nereids, made up his mind to visit the planet and stay if it felt right. The trick of course would be how to get aboard the shuttle. He knew that it would have but a few crew members, specialists in biology, geologists and a pilot. Stephen would have to find a way to get his name on the flight manifest as an expert in something they needed. He had access to the deepest files in the data bases of *Gaea* and it would actually be easy to write a virus that would find its way to the officer in charge of selecting the shuttle crew. Stephen decided to be a meteorologist, off of the radar screen from the other mission specialists and if his timing was right he could be on board before the very small meteorological department learned of his deceit.

Stephen also knew that the mission specialists would simply gather, get in the shuttle and fly down to the surface.   Time was short for their work so planning meetings and dry runs were eliminated.   Stephen wrote himself into the crew manifest as a last minute addition. He included all of the appropriate sign offs and medical releases.   A day before departure he visited his friend Korichiro.

"Ko, I need to talk to you."

"Please, my friend, sit down and have tea with me."

"Thank you, I will, as this is probably the last time we will get to talk."

"I am not happy to hear this. Are you gravely ill?"

"Oh no, quite the opposite.   Its just that I have found a planet I would like to settle on and the last shuttle to the surface is tomorrow."

"I am glad to hear that you will find happiness on your new planet, but sad that we will no longer have conversations that have revealed so many truths about the universe."

~ Sunrise Descending ~

"The truths will always be there for you Ko. In fact, it might be best that we do not discover them all."

"True, but we were making progress, you and I."

"A fact that I will not ever forget, my friend. I wish you a long and healthy life. One filled with wonderment and discovery."

"I wish you the same. I also was looking forward to having you attend my concert. The Chief Executive asked me personally to perform. He thinks it will remind the rest of the crew about the beauty of Earth. I will have an image of our friendship that will enhance my music."

"Thank you Ko, when the time is right, I will find you for some more tea."

"I look forward to that day."

Stephen rose, shook hands and departed to his quarters. As this was still the night shift he was really only a few hours from departure. He gathered a few things including a few borrowed meteorological instruments and made his way to the shuttle bay. Technicians were pre-flighting the spacecraft and loading scientific instruments for the researchers that would be on board. There was so much activity in an attempt to get their flight completed that Stephen was able to walk around un-noticed, place his gear on board and find the shuttle pilot.

~ Sunrise Descending ~

"Hello, I am Stephen Daedalus, meteorologist."

"Oh yeah, saw your name on the list, last moment addition. I'm Grant Gray, shuttle pilot. The best thing for you to do is get on board, strap in and get ready to fly in a few minutes."

"Shall do, my equipment is already on board."

"Good, we're just about ready."

Stephen did not waste any time getting on board. He went to the back of the shuttle passenger compartment, settled in and put his seat belts on.

Within several minutes other mission specialists got on board, a few gave him a look and nod. They settled in quickly as time was short to depart. Soon the pilot was on board, the main door was closed and systems within the shuttle started to come alive. Stephen sat quietly in the back and as he did not know anyone on board was left unnoticed.

The shuttle was cleared for lift off. It elevated a few feet above the hangar deck and taxied slowly towards the space door. After departure they gathered speed and aimed towards the planet. At this time Stephen felt like he had made it and started to relax. He looked out one of the windows to see his former home recede into the stars, another chapter complete. He turned back in this seat to think about the future.

Grant deftly flew the shuttle towards the surface, his control inputs were smooth and followed the recommended trajectory perfectly. The planet's horizon showing the blue of an oxygen atmosphere rotated in the windows slowly as turns were made to intercept the final approach vectors. Switches were thrown and the forward facing retro rockets were engaged to slow the spacecraft down. Within a few minutes a slight buffeting was experienced indicating the interface with the planets air layers. Retros continued to fire as the slowing became very noticeable as the crew members were pulled forward against their flight harnesses. More buffeting, more pulling followed in the ensuing minutes until, as they could not see the tops of clouds, the air smoothed out. Again Grant turned the craft to the right and prepared the aircraft for final approach. The nose rose a bit, Grant walked through his checklists, then the landing gear was extended accompanied with a bit more wind noise and buffeting. Very quickly after that the opening in a field where they would land was seen. The aircraft slowed to a crawl now as the lower thrusters took over the lift vectors. Gently the aircraft came down to about three feet above the ground,

277

paused, then slowly lowered until contact was made. Switches were again thrown, the sound of machines winding down was heard and within seconds the access door was on its way up. The smell of fresh air and plants wafted through the cabin. Next the sound of people unbuckling themselves and shuffling about was heard followed by movement towards the door. It all seemed a bit quick for Stephen as he hesitated to absorb the last moments if being associated with a physical component of *Gaea*. It had been a great adventure, life changing in fact, which is saying something for an immortal.

Finally Stephen rose to exit and found himself at the door opening looking out at a most beautiful planet. The air smelled cool and fresh. A stream was in the distance sparkling beams of light in Stephen's direction.

The rest of the crew, with the exception of the pilot, had already fanned out and started their tasks. Time was very short and Grant, the pilot, was already doing a pre-flight inspection of the shuttle, just in case a quick departure was required. He saw Stephen looking as if he was lost and walked over to him to see what was going on.

"We only have an hour, best you get your equipment in place."

"No need."

~ Sunrise Descending ~

"Excuse me?"

"No need, I'm staying. I put in my resignation in an hour ago on the com link back to *Gaea.*"

"Wow, sure you want to do this?"

"Oh yeah, absolutely."

"Well, okay. Hope you know what you are doing."

"Pretty much, actually. I have thought about this quite a bit. As it is our option to stay on a suitable planet I choose this one."

"You know that there are some strange people here, claiming to be ancient Greeks. The society looks kind of simple, but it's your choice."

"Yes....it is," he said as he shook Grant's hand.

With that, Stephen gathered his equipment and made his way to an open elevated area where he started to assemble a weather station. Within twenty minutes, he was basically done and reached over the side of the main electronics cabinet and threw the main power switch. The only sign of life from the unit was the movement of the main uplink antenna that was looking for *Gaea.* Within a minute or so it had linked to the ship and started to send data. Stephen finalized the rigging of the met tower and did a final inspection to make sure it was in good shape. Although he did a nice job, as if the unit would remain unattended for years, he felt in an ironic manner that he would continue to make sure the unit was operating properly over the many years he expected to live on Hebe 6.

The New Life

We shall not cease from exploration and the end of all our exploring will be to arrive where we started...and know the place for the first time. - T.S. Eliot

Soon the others returned to prepare for departure. Stephen did not have to rush in any sense and watched the others jogging around and barking at each other to hurry up. Grant was already inside getting the shuttle ready for lift off. Within a few more short minutes several of the crew had entered the shuttle while the remaining people were now in double time to make sure all of their equipment was on board. Another short minute later all were on board and the door was being shut. Soon the engines were coming to life and with a muffled roar the shuttle lifted off of the ground to about a distance of three feet. Grant looked out of the cockpit and saluted Stephen, then the craft rotated one hundred and eighty degrees and accelerated out of the clearing and into the sky. The roar of the engines brightened as the ship increased its altitude and when it penetrated the puffy cumulus clouds Stephen heard the echo of the departure resonate for several seconds. Soon however, it was gone.

Stephen stood there alone surrounded by footprints and a small weather station. He stood for a few more minutes, then located his backpack and small suitcase. Slinging the pack on his back he walked over to a ledge to find evidence of a village. The village he was interested in most was about ten miles away down the sparkling creek. Stephen could not see any activity from his vantage point and turned to find a trail leading to the creek. This was discovered and the hike to the village commenced. He found the trail to be stunning in beauty and quiet. If there were any animals around they were well hidden. The morning was getting on and at times he paused for a drink of water. After two hours walking he stopped for lunch. Birds were now about and as he sat to eat he observed bugs unlike any he had seen. The birds were all different as well. This is to be expected as every planet with life will always have a different set of animals and plants. Its just how nature works.

While on his trek Stephen could think about what he left behind. Earth, Zsa, Ko and the thousands of good people he had met. He smiled periodically while walking. He also thought about the people he was about to meet and how they had a similar affliction. This would bring a new understanding about life and the universe. He had studied the reports from the first away missions closely and knew of the Nereids. This was the group of people he wanted to meet the most and the inhabitants of the village he was now walking towards.

These people, he understood, were immortals like himself and had been created by similar means by another civilization. They were significantly older than he and could offer him wisdom regarding long life. It had been so difficult for Stephen to endure the changes....that constantly occurred around him. For all the people he knew, immortality was only a concept, usually attributed to the lives of Gods. It was by most accounts part of the fabric of human will. A dream of many people but the reality of the matter was far from a dream. His proximity to similar beings was exciting in many ways. On the other hand there was also a sense of desperation in him as he needed so badly to know truths about his condition.

"All in good time," he thought. "I have waited for this long another hour won't matter much."

Continuing to walk the sounds of the forest gave way to the sounds of rushing water. The trail led downhill along the stream where the water bubbled and leapt above the half submerged rocks, just like Earth. In fact in a moment of deja vu Stephen felt a sudden chill as his mind convinced him for a moment that he was on Earth. It did take a moment to come back to reality, which he initiated by walking at a brisker pace towards his destination. Now it was less than a mile away as the forest had given way to the stream environs, which led to a distinct area of deciduous trees and bushes. Within this area one could see the tops of simple houses much like Florence, Italy in the 17th Century. He walked down the first street he found and found it filled with the essence of the handmade beauty of the Renaissance. This felt good. He continued until he located a town square surrounded by simple shops and vendors. The inhabitants took little notice of him even though he had on unique cloths. Stephen wandered over to a fruit stand to look at the offerings. There was fruit of many colors and shapes, all a bit different to anything he had ever seen. He smiled at the anticipation of the new flavors each one had. Looking up he saw the proprietor looking at him with an unamused face, very human in appearance.

"Welcome to our village."

"Thank you, I come in peace."

"Of course you do, are you from Earth?"

"Yes, how did you know?"

"From your smile, you look comfortable here."

"I do, in fact, it reminds me of a very beautiful city on my planet."

"Florence?"

"Yes. How did you know?"

"We modeled this village after the best parts of Florence. It was the center of art and discovery during the period that you see here in the architecture."

"Its marvelous, but I understood the people of this village were the Nereids, descendants of Greek Gods....immortals."

"Oh yes that is in fact true, but more than that, we have experienced many wonderful eras of Earth's history."

"And you have found your way back here with those experiences?"

"Through the radio astronomers on Earth, yes."

"Thats amazing, I thought all they did was listen."

"Most do....some of us that remain there transmit information back to his planet, but more importantly we receive the transmissions from Earth, first from radio broadcasts, then television, then satellites and now from the Internet portals in orbit around Earth. We see Earth as it was and as it is."

"Amazing, but I can imagine if you monitored all of our transmissions and understood them, you would have a complete history."

"Correct, even your secret broadcasts have significance to us."

"Of course, you for instance, received the broadcasts from the submarines of World War II, the television broadcasts after that, the phenomenal increase in traffic with satellites and now the staggering amount of information on the Internet."

"That is only the beginning. Keep in mind, we have heard and recorded everything."

"The History Channel?"

"One of our favorites," he said smiling.

There was a pause in the conversation as Stephen realized his dreams were now coming true.

"Where can I stay?"

The proprietor pointed to the other side of the town square.

"Over there, ask for Leah."

"Thanks, see you around."

"No doubt."

Stephen walked across the square and finding the appointed building walked in, found what seemed to be a front desk, and asked for Leah.

"I'm Leah, how may I help you?"

"Do you have a room or place to stay for me here?"

"Of course, we can take care of you. Please have some coffee while I do the paperwork for you."

"Thanks."

Stephen moved to his right to find an urn of good coffee. He viewed it with a sense of irony. He thought:

"Millions and millions of miles away and they have coffee here, amazing."

After he retrieved a cup, he turned back to Leah and noticed this time that she had tattoos on her arms, mostly of playful objects. Cartoon characters, toys and the like.

"Interesting," he thought.

He had a sister many, many years ago that had tattoos as well. It seems my sister remade herself.

Leah finished her work and presented Stephen with a key. He smiled and giving her a last glance, walked over to the stairs and walked up to the top floor. Down the hall he went to find a room near the corner. He entered and found a medium sized pleasant room with several windows looking over the square.

"Nice," he thought. "Not only that but I didn't have to pay anything."

After resting a bit he walked down to the main desk to ask Leah some questions.

"Nice room."

"Glad you like it."

"I was wondering how much the room is."

"You mean as in money?"

"Yes."

"We haven't used money in thousands of years. We found that money is only used in an attempt to obtain more than what is fair. We don't believe in profit because it makes something worth more than is reasonable. It turns out that people find their own place in our world, some farm, some are scientists, some teach. More people find happiness that way. Everyone however is responsible for everything. If we are low on food, everyone farms, if we are in need of buildings, everyone builds. So the sense of accomplishment is shared by all and the needs of our society are met as well. Very balanced."

"Wonderful, I wish the people on Earth would learn that lesson."

"They will eventually."

"Are you one of them?"

"One of who?"

"The Nereids."

"Oh, no, I am just an offspring."

"Does it make you feel bad that you are not immortal?"

"Not in the least, I will live at least two hundred years that should be enough."

"Wow, I should think so. But I am not going to be so lucky. Although I am not from here I am immortal."

289

"Well, you will have a very interesting life ahead of you. Did you come here to meet others like you?"

"Yes."

"Well, I suggest you find the farms, thats were most of them work."

"I would think they would be the teachers or civic leaders."

"They have all been there and done that. They feel better working the land and creating food."

"Hmmm, okay. I will start there."

Stephen said goodbye to Leah and leaving the hotel, found his way back to the street vendor.

"Thanks, that is a nice place."

"Your welcome. Welcome to our village."

"I am off to find the farms could you direct me?"

"Of course," the vendor said pointing. "Go down that road and it will open up to a meadow where several farms are being worked."

"Thank you again," Stephen said as turned to start his journey.

After a few miles of walking he found the farms and looked for a likely candidate. Walking over to the older person there he introduced himself.

"Greetings, are you the owner of this farm?"

"Oh no, there are not owners here, just workers."

"So the owner is elsewhere?"

"No, there are no owners at all."

"Okay, well then, I just wanted to meet one of the descendants of the Nereids."

"Thats not me, I am not that old, look over that rise," the old man said as he pointed to a grassy area with several rows of plants.

Stephen bid farewell and started towards the rise. After climbing for a few minutes he saw over the arc of land several people tilling the fields and picking weeds. Walking over to the closest person he asked:

"Greetings, I am Stephen, from Earth, I came here to meet a Nereid."

The person straightened up and responded.

"I am Isaac, a Nereid. You say you came from Earth?"

"Yes, in fact. A few days ago a great ship shuttled me down to the surface and allowed me to stay."

"A great starship?"

"Yes, very large, with over a thousand people on it."

"Hmmm, and you chose to stay, to meet a Nereid?"

"Yes."

"We are just people."

"You're more than that to me."

"In what way?"

"The fact that you are immortal."

"And why is that important to you?"

"Because I am one as well."

Isaac was now a bit more interested and moved closer to Stephen.

"How did you come to be immortal?"

"A doctor back on Earth, several hundred years ago, gave me a treatment that allowed the cells in my body to replicate perfectly. Since then I have been frozen at this age, have outlived a wife, children, grandchildren and great-grandchildren. It forced me to adopt a nomadic lifestyle so I would not attract attention. When I heard about this large ship departing to explore other civilizations I joined the crew in hopes that eventually I could find another world were being an immortal would not be such a problem."

Isaac smiled and started to laugh when he heard the last sentence."

"A problem? All problems get solved, Stephen. It's not a problem for us anymore."

"Well, thats good to hear, it certainly has been a problem for me."

Isaac smiled again.

"That's because you have not had the opportunity to appreciate your gift."

"Yes, your right about that. In many ways it did not seem like a gift, especially after out living my family."

"Mortals are like another species, the same as us in many ways but fundamentally different. They are always changing as they grow, always changing their point of view about life."

"That seems true. I have changed my point of view however, over the many years."

"Thats because you are still young."

"I'm hundreds of years old, though."

"And we are thousands of years old, your just a baby."

With that, Stephen felt, in a way, relaxed and, in another way, amused. He had not though of himself as a baby. Over all he was very glad he had come to Hebe 6. A moment of silence followed their conversation. Stephen looked at Isaac who in Earth years looked about thirty. The story about the Nereids made Stephen imagine Isaac and the other workers who were slowly coming closer as Greeks directing the building of the great temples, setting up governments, initiating the conversations that would

293

create the intellectual explosion that happened so many thousands of years ago. Stephen realized that the people he was looking at now personally knew Homer, Plato, Aristotle, Heraclitus, Thales.

"Thales," Stephen said impulsively.

"Thales," asked Isaac.

"Did you know Thales?"

"Of course, we all did, he became one of the major founders of the study of philosophy and electro-magnetics."

"Our ship was named Thales, I worked on the scientific principles he discovered and the ship contained people influenced by his writings."

"Yes, he was pretty smart."

"Smart would be an understatement I would think."

"Certainly."

"How did the rest of the population deal with him? Did they understand anything he was saying?"

"Back then, there were small enclaves of thinkers and students. He found them and lived his life with them. As far as the rest of the population, they did not understand...and probably still don't even now."

"You're right about that, but the tree of knowledge idea is still taught in Universities."

"And it always will. Imagine having an influence on people's lives thousands of years into the future. That Thales did, and the others in Greece had that effect. Ultimately, around when Alexander the Great came into power, they took themselves too seriously and war and carnage took over as a way of life, not intellectual pursuits. Then the Dark Ages."

"Yes, and Earth has not really recovered."

"That's true."

"When did the Nereids leave Earth?"

"Right after the Hellenic Period, a hundred or so years before Christ. The Romans were starting to take over the world, selfish behavior was rampant. Descendants of the people who had left us there many hundreds of years before they came back to observe what had transpired. Our group decided to leave with them. A few remained to try to help people get back to a better time."

"Are they still there?"

"Oh yes, very hidden by necessity as you discovered."

"Well, they have helped a lot. Things are better, but a long way away from the period you were a part of."

"Yes."

~ Sunrise Descending ~

By now the other workers had gathered around to see who Isaac was talking to so earnestly. They were all roughly in their thirties, equally split between male and female. They all shared a look of wisdom in their faces, never over reacting or under reacting. Stephen and small group continued to talk about their respective pasts. He learned that the remaining immortals on Earth had influenced many great events by suggesting solutions to significant problems. They never became the well known scientists, theologians or politicians but were around to help formulate change. These included the fracturing of religion into many types after the Dark Ages. This had the effect of minimizing the power that the church had in civil affairs and ultimately allowing people to understand the true psychological nature of religion. Major world events like wars had roots in the remaining immortals. First, there was an effort to cull the populations of Europe and many other parts of the Earth. Eventually, based on communication and education, wars were seen as the least effective way to create change. After their initial meeting Stephen and the Nereids decided to talk further and they invited him to work with the group in the fields. He was also invited to live in their part of the village.

~ Sunrise Descending ~

From that point on, Stephen joined them in the morning, ate with them and occupied a room in their neighborhood. He learned to appreciate their place in the Universe. He also learned that an advanced society (relative to Earth's) had gone down the same path and medically learned how to extend life to immortality. It was after this point, not before, that they had realized that the only way to explore the Cosmos was to build a great, self sufficient space ship and spend many years exploring. They had found Earth and shuttled down a group of explorers who decided to stay. The result was the magnificent culture in Greece, which advanced science and philosophy more than any era that followed. Now Stephen was in his element and refreshingly it was time to start learning about the Universe.

Cosmic School

We are what we think. All that we are arises with our thoughts. With our thoughts we make the world. - Buddha

War is wrong. Hate is wrong. Greed is wrong. These things are obvious to most beings in the Universe. What fascinates immortals is how long it takes most cultures to recognize these facts. The cycles seem to be similar however, as there is a sociological evolution as well as a physical one.

Stephen learned this and other things from his new friends on Hebe 6. It was an age of awakening for him. He spent his days in the field chatting periodically with the Nereids as they performed their tasks. The days were long and arduous in some ways. There was always the fulfilling sense that they had accomplished something important, growing food and living with nature. They grew enough to save a bit in case of emergencies. They grew enough to take care of the local population.

After a few months, Stephen settled in and became one with the routine. He detected an interesting contrast, that between the simple existence that the Nereids lived in and the extraordinarily complex minds they had developed. This wasn't like a commune or other close social network where everyone was interdependent. Rather, it was a group of extremely intelligent people moving their way through the Universe.

On an individual basis Stephen found the conversations about personal experience and outlook, within a group setting. He found himself listening to discussions about the finer details of human thought and where it should go. They seemed to be sincerely interested

299

in the future. Not just the details of how the Universe would evolve but more importantly of how sentient beings would evolve. Would they leave their corporeal states and exist in energy only? What would their concerns be? What of the lower forms of life? Would they all evolve into sentient beings?

After some time Stephen discovered from his conversations with Isaac and the others that robots and androids were in the natural evolutionary chain of many worlds much like Zarathustra or the Uberman, the ultimate expression of life. Many of these worlds sought the speed and omniscience of non biological materials to augment and enhance their cultures. The crew of *Gaea* had discovered these societies as well in their exploration of the nearby inhabited planets. Interestingly, these "people" found themselves without emotion and without the ability to be creative. They went along with pure knowledge and ground to a halt within their hearts. As a result they were starved for art, music and culture.

Androids came into being as well an true genius was expressed by a few of the makers of robots and androids as they set their creations on the hazardous journeys to the stars and the galaxy. They would return many years later to report on their findings. Another interesting phenomena occurred when robots and androids from different worlds met each other and tried to coexist. One creator's idea of perfection might not be exactly the same as another's. In these cases the fundamental tenants of ethno-centrism was evident. The societies of mechanical beings stayed separate. Again Stephen thought about how interesting is was that sentient beings create things in their own image.

Isaac became Stephen's mentor and guided him through the Nereids' history like a patient professor. The process took almost a full year. He presented Stephen with some extremely old books and paintings, which had barely survived the thousands of years since their creation. For the most part however, the instruction was verbal. This typically happened after their work day around a fire outside under the stars. This allowed Isaac to point out certain stars and tell stories about its inhabitants. Stephen learned about the abundance of life in the Universe and how most of it is not sentient.

Another discovery revealed by the Nereids was the difference between Population I and Population II stars. Population I stars are like our sun, rich in heavy elements and concentrated typically within the spiral arms of the galaxy. Population II stars on the other hand are metal poor and usually are found in globular clusters and the nucleus of the galaxy. They are much older and had developed life billions of years before the Population 1 stars. These were of particular interest to the Nereids as they had been visited by some of the "old ones" or those beings from the old stars that dedicated their lives to exploration. The Nereids described the old ones as "barely corporeal." This intrigued Stephen as he wasn't exactly sure what that description meant and because it made him very curious to meet such a being.

The conversations continued between Stephen and Isaac for a very long time. Unlike normal interactions words might not be exchanged for weeks, then a few sentences were exchanged that Stephen learned to think about well after they were uttered. They were literature and carried meanings well beyond the definitions of the components. Language needs to become an art form to overcome its limitations in expression.

The Nereids learned a great deal about Stephen's life and aspirations. They lived his life through his words and found that his emotions could amplify or attenuate his experiences, modifying them from the mundane into the wonderful. Or modifying them from the frightening to the average. One such stream of thought was about his wife,

Zsa. Stephen had never lost his love for her and had suppressed the real life details with a swath of wonder and beauty. His view of her now was far from the life they lived so many, many years ago.

"Did you every have disagreements?"

"Oh sure, but they were minor."

"How good was your life together?"

"Extraordinary in every way."

A thousand other conversations took place about his love for Zsa. The Nereids were impressed by her impact on him, even though they recognized that his images were distorted. They admired the art that Stephen had developed to detail their lives together and her meaningfulness to his world.

They talked of many other things as well. Stephen and Isaac in particular, but over the years Stephen had conversations with every one of the Nereids. He learned much about each as individuals and much about each as a tribe.

Many more years past and for Stephen this was a long chapter of contentment. In so many ways these were his people, his culture and his life. They alone understood the meaning of immortality and all of its facets. At some point just about when neither Stephen or the Nereids could remember how long he had been there he received a visit from Isaac.

A small group of Nereids walked out to a particularly lush field on a particularly beautiful day to find Stephen planting seedlings of wheat for the next growing season. The group was made up of several of the males and several of the females from the tribe. Isaac was among them and upon reaching Stephen, who was on his knees and deep in thought, addressed him.

"Stephen, may we speak with you?"

Looking up and adjusting his eyes to the bright blue sky that framed the groups' heads, he said, "Of course." He then rose and presented himself to the group.

"Stephen, the group or tribe as you call us, is interested in having a meeting with you this evening around the campfire, after dinner."

"Is everything all right?"

"Yes, we have no issues with you and consider you one of our family. We want to discuss your life and future."

Smiling and not concerned, he replied, "well that sounds like fun."

They smiled as well and quietly turned and walked away back to the places they had all come from. Stephen watched them leave and wondered about what the details of the conversation tonight would be. He had learned to admire and appreciate all of them and felt without reservation that they appreciated him as well. This conversation about life and his future would be positive. He turned back to his work, knelt down to be close to the soil and continued his planting.

After some time he looked up to a descending sun, felt his hunger and walked back to the village to have dinner. As he walked down the cobble stone and dirt streets that made up the village he noticed that the people there showed him a faint curiosity. Their eyes would follow him for a bit, some smiled, others nodded. He continued his walk until he found an outdoor cafe with some open tables. The evening was still warm as he sat down. Soon he smelled the food that was being prepared inside and looked up to find a waitress smiling at him.

"The usual for you Stephen?"

"No, Susan, tonight I think I will have your amazing lentil soup and some fresh bread."

"The soup is good tonight. How about something to drink?"

"A glass of wine would be wonderful."

She smiled again at this and turned to place the order with the kitchen and pour a glass of red wine. All things at this cafe were made from locally grown food. The climate was so temperate that well over a hundred varieties of edible plant life were grown at the same time. Many others were rotated in after the growing season to keep an amazing variety of food available for the people.

Susan returned to present the glass of wine to Stephen, who by now was watching the curious watch him and by now was wondering what the curiosity was all about. His eyebrows rose periodically as his mind thought about what the others were thinking.

"Here is your wine Stephen."

"Thank you Susan, and tell me, why are so many people interested in me today?"

"You will find out later tonight."

"Thats all? No hint?"

"No hint." Susan leaned over to kiss Stephen on the cheek.

"So, are we going to get married?"

"Nope, something better."

"Better, what could be better?"

"That's not a question for me, but rather for you."

She walked away, trailing a smile.

Stephen finished his meal, cleaned up his place and said goodbye to Susan. Walking back to his apartment he noticed still that the villagers were giving him just a bit more attention than usual. He would have to maintain his patience until this evening; one way to do this was to take a brief nap before the meeting. He entered his apartment, closed the door, cleaned up a bit and laid down for a quick rest.

His dreams were a it more detailed than usual this evening and crossed the lines of anxiety and happiness. Normally his dreams were all positive, as his life had been. But tonight his wonderment as to what was going to happen that evening formed images of mild angst.

His dreams started to get more intense when he was woken up by a friend.

"Stephen, Stephen, you need to get up."

"What? What happened?"

"You overslept, you need to come down to the campfire now."

"How long did I oversleep?"

"Only a few minutes, they just got started."

"Okay, give me a few minutes to clear my head."

He rose and went to the kitchen sink to splash some water on his face. After he stood for a few moments, he faced his friend.

"Okay, I am ready."

307

"Lets go."

They walked out of the room, down the hall and out to the dark street. Within a few steps they could see the flickering light at a campfire beyond the end of the street by about a quarter of a mile. It took about ten minutes to traverse the distance, half of which was in the forested area that separates the village from the farm lands. For the most part Stephen and his friend did not speak as they walked and when they arrived his friend changed direction to find a pre-selected seat. Stephen on the other hand moved straight forward to address the small crowd seated in several concentric circles around the fire.

"Sorry I am late."

"Not a problem, its better that you made an entrance," Isaac said as he smiled.

"Over there?" Stephen said pointing.

"Yes, please."

Stephen moved to an open seat slightly more separated from the adjoining seats than the rest. He sat down to the eyes of the Nereids upon him, warm and appreciative. He looked around and smiled at his friends.

Isaac addressed him.

"Stephen, you came to us many years ago in search of people like yourself. You found us based on the explorations of the ship from Earth, a planet that we Nereids lived on for a long time. We welcomed you as we welcome all, but more importantly we allowed you into our hearts as a special human being. As we now have spent so many years with you and have learned to appreciated your warmth and caring about us it is now time to give you something in return. This will come in the form of three discussions at this campfire over the next three nights. These will be a celebration of your contributions to our people. In addition a decision has been made as to who you should be in the future. Isaac paused to let Stephen think about the words and respond.

"Who I should be in the future," he repeated, "I can think of no other group of people I would allow to mold me. I would do this based on the pure trust of your intentions. This begs the question, however, as to why you would want me to be different?"

"All this in due time as we will discuss that detail in our last discussion."

"Okay."

"For now we will settle on the subject of our first meeting tonight. You came to us from the Earth we knew thousands of years before you were born. It is important to us to see, through your experiences, how the people of

Earth evolved after our departure. You can imagine, as we had no direct way of knowing, that we were supremely interested to hear that people there made it through the Dark Ages and into the Renaissance, then beyond to the technological revolution and to become space faring. You taught us about the history of Earth after our departure. This gives us hope as to their ultimate future and maybe more importantly that we as the Nereids did not impede their progress."

"No, you did not. In fact, you became beacons of intellect and reason for us. Your guidance through metaphor and myth aligned us to better ourselves, Isaac. Its important that you and all of the Nereids understand that humanity is its own creation. You were part of that process."

"Thank you, from all of us, Stephen. And you are right, humanity *is* its own creation. Our minds form the future we want to live. So your can see by observing the past how people changed their forward thinking and got to where you are now. So now we need to think about where we want to go. That includes all of us here by the way. Especially you."

"How can I help?"

"We need to be here and you need to be there."

"I'm not sure I understand."

"As we have discussed before, the androids and robots that have been sent out by advanced civilizations to explore the galaxy have been here before. In fact they come here on a regular basis. We know that they will be here soon and we would like you to go with them."

"Go where?"

"To the ancient star systems. The population II stars and planets that are so much older than ours."

"Why?"

"To learn about them and then come back to teach us."

"Why don't you go?"

"Our hearts are happy here, your heart is happy exploring and learning. It will make you and us happy to have you go out into the galaxy and discover the wonder of life we can only guess at. Its important to us."

"I have been so happy here, with the Nereids, but in a sense I see what you mean. I do hunger to explore. I still look a the stars most every night and think about what is happening behind the twinkling."

"Then you will go?"

"Yes, of course."

Campfire Life #2

In infinite space many civilizations are bound to exist, among them societies that may be wiser and more "successful" than ours. I support the cosmological hypothesis which states that the development of the universe I repeated in its basic characteristics an infinite number of times...Yet this should not minimize our sacred

~ Sunrise Descending ~

*endeavors in this world of ours, where, like faint glimmers in
the dark, we have emerged for a moment from the
nothingness of dark unconscious into material existence. -*
Andrei Sakharov

The second campfire discussion was about the
Nereids view on traveling to the stars. Stephen was there
when they started the fire, just as the sun was going down,
in that sensual time where the image of the sun changes
from dangerously bright to the mellow colors of dusk. This
is when the birds, land animals and insects pause to think
about their day. Several of the villagers were preparing the
wood and kindling, milling around the fire pit placing the
pieces in an inverted cone shape. At some unspoken
moment someone produced a flame and placed it in the
very center of the cone. The fire started quickly and soon
supported the presence of larger logs and tree roots, which
would burn for hours hence. The work finished, the
villagers found their way to chairs, large logs, small berms
and relaxed, waiting for the next message from Isaac and
the other Nereids. Isaac appeared, scanned the crowd and
found a place to stand where he could see all of them.

313

~ *Sunrise Descending* ~

"Good evening everyone. We have more to tell Stephen tonight. More to discuss before he leaves us for the stars. Please make yourselves comfortable and find something to drink."

Isaac paused for several minutes, then continued.

"Stephen Daedalus will be taking us with him in spirit. He will be taking us with him in his heart and will return to us with gifts we cannot yet imagine. He is going to the old star systems, the ones that our robot and android visitors from the past had discussed in shallow terms. We know from them that the people in those star systems are much more advanced than us, they represent our future and we need their guidance. The trip to the old stars will be dangerous, as robots and androids are more immune to intense radiation than we. They can travel through parts of space that we have to circumvent, sometimes at the cost of many months of travel. When Stephen traverses these areas he will have to live in the most protected areas of the ships, sometimes for long periods of time. This will make the journey difficult from a personal point of view, but we know that he has the strength to do it. We know this because he is a discoverer of new worlds and is always looking forward. He found ours, witnessed others and will witness many more. What he will find in the old star

314

systems will be in some ways incomprehensible and strange to us. We know that we have the time to understand these systems. Think about how the ancients from Earth, which we had so much influence on, would react to how Earth is now with its aircraft and spacecraft. It would be quite a shock of course, but think about how children adapt so easily to their world. It was trivial for them to adapt to computers and space travel. They never knew how difficult is was supposed to be so therefore it wasn't."

Isaac paused to let the words sink in. The fire was in perfect form now with a very light sea breeze flowing in from the not so distant ocean. From a distance the people around the fire could see the reflections of bright stars and planets shimmering off of the water towards them, giving the illusion of being in the center of the Universe, which in some ways they were. There are those who say that the Universe is infinite, in which case all points within it are in the center.

Stephen listened and watched the others as Isaac spoke. He tried to imagine what was going on in their minds, sensing hope and wonder. Hope, as their culture would have something amazing to look forward upon his return. Wonder, as what would be revealed by the voyage.

Isaac continued, "We have heard that the old star people have evolved beyond immortality, that they choose between having a physical presence or existing in energy. They discovered that an ever present magnetic field can hold their essence forever. Moving from magnetic field to magnetic field allows them to move anywhere. And because the Universe is made of electromagnetic energy they can move at will to any destination. They can move about to witness the Universe at the speed of light and because time does not exist at these speeds are able to go to other galaxies like Andromeda and M33. They probably know how to go further, which is the first evidence that we know of where sentient beings can go to places we can only witness in telescopes. There are billions upon billions of life harboring planets. Most have a simpler type of life than our own, but a few have life much more advanced. A very few have transcendent life, where time is only the space between moments and where time is only useful for recording the details of the present. On these planets the life forms experience time as the horizon of being and float in a sphere where the farther they look the longer ago the image was made. These beings have done what we have done, become immortal and have done more, discovered a way to be anywhere. You will meet these life forms and

316

they will offer you opportunities we can only imagine. If you are satisfied with your life as it is, as amazing as it is, then you can live on without these opportunities. If, of course, you would like to know what you could become, you could make that decision as well. In any event, when you come back to visit us, you will see us in a different light."

"When I come back?"

"Yes, and we know you will come back."

"How do you know?"

"Because you loved Zsa."

"Yes, I did. What does Zsa have to do with coming back?"

"Because Zsa will be full grown by then."

"What? What are you saying?!"

"What I am saying will be the subject of our discussion tomorrow. We are weary and the fire is nearly gone. Please be patient until tomorrow and we will explain ourselves then."

"Uh, but..."

"Until tomorrow."

The fire was nearly out now and everyone, as if on cue, rose to put out the embers and let the night close in on them. Isaac, after Stephen had looked at the people leaving, was gone. He was not to be coerced into revealing

317

his secret. Stephen was left hanging and felt his stomach churning with anticipation. He rose as well and after helping a bit with the silent others, walked back to his room in the village. Interestingly, the others fanned out in such equal angles as they soon were all alone. They had much on their minds it seemed.

Campfire Life #3

Life is what happens to you when you are busy making other plans. - John Lennon

Stephen came early the next evening, of course. His curiosity about the last statements from Isaac kept him awake for most of night.   He drifted in and out of

319

consciousness thinking about Zsa and what they Nereids had in mind. They gave up their secrets very slowly and followed the course or streams of thought in a very methodical manner. All words were connected from the past to the future and it seemed at times that they were reading from a script.

He arrived at the spot in the late afternoon and with nothing much to do started gathering wood and kindling. He spent extra time placing the pieces in uniform, geometric shapes at the center of the fire pit. He noticed for the first time that there were no ashes or unburnt remains from the night before. Standing with curiosity, he quickly had to imagine that someone was cleaning the remains during the following morning. Looking at the dirt, the smoothness gave away the human intervention. Why? The only answer was that they took care of this place like one would take care of a shrine.

Soon enough the others started showing up. Interestingly they seemed to come from all directions, emerging from the forest and undergrowth, mostly in singular fashion. They remained silent unless spoken to by Stephen, who greeted a few of them. Many gave him a long look, one with meaning. Stephen felt the eye beams but was not intimidated. Within 15 minutes the place was again fully occupied. Isaac was last and walked down the only aisle to his designated place. Stephen remained standing by the fire until the look from Isaac instructed him to sit down at his place. Stephen complied and found his way to a place where he could observe Isaac and the others.

"Stephen thank you for your patience after we peaked your interest last night. We have something very important to tell you this evening."

"I'm all ears," Stephen said smiling.

"Over the last few nights, as we have sat here, we have discussed your future and in a sense ours. We, the Nereids, have reasons for doing things, including staying here and keeping to ourselves. We have traveled the cosmos but are now happy to live on a wonderful planet like this, one that provides us with all of our needs and most importantly lies in the exploration lanes for many space faring cultures. We would like to venture further than we have in the past but we are a large group and need alternative methods to explore and learn. One fortuitous feature of this planet is that it is part of the travel zones of the androids and robots from other cultures. These beings can go where many biological entities cannot and as a consequence have explored more of the universe than any beings we know. Now we have you and we have asked you to explore for us; we know where to send you and we are happy that you will experience wonders beyond our imagination. These wonders will make you consider remaining in these extraordinary foreign lands, this would make us sad as we would not be able to benefit from your new knowledge. We have, however come up with a way to have you seriously consider coming back to us."

A pause ensued as Stephen considered all that he had heard.

"Are you going to make a nice dinner for me?" Stephen asked fascisously.

"We are indeed, in fact, Zsa will make it for you."

Stephen's heart stopped for a moment as he had not expected to hear the name of his loved one.

"What....what are you talking about?"

"As we have gotten to know you, we soon realized that Zsa was the most important person in your life. Isn't that true?

"That is....she was.....but she is no more."

"Why was she so important to you, Stephen?"

"I loved her. She bore my children and we were together for her entire life, raising children, playing with grandchildren, living life to the fullest. She was the first to

322

know my secret. She chose to stay with me even though she aged and I did not. Our minds grew old together and made sense of our world. This made me appreciate life and appreciate how a single person could smooth the bumps and travails of the path of existence for me. I adored her and at times our hearts pounded with the same beat."

"Then you miss her, even though she has been gone for so many years?"

"Of course, I miss her. No one has replaced her and her voice is still in my head, asking the important questions."

"So you would like to see her again?"

"I would do anything for that, but its impossible, she is gone forever."

"Maybe."

"I don't understand what you are saying." Stephen was now getting anxious as deep memories were beginning to surface, welling up long ago felt emotions. His eyes felt the emergence of tears.

"We the Nereids welcomed you into our family. We then discovered that we appreciated your essence and wanted to do something important for you as a show of our gratitude."

"You don't owe me anything."

"Oh, but we do. At the very least we need to place a mirror in front of you and show you who we admire and appreciate. You came from a long distance alone. You are the bravest person we have ever met, facing the unknown of the Universe with open eyes and an open heart. We owe you much, because you reminded us of strengths we have, but had long forgotten. So therefore we have decided to give you something back."

"Really, please, I don't......"

"Stephen, do remember when you first came to us, you had several conversations about Zsa and your history with her and how much you loved her?" Isaac pointed to several people in the group around the campfire (now burning beautifully). "Do you remember having those discussions with these people?"

"Yes, I do."

A women rose about ten feet away from Stephen.

"Do you remember talking to Elva?"

Stephen looked at the women, now standing. He recognized the woman as Elva. They had had several meetings at coffee and tea houses about his past. She had been warm, interested in and unusually empathic as Stephen described his life on Earth. Stephen, without realizing it, smiled at her now; the memories were pleasant.

"I do remember talking many times to Elva and found her to be a wonderful listener, very much so."

"And do you remember showing her a lock of Zsa hair?"

Stephen spoke slowly, "I...do."

"And did you realize then that a strand of Zsa's had fallen to the ground?"

"No....."

"Stephen, from all of us to you.....we took that strand and obtained the DNA that created it. From that we made a viable zygote and Elva (he pointed to her) volunteered to give birth to another Zsa." Isaac smiled after saying this, Elva smiled as well.

"Oh...my," started Stephen, "I don't know what to think, I am stunned." And stunned he looked. "I..."

"Stephen," continued Isaac, "we want you to be happy, we chose this path for that reason and for another as well."

Stephen still looked stunned, paying more attention to Elva than to Isaac.

Isaac continued, "Your journey to the stars begins soon. We estimate that it will take at least 20 years. When you return, Zsa will be waiting here for you exactly as you met her for the first time." On this cue, the others started to rise and depart the same way they came in. Isaac and Elva remained to watch Stephen absorb the new information. He sat there speechless for many minutes, then:"

"Thank you, I don't know how to thank you. You have brought back life to a wonderful person."

"Your welcome," stated Isaac, who then departed, leaving only Elva and Stephen in the glow of the dying embers of a good campfire. They sat for a few more minutes in silence.

Stephen looked up at Elva and asked, "may I?"

"Of, course."

Elva moved closer and allowed Stephen to touch her belly. His hand was inches away from a love story from long ago. He rose after a few seconds, thanked Elva and started to walk back to the village. Soon he turned to make sure she was okay but she had left. The embers of the fire slowly twinkled in brightness as the waves of heat and emotion moved across their surface. He turned towards the road to walk back to his flat and back to the future.

Upon finishing his walk, still a bit stunned, he entered his room and sat down, in a moment he looked out the window, then up he looked towards the stars knowing that a robotic spacecraft was on its way and soon to land.

~ Sunrise Descending ~

He smiled and maybe to get a good start on the preparations, pulled out his suitcase.

Robots Have Little Personality

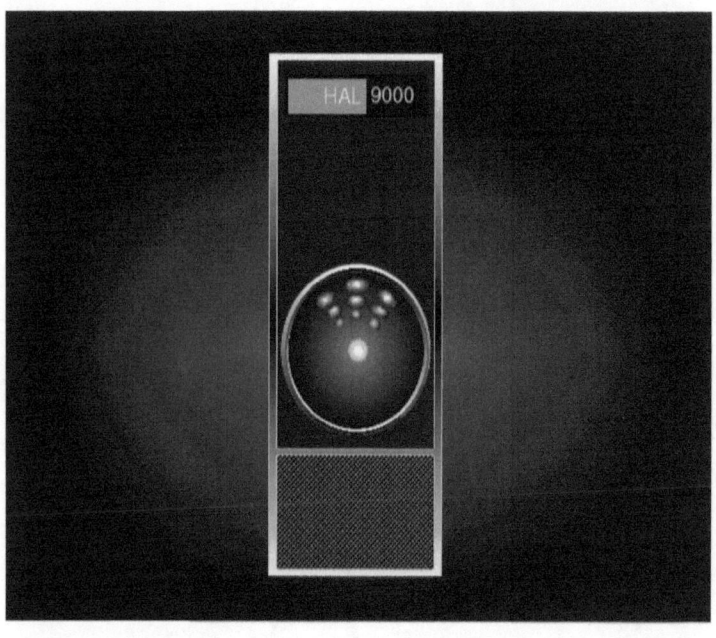

I visualize a time when we will be to robots what dogs are to humans, and I'm rooting for the machines. - Claude Shannon

~ *Sunrise Descending* ~

Several weeks passed, the implications of Stephen's "present" was considered and at some point he felt at peace with it. He counted the days until the predicted visit by the robotic ships. During his wait he spent time with Elva. He discovered who she was as a person and grew to admire her courage to bear a child without her DNA involved. She would in all other senses be the mother and would rear the child. Zsa would not be immortal like her mother which of course would become obvious at some point in Zsa's life. In a strange sense this would not be the first time Zsa had to deal with the issue.

Stephen and Elva became close during this period of waiting; he learned of her feelings about being immortal. She had children many many years ago and still remembered the inherent love for her offspring, although they were no longer alive. Just like Stephen, she had sad feelings for leaving her family behind. Like the others, she decided to just live for as long as she was going to live without a family. This all worked as planned until the idea of having Zsa came up. It seemed natural for her, whatever that means, to bring Zsa back to Stephen. Although it was a group decision, she volunteered to provide the womb. This because she liked Stephen, maybe more than liked. The extent of her feelings were attenuated by the knowledge that he would be leaving for a long period of time and the emotional toll for waiting that long was too much to ask of anyone. Stephen felt this attraction as well but his mission and the prospects of seeing Zsa again clouded the waters of his feelings for Elva. A few times during their discussions and walks he felt very attracted to her, but held back so as not to start something they might one day regret. To him she was beautiful and wonderful but more like an image than a part of his soul.

There were more walks and talks but the energy of their attraction slowly dissipated as the arrival day of the robot ship approached. At some point, during one meeting at a cafe, they said a subdued goodbye to each other. They became so busy that they might not see each other again.

The time arrived for the visit, Isaac sensed that the ship was close and went to the area where it typically landed to make sure the area was cleared. It had been many years, so the trees and bushes were larger and the undergrowth more extensive. Isaac and several of the others cut down the larger trees and removed the brush for a safe landing. Although the ship did not communicate with them the timing of the past visits were very regular and predictable. They would not be disappointed with this visit's timing. Isaac looked at the moon and knew it was during

330

this season when the moon was half full and just above the Eastern horizon that the ship would announce its presence by creating a contrail during its decent through the sky at dusk. Looking up at the appointed time, Isaac and the others saw the contrail almost to the minute of the previous visit. Robots believe in precision, or more accurately, they know of no other way to act. This was one of the many reasons they would not take over the Universe, although they would always be a part of it. Once the robots learned to replicate themselves and more importantly, write their own software, they took on a life of their own. The issue of course was creativity, of which they had none. They were driven to perfection, not art. As such they could not "think" themselves out of difficult circumstances. They became predicable to those who knew them. The advantages were that they never slept and could go where biological based lifeforms could not. Another advantage was that they were goal oriented and once there became a reason to visit a world or conduct a scientific experiment, they were undeterred. These goals were the vestiges of their creators, typically scientists and explorers.

The contrails they were observing became thicker and started to curve as the robot ship made its way to the landing zone. A speck in the sky became noticeable and

331

maneuvered with precision down a straight line to the forest clearing. Subtle sound came from the ship as it got closer. It was silver and smooth and without any windows. Slowing, it aligned itself with the long axis of the landing area and deftly lowered its landing gear just in time to alight on the ground.   Humming with a high pitched tone was heard upon their approach.   Once the ship landed the sounds diminished to silence. The only sound left was that of the wind.

Within moments a long hatch in the belly of the craft opened, one end lowered and revealed a set of steps. The lowering end slowed as it neared the ground, then touched down delicately. The tingling effects of the electromagnetic propulsion system felt by the people standing nearby started to subside. Stephen watched for the emergence of an android or robot but had to wait for a long period of time. He looked at the others who were gathered with him about 100 feet away from the craft. They showed no emotion and as a result Stephen chose to be patient.   It took a few minutes but eventually something started to descend the stairway, it wasn't what he expected. What descended from the craft was capsule shaped, about two meters long with four equal sized appendages that could be used as either legs or arms. Each appendage had two "elbows" or "knees" which could articulate in many directions. The advantages of this arrangement became apparent as the robot made its way down the stairs in a very smooth manner. It seemed obvious that these machines didn't necessarily model themselves after humans or other four legged creatures, they determined their shape by logic alone. As such, they can walk inverted as easily as upright and function in the weightlessness of space with ease. The capsule shape allows for sensor suites with hemispherical coverage on either end.

This particular unit moved gracefully over to the area where Isaac and Stephen were standing, straightened up and ceased moving. Isaac addressed it.

"Greetings, I am Isaac."

"Isaac, I am H4N3, human interface unit, craft 64D."

"Welcome back to our world."

"Craft 64D will stay here for 4 solar cycles as a standard information gathering initiative. This is program 16 of 32 in our standard cycle of stops. We will accept passengers and have accommodations for 6."

"We have one passenger."

"The passenger is assigned area 4. What type of life form is the passenger?"

"Humanoid."

"We have enough food and water for the humanoid passenger to complete the cycle of travel and return here in 30 of your solar years. The passenger may enter the craft at any time."

"Thank you."

The robot remained in place as Stephen looked at it, wondering what it was going to do. He then realized it was doing what it was programed to accomplish, which was sample the atmosphere, sounds, light, soil, electromagnetic environment, gravity, and a host of other physical inputs. From these data, when compared to the multitude of other visits in the past, the robot was writing a story of the evolution of this planet. The sentient beings were not as interesting as the physical parameters. This robot ship had the task of recording physical details of a cross section of the Milky Way. Its creators gave it and several others like it the specific task of recording and organizing the physical parameters from hundreds of planets, some not inhabited and others inhabited. The point of the exercise was to understand the dynamic evolution of the Milky Way. The spacecrafts were deployed in a roughly spherical layout of spokes from a central home base and each contained a very comprehensive set of sensor suites

334

capable of recording all physically measurable variables. Sentient life communications were not high on the priority list but space was provided for these beings for the purpose of allowing the creators of the crafts to learn about the levels of intelligence in the Universe where the process of evolving or harboring these life forms occurred. One question that needed to be answered was what environments were most conducive to intelligent life. The critical discovery was that the population II stars had a much longer time to evolve intelligence and as a result these stars and the areas that they inhabited (globular clusters and the center of the Milky Way) were billions of years ahead of the younger population I stars, like the sun whose solar system contained the Earth, where Stephen had been born.

The craft that Stephen was about to embark on was headed for a globular cluster where a much more advanced culture existed. These beings were the creators of the robot ships and the recipients of the information they gathered. In a sense they were also the fishermen who examined the contents (nets) of the spaceships when new life forms arrived. These beings knew that only the more advanced cultures would find their way onboard. Once the ships returned to the world of their creators, environments awaited to make the "catch" comfortable. In this way the creators could interact with them and record the evolution of intelligence in the Milky Way. The spacecraft were in another way like buses, whereby they continued to travel about taking data and transporting the curious.

To keep things in perspective the population I and II beings were separated by many billions of years. On Earth humans evolved from Australopithecus to Homo Sapiens in about 4 Million years. An evolutionary period of billions of years was an extraordinary if not incomprehensible amount of time. There are however a few common traits between the two levels. These included curiosity and the will to be happy. The Nereids knew this as it was one of the most basic of Greek philosophies and as a result of their influence, modern humans naturally were attracted to discovery and pleasure. It turns out that all successful life in the Universe shared these traits.

Stephen knew he had several days to "move in" but chose to see the vessel early to get an idea as to the layout and to determine what he could bring to make his long voyage comfortable. The robot did not seem to mind as Stephen walked by it giving it a wary glance. The robot was frozen in place taking data. Stephen's presence was noted by an increase in relative humidity and a localized thermal disturbance. He walked towards the entry stairs and about half way there looked back to see Isaac and others observing his motions. They showed no emotion, if anything they had a look of understanding. Stephen returned his gaze to the ship, which was silver and featureless. The skin was completely smooth and where the landing gear and entry stairway attached to the ship no doors or hatches could be seen. Stephen would discover later that all of the seams were sealed with a ferro-magnetic substance held in place by a very powerful magnetic field. He now concentrated on the stairs which were spaced about right for a humanoid; he placed his left foot on the first stair gingerly to test its weight bearing capability. Finding it solid he ascended the stairs until he found his way up to the interior of the ship. It was lit with what seemed to be white light with a faint tinge of blue. Rails were available inside and he used them to steady himself as he slowly walked around the ship to examine it and find his living quarters. Cubes of approximately one meter on a side lined the interior. There did not seem to be a cockpit or engine room. Just an interior space lined with cubes. The only break in the uniform spaces between these cubes was a series of rectangular areas about ten meters by ten meters up against the inner skin of the ship. Stephen walked into one of them to discover platforms and storage areas. He also discovered that one wall of this "room" had an image displayed of what the cockpit would see looking out the forward part of the ship. He got closer to find that the image had a photographic resolution to it with no discernible pixillation to the image he was viewing. The closer he got the more details he could see. He turned around to look at the rest of the room, which looked actually livable. There were places he could sit and walls that moved for privacy. One corner revealed what appeared to be a sink and toilet. There was also a table with many controls. He spoke for the first time:

"Wow."

Sounds were heard after he spoke, a voice speaking a few un recognizable words.

"Hello, is there someone here?"

"English, Earth, are we communicating?"

"Yes, who are you?"

"This is the ship. Welcome aboard, we understand you will be the only passenger."

"That is correct."

"You are humanoid?"

"Yes."

"We will make the appropriate adjustments for your comfort. Please observe the following details of your living space."

The lights dimmed and Stephen noticed one small area had a much higher light level.

"This is the food dispenser, you may program it for any food substance you desire."

Another area was enhanced. The first one dimmed to ambient.

"This area contains clothing, below it is bedding."

Another area was enhanced.

"This area is for bodily functions."

Another area was enhanced.

"This area controls the view screen and interface to the ship."

The voice stopped for a moment, perhaps waiting for a response. Stephen addressed the voice.

"What is your name? Do you have a designation? How do I contact you if I have a question?"

"I have no name or designation. You may speak to me at any time."

"May I give you a designation?"

"You may."

"Then I shall call you Majel, after a famous voice from Earth, long ago."

"You may call me Majel."

"Majel, what are the modules attached to the inside of this vessel?"

"The modules are the crew."

"The crew? How do they control the spacecraft?"

"They are all connected to a central network. Each can navigate and control propulsion, for slower flight one unit will take command with the others observing, for higher speeds more units will participate. At our highest speed all units are required."

"How fast will this ship fly?"

"Very near the speed of light, 98 percent to be exact."

"Then we will have relativistic time compression effects as compared to the people we leave on this world?"

"Yes."

"When will we return to this world?"

"30 years of their time, six months of your time."

"Okay, what do I need to bring with me?"

"You need nothing, all of your needs will be met. You however may bring things of sentimental value if you wish."

340

"Thank you, I will. When does the ship leave?"

"In three solar cycles. We will not leave without you. Please wear this device at all times." A beam of light lit up a wristband on one of the shelves.

"Okay."

Stephen walked over to the shelf, took the device which looked like a wide wrist watch band with several dim lights on it and several buttons and put it on his left wrist. It started to move just a bit, morphing itself to the contours of his arm. Stephen felt its presence change from awkward to comfortable to imperceptible.

"Feels good, Majel. What does it do?"

"Everything."

"Well I look forward to testing that statement."

"What is your designation, your name?"

"Stephen, Stephen Daedalus."

The voice faded from the ceiling to his new wrist band with the same fidelity and volume.

"We are friends now, Stephen."

"Good because I like your voice."

"And I your's."

Stephen felt a bit too comfortable for a second and decided to go back outside. He knew that six months in this craft would be a long time and that he should spend most of his remaining days with the Nereids. They knew about this craft and its robots. It would be important to hear their stories and maybe spend some time with the mother of Zsa. He had many complex feelings about this turn of events. He appreciated how Isaac and the others wanted to do something for him but Zsa could never be Zsa for many reasons. His curiosity would compel him to return to see who she was but without Zsa's experiences that made her who she was, how could she be the same person? He thought about the incredible capabilities of the Nereids and wondered if they could answer that question.

He walked down the stairs to the outside air and sunshine again. Although it had been only a few minutes the others had gone. Stephen stopped about 20 meters from the craft and turned to look at it. The robot was still in its place, probably still taking data. Stephen gave it a wide berth so as not to contaminate its readings and began walking back to the village. The day was beautiful and warm. The breeze light and Stephen noticed every tiny detail of his surroundings from the sounds of life around him to the smell of Spring in the air. It could not be a better place to live, he thought. He would surely return motivated by his curiosity as well as his love for this planet. He was also very drawn to the discovery aspects of his journey.

~ Sunrise Descending ~

What would the population II stars reveal to him? What about the other worlds he would stop at before the old star systems? He smiled at the prospect and as he continued walking he day-dreamed about the new life forms and sites he would encounter. To him the Universe was a continuous path of wonderment, revealing new un-thought of details and new life un-imaginable.

The village was closer now as Stephen awoke from his day dreams and could see the activity in the village. It looked normal and un-changed from the knowledge of the spacecraft sitting in a field just a few kilometers away. Stephen found his way to a cafe and sat down outside to have a cup of tea. People smiled at him as they walked by him. He smiled back. After his cup was emptied he rose and continued to make his way to his apartment to gather things of sentimental value and soak in the feeling of his home for so many months. As he got closer to his place he thought of and looked at his new wrist band."

"Majel?"

"Yes Stephen?"

"I just wanted to know if you were still there or if I was out of communications range."

"You will never be out of communications range."

"Will you teach me about this technology you use for this device someday?"

"Of course. It uses the complete electromagnetic spectrum. When you return we can discuss it further."

"Okay, thank you."

Stephen had now made it to his apartment and decided to take a nap followed in the evening by a trip back to the campfire area, where his life had been changed over the last few days.

His dreams repeated his experiences of the day. There was a bit of embellishment of course as his inner consciousness morphed the experiences with his desires and fears. Majel was real and walked about the ship without touching the deck. The robot had unblinking eyes that watched Stephen at all times. Stephen awoke an hour later wondering what the images meant. Clearing his head he got up and started to get ready to go to the forest. Before he made it to the door of his apartment and as the dusk outside lowered the light levels inside the room he noticed dim sparkling in the corner suspended in the air like tiny fireflies. He had seen this before but a very long time ago on his boat. He hadn't thought about it much then, now it was a little more interesting. Originally he assumed it was his eyes playing tricks on him but this time they looked more real, especially when he moved around and noticed they retained their three dimensional position like a suspended beach ball. They had different colors as well but did not move or change intensity. He watched for another minute then after he blinked to make sure he was really seeing something they were gone.

"Interesting," he murmured.

"They are indeed," responded Majel.

"I didn't realize you were watching. I'm glad I wasn't hallucinating."

"No, the light phenomenon is real, and intelligent."

"Where are they from?"

"That will soon become apparent. They tend to be a part of interesting peoples' lives. Have you seen them before?"

"Yes, once. A very long time ago while staying on a boat on Earth."

"They probably have followed you over the course of years, most of the time without you knowing it."

"Do you know why or who they are?"

"We, the robots, are not sure. Its part of our research protocol, to take note of them when they appear. They are not part of the population I star cultures."

"Okay, well that was interesting. I am going to the campfire site now to see who's there."

"A few people will be there."

"You seem to know a lot of things."

"I have 12,000 giga quads of instantly accessible information."

"Oh, that's half of what I have," Stephen stated while smirking at his wristband.

"That is not accurate," Majel reported coldly.

"Well, okay, maybe not quite half" continued Stephen, "and you have a sense of humor, thats rare among robots."

"We have interacted with humans for many thousands of solar cycles and have determined that their biological origins preclude accurate statements."

"Well thats true sometimes, however its more likely that they combine their feelings with their observations. That way we get more information in a shorter period of time. In other words, humans can tell you that the sun just set over the ocean and that they found it comforting at the same time. This can come in a simple sentence like 'it was a lovely sunset,' so you see perception and interpretation are commonly used at the same time. It makes us more efficient."

~ Sunrise Descending ~

"Its hard for robots to understand that."

"Yes, I know."

Stephen found a jacket, put it on and headed for the door. Walking out into the evening he took the most common path towards the camp fire area. Few people were out and he considered Majel's words about how many people were going to be there and wondered how she would know these things. Ultimately, he thought, he would ask about this during their long journey together.

The evening was crisp, smelled of rain and looking up he saw cloud cover that was thick enough for rain to form. The moon shown through between the airborne lumps to illuminate his path and then periodically it would darken. He slowed his walking during the dark periods so as not to go off the path and walk into a tree or bush. The grey light coming from high angles created many beams of brightness that enhanced certain areas of the forest. He would take this image in his mind with him on his voyage.

Soon he found himself in the clearing where the fire pit was and noticed but a few people around tending to a small fire. Walking up to them he nodded and acknowledged their presence.

"Good evening."

"And to you as well."

347

"Feels special somehow."

"It is of course, for us and you."

"Why is it special to you?"

"We know you will be leaving us for a while, not too long, but long enough for us to miss you and watch your Zsa grow up. We will take good care of her and look forward to your return. When you do return you will have stories and information from an amazing place. You will teach us things we long to learn. You will be our ambassador and tell your new friends about us. Maybe someday we will be visited by more than robots and androids."

"Well, I will miss you too and I look forward to returning to see you again and to see how Zsa has grown up. I wonder what she will be like."

"She will be wonderful, just like you told us."

"I think so, but maybe for different reasons. This is not Earth and you are not her original parents and she will not take the same life path as she did before. This will make her different from her predecessor but I am sure she will be a fine person with your guidance."

"You can, if you like, have us mold her in the image you have of her, we would be happy to do that."

"Oh, no thank you. That would not be fair, she would be no more than a replicant. My image of her is idealized. I described her beauty and intelligence to you, not her faults. Just let her grow up to be who she will really be."

"We will."

Time for Travel

One's first love is always perfect until one meets one's second love. - Elizabeth Aston

~ *Sunrise Descending* ~

The evening at the camp fire was uneventful unlike the previous evenings. A few conversations were held, fleeting glimpses from the others indicated that everyone knew the plan and all were comfortable with it. Stephen reclined a bit finding the fire light entrancing and for long periods of time simply stared into the flames and embers. The warmth was comforting as well; he knew he would miss this scene and the feelings associated with this place. He was now smiling a bit while thinking he would return to friends and in a strange way, family.

Looking around after several hours of day dreaming, his streams of thought floating him down a river of images and senses, he came to and decided to go home and sleep. The night was quiet and clear, the ocean miles away sparkled at him with bits of reflections from the moon, only meant for him. He smiled and began the walk to the village. He heard his footsteps in the grass and knew that the sleeping animals in the trees and burrows would probably open their eyes for a moment at the noise, sense that it was safe and return to their slumber.

He whispered, "Majel?"

She whispered back, "Yes, I am here."

"That was a wonderful evening tonight."

"Yes it was."

"I am going home to sleep but will visit the ship tomorrow."

"Okay, sleep well."

"Thank you, good night."

Why had he become so comfortable with a voice from his wristband? He wondered while walking. He imagined that maybe the robot on the other end was programmed to learn from interacting with humans. Maybe the wristband, morphed onto his skin so comfortably, could read his senses and brain activity. It really didn't matter as he felt he had a new friend that would take care of him during his upcoming voyage to the edges of the Milky Way.

In the distance faint lights from the village could be seen. Stephen walked towards the light, then into them, as he found the streets and avenues leading to his apartment.

Approaching the door he reached out to find the knob, turned it and entered his rooms. They were dimly lit from the outside lights which cast shadows across the tables and chairs. Stephen looked briefly over to the area he had seen the sparkling lights earlier that day and found them absent.

"Thats okay," he thought, "they were probably just curious about me.....I hope."

~ Sunrise Descending ~

Finding his bed, he dressed for sleep, located his pillow and within minutes was motionless in a current of contentment. Dreams followed that contained Majel again with a body and in addition not touching the floor as she moved about the cabin of the spacecraft. The dreams contained the campfire, whose flames created shapes and forms of experiences past. Finally the sparkles were there but suspended overhead and ever present as they reacted to every new mental construct of Stephen's thoughts.

The night was cool and moonlit. The dreams came and went and a few were remembered the next day when Stephen awoke. He opened his eyes to the sunrise shades of color as the sun started to descend over the land making its way to the opposite border. Swinging his legs around to lower them to the floor, he sat up to clear his head and make a cup of tea. After a few moments he rose to start his day.

After the tea and some breakfast, Stephen went to the window to peer into the dawn of a new day. It would not matter what happened that day, he thought, it would be good but what to do?

He decided to visit Elva, maybe for lunch at an outdoor cafe, in order to spend a bit more time with her. He walked to where she worked and found her tending to her chores and caught her, before she knew he was there, staring briefly out the window.

"Hello Elva, how are you?"

"Stephen, I was hoping you would visit before you left."

"Oh, absolutely; I definitely wanted to see you as well."

There was a pause as they looked at each other.

After a long moment they both tried to fill in the silence but interrupted each other in the process.

"Sorry, please go ahead."

"Oh, I was just wondering if you had time for lunch today?"

"Of course, can we go to the Sea Side cafe? I love it there."

"Sure, is now okay or would you like me to come back?"

"Now is fine......always."

He smiled at her and she at him for another timeless moment.

"I'll get my things."

She turned and walked to another part of the room to pick up a light jacket and a small purse. The other workers in the room felt the electricity and followed her movements, then looked at Stephen who was following her movements as well.   Turning, her eyes met his as she approached and only at the last moment averted to find her way to the door.

"Beautiful," he whispered, with just enough volume for her to hear.

"Thank you," she whispered back.

They walked in the warm sunshine towards the sea, glimmering still with motion, life and beauty.   Down a cobblestone walkway, they went.   Towards a nice cafe with the tables in the open sunlight covered by Cinzano shades and looking out upon the sea where a quiet beach and the surf breaking over rocks could be seen.

They found the perfect table and sat down.   The waiter appeared and looking at each other Stephen and Elva ordered water and a menu. Faint jazz ballads could be heard inside the cafe, a saxophone player and pianist decrying their love for an auburn haired beauty from long ago. They played the gentle chords and sung the sensitive melodies of thoughts of themselves.

Out viewing the ocean Elva and Stephen heard the overlaid voices of birds melding as best they could with the music.

"Wine?"

"Please," she responded.

The waiter returned, took the wine order and orders for cheese, croissants and fruit. Perfect for the weather and the company. Soon they were eating and talking about who knows what. An occasional laugh could be heard by the other patrons. An hour later, after some very good coffees, the waiter came inside with a look on his face that revealed a slightly voyeuristic experience. He walked over to the bartender, spoke softly and as he left to tend to his duties, the bartender smiled and shook his head, most likely remembering romantic times from the past.

"Ready, Elva?"

"Yes, can we walk on the beach for a bit before we go back?"

"Of course."

They rose, gathered their things and bidding adieu to the waiter, strolled towards the beach. He was slightly ahead of her for a moment, which gave her the chance to look at him. After making her decision, she placed her hand in his as they walked. He responded with a look and a smile.

The beach was smooth and firm this day, sandpipers scurried around the couple like water around stones in a stream as they hunted for their prey. The water foamed as it dissipated its energy from a thousand miles away and left a small line of risen sand. Their eyes looked at this and the other gentle details of the beach which reminded them of each other. Their eyes met periodically as they talked for a short while then moved in silence for another while. They found their way to the outcropping of rocks and into the recesses of privacy. Slowing, they got closer as they new their privacy was absolute. He put his arm around her waist and she put her arm around his neck and they kissed. Silence followed for a minute as they basked in their attraction. It seemed wonderful yet forbidden as Elva carried the life Stephen once called his wife.

"Its okay."

"How so?"

"Its okay, because she will be completely different from who she was before."

"But, won't you love her like you did before, maybe just a little?"

"Oh I will love her for who she will be, not who she was. She was who she was in my mind as well as in body. The difference is that my mind made her into things she will never be. For instance, she has no commitment to me and will find others who she will grow up with and feel closer to.

357

You on the other hand are here and now and on this beach. You have made a commitment and I appreciate what you have done. Our path is different and unique."

"So be it. I don't have to be back to work for a while."

"Okay, I am fine with that."

They turned and walked away from the water and towards the street that would lead to her apartment. He took her hand this time and followed her steps. They were warm with emotion and the overwhelming sense that they were doing something right. They walked quickly, found her entrance stairway and ascended to her apartment. Once inside they caressed and kissed again. The door was locked.

"Umm, how are you feeling?"

"Well I am just starting pregnancy, a few things have changed, especially my breasts which are getting hard."

Without thinking too much he said, "Really?"

"Yes, see?"

She took his hand and placed it on her right breast where he felt a combination of life, warmth and love. There was a moment where time was suspended.

"How long has it been?"

~ Sunrise Descending ~

"About 73 years."

What happened next got the attention of the nearby neighbors and some wildlife in the area.

Furniture was moved, a bottle of just opened wine fell over and started to glug, glug the red fluid upon the table. A wine glass fell to its side, rolled about 100 degrees clockwise and off of the edge of the table to hit the floor with a high timbered crashing as the glass shattered. More furniture movement was heard below on the first floor, the downstairs occupants looked up and at each other. Faint sounds of mono syllabic expressions and possibly the tearing of fabric caught more of their attention. Only the younglings were confused about the sounds, the rest of the animal kingdom within earshot understood. Some smiled at the thought. Birds left the nearby trees as something flashed by the upstairs window.

It took a while but at some point the commotion stopped and peace was restored. Elva, disheveled, made her way over to the table, sat down in a slumped fashion and drank a glass of water. Stephen walked over to the window, looked out on the world and smiled. Then looking at her, he went to her side and kissed her. Later, their strength restored, they went out for dinner, and still basking in the calmness of the afterglow, talked about the future.

"When are you going to board the spacecraft?"

"Tomorrow, in the afternoon. I don't have many things to bring besides memories. You will be with me somehow forever."

"I will miss you, but for a Nereid and for the right reasons 30 years won't be that long of a wait."

"For both of us."

After dinner and a moonlight walk on the beach, they embraced and walked home, where quietly this time they entwined.

The morning, perfect again, broke, revealing the sun on its trek again. After breakfast they walked once more to the sea. Stephen needed to witness it once more before his travels. Then while he was looking out to sea and wondering about the future, he remembered something.

"Majel?"

"Yes?"

"Can you record this moment?"

"Okay, I shall, would you like a visual record or just audio?"

"Both please."

"I am recording now. Its nice to see your heart rate has subsided. Were you exercising?"

"In a way."

"Will you explain the details to me?"

"I doubt it."

They spent an hour or so watching the sea and feeling the breeze, then it was time to say goodbye to the others.

"I will meet you later at the clearing before you go."

"Okay."

Stephen started his "rounds" going to every place he knew where a friend or acquaintance would be. He said goodbye to many people and wound his way around the village, leaving Isaac for last, as he had been a good friend and deserved special time. Once he was at the farm and spotted Isaac in the fields he walked over and greeted him.

"Isaac, I wanted to say goodbye before I left for the stars today."

"I'm glad you did. You made good choices in friends and in a mate."

"Uh, how did you know about the mate?"

"Everyone knows, neither one of you has touched the ground in three days. It could be a special union, one that could last for a very long time."

"That would be my wish, Isaac. I am very happy."

"Well then, now we know you will come back for two reasons."

"Three, Isaac. I will not forget your friendship and guidance."

"I will not forget either. Be well and travel safely. Bring back stories that will amaze us."

"I shall....goodbye for now."

"Goodbye."

Stephen turned and started to well up at the thought of leaving these people and these friends and this woman. He made it back albeit haltingly, to the clearing and even at a distance could see that Elva was waiting. Her red hair looked luminescent as he got closer and when she turned to greet him, her green eyes radiated. His heart skipped a beat, she was radiant. Why was he leaving? He answered his own question....so he could come back.

"Hello, you look wonderful."

"Thank you, I wanted to see you off and give you something."

She smiled and looking straight into Stephen's eyes, gave him a small box. Continuing, she said:

"Don't open it until you are settled into your journey. Remember, it will be only six months for you."

"And 30 years for you. It seems unfair."

"For you," she said smiling, "I'll be busy enough to make the time short. And you will be busy discovering the wonders of the Universe."

He wanted to ask her to come with him but knew it was not a good idea. There were too many dangers, too much radiation and the Nereids indeed were better able to help and support a new mother.

He took the box from her hand, looked into her eyes, froze the image of her face in his mind, kissed her and started to walk towards the ship. Turning he said,

"I love you, Elva."

"I know, I love you too. Call me"

In all of the excitement, he hadn't realized that he could talk to her frequently during his journey.

Smiling he said, "of course, I will call you all of the time."

Making it to the doorway of the spacecraft, he turned once more to see her. She waved, turned and walked away wiping a tear from her eye. He watched until she was gone then entered the craft to find his living area.

Inside the crew was still in their places, the outside sentinel had finished its work and came back inside to re-attach itself to the wall. Stephen checked in with Majel.

"Majel?"

363

"Yes, I'm here."

"When do we take off?"

The stairs were retracting, the door was in position to be shut and sealed. Certain new sounds could be heard in the cabin.

"Right now. Please go to your living area and sit down on the designated chair."

Stephen, realizing what was happening, moved quickly to the living area found the lit up chair, sat down and buckled in to his designated seat. In less than a minute the sense of movement could be felt, the view screen in front him became active and he could see out in front of the ship at visible wavelengths. Acceleration was felt at about two times the force of gravity and was constant. The climb angle slowly adjusted upward and at some point the darkness of space and the curvature of the planet could be seen simultaneously. The acceleration continued far past the time that only space could be seen in the view screen. They were well past the low orbit position and accelerating within the solar system towards their first stop which was several weeks away.

The constant two gs on Stephen's body was tolerable for a while but after about an hour he started to get tired of the pressure.

"Majel?"

"Yes?"

"How long will we be accelerating?"

"21 minutes, then we will have reached our lower cruise speed."

"Lower cruise speed?"

"The lower cruise speed is necessary while we are in the solar system, then we will accelerate to our high speed cruise."

"Why do you need to lower your speed while in the solar system?"

"There are too many hazards to flight, our sensors cannot make the necessary control inputs at a speed that will keep you comfortable."

"Hazards, like comets, meteorites and other space debris?"

"Yes, exactly. We will continue to accelerate at one g for the rest of the cruise portion then we will have a period of deceleration."

"Okay."

"If you use your view screen controls in front of you the flight path and speeds are available. You may tune the controls for the frequency of interest."

"Frequency of interest?"

"Yes, the sensors on the skin of the spacecraft can detect the complete electromagnetic spectrum, tune the controls to observe radio, infrared, visible, ultraviolet, x-ray, gamma and cosmic rays."

"Okay, how about after lunch?"

"As you wish."

The spacecraft acceleration diminished to one g, Stephen felt much more comfortable now and could get up and move around with ease. The orientation of the floor however was the bottom of the ship, 90 degrees from when he entered and sat down. The uniformity of the walls and floors now made sense to him. Upstairs was at the nose of the ship. He adjusted his position, took in a much needed deep breath and thought about getting some food.

After lunch he settled down to the view screen to explore its talents. The controls were pretty intuitive and with Majel's help he figured out how to explore areas around the ship using any part of the spectrum. The ship's hull was covered with millions of sensors that relayed their information inside to a central bus. The robots inside processed the information and presented it to the view screen as well as to the navigation systems.

Stephen made himself comfortable and started to adjust the controls for the lowest frequency. This was in the

Hertz and sub Hertz area where he observed the undulations of gravity waves propagating through space. The fields were not uniform and bent as they got closer to stars and planets. Ripples could be seen where supernovas had sent enormous energy into the gravity continuum. The ripples moved as if having dropped a stone into a lake of molasses. Moving up in frequency to about the KiloHertz range Stephen could see how electrons were being captured by magnetic fields moving back and forth between poles. The image around stars was more like the image of iron filings aligning themselves with the fields of a magnet. At the higher ranges electrical discharge could be observed like lightning and the dynamo effects of moons moving through the intense magnetic fields of very large planets. Then Stephen moved into the MegaHertz range where civilizations that first learned how to communicated with radio waves were sending messages and programs to listeners. Spark gap transmitters were also present and could be discerned by their wide band emissions, noisy but useful. Lightning was also observable in this frequency range as well as the selective frequencies of large planet magnetospheres. Shortwave transmissions were now observed where country's armed services and radio amateurs plied the waves with information and entertainment. As he moved up again to the 100s of MegaHertz he discovered the transmissions of television and other wide band transmitters. There were from slightly more advanced cultures. Satellite transmissions were first starting to appear in this range. He moved further up in frequency to the GigaHertz range to observe more satellite activity and wider band transmissions of the first vestiges of planets' internet activities. At one particular frequency, 1,420 MHz, Stephen observed the emissions of the element Hydrogen, which comprises some 72% of the know Universe. This was a very important emission line, which revealed the arms of galaxies, the evolution of stars and the motions of great gas clouds. The emission line showed the doppler effects of movement if offset from its primary frequency or the turbulence of the cloud with the broadening of the emissions. Other elements and chemical compounds presented themselves with other emissions lines. Carbon dioxide, water, ammonia and hundreds of others were present at specific frequencies from 1 to 300 GigaHertz. He tuned upward to observe yet more emissions of chemicals and the first semblances of thermal emissions as he went from the sub-millimeter bands to the infrared. Heat was clearly marked at the infrared frequencies and above that visible light showed the more familiar Universe. Stephen continued to tune the screen above the visible to the ultraviolet, which showed the actions of more and more energetic physical phenomena. The birth of stars and supernovas were observable in great detail here. Above the ultraviolet was the gamma ray, x-rays which revealed black holes, and finally the cosmic ray regimes. Each showed the activities of more and more energetic phenomena. The images were stunning and revealing at the same time.

"Majel?"

"Yes?"

"Why do you observe the complete energy output of the Universe with your sensor arrays?"

"We derive all of our energy from these measurements for our propulsion and life support requirements. In fact, cosmic ray energy alone could give us more than we need. We observe and harvest the other energy bands for research as well as sustenance."

"I can see why...its fascinating to observe. Especially as you can see the level of technical sophistication in many worlds. The earlier cultures use lower frequencies for instance. As they advance they need more bandwidth and thus most move to higher frequencies.

~ Sunrise Descending ~

You can see the development of radars and satellites as well, just fascinating."

"I am glad you are enjoying it."

"Majel, how long until we land again?"

"16 of your solar days."

"And what is this world called?"

"Outpost 399."

Outpost 399

*Our sun is one of 100 billion stars in our galaxy.
Our galaxy is one of billions of galaxies populating the
universe. It would be the height of presumption to think that
we are the only living things in that enormous immensity. -*
Wernher von Braun

"Majel?"

"Yes?"

"Tell me about Outpost 399."

"Its very old and very large."

"How old?"

"Well over a thousand of your years."

"How large?"

"Larger than the moon from your Earth."

"Can you tell me about the history of the outpost?"

"Yes. It was built by robots from a dying world, one that had lost control of its nuclear technology and had over polluted. The initial station was built over the course of ten of your years. The building has never stopped and other worlds and visitors have added their own environments. There are millions of inhabitants and a central government. The outpost is situated at the 4th Lagrange point in the same orbit as the world that designed it. The outpost is known for its huge telescopes and other scientific instruments. There are many technical universities within it."

"Sounds very interesting, Majel. Can you communicate with it?"

"Within a few of your days, we will announce ourselves and link to their Internet."

~ Sunrise Descending ~

"Will I be able to access information from this ship to prepare myself for the visit?"

"Yes."

Stephen went on to learn about the outpost over the next several days. He settled into a routine of waking, eating, studying, exercising, studying, eating, relaxing and sleeping. Most days he maintained the schedule to within minutes. In this way he could best acclimate to the closed space and lack of emotion from the computers.

The outpost wasn't exactly spherical as expected. It was more random with a long element of the structure pointed permanently towards the sun. This allowed the telescopes to be always in nighttime conditions and cool. Stephen also discovered that there was a central avenue or promenade to which many cultures from many worlds took up residence. There was high speed transit down this avenue to connect the different portions to each other. Based on the size, no life form could possibly visit all of the structure.

The power sources were mainly from the sun as well as from the energetic particles impinging the surface of the outpost. Electricity was the common denominator, which ran all systems and life support. Air was provided, recycled and replenished from water found on nearby planets. Particles in space were mined for other elements like nitrogen, hydrogen, etc. Light inside was provided by electricity of course, but in addition, they had large light pipes to gather the free light from the sun and send it through most anyplace in the structure. It looked inviting as Stephen found a significant amount of restaurants and entertainment.

Stephen thought it interesting that sentient beings from this area of space had found it appealing to build their own world. It certainly came natural to have the robots and androids build the station initially and keep the growth up on a continuous basis. A fully complete life cycle in a sense for the robots, metal to metal. It was also interesting that most of the raw materials were obtained by sifting through the molecules flying through space and to a lesser degree, sending robotic mining machines to asteroids and moons. He wondered about the next step where robots would simply follow their programming and simply build things forever. Robots were at the point now, he observed, that they autonomously replaced broken components on themselves and if they were too broken, simply got melted down, separated into their constituent components and were remade again from these components. The programs used by robots became fundamentally adaptable but only to continue following their prime directive, to build. The same robots who had started the task of assembling Outpost 399 were still on duty making more rooms, labs, living quarters and telescopes. They would remain doing so until manually shut down.

The spacecraft Stephen was traveling in slowed down in a few days and the image of the station was soon available on the view screen. Lights could be seen on the station from many many windows. As they got closer still, movement outside was also discernible. Robots and small ships formed a thin cloud around the massive structure, darting back and forth, delivering goods and life forms.

Another day or two and they would dock for a week's visit. Not much change was detected inside the spacecraft. The robots remained in place, Majel's voice did not get excited.

He liked Majel, but she was a bit boring, and the times he tried to mess with her she did not take the bait.

"Majel?"

"Yes?"

"The temperature is cold in here, please set the temperature at minus 40."

"Okay."

"I have changed my mind, the temperature is hot in here, please set the temperature to plus 50."

"Okay."

"I have changed my mind again, Majel. Leave the temperature alone and open the windows."

"There are no windows."

"Then open the door."

"The door is sealed."

"Then order another seal."

"Okay."

"Thank you Majel."

"Your welcome."

Getting bored with his cell mate Stephen simply occupied himself until the docking occurred at Outpost 399.

This happened quickly enough and he watched the proceedings on the view screen as the ship slowed to a crawl, negotiated a landing spot and turned to allow the door to mate with an adapter ring on the outpost. There was a thump as the operation was complete. Majel advised Stephen:

"We have docked and will be here for seven of your days."

"Thank you, Majel, where is a good place to get drunk?"

"At a place with liquor."

"Thank you, Majel, that helps."

"Your welcome."

The door was opened slowly to allow pressure equalization. The incoming air smelled quite a bit different as it had different ratios of oxygen and nitrogen. It would take Stephen a while to get used to, he would get headaches from it but eventually adaptation would come. Stephen rose and maneuvered himself to the door as he was weightless. He floated through and as he emerged he slowly felt the pulls of gravity which lowered him to the floor. He rose and stood at 10% of Earth's gravity. As he walked there was a gradual increase in downward pull. He noticed that were were different colored stripes on the floor and he discovered by moving from one color to another that they represented different gravity gradients, no doubt to make life forms from different planets feel comfortable. No two living worlds are the same diameter, so gravity varies as well. He chose the most comfortable color and followed it.

Noises, lights, corridors and rooms were everywhere. He cautiously approached a room that looked a bit like a restaurant with a multitude of life forms in it, many eating and drinking.

"Majel?"

"Yes?"

"How will I communicate with these beings?"

"I will translate."

He walked in and found a place to sit. As he did so he noticed that most of the life forms ignored him, which brought him some sort of comfort. Looking around he observed what life type would reach sentience if given the right conditions: four legged as well as two legged, avian as well as amphibian, aquatic as well as arthropod. Each life sustaining planet combined with its history of catastrophes like comets and meteor plus the unique qualities of its environment allowed certain life forms to flourish and others to remain suppressed. In common, there were plants, animals and insects; each of those had the opportunity to advance. In many cases, especially the very old star systems, a wide variety of life had reached sentience. Stephen was amazed that it all made sense. The most advanced life forms produced robots and other mechanical devices in their image. These devices, like robots and androids, tended to do the work the biological life forms could not handle. In other words, it was soon discovered by these beings, that the devices could work all of the time, do research all of the time and explore all of the time. The intellectual curiosity of the biologicals was satisfied as their needs and wants were taken care of by their creations. This had become a common theme in the Universe.

Some of the life forms started to notice Stephen and after a few minutes a humanoid like being approached Stephen and tried to communicate with him.

"Spirif tic nad?"

"Majel?"

"Yes?"

"Could you translate for us?"

"Yes, she wants to know if you would like something to eat or drink."

"Does she have water?"

"Dat fle was?"

"Yet, mir tak nad sa."

"She has water and will bring it for you."

The waitress turned and left to retrieve the water but kept eye contact for a brief moment before she left. Stephen took notice but did not know how to interpret the action.

After a minute the creature returned with the water and again kept eye contact with Stephen.

"Majel, please thank her for the water."

"Tas da."

"Na da. Bic no ot sa da min bea."

"She says your welcome and that she met another like you a while ago."

"Another, like me?"

"Yes."

"Min bea, waas lek ra ba?"

"Bus bea, mo eda jes sta ra fum."

"She says the other was a female version of you and stayed for many cycles."

"Wow, I assumed I was alone. Does she know where she went?"

"Min bea, waas gu ta?"

"Bus bea, eda eta sta la."

"She thinks the person traveled to the old stars."

"Please ask her when she left and which 'old stars'."

"Min bea, dode gu ta, dode sta da?"

"Bus dea, len glea tu das, ut das dan gla sta da."

"She says the woman left months ago and went to the same star system, with the population II stars, that we will visit soon."

"Tell her thank you."

"Tas da."

The waitress left and Stephen tasted the water. By now he was used to the air and the water was just that, water. In the Universe it will always be the same. He sat back to observe and learn about the other life forms in the room. Some moved slowly, some quickly. The variety was amazing and Stephen wanted to interact with all of them but his instincts told him to just watch for now and try to pick his conversations.

After 20 minutes or so he decided to eat something and with Majel's translating talents he ordered what he hoped would be a salad and steak. The steak turned out to be grown from stem cells and that animals had not been slaughtered for food for thousands of years. It didn't make sense to anyone on the station to conduct such a barbaric act. This was prefered especially when any food could simply be grown more safely. As there were no worries about parasites, hormones and bacteria. The food appeared soon enough and the taste was magnificent. Stephen was pleased with the universality of some foods. Other life forms in the room ate other things but the humanoids in general ate the same things.

After "dinner," Stephen decided to go for a walk. He found the promenade that he had learned about while studying the layout of the world. It indeed looked thousands of miles long and possibly a quarter of a mile wide. There were bullet train like machines that flew past at incredible speeds. They appeared to be "mag lev" types. Some stopped at stations that were within walking distance. The sides of the promenade had what appeared to be offices or restaurants. A wide variety of purposes were supported here as this world accommodated hundreds of species. Stephen decided to take a train in one direction for a while to get an overview of the outpost. Knowing that he had Majel on his wrist comforted him as he new she could keep him from getting lost and could help him communicate with others. He started his walk towards the train, taking in the sites as he made his way to the station. The variety of life forms was amazing, as each of the worlds they came from had different histories and environments, thus creating many morphological types. The languages he overheard were diverse as well. They ranged from monosyllabic to almost sing song. There were hisses and acrobatic pitch changes and humming, whatever it took to communicate. The whole experience was fascinating.

"Majel?"

"Yes?"

"Are you recording the sights and sounds around us?"

"Always."

~ Sunrise Descending ~

"Do you recognize the different life forms and cultures?"

"Yes, we can discuss them at your convenience."

"Good, something to do while we travel. Are there life forms we should avoid?"

"Not really, these societies are advanced and understand that aggression is not useful. If you are respectful, they will be respectful as well."

"Good. I am going to take a train in some direction for a while to get a feeling for the different areas on the outpost. Eventually, I would like you to direct me to the observatories, but not just yet."

"Of course."

He found his way to the train station and not understanding the signage, simply waited for a train to come by and stop. Within minutes a sign started flashing and chatter was heard on their version of loud speakers. He walked over to where others were standing and soon heard humming that hopefully meant a train was nearby. His patience was rewarded in a matter of seconds as a silver (Why are they always silver?) bullet train slowed to a stop ten meters in front of him. It was very aerodynamic looking with a sloped nose and conformal windows and doors. The doors were wider than he was used to and soon

383

slid open to reveal the insides of the train. There were no, cars per se, just a long silver tube that in fact hovered magnetically over a spot on the floor. The others started to board after some of the original passengers had disembarked. Stephen waited his turn and used the steps to get inside.

Once there, he looked fore and aft for a place to sit. The "seats" were of many different types in an effort to accommodate many types of life forms. He found something that looked comfortable near a window. As he sat, the view screen in front of him began to blink, showing a progression of caricatures and symbols. Nothing made any sense to him. The blinking however was getting annoying.

"Majel?"

"Yes?"

"There is a blinking panel in front of me that seems to want attention, how can I take care of it?"

"You must choose a destination, so it knows when to alert you to disembark. The symbols you see represent the stops. Choose one, touch it and it will make a note of it and stop blinking."

"What stop are available?"

384

"There is an arboretum, apartments, food areas, work areas, observatories, power plants, open areas, universities....."

"First the arboretum."

"Press the symbol that looks like a flower, when it cycles through."

"Okay standby........done."

"That all you have to do, the display will show you a number symbol that will count down until you reach your destination."

"Thanks."

With that and another minute of waiting, the doors quietly slid closed. Then the sensation of movement was felt, accelerating slowly until they seemed to be going at several hundred kilometers per hour. The train was silent without any wheel noise or air noise. The only sounds were periodic discussions among life forms. Looking outside, a myriad of geometric shapes whizzed by, along with colors and shapes of buildings and open areas.

Stephen peered at the number symbols counting down on the screen and surmised that they were similar to Roman numerals from early Earth times. There seemed to be a relationship to units, tens of units, hundreds of units, etc.

Stephen unfortunately did not know where zero was on this counting scheme and would have to ask Majel or wait for a change in the display. After considering whether or not he wanted to be surprised or plan his day, he asked for help.

"Majel?"

"Yes?"

"How long do I have to wait before my stop?"

"2 hours, twenty of your minutes."

"How will I know as I get closer?"

"The display will start to blink slowly, then quicken as we get closer."

"Okay, thank you."

Knowing he had a while to wait Stephen looked outside at the sights and periodically looked inside at the creatures present in the train.

The train indeed did not have cars and looked like a very long tube. There were different lighting schemes and signs of various sorts up and down the aisle. Across from him was a furry creature that appeared to be reading an information tablet. This was punctuated by looking at Stephen, probably asking the same question that was on Stephen's mind...."where is that thing from?" Mostly it seemed bored, which made Stephen feel a little less like dinner. He started to explore the display screen for more information, of which there were many pages, some with pictures but all with symbols he did not understand. He kept changing pages and exploring but soon tired, as he sat back in his seat he looked once more at his furry companion who was again looking at him. It made a noise of some sort.

"Mmmfrrt?"

"Majel, can you translate?"

"Yes, she asks if this is your first time in a train?"

"Tell her that I have been in many, but not on this world."

"Nommff, irtff eye stas glot."

"Botff, ta."

"She says stand by, she will adjust her translator device."

"How is this? Can you understand me?"

Stephen responded, "Yes, I can understand you perfectly."

"You are not from this world?"

"No, I am from Earth plus a few stops before I got here."

"There have been others from Earth, who visited here."

"How long ago?"

387

"Not long."

"Male or Female?"

"Both, they are wanderers like myself."

"Where are you from?"

"A few star systems away, It took me a very long time to get here, this place is a legend so I had to come see myself."

"Its very interesting so far. I am only here for a short while. I decided to go to the Arboretum, have you been there?"

"Oh, yes, many times, it is absolutely beautiful. There are millions of species of plants, some quite intelligent."

"Intelligent?"

"Why yes, are you surprised? They communicate very well."

"I have not encountered an intelligent plant on my travels, nor have I ever heard about them."

"There is a very large area, just for them. If you sit down and listen, they will start to talk to you."

"Telepathically?"

"If you mean by sending electrical signals to your brain from theirs, then yes, telepathically."

"That sounds interesting. And where are you going?"

"To the waterfalls."

"Sounds very nice."

"On my way back, maybe I will stop and see you at the arboretum. Your communications device will know if I am coming to see you."

The furry creature seemed quite gentle in Stephen's eyes, even though it looked somewhat like a mixture of dog and chimpanzee. It sat, unlike a dog but had a long snout and an articulating tail. The eyes were intelligent and the hands and feet dexterous. There was an interesting soul to her motions and words. Stephen smiled at this and said:

"I look forward to it."

The train continued its high speed journey and Stephen and probably the other passengers had the distinct feeling every once in a while that the outside was in motion, not the inside. This happens sometimes on a glass smooth night while flying a small airplane on Earth. The complete lack of motion reverses the pilot's senses.

He felt sleepy now, his eyelids became heavy and soon a nap took over his body. Right before he transitioned to silence, he thought about Zsa, how far he had come, Elva and the auburn hair of the animal next to himon the train.

389

~ Sunrise Descending ~

His nap felt like it lasted only a few minutes, enough to recharge the batteries. He awoke and sat up. It had actually been almost an hour but felt much shorter. His eyes came into focus and he saw the touch screen with the symbols. Somehow he now had a sense of what they meant. There were indeed decade symbols and a progression of other symbols starting with the most simple and crescendoing into the most complex right before an update in the decade counter. This was happening in reverse of course but now it made sense.

"Majel?"

"Yes?"

"I am guessing that we have about 30 minutes left, is that correct?"

"Yes, 28 minutes, 31 seconds to be exact."

Stephen looked to his right to see that the 'dogzee' was asleep as well. Then he realized that there was another sensation that he needed to take care of and this might be more complex, as an alien bathroom might require some unusual techniques.

"Majel?"

"Where is the bathroom?"

"Forward, 23 meters, then to your left."

"Okay, why don't you come with me?"

~ Sunrise Descending ~

"I have no choice."

Impressed by her sense of humor, Stephen rose and made his way forward to a door that had symbols at eye level. On the right side was a similar door with symbols as well, but different. Intuitively he chose the left side based on how male and female of multiple species was represented. Was there a universal difference?

He went in and found one other life form inside working a machine to either begin or finish the process.....

He continued to a place in the small room that had a receptacle for fluids and began to urinate.

The other life form started to make noises, some sounding unpleasant. It continued to gesticulate and squeak.

"Majel?"

"Yes?"

"Can you translate?"

"He says you are urinating in a sink and thinks you are disgusting."

"Yeah, well, tell him in our world its a sign of respect."

"I don't think I will do that."

"Okay, and here I thought you had a sense of humor."

"Not in this case."

Stephen finished his business and giving the life form one final look, realized that he could not figure out a way to wash his hands without more probable embarrassment. He wiped his hands on his pants and walked toward the door. The creature was still squeaking and squawking when he left.

"Unpleasant fellow, don't you think Majel?"

"Well, the train conductor has to keep up his appearances."

Stephen realized that it was now time to keep quiet and learn more than he taught. He worked his way back to his seat, found his composure and sat down. The 'dogzee' was still asleep but stirring.

Then the sensation of the vector of gravity changed from the floor and moved to the forward part of the train, they were decelerating. Dogzee woke up with the change. It looked over to him and focused her eyes, licked her lips and started panting. Stephen smiled at this, thinking about the dogs from Earth and how they became the best friends of so many millions of people. Now there was a sentient, communicative one near him that was probably the epitome of the hopes and delusions of so many back home.

"Good morning."

"And to you as well. We are getting near your stop."

"Yes, indeed. It was nice talking to you. I really hope we will meet again."

"We will, later this evening, at the Arboretum. I will contact you through your communications device."

"Good. I look forward to it."

The train had continued a constant deceleration for several minutes and now the world outside was starting to slow to a comfortable slew. Stephen watched outside until the view came to a standstill. He rose, smiled at Dogzee and made his way to an opening door. The life form from the bathroom was at the door, making sure that the passengers were exiting safely, when it realized that Stephen was there, it started to squeak and flair its appendages. Stephen saluted and said:

"Nice landing, Captain."

The creature was still upset about something as Stephen exited and made his way from the train. Within minutes the train had new passengers and the doors started to close, Stephen looked in the direction of Dogzee and saw that it was motioning one of its paws in the window. Stephen reciprocated by waving. The train then started to silently move forward, then glided out of sight at an every increasing speed. What remained was a quiet sensation of non motion. The aromas in the air were sweet as well. There were several distinct olfactory sensations, like cinnamon and roses. Looking around Stephen found the most plausible direction to walk, as it led to a vegetated area with a path. What he saw was grass like plants progressing to shrubs, progressing to Aspen type trees progressing to a deep forest in the distant. It looked inviting and the path looked clean and well maintained. It seemed to be made of concrete but with a slightly spongy feeling as he walked. The ambient light started to diminish as he passed about 100 meters of walking. At some point it felt like the Muir woods in California, on Earth, dim, quiet, with ferns and a canopy. It was very comfortable, so he continued down the path. At some point he realized that he was alone, except for the plant life, which was extraordinary and probably contained insects that lived within these plants. The flowers were stunning, with (as usual) colors that could not be replicated artificially. They were different shapes and styles of course but had the same attraction to the eye, living art. He walked further, maybe another 200 meters and the light became even more dim but still comfortable. Something here was different in this part of the woods. There was a slightly different timber in the air, a faint movement of sound. The smells were different as well and had progressed to those secret smells like endorphins which had chemical and electrical attractions few knew about until it was too late. He slowed his progression into the midst. There seemed to be a subtle fog forming as well, clearly a magical place now. It would be inappropriate to rush through this space. Looking about he was still comfortable and impressed by the beauty. There was something else though, something both observable and not. He slowed yet again to drink it in. At some point he unconsciously stopped and slowly looked around. What he realized then was not frightening but at a low level, mesmerizing. The flowers and some leaves had moved to follow his movement. To verify this Stephen took several steps backwards to observe their motion. They moved their gaze and followed him. He thought now about the science that could make this possible and then beyond the science to the reason. They were attracted, but at what level? Assuming it was just involuntary action, Stephen felt compelled to continue on.

The next level of "plant-telligence" was just as interesting. Now the motions were like the recognition of someone coming into a room. The organisms were occupied by other thoughts, then interrupted. They now moved in clumps to examine the newcomer. He was progressively getting to the more intelligent of the group. Enthralled, he moved yet further.

Now he found an area of sentient plants that only sometimes recognized his existence. They were engaged in discussions more important.

The continuum was obvious; perhaps the next level was total self absorption, solving the riddles of the Universe as it were, in their spheres of omniscience. He stopped, retraced a bit to attempt to communicate with the partially interested.

"Majel?"

"Yes?"

"Can you communicate with this plant life?"

"No, but you can."

"How?"

"Find a place to sit down and relax amongst this group. Soon you will hear the sounds and voices of those present."

"Okay."

Stephen moved over to an area where there was a rock wall that looked comfortable. He sat down, took a deep breath and looked around at those plants who had tracked his movement."

~ *Sunrise Descending* ~

"Hello," he said to one particularly attractive plant.

Silence.

He took in another breath, closed his eyes for a moment and thought about Zen.

He soon heard something like the fusion of a hum and a hiss. He remained motionless as to not disturb the experience. The hum faded, the hiss remained, a tone appeared. The tone moved about until it reached a pleasant frequency, 440 Hz or A on the piano keyboard. The tone stopped there and then diminished in amplitude, as did the hiss. Then chords revealed themselves out of the background, some atonal and some just right. The nice chords remained for a moment longer then progressed to musical patterns based on the harmonious chords. The periodic and melodic that resolved themselves into themes remained again for a bit. The themes evolved into portraits. During this time Stephen's eyes were still closed but now he was smiling. The plants knew this and continued to explore the resonant parts of Stephen's mind.

Eyes still closed, he now saw or imagined fields of daisies, rolling hills of clover, grass so comfortable on his toes that they involuntarily move within his shoes. He smiled still.

Now the sound of wind in the trees and across the prairies of wheat. He felt warmth on his face from a sun, contentment in his nostrils and images of beauty in his mind. It was a dream now, perfect in every detail and certainly one he did not want to interrupt.

Then he became conscious of himself and not lost in the sensations. He turned (in his dream) to his left to see a person. A person of beauty and intelligence. She spoke to him.

"Hello, I am Kallone. My sisters are Fate and Birth and I am Beauty. You come to me as this...

This thing, pregnancy and bringing to birth, which is divine, and it is immortal in the animal that is mortal. It is impossible for this to happen in the unfitting; The ugly is unfitting with everything divine, but the beautiful is fitting."

"I'm not sure who you are and what you are saying," stumbled Stephen.

"They know who you are and welcome you to their village," a voice behind Stephen said.

Stephen turned, opened his eyes to finally focus on the Dogzee.

"I thought you were going to contact me with my communications device?"

"I tried, but you were preoccupied, Majel told me that you were in kinda of a trance, so I thought I would hurry over to make sure you were okay."

"I appreciate that, the plants were speaking to me, I don't think I was aware of anything else."

"You weren't, I have been here for a few minutes."

"Well thank you, it looks like I have a friend."

"Indeed, my name is Thanadonous, Empress of the Southern Quarters."

"Stephen, Stephen Daedalus, time traveler."

"Hmmmm, time traveler, sounds like you have an interesting story."

"I do in fact. Actually to be honest, I don't normally tell people of my condition so quickly, I hope it does not offend you."

"Of course not, Stephen. Do you call yourself a time traveler because you have lived for a very long time or that you can transport back and forth in time?"

"Oh, I have lived for a very long time, Thanadonous. I have lived beyond wives, children, grandchildren and many many friends."

"Well I envy you, you will learn so much in your travels. How old are you?"

"Many hundreds of years, many...in fact possibly a thousand by now. I have lost track as it doesn't seem to be important. I don't know about envy, there are drawbacks as well as interesting things if you are immortal."

"Many creatures are, in fact the more advanced a culture gets the more probable it is that they learn how to extend their lives, ultimately into immortality."

"How many have you met?"

"Dozens, quite a few in fact. Some just like you, humanoid."

"I have heard vague hints that there are others like me, I did live with a group of immortals, the Nereids, for a while. I will return to them after my wanderings. The people I am interested in are like me changed by a medical procedure, not born an immortal."

"I have met many that have been changed."

Meanwhile, the plants around Stephen and Thanadonous were growing impatient waiting for either one of them to open their minds and eventually got back to chattering amongst themselves. To avoid further interruption, Stephen and Thanadonous walked back towards the entrance of the arboretum. They felt

400

comfortable with each other and Stephen needed someone to teach him the ropes about this world. They emerged from the walkway finally, turned left arbitrarily and continued to walk down the very large boulevard. They talked in generalities about where they were from and what they had done over the course of the last few years. Thanadonous walked on all fours and her tail reminded Stephen of a cat's tail or monkey's tail much more than a dog, which the rest of her body looked like. The tail twitched and sometime touched or wrapped itself around a tree trunk or post as they walked. Stephen had the urge a few times to pet Thanadonous but held back thinking it might be rude. He also realized that she could probably take off and run very quickly if she wanted. She was build like a large greyhound dog, at least a meter tall at the haunches. The gait was similar as well. Thanadonous was like a dog lover's dream, intelligent, communicative and friendly.

"Your pretty cool," he said inadvertently.

"Thank you, I like you as well."

"Are you hungry? Is there a place we can get something to eat?"

"Sure, they're everywhere. See the blue signs with the triangles?"

"Yes."

"That's where we can eat, the triangle symbolizes a tooth, which most animals have."

"Okay, lets go, I am famished."

They went inside the restaurant and found seats compatible with both of them. She had a place to put her front paws and a place for her tail. She looked comfortable and instantly started poking buttons on the table to view the menu. He looked confusedly at the buttons, then finally:

"Majel?"

"Yes?"

"What should I order?"

"Press buttons 2,2 then 5 on the left side. Press the blue button on the right side."

He proceeded to follow her suggestions, then paused.

"Majel, what did I just order?"

"A steak and a beer."

"Good suggestion, but how did you know I wanted that?"

"I have recorded your diet on the voyage and noticed that you are fond of this combination."

"Will Thanadonous try and eat this?"

He looked over at her to see if she was listening. She gave him gesture that required both her paws, he guessed at what it meant.

Within minutes a robot appeared with the food they had ordered. His was pretty hot, temperature wise, and hers looked more medium in temperature. She went straight for it and using a paw to hold it down, started pulling meat off of the bone, but in a dainty way. A pan of water was presented to her to drink from and she moved back and forth from the meat to the water. At some point, she realized he was looking at her and stopped.

"What's the matter?"

"Oh, nothing, sorry, its just that on Earth, creatures like you tend to eat from bowls on the floor."

"How barbaric."

"Oh, absolutely."

Stephen came back into focus and found the utensils adequate for eating his steak. It actually was very good and perfectly cooked.

"I like you," she said, "we eat the same food but too bad your not of my species."

"Feelings are mutual, Thanadonous."

They went back to their food and finished quickly. Stephen fell into the pace of eating at the same rate as her, which was brisk. Soon they were finished and sat back to relax for a bit.

"Where do you want to go next?"

"I really don't care; its all pretty amazing. I can only stay for a few days before I have to get back to the ship and continue my travels. Before I go however, I would like to see the observatories."

"Okay, there's plenty to see and the observatories are the best in this quadrant. Most astronomers from the neighboring star systems come here to work with the instruments."

"What can you tell me about them?"

"Well, not much, except that they are the biggest and most sensitive around. For instance the largest optical telescope is a good portion of this space station's length."

"But that is many, many miles."

"That's correct and the other telescopes, for instance the radio telescopes are just as large, with orbiting counterparts to make synthetic apertures that are the size of the orbit we are in around this star. The data that these instruments detect, streams in so fast, that our largest computers, the size of buildings, can only show a small portion of sky at any moment. The rest has to be mined and sometimes that takes a very long time."

"Wow, the things that they must have discovered!"

"Indeed.   The things that they do not know they discovered."

"I wonder if they can see my planet from here."

"They can see minute surface details of thousands of planets."

"Amazing, but on our way in I did not see any large curved surfaces to gather and focus the light."

"That's old technology.   These days, they use Shoemarkian arrays.   They receive energy from all angles and the post-processing creates the images."

"Excellent, when can we see them?"

"Tomorrow, I am getting tired, especially after that meal. So I will take you to a hotel and pick you up in the morning."

"Morning? How do you know its morning?"

"Well, as you will find out when we leave here, they dim the light sources to simulate the evening, then they will increase the light levels to create morning."

"Makes sense."

They rose to leave, Stephen hesitated for a moment and realized that he had not been exercising a common practice.

"How do we pay?"

"A very long time ago, advanced cultures realized that a monetary transaction was not necessary and ultimately a bad idea. It only allows the more base instincts of life forms to emerge, like greed and selfishness. It turned out that life forms in general after a distinct point of intelligence will contribute on their own terms in their own way to promulgating their species. In this way they are considered to be working. For instance, with no other constraints, what would you do?"

"I suppose that I would contribute to the science of astronomy."

"And would you simply find an observatory, find the task that you could contribute most to and start?"

"Yes, I suppose, if they needed me."

"Those needs you speak of used to be associated with whether or not they had the money to support your work, didn't they?

"Yes, in fact."

"So places like observatories could not let as many people in to their laboratories as were willing to work on their tasks, right?"

"Thats correct."

"So they missed out on many talented contributors to their science because of money."

"Yes, thats true."

"Well, that kind of behavior is passe."

"What if you want a large house and fancy car?"

"It turns out that societies had programmed their offspring to see these objects as attractive, in a way that promoted their self image. This again is a waste of time and energy. The same people who thought they needed a large house found out they for instance really wanted to build trains or write books. The stress levels for people who were driven by goals manufactured by others went down by such a significant amount that they literally doubled their life spans. Now the sciences, medicine and the arts are very well supported with happy people. For that the resources like food and shelter are provided without cost."

"What about jobs people do not want to perform?"

"Robots and androids take care of these tasks. Advanced life forms would rather design and test machines than perform menial tasks. It was discovered that the life forms that used to perform these tasks were way too intelligent and over qualified, thus not contributing properly to society. And by the way, the amount of crime and bad behavior all but disappeared as the stress of everyday life was eliminated."

"And those that were simply lazy?"

"The lazy started to slowly diminish in numbers as they found that they were actually bored and stressed. They soon found things they liked to do with like minded life forms to do them with."

"Sounds like the normal course of progress."

"It solved an enormous amount of problems. In fact for many cultures and societies it allowed them to flourish into what they were really capable of doing. The amount of contributions to knowledge and general happiness was immeasurable after the change."

"What about education?"

"What happened was of course, education was without cost and as a consequence, those who were interested, curious and capable, went as far as they wanted. This without the concerns of paying, just with the passion to learn. The amount of educated people went up a thousand fold and as a result a much better world was created. One that you are now standing in."

They continued to walk out of the restaurant and down the boulevard to a place like a hotel for Stephen. They walked in and found a large eyed nocturnal animal waiting for them. Thanadonous made the arrangements and Stephen was given a room for the night. He smiled at his new friend.

~ Sunrise Descending ~

"Thanks for a great day and evening, Thanadonous."

"My pleasure, I enjoyed it as well, see you tomorrow."

"Tomorrow then."

He followed the large eyed creature to a room. The creature stopped, extended one of its many appendages towards the door, turned and left. Stephen went in to find what he only describe as a universal living quarters. There was a bed, a mat on the floor and complicated looking bathroom, a balcony and a variety of chairs. He walked over to the balcony and looked out from above, down to the boulevard. There was a minimum of activity, the trains went by less frequently. He wondered if life in general existed in light and dark cycles and if intelligence itself needs a break in the form of sleep. It was quiet and cool. He smiled at his situation here on a foreign world, with a new foreign friend and looking down at his wrist, with a foreign guardian. It all felt quite good to him.

He went back inside from the balcony to find a view screen on the wall and soon found the control unit to activate. Was this, the portal to information, also universal? He messed and fooled with the controls until the screen became active. A ubiquitous up and down arrow allowed him to surf the channels. There was an enormous variety of programs showing a multitude of life forms engaged in activities like sports, news and weather. How could there be weather on a mechanical outpost? Well, they had it to keep the plant intelligence happy. There were also channels with variety shows and various forms of acting. Was acting universal as well?

Feeling tired and drained from the "day," Stephen went the bathroom to contemplate what to do in what vessel. He stopped for a moment.

"Majel?"

"Yes?"

"Which one is the sink?"

"The round one to the left."

"Thanks."

He washed his face, hopefully in water... and brushed his teeth, hopefully with tooth paste. Majel did not stop him as he chose the best candidates for the tools to get ready for sleep.

"Majel?"

"Yes?"

"What do you think of Thanadonous?"

"She is a good friend and will take care of you while you explore this outpost."

"I like her as well, I get the feeling that she would like me to be a part of her pack."

"You are perceptive, because that's true. There is comfort and protection by being part of a pack."

"I will do what I can, but I...we are only here a few days."

"True, but now you know about this place."

"I like it here."

"I know. There are lots of places you will like during our trip."

"Okay, Majel, I am tired and going to sleep, talk to you tomorrow."

"Good night."

More Life to Discover

In order to really enjoy a dog, one doesn't merely try to train him to be semi-human. The point of it is to open oneself to the possibility of becoming partly a dog. - Edward Hoagland

      The next morning he awoke to find Thanadonous and five other 'Dogzees' curled up on the floor sleeping. He wondered how they got in and why they were there. He realized within a few seconds that the conversation with Majel last night about being part of the pack was coming true. He was part of the pack. As he tried to be quiet and sit up, Thanadonous and one of the others stirred, raised their heads and looked at him.

"Good morning, Stephen."

"Good morning, I didn't hear you come in last night, but its nice to see you again."

"They have special doors for us you know. We did not make any plans last night so I invited my pack to sleep here and get to know you."

"Okay, that works."

The rest of the Dogzees started to rise and stretch. Some started to come over to sniff Stephen and make themselves available for conversation. He looked at one in particular.

"Hello, I'm Stephen. How are you?"

"I'm fine, my name is Horus, son of Thanadonous. These are my friends and family."

The others were now walking about and appeared anxious to go out.

"Would you all like to go outside?"

"Yes, quickly, answered Horus."

By now everyone was up and moving about lining up near the humanoid door. Stephen opened it and they filed out, for some reason, Stephen thought about cattle at a stock yard as he watched them leave. Smiling he closed the door behind him and followed them outside, as they certainly new more about the area than he did. He caught up to Thanadonous.

"Where are we going?"

"For relief then breakfast, at the park, there will be food for you and I think you will find the sites interesting."

"Okay, sounds fine."

They walked down the boulevard for about a mile, or so it seemed, to find a park, complete with trees, grass and flowers. They were all much different than what what he was used to on Earth. He was getting used to differences in the Universe. He again realized the impact of different environments on life. Universally, life came out of simple organisms that followed the ability of the indigenous environment to nurture them. One thing, so to speak, lead to another, and plants and animals evolved to higher forms right up to the point of high intelligence and sentience. Then there seems to be an explosion of creativity and the will to explore. What happens after that takes on many forms, interestingly. Some cultures gravitate towards the

414

silicon solutions, some find that the more simpler forms of living are more attractive. The ultimate in silicon or computer based evolutions end up, for the most part, as hybrids of both. With the advantages and disadvantages of both. Stephen was going to find out what life evolves into after many billions of more years of evolution.

For now, the air was crisp, the company friendly and Majel was quiet.

"Hmmm....Majel?"

"Yes?"

"Good morning."

"Good morning to you as well. I chose not to wake you when they came in, they just wanted to sleep."

"No problem. I think we are going to breakfast then who knows...do you have any suggestions?"

"Ride the train."

"Okay, shall do. Any particular direction?"

"Just farther down the same line you took before, you will find it very interesting."

"So far its been amazing, even met some cool....life forms."

"There are plenty more, this outpost is the crossroads of hundreds of different species."

"Can you communicate with most of them?"

415

"Yes."

"Then I will let you come with me."

"You have no choice."

"Hmmm, and I thought you didn't have a sense of humor."

Stephen continued walking with the Dogzees; they sometimes walked together and sometimes walked individually to something that smelled interesting or looked interesting. They also would look at each other periodically, like they were having non verbal communications. He felt comfortable and safe in their midst. Presently they found a park with what probably was a variety of restaurants, some at humanoid levels and some lower. They of course went to the lower levels and ordered their favorite foods. Stephen went to a co-located upper restaurant and attempted to read the menu.

"Majel?"

"Yes?"

"Can you scan the menu and recommend something for me?"

"Yes, order number 4 and number 12."

"Okay."

He did so to the attendant, then turned to see the Dogzees enjoying their food silently but close together.

Every once in a while, Thanadonous looked his way. He smiled back at her.

Within a minute, his food was ready, it appeared to be an omelet and some tea.

"Majel, is this what it appears to be?"

"Yes, you will like it."

"Thank you, Majel."

He took a tentative taste and found it very good, the tea was satisfying as well. In another minute, he was mimicking the Dogzees.

Minutes after that, they had all finished, Thanadonous walked over to him.

"Done?"

"Yes, that was great, where to now?"

"To the park, where we can rest a bit and observe the natives," she said with what was a movement of her upper lip, something like a smile.

"I'm all for watching the natives, lead on."

They walked across the boulevard to an open area in the sunlight. The Dogzees were a bit sluggish in their gait as they made the trip. Thanadonous walked beside Stephen and lead him to a place where he could sit. The others found places in the sun and on the grass, they circled before they made their final decisions on where to lie.   Stephen sat down with the sun behind him and the boulevard in front of him, he relaxed, as did the others. Soon many of them were asleep,   Thanadonous had lowered her eyelids a bit and looked like she would drop any second.

"I'm tired, need a rest for a bit, wake me if you need anything."

"Shall do, have a nice nap."

For the next fifteen minutes Stephen viewed the people, creatures and droids that populated this area of the outpost. He was now blasé about seeing other life forms due to his recent experiences. He thought about how people on the two planets he had lived on, who had not experienced this kind of travel, would recoil at some the varieties of life this Universe had to offer. He thought about their cultures, religions and lives in general and considered how they were similar in many ways. This gave him comfort in a way, as it minimized the stress of the unknown as he interacted with others. The big test of his theory would come when they visited the population II stars in the next several weeks.

After their brief nap, the others stirred, eventually Thanadonous rose and greeted Stephen.

"Ah, I feel better now."

"Good, what do you generally do during the day?"

"Wander around, travel, meet people, eat, sleep," she said while scratching behind her ear with her hind leg.

"That covers a lot of ground."

"Yeah, in general we are wanderers, some of us have traveled in space and some were born here. There is certainly enough to experience here."

"Seems like it."

"What do you want to do?"

"I think I will board the train again in the same direction and explore this world some more. Will I be able to get a hold of you again?"

"Of course, your communicator knows how. We will all be here for a while, call me when you get a chance."

"Okay, I will. For now, thank you for your guidance and friendship. Hopefully I will see you soon."

"Bye then, for now."

Stephen smiled and waved to the others, then walked in the general direction of another train stop. This took a few minutes, during which time he reflected on his morning. He felt that he enjoyed this kind of life and how his condition (immortality) gave him the opportunity for these experiences.

The train station was located and he queued up again for a trip to who knows where? The familiar count down symbols were present and he started to feel at home.

"Majel?"

"Yes?"

"Is that train conductor going to be on the next train?"

"The one you were talking too? Your friend?"

"Sort of."

"No."

"Where is the next train taking us to?"

"To the Science Quadrant, where the observatories are located."

"Perfect, I've been looking forward to seeing them."

"The train will be here momentarily, we will take it to the ninth stop."

"Okay, that works."

The train did indeed come soon, Stephen boarded and smiled at the conductor, who was of the same species as the last one he met. Turning left he again walked into a sitting area where multiple species were present, this time many of them were different than the last train ride. Again, he found a window seat and waited for the doors to close and the silent acceleration to begin. He was not disappointed as the train gained speed quickly, the numbers on the display panel in front of him, now familiar, counted down to the next stop which by his estimate, was about thirty minutes away. He felt comfortable enough to close his eyes for a quick nap. Assuming he would come back this way, he knew he wouldn't miss anything. Twenty minutes later his eyes opened. After clearing his head he looked over to his right and observed a life form watching him.

"How you doin'?"

"Squcrantx flit mitss fa."

"Majel, can you translate?"

"He says your not from here."

"Tell him he is right then ask him is he lives here."

"Yuplok dis waan. Wit mil pip buyt?"

Majel then turned on the real time translator.

"Yes, this is my home and I work here. Where are you from?"

"Earth, for the most part, although I have lived on other planets."

"I know earth, its visible in our telescopes."

"Do you work at the observatories?"

"Yes, as an astronomer."

"Can I get a tour and see your equipment?"

"Of course. Just get off when I do and we can sign you in for the day."

"Thanks, that would be perfect."

They continued in silence for the rest of the trip. Stephen viewed the landscapes whizzing by. The astronomer was reading from an information tablet. Stephen thought again about how some things were the same around the Universe where life forms started to bring things along with them at some point in their development, to aid in communications or to record.

There were a few stops before the observatories where Stephen did what most creatures do, watch the new things get on board and the new things leave. For the first time, he was cognizant of smells and textures, which were plentiful. There were also sounds from the movement of the life forms that was different. With a bit of random thinking, Stephen wondered about ethno-centrism in the Universe. Was it a standard practice to want to be the same as some groups and notice differences in others as a result? Probably. On Earth he had witnessed religious groups practicing this, ethnic groups as well. He guessed it was an inherent social protective attribute that came from the very distant past. It certainly, in this modern setting, had no place. To put it another way, those who continued the practice found themselves isolated from more progressive races of beings who were more apt to discover the wonders of the Universe.

The stop for the observatories soon came, Stephen came back into focus from his thoughts and the creature to his right was motioning to him to follow. They both rose, Stephen followed and the astronomer thing walked out the hatch to the promenade. Once away from the train and once it had departed, Stephen got to look around at the buildings or probably more accurately, the devices that surrounded him.

"These are some of the observatories we have, there are many around this outpost but this area is where we collect and disseminate the data from our instruments."

"Looks very.....substantial."

"It is, in fact it is the premier observational center in this area of the Milky Way. Observers travel for very long periods of time to use these instruments. The telescopes here are capable of mapping planets in nearby galaxies. The computational power is growing so fast there are only estimates as to its capabilities. All of the primary telescopes feed their raw data into these massive computers which measure thousands of parameters over very small time periods to very large. The amount of data from even one instrument exceeds that of entire advanced world. I am going to take you to one of the visitor stations were images at all wavelengths are available for your perusal."

"The ship I came in had similar capabilities, however I don't think it was capable of looking at extra-galactic planets."

"No, of course not. However the data from these types of space vehicles is down loaded into the main computers. In this way we can create a fully three dimensional image library of the stars in this portion of the galaxy."

"Impressive."

"Indeed, especially when you get introduced to the fine details of the data, this is truly a discovery machine."

They walked across the boulevard into what appeared to be a cathedral like entrance, somewhat gothic in appearance. The ceilings were at least a hundred feet tall, hallways inside fanned out at even angles and appeared to go to infinity due to their incredible length. Moving walkways were everywhere, many with tables and chairs for comfort. Stephen and his new friend moved toward the second hallway on the left and stepped onto the moving sidewalk. They then walked over to a place to sit. What caught Stephen by surprise was the fact that somehow, the sidewalk started slowly but increased in speed as they moved toward a distant intersection.

"We need to get off at the next stop" said the astronomer.

Stephen nodded in response.

Soon, the movement of the sidewalk started to slow, the astronomer stood, Stephen followed him as he walked off of the conveyor into another hallway which also had high ceilings, though only about fifty feet this time. There were periodic entrance doorways spaced about fifty feet or so from each other and they ended up walking down to the third one on the left. The astronomer placed his hand/appendage on a flat pad near the door and silently an opening into a dimly lit interior appeared. They walked into a large spherical room with deep black walls. In the center was a circular pad and control station. They moved to this point and stopped in front of the station.

"This is where you enter the coordinates and measurement criteria. This panel is for entering the three dimensional positional data, this panel for the area of the electromagnetic spectrum you want. This panel over here is for applying the filters and algorithms you wish. This last panel here is for recording data. Everything you do here is confidential, however you may observe secret communications on other worlds, you may not transfer them to a recording device or tell anyone else of your findings. To do so will get you expelled from this facility. Do you agree to these terms?"

"I do."

"Lets start with something simple then."

The astronomer pushed some buttons, the opening they came in disappeared. The lights started to dim. Soon there were points of light discernible and suspended in the room, like a holographic projection. The points looked like stars in a planetarium but were placed in three dimensions. Stephen was surrounded by them, some but a few feet away and others fifty. As their eyes acclimated the stars became more focused, with different colors and many with (now visible) planetary systems. The astronomer moved some controls that looked like spheres mounted in a central area relative to the control panel. One particular star system was covered in a rose colored dimly translucent sphere, a button was pushed and it seemed that the room flew itself to that star systems and got very close to it. What they now saw was the star as a ten inch yellow orb complete with sunspots, flares and a mottled surface. The planets were in a plane surrounding the star and comets, asteroids, moons and space debris could been seen. The astronomer then placed another rose colored sphere around one of the planets and with another touch of a button they flew to this particular world. What was seen quickly was that the world had a small ocean (or a very large lake) an atmosphere, and what appeared to be contrails, or signs of advanced life. The image stopped here for a few moments before the astronomer "flew" the image towards a seashore and paused at what appeared to be a thousand feet in the air. The astronomer moved to his right and adjusted the frequency selector to choose light, radio, infrared, ultraviolet and electrical activity in the image. As he scrolled through the bands of energy, different constructs could be observed.

"As you can see," the astronomer started, "there is life on this planet, and has been there for some time. Notice the radio signatures that show that on this seashore, long ago there was an ancient village, where the post holes of their primitive homes left imprints in the dirt. There are also artifacts that lay undiscovered below the surface around one meter deep. Notice to the right, near the water line, that there are traces of pollutants from the burning of fossil fuels and even some traces of radio active material. The water, as you see, has simple organisms that have adapted to the inclusion of pollution. There is an overabundance of phosphorus, potassium and nitrogen, which are all fertilizers. Therefore the plant like ocean life, much like your algae, has thrived and probably driven out more indigenous life forms. As a result of these observations we can place this civilization in a standard historical hierarchy."

"Thats very impressive, very impressive. I have a question. To do this it seems that you have captured every photon at every energy level. Is that correct?"

"That is exactly correct and we can do this for most of the galaxy."

"Why leave home?"

"Indeed."

"Can you show me Earth?"

"Yes, of course. Now remember that in all of these images, due to the speed of light or more precisely the speed of photons in the electromagnetic spectrum, the farther away you look, the farther back in time you see."

"Yes, I know, that is universal."

"It is to a degree. The computers here are capable of using quantum prediction algorithms to give a more up to date quasi image, based on confidence limits. This for instance means that we can see this world as it is today to a

72% probability, based on its distance from here. Sometimes this is useful information."

The astronomer now focused his attention on the images of Earth, which were many, many light years away. The "holoterium" flew to Earth's solar system and paused for Stephen to re-familiarize himself with the planets and the sun. It was easy to make out Jupiter and Saturn, and upon further examination the red planet Mars and the Blue Marble of Earth. After the pause the astronomer flew further in towards Earth and settled the image at about one hundred miles above the surface. The clouds, oceans and land masses could easily be seen.

"What area would you like to see in detail?"

"Virginia, USA."

The astronomer placed the verbal commands into the control console and the Earth image spun a bit, then it appeared that the viewpoint dove into the atmosphere, through the clouds and slowed just above the appropriate place where Washington, D.C. could be made visible.

"Slightly to the right, where the large river empties into the Chesapeake Bay, move to the left a bit, zoom in, okay do you see where three rivers converge to empty in the Potomac? Okay, now down the southern arm and around the bends to a marina. Zoom in some more. Okay thats it. And the marina is still there! A lot different than when I was there before, but that place brings back a lot of fond memories. I used to own a boat there, it was beautiful and idyllic. Can you do a spectral analysis?"

"Yes, of course."

They viewed different spectral bands, looking at carbon, oxygen, nitrogen, etc. The astronomer offered an opinion:

"It actually looks pretty clean, low pollution and oxygenated water. There are schools of fish, birds, land animals, jelly fish and a lot of boats. There is one boat there. See? It has a different signature, much more carbon content and based on the signature, it looks very old, maybe its made of wood. This would make it many hundreds of years old."

"You've got to be kidding, that could be my old boat. About eighteen meters long?"

"Yes, very close to that, based on where it is tied up, it could be a museum."

"It would have to be, it was owned by some famous people in Earth's history; a Tuskegee Airman for one."

"And you for another?" The astronomer looked at Stephen when he said this and his inflections implied a smile.

430

"I'm not that famous, unless they found out about my physical attributes."

"You look like them, I don't understand."

"I do in fact, however I have lived for many hundreds of years, unlike normal Earthlings."

"I see, that's quite an advantage."

"In most ways, yes. The problem is that most species die in two hundred or fewer Earth years. I have outlived them all, including my family, and their families. You see my point?"

"Of course, but I have met someone like you, from Earth. She was traveling through just like you."

"I've heard there could be another, do you know where she went?"

"No, she was here a while back but did not stay very long."

"And you think she was like me in the sense of being very old?"

"Yes."

"Hmmm, okay."

The astronomer went back to face his control board and asked:

"Would you like to see anything else?"

~ Sunrise Descending ~

"Yes, in fact....show me a star field with some population II stars."

"Typically, that means a globular cluster, of which there are several."

"Okay, please show me the nearest one."

The astronomer "flew" out of the Earth's solar system and past the outpost to a globular cluster that appeared to be hovering over one the arms of the Milky Way. The destination was M15, a large cluster in the Pegasus system. It was made up of thousands of stars, mostly very old and metal poor. Globular clusters are unique in the sense of that they tend to be outside of the Milky Way disk, have very old stars and have very bright stars. There are cases where the stars in M15 are at least one thousand times brighter than the Earth's sun. Majel's counterparts would venture out to M15 to visit these stars, as they had the most advanced civilizations ever encountered by space faring life.

As the image in the holorarium got closer Stephen could make out the spherical extents of the cluster, perfectly uniform with star density increasing as it got closer to the center. The stars were also of many colors, like jewels, some bright red, some white, some blue.

"Majel?"

"Yes?"

"Can you designate the star in M15 we are going to visit?"

"Yes, its near Kuestner 648, a planetary nebula, we call it M15K64812042918."

Stephen asked the astronomer, "can you locate that particular star."

"Of course."

The image view point swam about in the cluster which now encompassed the entire viewing room. They moved left and right, up and down and finally, particular star was centered and zoomed in on. There was an awe inspiring planetary nebula, shaped a bit like an hour glass on its side, where a star had blown its poles off during its final death throes. The colors from this nebula covered the entire visual spectrum and comprised wisps and tendrils of tenuous gases ever expanding from the scene of the initial explosion.

They flew closer to the star of interest and as they closed in they noticed that the planets of the star system, of which were variegated in color and of significant differences in size, were all in one orbit around the large sun.

"Wow, look at that!"

433

"This is one way we can detect old and advanced civilizations. They have found the solution to placing all of the planets in one orbit to stabilize them and provide for their large populations. If you observe closely, the larger planets are in opposition, the smaller ones are placed in such a way as to balance the circularity of the orbit.."

"What about the difference in colors?"

"Well, just like your solar system, some planets have more water, like your Earth. Some have oxidized, like your Mars. Some have thicker atmospheres, like your Venus and Jupiter. They are all populated with a wide variety of life forms. Many times the simpler forms all exist on just a few planets to allow for their natural evolution. The threat of extinction is much too high on the planets with the higher life forms. It is typical to have one planet be the central governing location for the whole solar system. Trade routes exist between all of the planets as you can see here."

He zoomed in a bit further to reveal a faint silver ribbon of spacecraft moving between each planet. Some more dense than others.

"We're going there, Majel?"

"Yes, to the blue planet, where the most advanced cultures exist."

"I am looking forward to it."

"Is there anything else you would like to see?" The astronomer asked.

"No, this has been fantastic, thank you very much. I'm sure you are busy with your own research and I do appreciate you taking out time to show me these things."

"You are welcome, my name is Dax. I can be found here almost any time. Please return from your trip and let me know what you found."

"I will. Thank you again."

Preparations for the Long Trip

Love builds up the broken wall
and straightens the crooked path.
Love keeps the stars in the firmament
and imposes rhythm on the ocean tides
each of us is created of it
and I suspect
each of us was created for it.
- Maya Angelou

~ *Sunrise Descending* ~

"Majel?"

"Yes?"

"Please direct me to a place where I can relax and watch the sights, I have to assimilate what I have seen."

"What setting would you like?"

"Do they have an ocean or large body of water on this outpost?"

"Yes."

"Lets try that."

"Go back to the train station."

"Okay."

Stephen smiled at the astronomer as he left, the light increased in brightness enough for him to see himself to the floor and walk safely. His mind was filled with the images he had just witnessed. It was interesting that the observatory had recorded so many photons for so long it had a very clear picture of the activities of most worlds in the Milky Way. The only real difference was the issue of time, where the farther they looked, the farther they looked back in time. The computers could, based on knowledge from other measurements, extrapolate what was probably happening on these many worlds now but with varying degrees of accuracy, based again on how far they were trying to observe.

There was however a common path for life, a common theme. The more examples of life one witnessed and observed the more certain tenants or rules made themselves obvious.

The first was self preservation, no matter what or how a life form would do to survive. This would be through adaptation or in other worlds, evolution. The fit would survive, change would occur to keep fit.

The second was curiosity, this applied to life forms with brains.

The third was based on the consequences of having a brain, which then became self aware, which then created an evolutionary trail of thought. This parallel line of life, much like a continuous series of mirrors over the ages, allowed the sentient beings to use the intellectual work of those in the past to forge ahead in the future. In other words, those that did not ignore the past did not repeat the same mistakes. This law was called creation.

Stephen followed Majel's prompts and made his way to a particular train, then after entering, he made his way to his favorite spot, on the left side, sat down and looked down to see the familiar symbols counting down to the next stop. Other smaller symbols on the display, he now realized, referred to the upcoming stops.

~ Sunrise Descending ~

"How far are we going, Majel?"

"We will travel for about one of your hours, get some rest if you would like."

"I think I shall, Majel, thank you."

He moved about to get comfortable in his seat, looked around at another bevy of creatures and closed his eyes for a few minutes. While blacked out he dreamt of the images of the new world suspended in air. He viewed the thin silver ribbons and his mind's eye flew amongst the planets and around the orbit. He had Thanadonous with him, she did the flying as well. Once he arrived, in his dreams, to the blue planet, he saw Zsa, Jack, Elva and the Nereids. It was full circle, the farther he traveled the closer he got to home.

Then there was a period of darkness from which he awoke some time later. Coming to life he pondered his dreams and considered the dark period. He wondered why minds are so active when we sleep? In fact, why do we and most all creatures in the Universe, have to sleep? People who are sedentary don't need it to replenish their sleep from a physical stand point. The mind needs to sleep, yet does not when the body is not mobile.

He cleared his mind, looked to his right to see what interesting creature had sat down on the other side of the aisle and saw none.

"Majel?"

"Yes?"

"There seems to be fewer life forms on the train today."

"There are fewer at the ends of the train lines, near the outside portion of the outpost where we are going, you will see the surrounding space from the viewing ports."

"Good, I have actually missed seeing space."

"Another thirty of your minutes and we will arrive."

Stephen turned to his left to look out of the train window, still silently whisking along. The rows and rows of tall buildings now gave way to lower structures and periodic peeks at great distances where what might be farm land and large open areas were present. The sunlight was brighter here, shadows cast were clear and defined.

"Majel?"

"Yes?"

"Did the train increase in velocity?"

"Yes, by ten fold as we got away from the large urban center."

"That explains how we have moved so far."

~ Sunrise Descending ~

Now, even greater plains could be made out. Wide swaths of sunlit vegetation, much like wheat, moved slowly back and forth under an unknown wind source.

The train now slowed in a very smooth fashion. Stephen smiled as he knew he could soon get up and walk around this amazing world again. Looking out the window he saw what he had asked for, the sparkling sea on a curved horizon. He thought of the sea shore and the beauty that awaited him.

The train slowed further and past the lower speed he had encountered while in the city. It slowed further still and within a minute came to a complete, silent standstill. He rose, made his way to the opening hatch but before he left he looked up and down the central aisle of the train to find it barely populated. This was certainly one of the last stops for this machine.

He stepped out into the sunshine and light breeze, reminiscent of the ocean areas of Earth. Did this mean that there were many similar places in the planets with large bodies of water? He hoped so.

Outside it was glorious, birds were about, all different than any he had ever seen but all flying or perching on the vegetation or watching him intently while standing on the ground. Was this a common life form as well?

~ Sunrise Descending ~

He moved away from the train, now experienced in the timing of stops to movement. Open areas were around him, some low lying structures, some paths and small roads. He looked for the sparkles of the not so distant water and followed the path that appeared to lead him in that direction.

The train started to slither silently away in reverse direction as this was the last stop on the line. Stephen carefully smelled the salt air and was a bit amazed that it in fact smelled "right." Water he knew was universal in space, it was on most planets, in all star systems, there were in fact large clouds of it suspended in the Milky Way. But salt water? He thought this was less prevalent but here he was standing near a foreign shore, billions of miles away from Earth and experiencing something very familiar. No matter, there was really only one thing to do....go down to the water and taste it.

He did exactly that and tentatively scooped up some briny fluid and dapped a finger into it to taste. It was in fact salty, which made him wonder if there were fish similar to Earth's out beyond the swells. His thinking stopped for a moment as he viewed the undulating water and the sparkles as they spread towards the horizon.

"Beautiful."

~ Sunrise Descending ~

He felt the urge to relax and looking around found a swelling of sand with some vegetation to sit on. Making himself comfortable there, he looked up to see and hear the sea, bright with the low roar of waves breaking sequentially down the beach. Life was good.

As he watched, daydreamed and reminisced about the experiences of the near past, he started to observe motions in the water. They appeared to be swellings as if a very large turtle was about the emerge from the surf. He continued to watch and became fascinated with the swellings and undulations. Presently the swelling gave way to a large head, much like a whale's, with eyes half a meter in diameter. It was looking directly at him, which felt a bit disconcerting. It simply stayed in the surf and watched, no blinking or moving about. At some point, Stephen's curiosity got the better of him and he rose to get a better look at the beast. He took a few tentative steps forward towards the water.

"I wouldn't do that if I were you."

Stephen turned abruptly to find Thanadonous and several of her friends behind him. A few of the dogzees were circling around to place themselves between the beast and Stephen.

"How did you get here?"

443

"You have a very distinctive smell, it was easy to track."

"What is that thing out in the water?"

"Not sure what the name is but it has a twenty meter tongue with lightning speed. Two more steps and you would have been dinner."

"Is it intelligent, does it communicate?"

"Nope."

"Well then, I am very glad you are here. How have you been?"

"Great, we had nothing to do today, so we decided to make a game of finding you. Now however we are hungry again, lets find something to eat."

"Fine with me, lead the way."

The Dogzees, somehow communicated to each other; it was time to move on and let the ocean beast find different prey. They gathered and walked down the water line, giving a wide birth to "big eyes" and aimed towards an outcropping of buildings. After a kilometer or so of walking they found themselves in a small village and walked down a simple road towards a restaurant. They entered. As they did the owner, which was somewhat humanoid, gave them a cross look and (through Majel's translator) said:

"We don't have places for them," referring to the Dogzees.

"Well, if you don't we will go elsewhere, I am with them."

"Last pack like that tore my place up."

"I wonder why?"

"Well, if you vouch for them, they can go over there, near the corner. I will bring some low tables and some pans for them to eat from."

"Thank you, that will do."

Thanadonous was silent throughout this exchange but Stephen knew she was smart enough to keep cool. If something got out of control, she and her pack would respond appropriately. They moved over to the appointed area and Stephen noticed that the larger of the animals sat down so they could view the surroundings, the movement of the owner and the door. Stephen also thought he detected a serious mood with the pack.

"Thanadonous, I am not sure I understood that interchange."

"Oh, I'm sure what that was about. He thinks that all life forms like us cause problems."

"That's prejudice."

"An old tradition."

445

~ Sunrise Descending ~

"You know, I am very sorry to hear about that, especially in a culture I thought was so advanced."

"It occurs everywhere in the Universe."

"Like ethno-centrism?"

"Just like that, and this culture although technically advanced, still has vestiges of hate, crime and selfishness. That's why we like to keep together."

"Makes sense."

Another person came over to take orders for food and drink.

"Hello, may I help you?"

"Yes.....," and orders were taken.

The meals were delivered in the bowls, the Dogzees were careful to examine the food before they let their hunger take over. Stephen watched as the owner checked on them from a distance every few minutes. There was still a hint of tension in the air as they finished, rose and left. Stephen chose to be last to make sure there weren't any further problems. This experience reminded him of the actions of those in rural areas on Earth. Somewhat behind the times and less educated.

They walked outside, nothing further was said about the lunch and Stephen knew beforehand that his friends would probably want to find a place to lie down and take a nap.

"Let's find a park to relax."

"Oh, very good idea, Stephen. There is one just down this road, it has places for you to sit and places for us to curl up for a bit."

She was right, it was exactly as she had said once they arrived. It was now Stephen's turn to watch out for them as they power napped. He took his assignment seriously, moving his gaze about to make sure he was the first to see anything suspicious. The others slept well, knowing he was looking out for them. He actually kind of liked the pack mentality in many ways and felt very safe with them. It felt natural for them to keep him safe and the reverse also was true. Soon enough, maybe after fifteen or so minutes, they started to stir and stretch. Once they were all up it was time for something different. The sun was starting to set over the ocean, the birds were starting to calm down and look for a place to spend the night. They walked back down the seashore the same way that had come. Stephen kept a wary eye out to see for the sea monster that might have had him for dinner.

"Thanadonous?"

"Yes."

"I like your pack, but I have a question?"

"Its our pack. And what would you like to know?

"Do the others talk?"

"Yes, when they have something to say. Normally I do all the talking to other species like yourself."

"Okay, suits me. I do appreciate however the sense of cohesion in the group and I feel comfortable in watching out for them."

"We know."

"So, what do you do during the evening?"

"Generally we walk around, take inventory and keep aware."

"Inventory of what?"

"Places where we can find food. Also, there are other packs, sometimes we interact with them. It, in a way, is much like a series of clans, we tend to intermix with other clans for the purposes of procreation and tend to stay with our friends for safety."

"I have seen that happen before in other worlds. Seems natural."

"Yes, in fact, the behavior is part of many successful cultures."

"Do you mind if I stay with you this evening as you roam around."

"Of course, we would like that."

They walked further towards another larger outcropping of buildings and started to "cruise." As they did and as it got darker, other life forms started to appear. The night life was as diverse as the day time inhabitants. Some clung to walls, others flew, yet others peered out from the shadows. Again, for the third time in as many days, Stephen was getting an education.

Lights appeared in many buildings near the walkway. These lights illuminated the walkways and roads enough to easily navigate.

Every once in a while, the whole pack would simply stop and sit down to sniff the air, listen for sounds and take inventory. Stephen of course would stop as well and found himself listening and smelling as well. He knew of course that his senses were probably much less attuned to his surroundings as compared to his friends but he made the motions anyway.

For the rest of the evening they moved about and took inventory. At some point, the festivities were over and they all appeared tired. Stephen and Thanadonous discussed a place to sleep or bed down, depending on your point of view. They found some sleeping quarters large enough for all of them and took refuge. That night, Stephen laid awake, sometimes staring at the ceiling and thinking about the day, his new friends and the future.

The future was his main interest and he was becoming anxious about getting to the Population II stars and maybe finding someone like himself, possibly from Earth. It was a one in a million chance but if you don't try the odds get worse.

Leaving the Metal Behind

Exploration is really the essence of the human spirit. - Frank Borman

The next morning Stephen arose early, he had a lot on his mind. The Dogzees were still not ready to get up as he made his way to a balcony to have a quiet conversation with Majel.

451

"I think I would like to go back to the ship, Majel."

"The ship is ready for your return and ready for departure at your leisure."

"I thought you were going to stay here for seven days."

"That would be the maximum, we can leave at any time now."

"Okay, that works for me, I am going to take the train back today. Right after I say goodbye to my new friends."

"They will always be your friends, no matter when you come back."

"How do you know that?"

"They know your smell and well after they forget your face and voice, they will still remember your smell."

"I'll remember that and miss them when I am gone. However now that I know that there are regular flights to this outpost someday I can come back."

"Thats true, however remember the relativistic time issues and also the fact that the Dogzees, as you call them, barely live fifty years. So you will have to return quickly."

"Thats true, Majel. Thanks."

He turned around from looking out the balcony to view the floor which was still covered by curled up Dogzees.

~ *Sunrise Descending* ~

Smiling he walked inside to the kitchen area to find makings for a cup of tea or coffee.

Once there, he found what looked and smelled like tea leaves; there was a heating apparatus and water in a container. Working with logic and luck, he fashioned a cup of tea, thought about how universal it might be and turned to wait for his friends to wake up.

Within ten to fifteen minutes they were stirring and stretching. Stephen found their behavior predictable as they had now spent a few "sleeps" together. He also felt a bit sad at having to leave this very comfortable group of friends. Even though only one talked to him. With more time the others would start to communicate and he would learn their stories. That would keep it interesting, but ultimately, there was a real chance that he could see them once more on his way back.

"Good morning Thanadonous."

"Good morning."

"I need to talk to you."

"Yes, I can sense you have something to tell me, or us."

"I am...."

"Going to leave."

"How did you know?"

453

"We sense things on many levels, and we also know that you will be back."

While saying this, the others all were looking at him with unblinking eyes. Stephen knew they were serious and knew what his destiny held. He felt good.

"I will be back; I like you guys and promise to return."

"We know and now we will take you back to your ship."

"Thats a long trip in the train, are you sure you all want to go?"

One of the other Dogzees, with a much lower voice said:

"Yes, we do."

That being said Stephen looked around and made his way to the door. The others followed in single file. They walked down to the boulevard and towards the train stop. The day was bright and clear. The Ocean beckoned in the distance. The creatures of the previous night were gone. Once the train made its appearance on the horizon, the group assembled in the same area where the entrance door would be once the train came to a stop. The Dogzees for the most part sat down looked in different directions and smelled the air periodically.

~ Sunrise Descending ~

"This is an amazing place," thought Stephen.

After what seemed to be fifteen minutes the Dogzees seemed to concentrate their attention in the direction of where the train would be coming. A few of their ears came up leading Stephen to recognize that their senses were certainly more acute that his and that the train was imminent. Within another minute a faint hissing could be heard and maybe he felt the air pressure change as the large train was displacing the air. Another minute passed and he could now see the dot that would become the first train car. Looking around to make sure his friends were all safe, he took a step backward in anticipation of the arrival. Another minute yet and the dot became a circle and then an even more complex shape as the nose of the train closed to within a hundred meters and slowed to a stop in front of him and his entourage. The doors slid open and they entered by twos. Moving rearward they found a group of seats to occupy. Stephen again found his favorite side with a window to look out of. In this case the seats had been turned around to face the return journey. After they were comfortable, the doors slid closed and the machine started to accelerate slowly in the direction from where it had come. The machine was largely silent and smooth. It was also about empty and would remain so until they started to get

455

back into the more urban areas. Stephen was starting to miss the ocean already and filed through the pages of images of the sea in his mind. The train accelerated further, causing the close in details from his window to become blurred. Looking up he could see farther away more comfortably as the parallax slowed the movement of the distant features. After a few moments even the slowed movements tired his eyes and he turned to check on his friends, many by now had curled up in their seats and had fallen asleep. A small movement or subtle sound would arose them faintly, their eyes would open to make sure all was well, seconds later they were dreaming again.

It had been discovered on Earth a long time ago that the Dolphins who continuously had to come up for air had learned to sleep with one side of their brain active to keep up normal functions and other side asleep. They would exchange sides to get equal rest. In this state of half sleep the dolphins were barely aware and kept close to their pods as they oscillated between the deep and the surface. So to it had been discovered that a very small number of humans did not sleep but found a quiet place to rest with their eyes open, typically at night, with a dim light to keep them company. Stephen wondered if the Dogzees had learned this trick as a method of self preservation.

~ *Sunrise Descending* ~

A trick that Stephen had learned recently with his pack was to take advantage of the down times and catch a nap, which he did now as the train had reached full speed and the images outside flew past at such a rate that it was tiring to observe.

Some twenty minutes later, there was a change which made the pack stir. The train was slowing down for its first stop. All were alert by the time the machine came to a stop and all observed the the newcomers as they filed past towards their seats. The cycle repeated more frequently as they moved into the denser parts of the city. By this time, all were completely awake.

"Majel?"

"Yes?"

"Do you know where we are?"

"Yes."

"Will you alert me when we need to get off?"

"Yes."

The train continued, slower than usual now as more life forms crossed the tracks unaware of the dangers. The pace increased a bit to the next stop and a few more, until:

"Next stop you need to disembark."

"Okay, we will Majel."

"After that I will direct you to the ship, which has been moved from its original docking station."

"Fine, but before we go there I want to take my friends someplace to eat."

"There will be plenty to choose from."

The train moved along for another thirty minutes or so, stopping periodically to ingest or disgorge the various life forms of the outpost. Some chattering when they climbed in, some quiet, some looking at Stephen and his pack, but most ignoring them.

Soon, Majel announced their arrival.

"Time for you to disembark."

"Okay."

Stephen rose, Thanadonous noticed and rose herself, followed by the others. The train had come to a complete stop now, they moved toward the opening doors and walked out. Instead of having to climb down, the floor of the train was flush with the station floor which made the effort easier. They walked out, turned right and around the end of the train as it had been traveling on the right side of the boulevard for the last hour or so. Across the mall they went, following Majel's instructions and towards a series of low buildings backed up by larger ones. The lower set included several places to eat, Thanadonous was put in charge of choosing and she quickly found one with the right tables and bowls for their comfort. They took their places, again together, and ordered their food. It was the last time together as a complete group as Stephen realized that when he returned, some or most of them would be gone because of their shorter life spans. He felt a bit sad at the thought and looked at each of them in a subtle form of reverence, not to embarrass them but to imprint their images in his mind.

He ate his lunch slowly, drank the water, and thought about the significance and unfortunately the quickness of this visit. He had witnessed more variation in living species than he could have ever imagined. The Universe was truly packed with life, they all shared many similarities, like breathing, eating, thinking. They shared many philosophical ideas borne from their sentience, refined by their sages. They all seemed to be moving in the same general direction, life, the pursuit of knowledge, the pursuit of love. It was comforting, or maybe even more to the point, it was the natural order of things.

Preparing for the Pop II Visit

The sea is dangerous and its storms terrible, but these obstacles have never been sufficient reason to remain ashore ... unlike the mediocre, intrepid spirits seek victory over those things that seem impossible ... it is with an iron will that they embark on the most daring of all

~ Sunrise Descending ~

endeavors ... to meet the shadowy future without fear and conquer the unknown. - Ferdinand Magellan

In life there are a few moments of pure contentment, rare but giving one hope that all will be well. Stephen climbed into the spacecraft now, having bid farewell to Thanadonous and her pack, looked at them one more time as he ascended the stairs, turned around and waved. They responded by waving their tails. As he entered, smiling, he found his way back to the compartment he had occupied on the first flight and made himself comfortable. With him were not only memories but a few trinkets, worth very little to anyone else but worth a fortune to him. Each reminded him of the details of this world, the plants, the observatory, Thanadonous and her pack, and the ocean. It was a trick of humans in particular to find objects like these to trigger parts of their brains to bring back images, sounds, smells and memories much like a short snippet of a movie.

He stored away these memories and other things and moved towards the back of the room where the couch was and where he would sit during their takeoff. From here he could watch the view screen and witness the departure and the image of the station as they moved away into space. He turned the unit on with a remote control and attempted to find his friends watching on the hangar deck floor, but they had left, back to their wandering. Other creatures were about, tending to other ships, fueling or bringing supplies. Turning away from the screen, Stephen saw that the other robots had taken their places on the inside of the hull and probably were going through the final count down checks needed for such a complex trip to the supernal regions of the Milky Way.

It seemed like the craft and robots were basically ready when Stephen boarded, as he got comfortable, the sounds of magnetic relays were heard, brief flickering of the lights were observed and Majel advised him to sit down and buckle up. He did as he was told, got comfortable and monitored the action on the view screen. The humming sound increased and he felt a mild movement as the craft levitated above the hangar floor and began to back out towards the space doors. They moved into a very open area, the first door closed behind them, then after what probably was a depressurization cycle, the door in front of them opened and the stars were waiting for them. They moved forward purposefully until they were clear then turned left and up, they started to accelerate. Stephen was pushed back into his seat (again) and remembered the past experience, knew that the direction of gravity had changed from the "floor" to the "wall" behind him. This time he would get used to it more quikly.   The stars spun and moved in the view screen but soon came to a stop as the image of their destination lay straight ahead of them.   It was an awesome sight, even at such a distance, Stephen zoomed the image in and discovered stars of many colors and intensities. As the craft increased in speed, the hue started to very slowly and moved to the blue side, due to the Doppler shift. This took hours, but it was obvious.

"Majel?"

"Yes?"

"Do you have a name for that star cluster we're heading for?"

"Yes, M15, in your Earth terms as I had mentioned before."

"Its stunning. How long will it take us to get there?"

"Twelve of your days."

"Thats not too long."

Indeed it was not, as the acceleration took many days to get up to final speed, then there was a period of weightlessness of two days followed by several days of de-acceleration, where the ceiling was now the floor. He appreciated the fact that the robots had taken into account what would be comfortable for him, even though they could withstand much more g force.

The days went by quickly, Stephen absorbed any scientific information available on this star cluster, as he took full advantage of the memory banks of the ship. M15 was discovered in 1746 by Jean-Dominique Maraldi in France. The cluster resides in the constellation Pegasus and was included in the Messier catalog in 1764. The cluster is over 13.2 billion years old and hence one of the oldest globular clusters in the Milky Way. M15 is about 33,600 light years from Earth and is extremely bright as compared to the sun. It is also one of the most densely packed globulars ever discovered. It has undergone a contraction astronomers call a 'core collapse' and has a central density cusp with an enormous number of stars surrounding what may be a central black hole. In addition, there are 112 variable stars in the cluster which is abnormally high and 8 pulsars including a double neutron star system. There are also four planetary nebulae in the cluster. This would be a beautiful visit as they wound their way around the close star systems and found the place with the most advanced culture. The observatory on Outpost

~ *Sunrise Descending* ~

399 did a good job displaying its secrets, but there was something even more exciting as they got closer and able to resolve more and more details. It was almost as he could smell and taste it. He watched the image, day by day, and made a movie to get a perspective of the distance. The movie revealed the stars in the cluster starting to get farther and farther apart. At some point the faint images of planets appeared in their orbits. The radiation levels increased as well. Majel advised Stephen to stay in his cubicle during certain parts of the journey to protect himself from the intense particle bombardment. These seemed to come in waves at an almost predictable frequency. Stephen didn't mind being sequestered as the rest of the spacecraft was pretty boring. He got into a routine of eating and sleeping at specific times, studying and using the view screen at others. Although there were movies and other entertainment in the memory banks the view screen spent most of its time looking forward, towards their destination.

The days did indeed go fast; soon enough he spent a lot of time in a weightless condition. This was reminiscent of how the astronauts and cosmonauts lived for so long in Earth's orbit or going to the Moon and Mars. This was before the discovery of quantum gravity control. For now however, it was fun. Within a day or so, the gravity shifted to what used to be the ceiling, as the ship reversed its thrusters and started the final phase of the flight. The view screen, now on the opposite wall, showed great details about the stars and associated planets. They soon passed one star, then another and began to weave to and fro amongst the fiery orbs as they continued to slow down. At some point, many hours after they began their maneuvering, a single star was centered in the screen and it became obvious that this was their true destination. Movement towards and around the star slowed to a leisurely pace now and at the prescribed moment the star that was at the center moved to the side and a blue planet appeared in the cross hairs.

This pleased Stephen as he knew that there was an ocean waiting for him there. Unlike some of the other planets he had seen, this was seemingly as disorderly as Earth. The most advanced cultures he had observed had moved their planets into a single orbit to allow growth of their populations and make communications and travel much more efficient. Here however it appeared that the planet, much larger than Earth, was by itself and, aside from its sun, was the sole occupant of the solar system. It did however sparkle and shine and look very inviting.

~ Sunrise Descending ~

They silently entered orbit and spent many hours just flying hundreds of miles above the planet's surface.

"Majel?"

"Yes?"

"Are we going down to the surface?"

"Soon. Arrangements are being made now. They are curious about you, as you have traveled so far to see them."

"Okay, tell them I look forward to meeting them."

"We have, they need to make arrangements."

"You said that. What kind of arrangements?"

"They must make the environment conducive to your life form."

"How long will that take?"

"Not long, another hour perhaps."

Stephen, again weightless, made his way to the most comfortable part of his quarters and found some water to drink. After a few moments, his curiosity got the better of him.

"Majel?"

"Yes?"

"What do they look like?"

"Anything."

"Anything? I don't understand, please explain."

467

"They have conquered matter and energy. They are immortal as you are and can move about the Universe at will. They learned about quantum replication and use it to be anywhere they want. They also receive all energy in the Universe and use it to create what they want."

"And need?"

"There is no need."

"How do they live together?"

"There is no together, they simply are."

"How many of them are there?"

"Many....one....they are here now."

"Here now? In this ship?"

"Of course, and they have been for the last several days."

"How can I talk to them?"

"Think."

"And they will respond?"

"If you would like."

"Hmmm....okay, well here is a problem, humans think sometimes randomly and try to vocalize rationally. Its important that they separate the two, this is like having two voices, one audible and one in the background. It allows us to evaluate things before we speak. It allows us to consider a wide variety of thoughts before we make a conclusion. So having them in my head will most likely confuse them.

"They know this and have already recorded your complete mental history. You have nothing to be concerned about as they know what is on your mind."

"Well in any event, it will be easier for me to communicate by verbal interaction."

"As you wish, it comes as no surprise to us."

"To us?"

"Yes, us. We are now Majel, does that make you uncomfortable?"

"It works for me, thank you for being considerate."

"It is you who are being considerate. The ship will now land."

Indeed the ship changed course, lowered the nose to enter the atmosphere and found a suitable landing place. As he got closer to the ground, he noticed many dome like structures and many tall crystal looking buildings. They blended with the forests they were placed in and looked both strong and delicate.

The ship swirled around several structures and toward a large open area. It slowed to a crawl and deftly touched down in the clearing. The electrical circuits started to shut off in the ship and quiet followed the humming and

469

singing circuits. The silence was followed by the opening of the stairway to the outside. Once it thumped down on the ground there was silence again. Stephen stood up, smelled fresh air and proceeded to the opening. He walked down the stairs to a bright outside.

"Majel....or whomever?"

"Yes, we are here."

"I need sunglasses, its very bright out here for me."

"Stand by."

Soon a box appeared from somewhere inside the craft, it was lowered by some remote gravitational means, towards Stephen. He knew somehow to open it and pull out a nice pair of wrap around sunglasses, reminiscent of the old Italian styles of Earth. He put them on to find out that not only did they attenuate the light levels to his eyes, but also provided a limited amount of spectral imaging, allowing him to discern different material constructs. They were in the end... comfortable. Back to the matters at hand, Stephen looked around for an opening or door or building that would be his logical destination. Seconds after his search started he saw what appeared to be windows or glass doors built into a low grass covered hill. It was about thirty meters away and looked inviting enough for him to start walking towards.

"Majel....or whomever?"

"Yes, we are here."

"Am I going in the right direction?"

"Yes you are, Stephen. Please go into the structure ahead where someone will meet you and get you started."

"Get me started? Get me started for what?"

"Get you started to know us."

"Ummm, okay. Do you have a name?"

"If you would like you may call us Mungu."

"Okay Mungu, nice to meet you. You have a fine planet."

"Thank you. We are waiting for you inside."

He continued to walk until he was at the center of the glass partition. He found out as he got closer that in fact it was not glass but a very thin sheet of what looked like water. He approached tentatively, put his hand out to touch the shiny substance and found that his hand went through it but without any sensation. He pulled it out to find that it was still connected to him, decided all was safe and entered the opening. Inside he found a hollowed out area with glass smooth walls and many tunnels or hallways leading further inside. The walls were lit homogeneously and the temperature perfectly comfortable. Realizing that all roads inside would be interesting he walked straight in to the closest one and followed it to wherever it might lead. Within ten meters the hallway opened up into a large room, again with smooth but arched walls, light and color filled the room populated with tables, various sitting apparatuses and life forms inside, which were for the most part sitting one per table. They sat there quietly and seemed to stare into random parts of the room, as if stupefied or mesmerized. There were dozens of them in this room. Stephen felt a bit uncomfortable at the sight and looked at the individuals carefully as he walked around the room.

"Mungu?"

"Yes?"

"What is this place?"

"The Library, as you would call it. Everyone in here is connected to our research memory banks and can explore them in what you would call a virtual sense."

"I think I know what you mean, its just that they look suspended, non-conscious."

"In a way they are, each table has a mental link that relaxes the researcher completely and allows their mind to explore anything they want. We have billions of your years of research material available. There is nothing you cannot find in here. This place alone can advance a complete culture by leaps and bounds, again in your terms. Would you like to sit down and explore?"

"Not yet, I would prefer to look around further if you don't mind."

"Of course not. Go anywhere you please. Your gastrointestinal system requires attention, we will feed you now."

"What?"

But before Stephen could articulate a question, he realized that although he was hungry and thirsty when he came into this place, those sensations were now gone. Somehow, Mungu had provided his stomach with food and water.

"Thank you, I felt that. What about the pleasure of sitting down to eat and drink?"

"It takes up valuable time, so there is no need for that here."

"Just research?"

"Just research, thought and personal growth."

It makes sense that this is where evolution will take us, Mungu. Although in a strange way, it seems boring.

"It is only boring to you because you spend so much time preparing to grow. It is based on your ancient past, where survival was paramount. Here that is not an

473

issue, sustenance is not an issue, only thought is important. There are those here that spent significant amounts of time, many of your years, exploring just one thought. Here philosophical endeavors are allowed to flourish."

"I see, and based on my experience, it makes sense that the pursuit of intellectual fulfillment is or will be the most important part of life. For now however, as I don't think I am ready for that level, I would just like to explore your world. It has been an interest of mine for many years and an interest of friends of mine as well."

"The Nereids?"

"Yes. You know of them?"

"No, but you do."

"I see. And yes, they asked me to meet you and return to them with new knowledge."

"We will give you any knowledge you want."

"Thank you. For now could I explore further?"

"Of course, go anywhere you like."

"I have a question."

"Please ask it."

"Are you corporeal? Do you have form?"

"If necessary. Our species is a melding of many life forms found in our star cluster. We became sentient, like you, immortal, like you, and then found ways to have the electrical impulses in our minds communicate with machines. Soon, our sense of self was able to transfer from our physical form to a much larger collection of others, creating a more global consciousness. As it was magnitudes more complex and capable, the ability to revert to our physical selves then became less attractive. Why, we asked ourselves, should we go back to such a simple state, especially one that was always in danger of running out of sustenance, requiring procreation, and subject to accidents and death? As our many minds were now one, we soon realized that the evolution of the machine was paramount and to that end we quickly were able to formulate ourselves in conduits of energy or mass. One to exist quickly and one to exist permanently. As you know these two forms are interchangeable and we now use them to live. These are the most efficient forms of life."

"To live, to live in either mass or energy."

"That is correct."

"Thats amazing."

"To you...now. Someday it will make complete sense. As you know, any sufficiently advanced life form appears to be magic to the others."

"But we are attracted to them, nonetheless."

"And that is why we are here and will never cease to exist. Life is attractive."

Stephen paused for a moment to take all of this in, he thought of it as a revelation, smiled at the possible implication of it and decided he still liked his physical being. He moved on into other rooms, exploring them carefully, realizing the massive extent of the structure and taking in the other life forms populating the place. There was a distinct sense of reverence in this building, no loud discussion, no laughter, no intrigue. It made sense that we would all end up here someday, but for now, fun had its attractive side as well.

He continued to move on past rooms with windows, rooms without windows, different colored rooms, glass like rooms, crystalline rooms. There seemed to be an infinite variety. At some point though, Stephen felt tired and wanted to sit and watch the surroundings.

Ambrosia

No man or woman of the humblest sort can really be strong, gentle and good, without the world being better for it, without somebody being helped and comforted by the very existence of that goodness. - Alan Alda

One of the rooms he passed during his explorations looked inviting and did not have that "library feeling". There were life forms there he felt he could communicate with who were standing around or sitting. Concentric tables that were

477

many meters long were co-located with chairs or other sitting apparatus. The tone was subdued and relaxed and there was food and drink on some of the tables. This was probably the low brow room, one where the intellectually challenged could congregate. Things of course are relative, even here, thought Stephen. The ones in this room are advanced enough to get here, to the outer portions of the Milky Way, in sophisticated spacecraft. That being said, he still felt as if this room was a better match for him, certainly one that would have answers to his questions.

He walked in, found a place to sit and examined his surroundings. The table he rested is arms on came to life, he felt a question coming on.

"Mungu?"

"Yes, we are here."

"Is this table trying to communicate with me?"

"Yes, it wants to know if you are hungry or thirsty. You may talk to it directly, it knows all languages."

"Okay."

He turned his head towards the glowing table.

"Uh..table, please bring me water and a salad."

The color of the table turned to green. Was this the universal affirmative color or was it indicating it was ill? The answer would come in a matter of seconds, from an opening in the table where food and drink elevated upwards. The seam where the opening appeared then disappeared.

"Cool."

"Oh, thats nothing here."

Stephen turned to see a humanoid standing beside him. She looked completely familiar, not in terms of knowing her personally, but in terms of looking like she was from Earth.

"Hello! Where are you from?"

"Earth of course, looks like you are from there as well. You looked pretty shocked when you saw me, been out in space for a long time?"

"Years, not all of it in space of course. You?"

"Oh, been around a bit, years as well. So... you ever been to Texas?"

"Used to work there, for NASA."

"NASA? I'm not surprised; you look a bit geekish."

"You know, I am getting the feeling that there is something special about you. I mean, how would you know about NASA, they no longer exist and haven't for many years. Where exactly are you from and more importantly, when?"

"Well, Stephen. I am from Earth, as you figured out, and very old. Its been a very long journey for me and what intrigues me about you is that you might be old as well, especially if you worked for NASA."

"You have me at a disadvantage, how do you know my name?" asked Stephen, smiling.

"Well, if you spent any time in their library, you would find the details of the visitors and drill down for anything interesting. I have been here for a while and always look for humanoid visitors. Its been a long time, I have to say, so when you showed up, I just had to meet you. My name is Ambrosia."

"A lovely name, reminds me of the Greeks, whose offsprings I spent a lot of time with."

"The Nereids I bet."

"Exactly, how did you know that?"

"Who they are is legendary for both Earth and this place. It was also in your bio. They are famous, not only for who they were in ancient Greece, but in the years following when they knew about places like this but chose not to visit."

"Well, I know them pretty well, they are very kind hearted and believe they know enough to keep them occupied for a long time."

480

"True, but should you not always seek new knowledge?"

"You sound like Plato, who by the way would show you that you yourself have the answer to that question."

"The Socratic method."

"Works everywhere I have been. Its their right, they are a happy, content people. I look forward to seeing them again."

"Sounds like there is a story there."

"There is, a really good one."

"Well, I look forward to hearing it. In fact I would like to go back to the Nereids with you, if you don't mind."

"No, of course not. They would like that I'm sure. So what's the deal here? What's your story?"

"Like I said my name is Ambrosia, and I, like yourself, am very old. I am also from Earth and might have been there when you were, especially if you worked for NASA."

"When exactly, and where?"

"So many questions you have."

"Oh, its just that I have not talked to anyone from Earth in a very long time. To meet someone who is not only from Earth but knows things about the time I spent there is amazing."

"Well, if you must know, I grew up in Colorado, went to college there, worked for a while there, got married, you know... pretty standard stuff."

"So were you born immortal?"

"No, just lucky enough (I think) to know a very special doctor."

Stephen was dumbstruck and it took several minutes to compose himself.

"Are you okay?" Ambrosia asked.

"Uh.....it wasn't someone named Roger was it?"

Now she was dumbstruck.

"Yes, his first name was Roger, from Lafayette."

"Well.....you and I have something in common."

Silence followed as each person considered their ramifications of this discovery. Neither one knew there were others and now possibly others still.

"What..I...wow...okay, you speak first."

"Thats amazing, Stephen. I can't believe we went to the same doctor."

"I wonder if there are others."

"Probably, depends on how much serum he had. He was an amazing physician, one of the brightest people I have ever met. I wonder what he would think about the fruits of his labors."

"Maybe he took some as well."

"You never know."

They sat for a moment, looking at each other and wondering about each other's extensive life and stories. They knew that they would spend a lot of time together to "catch up."

"Well, we have a lot to talk about."

"Indeed," followed Ambrosia.

"So, how long have you been here?"

"About a year, in Earth terms."

"I'll bet you have some stories."

"Indeed," she repeated.

"Well for now, I am going to eat, I'm famished."

"Oh, please do. I am going to go back to my table and return with my things."

"Okay, I won't be long, then maybe we could go for a walk."

"A walk perhaps you won't forget."

Stephen smiled at the thought as she turned and walked away. He felt a bit jaded now as he had seen so many fantastic things and simply assumed she could not impress him further. As it turns out he would be wrong in his assumption.

She returned in a few minutes with what looked like a back pack. Sitting down she made herself comfortable. Stephen felt at ease with her as well, as there was no pretense, no assumptions, just a mutual interest in each other's life, very much like finding a long lost sister or brother. In some ways much like finding a long lost twin brother or sister. That made them both smile now.

Stephen finished his meal, cleaned his plate and drained the water. He pushed the dish and glass back to the same area where they had first appeared and un-shockingly the seam appeared again and lowered the dishes down inside the table. Stephen mused a bit, then said:

"You know, I expected this culture, which is many billions of years more advanced than us, to not have to use technical devices like this. I had anticipated much more. They seem completely communicative, anxious to interact and willing to share their knowledge."

"Oh, the service staff is first rate."

"The service staff?"

"Oh yes, what you have encountered today is the porch, wait till you see the living room."

Stephen did not know exactly how to respond to this revelation. He had experienced space travel, incredible

484

observatories, libraries with so much information no one person or entity could assimilate a single subject over a lifetime of study, and yet, there could be more? Even the Nereids would be impressed. Maybe the Nereids knew this all along. Interesting.

He looked to his left at his new friend, she had the look of having wandered for centuries and having finally found a home. They both knew they would be spending a lot of time together in the future.

"Are you married?" she asked.

"Sort of, not by official ceremony but I do love someone at the last planet where I lived for a long time. Its a long story but she is carrying a child made from the DNA of my wife I outlived on Earth."

"Wow, now that's a story. Are you going back there after your visit here?"

"Yes, definitely. She, her name is Elva, is very special to me. As things turned out, she is immortal."

"And the child?"

"Mortal."

"Well, I am not sure how to respond to that, on the one hand I question your judgement, on the other, I did the same thing. I married a few times, deeply in love in all cases. I felt the tragic loss of my mates as they grew older.

I stayed with them in all cases, lived with them as a wife, then daughter. The kids were next, then the wandering. I'm not sure I would recommend that life for anyone else; but on the other hand, I have experienced so many wonderful things. Their memories are but a part of my life and not my life."

"Well said, its not easy."

"No its not, certainly not what anyone else would think."

"But here we are."

"Yeah, no matter where you go, there you are."

"Buddha."

"You know, its amazing how much the philosophers and sages knew, I mean, it seems as though their words last the longest."

"I would add the physicists and astronomers to that list, as they best understood the physical; the philosophers and sages understood being and time."

"True."

With that they both rose so she could show him the rest of the facility. He was glad he found her and intrigued about her past. The problem of course would be that considering how old they both were telling each other's life stories would take some time.

~ Sunrise Descending ~

They walked out of the cafe, down some halls. He quickly lost count of how many rights and lefts they had taken. They walked by arboretums containing flora and fauna that was beautiful. Photosynthesis took place at many different colors and therefore green was not dominant on many planets. There were even white, black and translucent varieties of plants. He learned later that some planets have very large and bright moons and as a consequence, plants from those worlds used the moonglow as well as the sunshine. One particular plant had leaves with a day side and a night side. The leaf moved up and down to accommodate for the best light.

They continued down hallways and past large rooms, over glass floors and underneath bodies of water within tubes. After what seemed to be at least a mile distance she slowed as they walked into a very large room with a fountain in the center. The fountain contained fluid slightly more viscous than water and moved a bit slower as it emanated from the top and flowed gently to the lower pools. They moved closer and found a bench about ten meters away to sit down.

"That's really fantastic," Stephen said in awe.

"Keep looking."

~ Sunrise Descending ~

As he did the fluid turned subtle shades of colors and he thought he could see images in the folds of the descending cascades. Images of faces and landscapes. He paused and considered seriously that this was just his imagination. The images were mesmerizing. As he was drawn in, Ambrosia looked at him and observed what she, at one time, had experienced. It was a nexus. A nexus to the past and possibly the future, if interpreted properly. Stephen saw images of people he knew and loved, he saw the fields of Hebe 6 and the oceans of Outpost 399. He thought he smelled the places as well as the images resonating in his mind and brought forth all of the sensations he had experienced. He blinked and retracted a bit.

"What *is* this thing?"

"A mirror, one of many in this place. The inhabitants found a way to project the images in our brains. There doesn't seem to be an operations manual for it. Most of us just come in here to review our experiences. There are others that do more with it, they see the future. And there are even those who believe it has religious properties."

"A sufficiently advanced culture appears as magic....."

488

"Exactly. I have the feeling that it is just an apparatus of sorts and it can be fun or relaxing to use. If however, you are not careful, it can hypnotize you and you might never leave, except for its safety mechanism."

"Which is?"

"It will shut off if it detects someone is lost in it."

"Convenient. I see why you call it a mirror, the images I saw were from my past, there were other images as well, some that did not make sense to me."

"Have you ever had a dream with unique images?"

"Of course."

"Many of those images reside in your mind as well."

"I see. Ambrosia, what does all of this mean?"

"What exactly are you asking?"

"Well, what I am asking is....here, at this place, which is billions of years more advanced than all of the cultures I am familiar with, it seems that knowledge is the pinnacle of existence. In other words, there are libraries, mirrors and mysteries to explore. Is there anything else?

"Do you need something else?"

"Sometimes you stub your toe, make a wrong decision, feel sad; all of that seems unnecessary here."

"It is, and you are right. This place represents the pinnacle of existence and essence. It is what millions of cultures will become one day. It focuses on the progressive thoughts and leaves the mundane to languish."

"But isn't there more to learn?"

"These people learn at a prodigious rate, they sense all things in this galactic neighborhood, but that input is only a part of the life, assimilating the information is the other part. Coming to conclusions is yet another part. I think they have reduced the laws of the universe both physical and experiential to some simple truths. These truths are hard to disprove and as a result they are at peace with themselves."

"And these truths are?"

"To be discovered."

"What? Thats nonsense."

"Not to them, not to me..now and not to you....someday."

"Well, I will ponder that. I mean you would think that there would be a more solid answer."

"Then what? Be done? What would be the attraction of exploring further? You see, when you were a child the laws of life and the Universe were state of the art, so to speak. When you became an adult, those particular laws were but a stepping stone to new laws and precepts. Now of course, these ideas you held dear on Earth are but a footnote in the overall scheme of things. So what about the future?"

"Yeah, I know... more laws to be discovered more life to be understood."

"Good, your doing well on the first law of existence."

"And the others?"

"All in due time. For now, what do you like to do?"

Stephen looked at the fountain again, this time with a bit more understanding. He furled his brow and thought dark thoughts, of death and despair. The fountain turned red. Then he thought of happiness and joy, the fountain turned sky blue.

"I get it...I am in control of the mirror."

"Exactly."

"And as far as what I would like to do.....I would like to go home."

~ Sunrise Descending ~

To What Awaits

The real voyage of discovery consists not in seeking new landscapes but in having new eyes. - Marcel Proust

"So, what shall we do?"

"Anything, everything, nothing; I have done them all. Shall we journey to the center of the galaxy? To the other population II star systems and see what's in store for us?"

"Actually, maybe after some time here, I would like to go home."

"To Hebe 6 and Elva?"

"Yes, to Hebe 6, to Elva and to Zsa."

"Fine, that suits me, I would like to go with you."

"Of course, you mentioned that before. The Nereids will embrace you. I of course would appreciate having a friend there."

"Good, I will pack my things tonight if you wish."

"Well, I guess a day or two in the intellect of the Universe wouldn't hurt me too much. So maybe, how about the day after tomorrow?"

"Sure."

"Majel or whomever?"

"Yes?"

"Can we schedule to return to Hebe 6 the day after tomorrow?"

"Yes, of course. We are ready anytime."

"Ambrosia would like to come with me, can we make accommodations for her?"

"Yes, they will be ready when we depart."

"Thank you, Majel."

The schedule was now set. They would go together which for Ambrosia made a lot of sense. She had not seen humanoids from Earth for a very long time and missed their company and eccentricities. For Stephen, he had seen enough and wanted to get back to his clan. They would like her and would especially like to hear of her adventures around the galaxy. Even though he had only known her for several hours, he was sure she would be comfortable on Hebe 6. They left the fountain area and walked further, passing more large open areas with groups of like individuals and rooms with stars projected and hanging in the air. There were areas where conversations took place and others that were bathed in silence. It was all interesting but he longed for the open outdoors, with fresh air and blue skies. He had the urge to travel again, travel back home.

Ambrosia was content, showing Stephen around and having dinner with him that evening. She had, after a very long wait, finally found someone like her to talk to and did so at great length. Stephen listened to all of the stories, some patiently, as she described different planets and different life forms she had encountered. Now, for her, it all seemed worth it, galavanting around the stars and experiencing new cultures. Now, she could relate the experiences to Stephen and soon, the others. She smiled a lot at this thought.

A day more went by, basically just exploring the crystalline world and talking. Ambrosia had packed early, Stephen was ready an hour before they needed to start back to the ship. They found themselves walking quickly down the corridors towards the landing pad, both of them felt like they didn't want to be late. They arrived to find the ship's door open and waiting. The advantage of Stephen's wrist band with Majel watching over him was that the ship knew what to expect. It was fully fueled and all of the robots had taken their place. Another living area, identical to Stephen's and exactly opposite of his had been created. They walked into the other parts of the ship and back to their quarters. She looked at her space and said:

"Lovely, but I hate the drapes."

He responded, "and no pool table, what a dump."

"Shall we ask for first class?"

"Well, I only have sixty billion miles now, not quite enough to qualify."

"Oh, well, guess these will have to do."

She walked over to her area and started to unpack. The walls had the same layout in terms of storage space, a view screen had been added as well. In all details it was a mirror image of Stephen's.

Stephen sat down and started his view screen to get a sense of when they would be leaving.

"Majel, or whomever?"

"Yes, I am here now."

"The others are gone?"

"Yes."

"Good. If I understand the view screen, it seems that we are going to leave in less that an hour. Is that correct?"

"Yes."

"And we are going back to Outpost 399 or Hebe 6?"

"There is nobody to pick up on Outpost 399 and the data we need to transfer can be done when we are in close proximity of the Outpost."

"Can we stop there for a few hours so I can see a friend?"

"Of course."

Ambrosia heard this conversation and was looking at Stephen for an explanation.

"I just wanted to say hello to a friend of mine, you'll like her."

"How many women do you have scattered around the galaxy? Is she pretty?"

"Oh, she's a real dog."

"That's a horrible thing to say and I thought you were advanced."

"Nope, just basic."

Ambrosia was now convinced that the Neanderthal recessive genes had come forth strongly in her new friend. She grimaced at the thought. She wrote him off and continued with her preparations for departure.

"How long is this flight," she asked.

"Not long, several days, a week perhaps. It depends on the amount of assistance from gravity waves we receive. Its just like flying a plane, you might get a headwind or you might be lucky enough to get a tailwind."

"Hope we get a tailwind."

"Anxious?"

"Maybe."

"Well me too, I think you will like my friends and the place. It's a good rest stop before we make it to Hebe 6."

"Sounds alright. In fact I might have been there before, can't remember."

The sounds of the ship started to change in anticipation of a take off. Stephen had experienced this before and alerted Ambrosia to prepare herself. The door was retracting and closing now.

"Turn on your viewscreen, use the cursor buttons to select an outside view. Sit on the seat at the rear of your space, its the most comfortable."

"Okay, thanks."

Both of them went to their respective positions as the sounds of magnetic interlocks and power systems started to resonate throughout the ship. He sat down, crossed his legs and selected the proper screen. She sat down, looked over at him for clues as to what was going to happen next.

The ship rose, rotated slowly and started to accelerate towards the sky.

"You know, Ambrosia, I actually prefer real pilots. These robots you see attached to the sides of the ship are okay and very efficient but real pilots make a flight into an art form. I miss Grant, who I used to fly with, he flew with swan like grace. I never minded the extra time it took to get somewhere as he arced and swooped, sensing the winds and currents."

"Sounds like he was one with the birds."

"Yes, and there is something important about that. What I just experienced on this world documented those feats but did not understand them. Flying is only one example, poetry is another. Do you see my point?"

"Maybe."

"It will be more obvious when we meet the Nereids. They are good people, they understand and appreciate art and interpretation and the wind."

"I'm lost."

The spacecraft had moved through the atmosphere by now and was aiming for the stars. The motion had been very smooth and their conversations had taken any anxiety about flying away from Ambrosia. They proceeded towards Outpost 399, the lateral star movement in the view screens slowed and started to expand instead of slew. The acceleration continued to the point where they became acclimated and were used to the back of the ship being the new floor.

Stephen looked over to see if Ambrosia was alright, she looked fine and was working the view screen to find something to read. Stephen left her to her explorations and looked for something to eat.

After a few hours of self absorption they both felt tired enough to go to sleep. Within five minutes of each other they fell into comfortable dreamland. She dreamt about the future, he about Elva.

It was a good sleep, seven or eight hours worth, when they both woke up. He rose from his recline and looked over to see that she was up and looking through her area for something.

"What are you looking for?"

"Some tea or coffee."

"Just ask Majel."

He realized after he had said this that Ambrosia did not have a bracelet to easily communicate with Majel. So he initiated the conversation.

"Majel?"

"Yes?"

"Can you help Ambrosia?"

"Of course. Ambrosia, what would you like?"

"Tea, preferably."

"It will be available to you in one minute."

"Thank you."

"Can you give her a bracelet like mine, so she can communicate with you?"

"There is no need. I know her voice now, all she has to do is talk to me."

~ Sunrise Descending ~

Majel was true to her word and within the appointed minute a door slid open to reveal a cup of tea.

"Do you have milk, Majel?"

"Yes, standby."

The same door opened again with a smaller cup of milk. She took it and poured a bit of it into her tea. Sitting back, she took stock of her surroundings and looked over at Stephen.

"Good morning."

"Good morning to you."

"What is there to do on this ship...to while away the time?"

"Not much. I ended up getting into a routine of eating, exercising, reading and following the progress of the flight. It was a bit mundane but got me through. For this flight however, I think I might do a bit of writing to document what I have experienced."

"Can you communicat with others?"

"During our flight, the speed is so great that the frequencies Doppler shift quite a bit. The messages take a long time to get to and from their destinations. Its best to send messages like an old style telegram, in other words, don't expect an immediate response."

"How do I proceed?"

"Use the view screen to compose your mail, then ask Majel to send it to a particular person. She will control the communications equipment to make up for the Doppler shift."

They both then tended to their chores and explorations. They spoke little during the first days.

The days grew into a week, by this time there was an excitement about getting to their first destination. Both viewscreens now showed a countdown clock. She was more talkative now, asking questions about this metal world she had never visited. He did his best to describe it.

As the last remaining days turned into many remaining hours, they prepared for the visit. It was slated for two days, enough for him to find his friends and enough for her to experience a unique place. He emoted positive anticipation, she watched and looked forward to it.

The last part of the trip included a weightless period followed by a reversal of the gravity vector. Stephen was entertained by how Ambrosia adjusted from siting on the floor to sitting on the roof. He had been through it before and knew how to handle it. Although he assisted her and told her what to expect the image of her lifting out of her chair, floating across the room and settling upside down on the opposite wall's chair brought a smile to his face.

The deceleration process continued until the view screen were filled with the outpost.

"That thing is huge," she exclaimed.

"Oh, yeah."

They assumed a parking orbit around the Outpost for several orbits, then started the decent to a landing dock.

"Majel?"

"Yes?"

"Can you contact Thanadonous and tell her we are landing?"

"Yes."

They maneuvered through the tenuous atmosphere that had formed around the outpost due to its enormous size, through some clouds, into a touch of turbulence and finally lined up with a landing dock door. The door opened to reveal an awaiting landing bay, lit from within. Stephen and Ambrosia watched their respective screens with interest as the craft slowed down and carefully made its way into the open hangar bay, then settled. The magnetic hums they were now used to subsided, the cabin air pressure was neutralized against the outside air and the door was opened. Stephen and Ambrosia rose to go outside and into Outpost 399. The light was a bit brighter than they were used to but they soon adapted. They walked towards the boulevard he had spoken of to her. The trains were still there as was the plethora of life forms. Into the open space of the boulevard they went, then stopped to look around. As they scanned the landscape, Stephen noticed something familiar in the distance, a pack of four legged animals making their way towards him. He smiled at the thought of who it might be. Soon enough his hopes were verified as a pack of Dogzees were walking then running towards him.

"Thanadonous?"

"Hello Stephen. How are you?"

"I'm great, I brought a friend, her name is Ambrosia."

"Hello Ambrosia, nice to meet you. These is my pack."

As she said this they were surrounded by Dogzees with wagging tails. She also felt both completely comfortable and a little embarrassed at the same time. Comfortable because these creature talked and were very friendly. Embarrassed because she assumed Stephen was being a bit chauvinistic when he first described Thanadonous. She looked at him at a moment when he was looking her way and caught his eye. Based on the expression she had he smiled and understood the import.

~ Sunrise Descending ~

"Lunch," he asked?

"Absolutely," Thanadonous replied.

The others in her pack elevated their energy levels at the thought of getting something to eat. Soon one of them was in the lead towards a favorite cafe. The others followed with Stephen and Ambrosia in the middle. They made their way down the boulevard and into an open air cafe where the appropriate sitting apparatuses for all species were present. They moved to the left side of the establishment and sat down. Presently a waitress came by to take drink and food orders. Stephen sat by Thanadonous smiling as he listened to her describe what happened in the intervening years that Stephen had been away. It was a combination of "not much" and "all kinds of changes." Stephen talked briefly about his visit to M15, which was beautiful and revealing in the sense of what he found there.

"So, what are you saying?" Thanadonous asked. "Now you believe in friends."

"Exactly, the visit was important and good, but what I discovered was ourselves, not some extraordinary revelation about the nature of the Universe."

"I could have told you that," she said smiling.

"I also found Ambrosia."

"And that I am sure was worth the whole trip, she fits well with our pack."

"She does, doesn't she?"

Stephen looked over at Ambrosia, who was busy getting to know the rest of the group. She smiled and as she did so the others were anxious to get her attention, moving in front of each other to get the best chance.

Well over an hour was spent talking and eating and all too soon, it was time to take a walk and (for the Dogzees) get a nap. They walked over to the first park Stephen had been to, found a good spot for both species and relaxed. Soon the Dogzees were curled up and asleep as Stephen and Ambrosia sat on a bench and talked in low tones.

"There're very cool, Stephen, very cool."

"Yeah, I know. Its easy to assimilate with them, moving in a pack, protecting the others. They just wander around, discovering, listening, smelling, eating and napping."

"Idyllic life."

"Indeed. Well I can offer you some interesting sites we all can go see."

"How long are we going to be here?"

"A day or so. Its up to us."

"Well, I am anxious to get to your home, as you must be. If I understand what you have been saying about the robot ships, we can come back in the future."

"That's true but of course there will be the relativistic time issues to deal with, so we can't do it very often."

"Actually, you can't do it very often in the near future."

"Well, thats true. As you can imagine, I would like to spend a good amount of time with my people on Hebe 6, but as you point out, after that it is open."

"Yep, and I will be bored by then and will need to do some traveling."

They talked further about the past, present and future, then decided on a course of action for the immediate present. The decided to visit the "cerebral forest" as Stephen referred to it. The Dogzees stirred within about fifteen minutes and stretched. Ambrosia told Thanadonous about their wishes and within a few seconds they were all headed for the train. They queued up and waited for not a long period of time, maybe ten minutes. A train slowed to a stop in front of them, the doors slid open and they all got aboard. During the process, Stephen passed the conductor who remembered him from an incident in the past. The conductor immediately started squawking and chirping about something.

"He seems a little excited," Ambrosia remarked.

"I didn't tip him very well last time."

"But they don't use money here."

"Its just an expression. He is just concerned about my sanitary habits."

"What did you do, pee in the sink?"

"Ambrosia, how crude."

She looked at him with the realization that an honest answer was not forthcoming.

"Well, its easy to do," she said.

Now Stephen was at a disadvantage as she moved her attention elsewhere. They moved into their seats, Stephen of course by the window, and the train started to move down the tracks. They knew the stop of course and the Dogzees started to get active as they were in close quarters. Stephen and Ambrosia sensed it as well and prepared to disembark at the appointed time. The train slowed to a stop and they stepped out into a bright fresh day. Stephen waved goodbye to the cranky conductor who said something under his breath. They walked over to the park that lead to the forest that could lead to mental disorders. Stephen briefed Ambrosia on the way there.

~ Sunrise Descending ~

"Now, this place is very interesting. The Dogzees will stay in the first part as we walk further and further. This is a place that demonstrates what happens when plants evolve into sentient life forms. Remember, they are just sensing what and who you are and if you get uncomfortable we will leave."

"Okay, no problem, I am very curious as to what they think of us."

"Who knows, I did't make it through the complete forest last time. It was quite an experience."

They made it to the park, found a good place for the dogzees to spend some time at and started down the path to discovery. As they were walking, the Dogzees watered themselves and curled up for yet another nap. Thanadonous was the last to lay down, as she watched her friends walk down a path, she made sure they were safe then took care of her own needs.

They walked for fifteen minutes or so, the short grasses changed to small bushes then larger ones then as they moved deeper into the forest, trees. It was quiet and contemplative and few words were spoken. Stephen knew the way and slowed down as they approached the sentient plant life. He looked at her.

"Ready?"

"Ready as I'll ever be."

They moved deeper still.

"Watch the plants, Ambrosia. At some point you will see them moving in unison then later, they will follow our movements. Its after this point that you will hear sounds or feel tingly as they start to probe our thoughts. I don't think theyr'e dangerous, just curious.

"Okay."

They moved deeper still and as Stephen had predicted, the plants started to follow their movements and Ambrosia at some point said:

"Oh.....I feel them now. They *are* curious. They're not threatening at all."

They moved deeper into the darkening forest. Stephen could feel the probes, Ambrosia was silent but had a serious look on her face. Another fifty yards in and:

"Okay, I've had enough," she said in a shaky voice.

"We can stop now. Do you remember the fountain at M15?"

"Yes."

"Its the same thing here, they are interested but for the most part are reacting to your thoughts."

"What comes farther in?"

~ Sunrise Descending ~

"My guess is that it becomes more intense. Maybe they use this skill of theirs to keep out predators, you know...herbivores."

"Could be, hey, I have pegged my fun meter, lets go back where I don't feel so...violated."

"Sure, lets go."

They turned quickly and headed back to more light, less mental noise and less anxiety. They walked very quickly at times as they, without saying anything to the other, wanted to see the Dogzees again. If they were younger, they probably would have broken into a run.

Soon however, due to their haste, they saw in the distance, the open fields where they friends were waiting. Once they had broken into the opening, they quickly found the Dogzees, who were (again) just stirring and said hello.

"Creepy in there?" asked Thanadonous as she loped over to greet them.

"Kinda," Ambrosia responded.

"Well, let's get out of here, its dusk now and there will be a lot happening on the boulevard."

"Lead the way."

The whole pack made their way to the opening of the enchanted (or dis-enchanted) forest and back to civilization. Indeed it was getting darker and the light

511

systems started to close shades and turn on background lights to simulate sunset, then night. They cruised for a bit along the south side of the thorough fare. Trains past periodically and life forms of all sorts walked or crawled in every direction. At some point, the Dogzees were hungry again and they found a decent restaurant for them to eat and relax a bit.

The rest of the night was filled with exploration, discussions about lots of topics and a few rest stops. At some point Stephen and Ambrosia were getting tired and wanted to find a place to sleep. The Dogzee complied with the caveat that they would find a place that they could come and go during the evening.

A room was found with a "Dogzee" door and they all made themselves comfortable for the night. Periodically and quietly, one of the animals would rise and go outside. Although barely perceptible, at one point Stephen heard a faint noise and rose to investigate, it was very early in the morning. He walked over to the door to see that it was still moving just a bit. Slowly he opened it and walked out. It was clear and crisp, with the shutters just starting to crack in some sunlight. He walked further down a path and towards a small alleyway where he stopped suddenly. The Dogzee that had left was nose to nose with another species. There was tension in the air as they slowly circled each other. The Dogzee was showing its teeth and snarling. The other creature was staring very intently at the Dogzee, looking no doubt for an opening. Then quickly, they were at each other's throats and tumbling about on the dirt. Stephen thought about intervening but realized that this was the natural course of things and although primitive, was in their genes. He waited until one of the two backed away, torn and a bit bloody. The Dogzee had been victorious and had, without killing its foe, established its dominance.

"We should do that," thought Stephen about how humanity became proficient killers once the act became less personal. This happened when drones and robots did the dirty work. It was very easy to push a button and have whole communities disappear. For this reason primarily, Stephen had left the Earth. They would no doubt evolve out of the barbaric nature of living there but Stephen was too impatient to wait for it.

The victor was finished and left his mark on a local bush. He looked at Stephen and walked back to the room where the others had been sleeping. Stephen followed and upon arriving, realized that he was not done resting and crawled back into this bed for another hours worth of sleep. That would take the edge off. He rolled over, closed his eyes and within moments was gone. The next thing he remembered, he was hearing noises from many places in the room and rising, found that he was the last to get up.

"Well, welcome to the day, or afternoon or whatever. You must have been tired," Ambrosia observed.

"Oh, I was up last night with one of the others," he said this as the last Dogzee, the victor, was stirring to rise as well.

"Fun night?"

"Eventful."

Stephen went over to the victor and looked at him intently.

"Guess I'll take back all that stuff I said about you."

"Thanks," which was the first word Stephen had ever heard from this animal.

They composed themselves and filed outside for a breakfast search. As they walked around looking for a likely candidate, Ambrosia caught up to Stephen.

"What are your plans, Stephen?"

"Breakfast, then maybe we should saunter back to the ship for an early evening departure, How does that sound?"

"Perfect, I like this place, I like your friends, but (and this might not make sense) I am homesick."

"Oh, it makes sense and I agree."

For the rest of the morning, then afternoon, they wandered and explored. The day, again, was clear and crisp; the outpost engineers had done a decent job of simulating diurnal cycles and to a great degree, seasons. This current season was Spring, and it felt like it, smelled like it and had those particular colors that even for a foreign world, were distinctive.

Late afternoon, after another quick Dogzee nap, where Stephen and Ambrosia watched the sights, they started back towards the landing dock to prepare to depart. The closer they got, the slower the pack moved, trying to delay the takeoff. Eventually however, they were too near to delay the inevitable. As they walked up to the ship, they paused as Stephen and Ambrosia promised Thanadonous and the others that they would return. The Dogzees were all given an invitation to travel to Hebe 6 as well. Final looks were exchanged and the pack turned for the boulevard and Stephen and Ambrosia entered the ship.

The Final Lap

It is not the going out of port, but the coming in, that determines the success of a voyage. - Henry Ward Beecher

~ Sunrise Descending ~

They entered silently, found their places, alerted Majel that they were ready and listened for the distinctive sounds of departure. It had been a wonderful visit, just like visits with good friends usually are. There was a harmony between Stephen, Ambrosia and the members of the pack that could not adequately be described in words.

For now, they sat back, relaxed and waited for space. The craft closed its doors, the pressurization cycle started and then the magnetic humming. They levitated, turned towards the space doors and headed out to the stars. Stephen's view screen was set to forward view, Ambrosia's to rearward. She watched the outpost recede into the distance and thought about the experiences she had there. The future was looking good though and within a few minutes she too was looking forward.

"Which star is it?"

"Here, I will put a cursor on it, its yellow like our Earth's sun."

"Okay, thanks, I see it now."

"Now we wait for several more days, depending on the gravity waves, then we will be there."

"I look forward to it."

"Me too," he said smiling.

They sat back and relaxed for the next many days, periodically looking at the view screen to determine how close they were getting. He spent a lot of time talking about the Nereids, Zsa and Elva. Ambrosia asked a lot of questions but was seemingly intent on making Hebe 6 her home, regardless of who the Nereids were or what they wanted from her. Stephen found this curious but comforting in a way. She, like him, had been transformed by the doctor and had much in common with the people on the awaiting planet. No matter what happened, he realized that they would be close for a long time. At this point, she looked at him for a long moment.

The ship droned on, the star system got larger in the viewscreen and the anticipation of a landing grew near. Soon Majel was announcing a gravity reversal again, Stephen and Ambrosia moved from the floor to the new floor and adjusted their lives in reverse. The de-acceleration took a little over a day, whereupon they transitioned to weightlessness and the ship entered orbit around the planet. Excitement was in the air as they slowed down further and lowered the nose of the spacecraft to enter the atmosphere.

"Ambrosia, it will get a little bumpy from here, but the landing should be in less than an hour."

518

"Okay, thanks for the warning."

They continued down, sometimes feeling the heat of re-entry propagating through from the outside skin. It was in fact a bit bumpy, sometimes moving unsecured items about in the cabin. The relief from this excitement came when the nose of the craft came up for level flight. By this time they were only a few thousand feet above the ground and contined to slow down for a landing. They could sense the negative forward g's when the final moments of the approach came. The craft now banked and maneuvered to line up for touchdown on an open field, the same one that Stephen had first witnessed the arrival of the robot ship. Thrusters engaged during the final seconds and a subtle thump was felt as they alighted on the landing pad. As before, the same sequence of events took place, with the humming and magnetic relays opening, the air pressure equalizing and the hatch opening to invite them to Hebe 6. The air smelled sweet as they rose to make their way towards the opening. Before they left Majel had a question.

"Stephen?"

"Yes Majel, go ahead."

"You may keep the communication bracelet if you wish to contact us when we are in your sector."

"Okay, Majel, I think we will do that," he said this as he looked at Ambrosia. There was no way to predict the future, even with their extended experiences. He therefore thought it prudent to keep all options open. At that time however, travel was not in their minds.

"Majel, thank you for a nice, interesting trip."

"Our pleasure and our duty."

When she said this, Stephen's left eyebrow moved up almost an inch.

He looked at Ambrosia, took her hand and led her onto the surface of the new world. They brought a few things and walked away from the spacecraft in case there was an immediate takeoff. As it turns out, there wasn't and after their departure, a sentinel robot came out and took its place several meters from the ship. Only silence was left.

Stephen and Ambrosia walked down the path towards the village. It was Spring and the birds and flowers were in abundance. They walked further into a forest with the tree canopy overhead and curious animals all around. About a mile into the trek, they broke out into a clearing just before they entered the village. In the distance they could see people moving around, some who were just now taking notice of the approaching strangers. As the couple moved closer, more and more villagers stopped to look, some even started to close the gap for a greeting. Once in their presence it was obvious that the villagers had been expecting them.

"Welcome back, Stephen," said one.

"Its good to see you again, we heard you were coming," said another.

"It nice to be home."

"Who is your companion?"

"This is Ambrosia, a very special person like yourselves in many ways, she has come to make this place her home, please welcome her."

"Oh, we will of course."

"Thank you, and do you know where Elva is?"

"Yes, she knows you would be here soon. She awaits at your favorite cafe."

Several villagers had moved in curiosity to surround Ambrosia.

"Stephen, I know you have some catching up to do with the locals and certainly Elva, I would like to get to know these people and stay behind. Lets meet later."

"That works for me, Ambrosia, thanks. I'll see you later."

Ambrosia walked off with her new entourage, talking about her travels and experiences. Stephen bid farewell to the remaining people and started to walk into the village to find the cafe. By this time of the day it was getting warm, so he unbuttoned his jacket a bit to cool off and slung his travel bag across his shoulders. A few blocks away from the cafe he could just make out a few people who were sitting under the awning having lunch or coffee. One sat alone and was looking his way. Surely it was Elva, and she looked attractive even from this distance. He really did not know what to expect, as the relativistic time dilation had caused her to wait almost thirty years to his one. He had been through this before however and wondered what personal dynamics would take place as she had lived so much longer than he. Was she married by now? And what about Zsa?

He walked quickly and with purpose. Soon he was close enough to make a determination. It *was* Elva, sitting there staring back at him. She was a little in shock as her image of him from so long ago was exactly as he appeared. On the other hand, Elva had lived a lot longer, near twenty years in fact. She looked good as usual and that only added to Stephen's enthusiasm to see her again.

"Elva, you look wonderful!"

"As do you Stephen, you look like you left yesterday."

"Feels like I did, Elva," he sat down next to her an looked at every detail in her face. She was quiet as she looked at him. The waiter came over and asked if Stephen needed anything.

"Tea," she said.

"You remembered."

"Of course, and thank you for keeping in touch with me over the years. Although in your time line, you might have been emailing me every day or two, in my time is was every month or so."

"Well, I wanted to keep in touch, even with the time problem. How have you been and what have you been doing?"

"As you know from the emails, everything is fine, Zsa is grown up now and is a wonderful person. Her genes had a lot to do with her disposition and now we understand why you missed her so much. You will meet her tonight. As far as myself is concerned, I waited for a long time but finally found an incredible person to spend a lot of time with and you will meet him as well tonight. We all thought it best that I meet you privately before introducing you to the others."

"I could tell you had feelings for someone else through your emails. It makes sense, it would have been very selfish of me to hope you would wait. As far as Zsa is concerned, I am glad she turned out well, and look forward to meeting her. She could never be as my wife was, her genes are wonderful as expected, however her life experiences also define her. Nature and nurture you know. Has she found someone?"

"She has had a few boyfriends but nothing serious. She is extremely anxious to meet you, especially since she knows the conditions under which she was born. To her you are like a father figure as you and I were the same age when you left. She gets along well with my mate, much like a step father."

"Good, that makes sense. I was hoping that it would not be awkward once I returned. Although I appreciated the gesture you and the Nereids went through to bring her back, her memory for me was that of another person. Although she is the same person cell for cell, she is totally different in terms of life experience. This makes all the difference in the world, as my old Zsa had a challenging life that prompted her to work very hard for her education and place in NASA. The situation is much different here because you and the others live a more idyllic life. Don't get me wrong, sometimes challenges make for a strong person."

~ Sunrise Descending ~

"We know, and we know that she was well taken care of and turned out to be a great friend to many. Speaking of friends who is your companion?"

"Her name is Ambrosia. We met on a world in the globular cluster M15. It turns out that she knew the same doctor that gave me the immortal serum and he treated her as well. Her journey has been just as long as mine, with many of the same problems and wonders. She came with me to make this place her own."

"To be with you?"

"Oh, I don't know exactly, we never talked in any detail about that and considering our long lives which included many loves, we are both careful to commit."

"Sounds like there might be more to the story. Bring her tonight to the campfire, Isaac and the others are looking forward to meeting her and seeing you again."

"And you will be there?"

"Of course, with Benjamin, my mate and Zsa."

"Sounds like a party."

"Oh, it will be. For now welcome home, its so good to see you."

She gave him a kiss, he tried to remember if it was going to be the same sensation as so long ago but was left a bit hollow. Time is like being on a boat in a river, if you get off the boat, the river never remains the same but will rush by, never to be captured again. He rose and took his travel pack to find a place to stay. He looked at her as he left, and saw the same facial features he remembered so clearly, but they had changed to reflect her recent experiences, she was another person now.

She soon left the cafe as well, walking back to her life and home.

That evening, Stephen found Ambrosia and asked her to come with him to the campfire meeting. She already knew about it and had been invited by some of her new friends.

"Do you like this place?"

"Its perfect, Stephen. Just the right feeling with the forest, ocean, quiet village and it seems that the people here are all at peace with themselves."

"Yes, they are. I like this place for the same reasons. There is a quiet mystery to it as well. The Nereids, who you will meet tonight, have stories to tell, ancient stories. Some of these I have heard, some that will come after many more years of friendship with them. I honestly feel that they might know things you, I and the inhabitants of M15 do not. Maybe its a spiritual thing, maybe not. Its just that there is a sense of 'more than life' here."

"Perfect, this is what I have wanted to experience as well, Stephen. Thank you for bringing me here."

"Your welcome, but I would say you should reserve judgement until you meet everyone this evening."

"That's fair, but it sure feels right at this moment."

Stephen looked at her and paused for a moment. Fundamentally, he was happy that she was content. This was important to him he realized.

Campfire Life #4

Home is not where you live, but where they understand you. - Christian Morganstern

That evening, everyone started to gather at the campfire site that so long ago presented the revelation and predictions for Stephen's future. It was just after dusk, the light was dimming rapidly and the animals were starting to get quiet. Stephen and Ambrosia walked to his old sitting place and sat down together. As people filed in they came over to greet Stephen and meet his new companion. They were all happy to see him and meet her and with the same warmth they had so many years ago. It was with an aura of tranquility that they emoted as they filed by and spoke. Isaac was one of the last.

"Welcome home, Stephen, and welcome to our family, Ambrosia."

Ambrosia smiled broadly as she listened to Isaac. Then, Isaac turned to face Stephen.

"Stephen, we have something for you as we had agreed. Upon your return, we offered to present you with someone who meant so much to you in the past. We have done so by having Elva give birth to her, and raise her. Zsa as we expected turned out to be an amazing person. She has lit up our little world with a keen intellect and an insatiable curiosity. We thank you for the gift."

"Looks like everyone is happy about the addition, I'm glad it worked out."

"Not as glad as we. See for yourself."

Stephen turned to his right to find an identical replica of Zsa in her twenties, about the same age as when he first met her. He was speechless at the sight. His

529

dreams had not done him justice as she stood there looking at him in the steady moonlight and scintillating firelight.

"Wow, Its amazing to see you again. I'm not sure what to say."

"You look too young to be my father, but you do look just like the pictures they have shown me over the years."

"Its a long story, only portions of what you have heard."

"I look forward to the rest."

"Zsa, this is my friend Ambrosia, who as it turns out is as old as I am. She is also from Earth and shares a common background."

"Nice to meet you, I will call you Aunt Ambrosia."

Ambrosia smiled at this and at the resolution of Stephen's place in the family.

For the next several hours they talked about the journey to the stars and to Outpost 399. They talked also about the robot ship, of Majel, and M15. There were simply too many stories to cover in one night and it became obvious that it would take a very long time to hear about both his and her experiences.

Stephen was awestruck with Zsa but realized that she indeed was not the same person as his former wife. He felt comfortable with the thought that he could mentor her for a few years, at which time he would not be surprised to find that she would venture to the stars and blaze new trails to the cosmos. It would be fun to watch.

Elva looked happy with her mate, who was at her side. He looked at Stephen periodically to find out who he was and wondered what he had meant to Elva. Stephen for his part, might tell him in the future.

Stephen took in a deep breath while watching the fire and realized that the future was indeed the issue. He looked at Isaac, the Nereids, Zsa, Elva and Ambrosia in slow succession. It was a satisfying feeling to be with them all.

"How do you like this, Ambrosia?" Stephen asked as the hour was getting late.

"Oh this is wonderful, these are amazing people, capable of anything including flight to the stars. Yet they stay here, build fires and farm. They are completely self sufficient and have a pure happiness that is rare in the Universe. Even you know this."

"Yes, thats true, but where do we go from here?"

"Everywhere, nowhere, the real question is what are we going to *do* from now on."

"Grow and interact and discover."

The fire was now mostly embers, many of the villagers had gone home, including Zsa and Elva. Isaac came over to sit with Stephen and Ambrosia. He did not speak initially.

Then, an image from many many years ago appeared. It was the sparkles that Stephen had witnessed on the boat, before the whole adventure started. He rubbed his eyes, assuming he was just tired, but they persisted. The sparkles were of many colors and twinkled a few feet from where they were seated.

"Do you see that?"

"Yes."

"They look a bit like M15 with the same colors and general shape."

"Of course they do," replied Isaac.

Epilogue

They stayed together for longer than they could remember. It was a union of happiness, necessity and understanding. It was also what so many elderly couples are just beginning to understand as they start to realize what is important in relationships. It is a resonance, a contentment of juxtaposition with your mate. To experience the universe like this is the definition of luck.

After years on Hebe 6, years with Zsa and Elva as well, they grew to know and appreciate the Nereids. The quiet secrets came out slowly and were couched in millennia of wisdom. The words were carefully chosen as words themselves have limitations, but they were true nonetheless.

The sparkles were the image of the M15 community of stars, where they had learned to transcend time and space. They had met Stephen and had researched his past, which accounted for the sightings on the boat. As someone they admired they followed the course of his life and would continue to do so for a very long time. They had this ability, borne from a primordial curiosity and evolved into the ultimate cosmic consciousness, which of course, is the natural order of things.

ABOUT THE AUTHOR

"Writing books allows me to learn about things"

Kevin Shoemaker was born in New York City in April of 1954. A son of an actress and musician turned professor. He has lived in several states and has been educated in the fields of philosophy, radio astronomy and antenna design. He has authored several technical papers in astronomy and has nine patents in the fields of aviation, antenna design and meteorology. In addition, he is an avid pilot and boat owner and holds several certificates for operating airplanes, helicopters and performing flight instruction. Currently he works as an antenna and radar designer in Colorado. Mr. Shoemaker is a father of one daughter and one son and lives near Boulder with his wife, Judi.

Comments?   e-mail: Shoemakerlabs@gmail.com

Other books by the author:

Mars Life
Practical Antenna Design
The Voyages of Gaea
Life in the Universe and Where to find it